Beyond the
Cherokee Trail

Other books by Lisa Carter

Aloha Rose, Quilts of Love series

Carolina Reckoning
Beneath a Navajo Moon
Under a Turquoise Sky
Vines of Entanglement

BEYOND THE CHEROKEE TRAIL

Lisa Carter

Abingdon Press
Nashville

Beyond the Cherokee Trail

Copyright © 2015 by Lisa Carter

Published by Abingdon Press, 2222 Rosa L. Parks Blvd.,
PO Box 280988, Nashville, TN 37228-0988

www.abingdonpress.com

Macro Editor: Teri Wilhelms

Published in association with the Steve Laube Agency

Library of Congress Cataloging-in-Publication Data

Carter, Lisa, 1964-
Beyond the Cherokee trail / Lisa Carter.
    pages ; cm
ISBN 978-1-4267-9546-6 (binding: soft back)
I. Title.
PS3603.A77757B49 2015
813'.6—dc23

2015008547

Printed in the United States of America

1 2 3 4 5 6 7 8 9 10 / 20 19 18 17 16 15

Dedication

To my Aunt Julia—Thank you for your encouragement through the years. Your smile lights our family gatherings. Thanks for contributing what became one of my favorite Ross lines the day we ate barbeque at your house. I love you.

Readers—Blessings to you and I hope this special place in the mountains of North Carolina and the Snowbird people will capture your imagination and grip your heart as they do mine. Though the characters in this story are fictional, the historic events recounted are not.

This story is not mine, but one of those things which you know beyond a shadow of a doubt is God's story. An eternal story of His mercy and grace, not just to Linden, Sarah, Walker, Pierce, Touch the Clouds, or Leila, but to all who've been broken and felt abandoned by the guilt of their transgressions or the pain of loss.

If you've ever felt unwanted or unloved or weary, God invites you to come. Because in Christ, there are no outcasts.

My prayer for you today, if you've fallen or if you grieve, is that you would discover for yourself the God of all peace and all comfort. That you would lay hold of the God who offers grace in the hour of your greatest need.

And Beyond.

Acknowledgments

For his help in the historical research of this project I'd like to thank **T.J. Holland,** Cultural Resources Manager for the Eastern Band of the Cherokee Indians in North Carolina and curator of the tribally owned Junaluska Museum. A renown Snowbird Cherokee artist, he patiently answered my many questions and helped me to locate what remains of the Tatham Gap Road where the gouged wagon ruts made on the Trail can still be seen. Deep in the woods outside Robbinsville, it is a painfully beautiful yet slightly haunting place. As if the earth itself remembers the suffering of those who once trod this path.

Jesus—Here I raise my Ebenezer. By Your help I've come. You are the beginning and the end of my journey. For truly the further we travel together, the sweeter comes the end.

*So now you are no longer strangers and aliens. Rather,
you are fellow citizens
with God's people, and you belong to God's household.*
Ephesians 2:19 CEB

*Therefore, let us draw near with confidence to the
throne of grace,
so that we may receive mercy and find grace to help in
time of need."*
Hebrews 4:16 NASB

*Blessed be God, even the Father of our Lord Jesus
Christ,
the Father of mercies, and the God of all consolation.*
2 Corinthians 1:3 KJV (1833)

Reader's Note

In 1835, members of a minority faction of the Cherokee Nation brokered a compromise settlement with the United States' government known as the Treaty of New Echota, ceding its claims to the entire Cherokee Nation in the states of North Carolina, Georgia, Tennessee, and Alabama. The treaty agreed to the removal of all Cherokee citizens to beyond the Mississippi River in Indian Territory. This deal—without the official authorization of the Cherokee National Council—became the legal basis for the enforced removal of an entire ethnic group from the only home in which their people had lived, farmed, and roamed for hundreds of years.

John Ross traveled between New Echota and Washington urging President Andrew Jackson to reconsider. Daniel Webster, Henry Clay, and Davy Crockett among others argued for the Cherokees' right to stay. But Congress ratified the agreement in 1836 in the face of mounting pressure to seize the valuable Cherokee lands. And although the Supreme Court upheld many of the Cherokee claims, the fate of the Cherokee Nation had been sealed once gold was discovered within its borders.

The government granted the Cherokees two years to prepare themselves to be removed. But Ross promised an eleventh-hour intervention. And so, in May 1838, most of the Cherokee were caught completely unaware. With crops planted in the field, laundry hanging on the line, breakfast waiting on the table . . . soldiers appeared at their doors.

Of the sixteen thousand removed—a virtual death march—six thousand men, women, and children perished along the twelve-hundred-mile route that became known as the Trail of Tears or Trail Where We Cried. The removal ensured the land, which had been their ancestral birthplace, would become nothing more than an oft-repeated story around hearth fires of a time and a place revered and longed for, but outside the scope of living memory. The Trail came to symbolize the oppression of all Native Americans in the American expansion to the Pacific Ocean.

In the isolated mountain terrain of western North Carolina in what today comprises the Qualla Boundary near the town of Cherokee, some refused to surrender to removal. These few hundred became the Eastern Band of the Cherokee.

An even smaller number secreted in a pocket of the rugged Snowbird Mountains—still considered one of the last wilderness regions within the United States—also successfully eluded capture and became known as the Snowbird Cherokee . . . This is their story.

1

April 2018

Glass crunched underneath her feet. Linden froze, catching sight of the jagged glass shards protruding from the French doors.

"Quincy?" Her voice echoed across the deserted parking lot of the Trail of Trails Interpretative Center.

She swallowed, glancing over her shoulder at the trees shrouded in darkness. An owl hooted. She shivered.

Maybe she'd come back tomorrow. In daylight. Raised in the flatlands, she wasn't used to how night in the looming mountains engulfed the valleys in one fell swoop.

Rhododendrons rustled behind her. She tensed, but someone within the darkened interior moaned.

"Quince?" she whispered.

Stepping around the broken glass, she crossed into the Center and fumbled for the light switch. Something drifted in the air past her nose. She swatted it away.

The overhead light flickered to life. She gasped at the chicken feathers plastered against the smashed display cases, as if tarred and feathered. And then she spotted the words spray-painted on the far wall. The dribbling red lines gave the message the appearance of oozing blood.

Don't Come Back Prairie N——

Her breath hitched at the racial slur. Something bumped behind her. She wheeled as a bloody hand appeared, rising, grasping the top of the case. Linden screamed.

Quincy, his glasses askew on his face, hoisted himself upright. "Linden?" Blinking, his eyes dilated in the artificial light. He wobbled.

"What happened?" She rushed forward, grabbing his arm. "Who did this?"

He shook his head and would have fallen except for her support. "They jumped me." Touching a patch of blood at the back of his head, he winced. "Never saw their faces. But they were skinheads."

Linden's eyes widened. "In Cartridge Cove?"

His eyes darted, accessing the damage, and flitted to the encroaching darkness. "Said they'd be back if we didn't stop this nonsense."

"Nonsense?"

He nodded. "Bringing the divided tribes together for the commemoration."

She frowned. "The Oklahoma band? The ones they called the prairie . . ." Her lips tightened. She wouldn't use that word.

"We need to get out of here, Linden. It's not safe."

She draped his arm across her shoulder. "My car's outside." She lugged him toward the shattered door. "Then we'll call the police."

Linden felt the weight of eyes boring into her from the edge of the forest. A frisson of fear prickled against her skin. Her heart pounded. She dragged Quincy through the twilight around the corner of the building.

She pointed to the hood of her car. "They left something." She stared at the paper trapped against the windshield. "It wasn't there when I parked a few minutes ago."

"That means they're still here." He shuddered. "Watching."

Linden reached for the message.

He hunched his shoulders. "What does it say?"

"It says, 'Shut down the festival or next time you'll burn.'"

She frowned. "What does that mean?"

"Welcome to Cartridge Cove, North Carolina." Quincy cleared his throat. "Sure you don't want to go home to Raleigh?"

She crumpled the note in her hand. "Their kind drove out the Cherokee a hundred plus years ago."

Narrowing her eyes, she jutted her chin at the deepening darkness. "Nobody's driving me out."

"Would you look at what I've found?"

Her elbows resting on the sill of the attic window, Linden dragged her gaze from her contemplation of the majestic Snowbird Mountains. "What now, Gram?"

A Beach Boys tune from the Oldies But Goodies channel blared from the portable radio. Linden wended her way through the stacked piles of heirlooms. The junk her ancestors had accumulated—ahem, hoarded—like a bunch of pack rats.

Her sixtyish grandmother sat cross-legged and limber as a teenager beside the enormous, brass-studded trunk they'd unearthed under the eaves. Her Italian loafers keeping time to the beat, Marvela belted out her own gutsy, contralto rendition at "the Southern girls" part.

A smile flitted across Linden's face. Nobody did youthful like the baby boomers.

"Did your people never throw anything away, Gram? There's counseling for that now. Intervention strategies. TV shows."

Marvela raised one sculptured eyebrow. "What? And deny us the pleasure of a treasure hunt?" She shrugged her shoulders. "Besides, this isn't just Campbell heirlooms. When Fraser's parents died, he was busy commuting between D.C. and Raleigh. I was busy having your father. We hired a company to box up the Birchfield place and stored everything in the attic like my grandmother always did."

Linden snorted.

Gram gave her a pointed look, a by-product of graduating from Miss Ophelia's School for Young Ladies. "Really, Linden. Snorting is so unladylike. And at your age . . ."

Only Gram cleaned out the detritus of decades—make that centuries—in Calvin Klein designer jeans and a Ralph Lauren sweater knotted gracefully over her blue Talbot blouse. And, still managed to look ready for a ladies' tea or political fundraiser.

Linden sighed, wishing—not for the first time—she'd inherited Gram's thin elegant form and classic, model-like features.

Gram could make a trip to the bathroom resemble a glorious adventure. And now, she'd gotten sucked into this latest scheme of Gram's, to convert the old family home into a bed and breakfast in the far western corner of North Carolina.

Not that Linden had anything better to do when Gram announced her "retirement" plans to return to her childhood home in tiny Cartridge Cove, population five hundred. Nothing better to do in this economy after she'd lost her job during that PR fiasco.

And with her fledgling public relations company on the verge of going under, Linden had been sent by the family to act as a cushion—foil or field hand, take your pick—to balance her grandmother's "youthful" exuberance. But at least, thanks to Gram's influence, she'd managed to snag the Cartridge Cove commemoration as a client.

"Look, Linden, darlin'." Marvela thrust two bundles of fabric, one in each hand, at Linden.

"A Union flag?"

Marvela's eyes danced. "And a Confederate one, too."

"You don't mean . . . ?"

"One son fought for the Union. The other for the Confederacy." Marvela fluttered a hand in the direction of the window. "A lot of families in the mountains split according to conscience."

Linden fingered the dry, brittle fabric. She hoped her own mother would never receive a flag on behalf of Royce, Linden's younger brother, currently stationed in troubled Central Africa.

Marvela brushed a strand of her silvered hair from her face and reached once more into the trunk. "Maybe this book I found underneath the flags will tell us more."

Linden grabbed for the book. They swapped items. Marvela placed the flags alongside the other treasures she'd unearthed—a silver pocket watch, a doughboy-style helmet, and an Art Deco brooch.

She plopped down beside her grandmother and brushed her fingertips over the dark, leather cover, the edges and binding frayed and crumbling with age.

"It's a journal. Somebody named Sarah Jane Hopkins."

"Is there a date?"

Linden lifted the book toward the dim light of the lone light bulb dangling from the ceiling. She squinted, trying to decipher the spidery, old-fashioned handwriting with its flourishes and curlicues in faded blue ink. "First entry, 1837. December."

She grinned at her grandmother.

Marvela reached into the cavernous depths of the green leather trunk. "Cool."

Cool? She threw her grandmother a fond look before turning her attention once more to the book.

"Time period's right for Quincy's museum and the commemoration. But too early to explain the flags." Linden thumbed to the last page. "Last entry is dated—huh?"

Linden let out a gust of air. "1900. Perhaps a diary where she recorded only the milestones of her life. Maybe she'll explain the flags, after all."

Marvela popped her head out from the trunk. "Did I tell you how much I like that young man of yours, Dr. Quincy Sawyer? I'm glad he's going to be okay."

Linden cut her eyes at her grandmother. "He's not my young man, Gram. Stop playing matchmaker. Been there, done that." She tossed her head, sending a wave of tendrils tumbling out of her chignon. "Never again. And at my age . . ."

Marvela snorted. "Twenty-nine. And just because of one jerk, you're hardly too old to lock your hope chest away for good."

Graduates of Miss Ophelia's, like Marvela, refused to understand in the twenty-first century, girls didn't have hope chests. Or dream of love and take-your-breath romance in the crazy world of modern life.

Especially not after an experience with someone like The Jerk.

Marvela patted the side of the trunk. "Why, I bet this might've been Sarah Jane Hopkins's own hope chest." She gave Linden a sly, sidelong look. "And none of us are too old for romance."

She made a show of smoothing the non-existent wrinkles from her perfectly creased jeans. "Not even me. Why, at my advanced age," Marvela drawled in that cultured Southern belle tone she learned at Miss Ophelia's, "you never know what I'm liable to do."

Truer words had never been spoken. Linden fought the urge to smile.

"'Cause," her grandmother laid her French-manicured hand on Linden's knee, "you never can tell what adventure might be just around the corner. When you least expect it—"

"Like a tornado or E. coli?"

Marvela rolled her eyes toward the rafters.

Smothering her laughter, Linden stuck her nose into the pages of Sarah Jane Hopkins's diary.

◆

"Like this, Eli." Walker tossed the small, deer hide-covered ball into the air and lobbed his netted hickory stick, propelling the ball in the direction of Eli's outstretched stick.

"I'm open," yelled Matt, another one of Walker's stickball recruits. He sprinted forward, and then side-to-side dodging his opponents in the scrimmage match.

Eli spun and leaped, stick stretched high, into the air. With a whoosh, he sent the ball careening through space, over the head of a charging player straining for the interception. Matt, fending off another player in this down-and-dirty Cherokee version of lacrosse, made a leap worthy of the great Michael Jordan. Catching the ball in his net, he shook off his impending foe like a coon dog shook off bath water.

Walker, Eli, and their team cheered, hickory sticks stabbing the air, as Matt blasted the ball between their opponent's goal posts to score. Amidst much jubilation, Eli and company performed a small victory dance with Matt perched atop their collective shoulders.

The rest of Walker's Boys Club crew leaned over, hands on their knees, drawing in great gulps of air as sweat dribbled down their bare backs. Walker ambled over and clapped a hand on the nearest teen's shoulder. "Better luck next time, Owle."

Jake Owle straightened, mischief in his brown eyes. "Better luck if next time Matt Cornsilk's on our side of the scrimmage."

Walker laughed. It was true. Matt Cornsilk possessed an incredible agility coupled with explosive bursts of speed.

"I promise we'll mix it up next time." Walker caught sight of his mother, Irene Crowe, leaning against the chain-link fence that surrounded the high school baseball field they used to practice for the stickball tournament.

Walker's smile faded.

He understood why she'd come. And it wasn't to watch him coach Cherokee stickball.

Walker angled as the guys gathered around for further instructions. "Great practice. Don't forget we play Wolftown next Saturday."

Several of the guys groaned. "They're big."

"And fast," added Eli.

Jake smirked. "Not as fast as Matt."

Matt ducked his head, but grinned and scuffed his big toe in the grass.

Eli expanded his skinny chest and pounded his fist against it. "We're big, too. Real Snowbird Cherokee mountain men, not like those city boys."

Walker's lips twitched. "I hardly think Wolftown qualifies as a city, and those boys are as Cherokee as you or I. Anyway," he pinpointed one or two of the boys with a look, "don't forget to practice your drills this week."

The boys groaned again. He held up his hand. "They build stamina and increase cardiovascular performance." More groaning, like he'd assigned algebra or something.

"No pain, no gain, no trophy at the festival. See ya next weekend. Ten A.M. sharp. And . . ."

The boys had already started to shake their heads. They knew what was coming.

Because he said it every week.

He planted his hands on his hips. "If any of you, lazy bums, ever have a hope of getting a girlfriend, I'm begging you, please . . . hit the showers."

The guys rolled their eyes.

Eli, his smart-mouth second cousin, jabbed him in the ribs with his elbow. "Like why don't you follow your own advice, Coach?" He held his nose. "How about you set a good example and show us how to catch one of them sweet thangs?"

"Not going to happen, dude." He nudged Eli with his shoulder. "Too busy babysitting you sissies."

The guys laughed and fanned out to collect their equipment.

Matt, team captain, initiated the rousing war chant the boys composed when Walker formed the group three years ago. They believed it made them sound more Cherokee, fiercer, warriorlike and that the chant struck terror in the hearts of intertribal teams like the Choctaw group from Georgia.

Fighting a smile—because the only thing their proud war cry accomplished was to disgust the fairer sex of all races—Walker strolled over to where his mother waited.

Shaking her head, she handed him the Cartridge Cove Volunteer Fire Department t-shirt he'd left draped over the fence. "Yeah, son, why don't you follow your own advice and provide your old mother some more grandbabies before I expire from this earth?"

He hunched his shoulders as he slipped the shirt over his head. As if his indomitable mother would ever be old. Like many of their Cherokee forebears, she'd probably still be kicking up her heels at the ripe old age of a hundred.

Not to mention, nagging him to his early death about this police thing.

"You didn't file an application with the Sheriff like you said—"

"Like *you* said." He poked his head through the neck hole and shrugged his arms into the sleeves. "*I* never said. You know how I feel about that subject, Ma."

Irene placed her hands on her hips in a familiar, if unconscious, imitation of her son. "You're more than qualified, John Walker Crowe. And, viewed as an up-and-coming leader among The People."

He untied the leather thong holding his shoulder-length hair out of his face. "Not by choice, I assure you."

Irene's eyes narrowed. He'd seen that look before. Like when he'd tried her patience and she sent him out to cut his own hickory switch. "The elders have done their part for the tribe. It's time for younger blood. Time to let the Old Ones retire to their farms and—"

"And to checkerboard games at the Mercantile."

Her lips pursed.

Walker possessed the good sense to take a step back at the expression on her face. At thirty-two, he'd been too old for hickory switches for years. But on second thought, did one ever get too old for a mother to snatch a knot in her child?

"To whom much is given, much is required, John Walker. And after what happened this week at the Center . . ."

He shook his head. "After what happened to me in Afghanistan, I swore I'd never pick up a gun again. And for the record, the abilities I've been given, I don't want."

Some of the fight went out of her eyes. "Here," she made a circling motion with her finger. "Turn around and let me scrape that hair out of your face. You're making a right mess of it."

He handed her the leather band and pivoted. He bent his knees to accommodate her lesser height.

"It wasn't your fault, son."

He grimaced. She wasn't going to let this go. Her hands finger-combed the strands of his hair.

"Maybe like the elders, I've done my part, too, Ma. You ever think of that? For my country. Above and beyond. Time for me to retire to *my* farm."

She grunted. "You and those trees."

His knees were beginning to ache. Proof he wasn't getting any younger, either. Probably a result of the uncomfortable, crouched position he'd often assumed in carrying out his specialty within the unit. Time for a new tactic. He'd learned a little something about strategy during his two tours.

"I'm not warrior material like Uncle Ross," he continued. "I've wished my reflexes had been a second slower, my aim a trifle higher . . . Hey—ow! Stop Mom. You're hurting me." He squirmed, trying to loosen her stranglehold on his hair—and his scalp.

She shoved him away. "So you could've been the one brought home in a body bag?"

Walker fell against the fence before righting himself.

Her eyes welled into pools of liquid chocolate. "You'd rather your mother buried her son? As if I didn't practically wear out my knees the whole time you were gone, praying, begging God to spare your life. You'd prefer more of your buddies had been blown away because you failed to stop that . . . that . . . ?"

"Better me than somebody's child," he whispered.

Irene's shoulders slumped. He pulled her into an embrace. She returned his hug and then, punched him in the arm.

Walker smiled. That was more like the tough, never-say-die bulldog of a single mother he'd always known.

"Speaking of the townspeople and this festival . . ."

There was more?

She had that look in her eye again. He might not have been cut out for army life, but his mother, the gifted Cherokee quilter and potter, would've made an outstanding drill sergeant.

"The council's decided since you're the head of the community development club this year, you're the perfect tribe liaison for this PR woman the committee hired to spearhead the 180th commemoration of the Trail of Tears."

He'd been hiding out on his farm all winter, avoiding the joint tribal and town council planning meetings, hoping, praying such an eventuality wouldn't come his way. "Why me, Ma?"

She held up her index finger. "One—because this is your slow time of year and you don't get busy again till late summer after the festival's over."

"Hang on a minute," he protested. "I got plenty to do. Fertilizing. Weeding. Shaping the trees."

She ignored him and pushed up another finger, making a V. "Two—as *gadugi* leader, you know The People, especially those old-timers in the hollows who can be . . ." Irene gave a delicate cough, ". . . difficult if the notion strikes them. A united front, Cherokee and Appalachian, you and the PR lady. Not to mention it's your civic and tribal duty," she threw in for good measure.

He groaned.

"Three," she ticked off on her fingers. "Your uncle Ross, since he returned home, is overseeing the arrangements for the Western Band Oklahoma delegation to retrace the Trail and coordinate the historic reunion from this end. I figured you'd want to spend all the time you could with Uncle Ross, since you two don't get to see so much of each other these days."

He frowned. That struck below the belt. Dangling his favorite—okay, his only great-uncle—like a carrot in front of his nose.

"You know what I think of this reunification scheme. It's a bad idea to stir up those long ago resentments between the Cherokee and the Appalachians." He made a face. "The ones waiting in the wings to seize our land—our farms—as soon as the soldiers dragged us away during the Removal."

She folded her arms. "A lot of those settlers helped the Eastern Band hide out in these mountains till the soldiers left."

Walker reached for the sneakers and gym bag he'd left at the fence before practice. "You mark my words, no good's going to come from reliving that pain, misery, and racial prejudice. Case in point what happened at the Center this week."

"A lot you know, Walker Crowe, holed up from life on that mountain farm of yours. Everybody's coming together to make this festival a success. Families, Cherokee and non-Indian alike, are excited about the Western Band coming home to the ancestral place."

She flipped her stick-straight hair over her shoulder. "Sorta figured with all you've been through, you'd have a certain understanding of that. That longing to come home."

On a nearby bench, Walker stuffed his feet into his Nikes. "Even after 180 years?"

"Home is home, John Walker."

Walker tugged the shoelaces tighter. "No matter how far you've roamed?"

"The farther you've traveled, the sweeter comes the end of the journey," she countered. "Besides, no fair the Qualla Boundary up the road gets all the tourist trade with their outdoor drama and recreated Village."

He cocked an appraising eye her way. "Festival won't hurt your quilt shop either, will it, Ma?"

"Festival won't hurt anyone's business, Cherokee or white, in this economy, son."

He chuckled. "Leave it to the Almighty Dollar to bring white and red together at last."

She slid beside him on the bench and tucked the folds of her wraparound skirt under her bare legs. Late April at four thousand feet still packed a chill despite the midafternoon sun. "Seeing as money divided us in the first place . . ."

He'd deflected—for the time being—her ambitions for him as well as her less-than-subtle hints to be fruitful and multiply. The festival was a battle he reckoned—in light of the others—that might be the better part of valor to concede.

"In everybody's financial interests, you say?"

She nodded. A smile played across her lips. "Won't hurt that agribusiness of yours, either. Because when you're dealing with the tourists—"

"The only color that matters is green." He gave a huge sigh. "What time, Mother?"

"Four o'clock. At Miss Marvela's. Uncle Ross said he'd liked to ride shotgun with you."

"Good ole Uncle Ross," he muttered between clenched teeth. "At least he's always got my back."

Irene sniffed the air like a bird dog. Scrunching her nose, she waved a hand in front of her face. "Phew, John Walker. Those boys were right. You stink. Make sure you go home first and hit the shower yourself."

2

Late December 1837

Sarah Jane pierced her finger with the sharp edge of the needle. Stifling a cry, she laid the quilt square in her lap and sucked the tiny, red dot of blood from her forefinger.

"No blood on the quilt." Leila smirked from across the drawing room.

Glancing over to the mantel clock, Sarah Jane smothered an inward groan. Papa had promised he'd return from Charleston with his new apprentice this afternoon. But still no sign of Papa's carriage.

"Maybe a snowstorm hindered their return home," Leila speculated.

Sarah sent a prayer heavenward the apprentice doctor had the wherewithal and good manners to do most of the driving on the long, country roads between the bustling port city of Charleston and the backcountry trails in this isolated corner of the Cherokee Nation.

"Your father's getting slow in his old age." Leila flashed even, ivory white teeth at Sarah.

Sarah Jane silently concurred, not that she'd give Leila the satisfaction of knowing they agreed upon anything. Papa *wasn't* getting any younger, although like a good plow horse he'd rather die in the harness than admit it.

"Do you think Dr. Hopkins remembered to buy the blue silk for me?"

Sarah Jane withdrew her finger from her mouth and studied it for any further evidence of blood before picking up the Carolina Lily square again.

"I'm sure he did. Papa wrote it in his little notebook, and you know how careful he is about such things."

Papa wouldn't be pleased to learn that, less than a day after his departure, Leila's own father had been called away to yet another Cherokee council meeting.

Her face clouded. And when Papa returned to find her alone with Leila and old Kweti? An inappropriate chaperone, he'd say, not thinking too highly of Leila's tradition-bound Cherokee nurse with her chants and potions.

Leila poked her aristocratic nose in the air. "I'm going to add this quilt to my hope chest." Her eyes narrowed at Sarah's paltry quilting effort.

Those enormous, lively dark eyes the boys—Cherokee and white—found so bewitching.

"Hard to believe you and I both took two years of needlework together at Salem Academy."

Sarah Jane decided it was best to let that remark lie.

Leila fluttered her lashes, failing in her first attempt to rile Sarah and alleviate her boredom. "My father brought me a green trunk the last time the delegation went to Washington to plead our cause with the President. You do have a hope chest, don't you, Sarah Jane?"

She giggled and wound a curl of her rich, flowing blue-black hair around her finger. "Or do you no longer entertain any hopes?"

Refusing to respond to Leila's usual jabs, Sarah Jane inspected the clock again, skimmed across the book-lined walls, and then gazed out the parlor window. She fingered the scratchy wool homespun she'd donned this morning. Leila understood full well Sarah Jane's father, a medical missionary to the North Carolina contingent of the Cherokee Nation, didn't have the lavish funds the slave-holding planter, Ambrose Hummingbird, had at his disposal for his daughter, Leila.

She stabbed the needle through the cloth, pondering the unfairness that plagued her life. When God gave out beauty, Sarah Jane figured Leila had not only pushed her way to the front of the line, but probably shoved one or two more—including herself—out of any chance of receiving any beauty at all.

Leila, she suspected, had befriended her because Sarah Jane was the only white girl within a hundred miles of the Hummingbirds. And Leila Hummingbird, despite being a full-blooded Cherokee, was the "whitest white" Sarah ever met. Whiter than her. With the red brick manor house, the finest silk clothing and finishing school education to prove it.

A five-dollar Indian, as the more traditional Cherokee referred to Ambrose Hummingbird. And it wasn't meant as a compliment. He looked like an Indian. But acted like a white man. Neither he nor Leila spoke a word of Cherokee.

Leila's father wasn't much of a churchgoer, and some of the things Leila said were nothing short of shocking. Leila didn't practice traditional Cherokee beliefs despite Kweti's best intentions nor evidence much spirituality in the Christian faith of her deceased mother, either.

Fact was, sad to say, Leila Hummingbird didn't believe in much of anything. Except herself.

And bless his dear, always-believe-the-best heart, Papa actually maintained she, Sarah Jane, provided a settling influence on Leila.

"Humph." As if anything could contain a force of nature like Leila Hummingbird. One could about as easily harness the wind.

"What did you say, Sarah Jane?"

"Nothing."

Sarah Jane set her lips in a line as thin as the green stem of the lily and bent her head over her appliqué. What she wouldn't give to be in her own house. She'd left her journal there, fearing it would fall into Leila's meddling hands if she brought it with her to Chestnut Hill.

Not that she'd written anything in it in the month since Papa surprised her with the birthday gift. He knew how she loved to "scribble" and vowed she might miss the rapture if she had her nose in a book at the moment of the Twinkling Eye. The journal, to Sarah Jane's delight, combined the best of both of her passions.

Who knows? Someday, somewhere, someone else might read what she hoped would be pearls of wisdom gleaned along the path of her life's journey. And so, she'd resolved to record only the most momentous of events.

As if anything of any importance would ever happen among the sleepy Snowbird Mountains.

Her father contended Leila merely lacked the fruit of self-control—in Sarah Jane's opinion not the only fruit of the Spirit Leila Hummingbird lacked. Then her conscience—and the voice of her own dead mother—smote Sarah Jane. She closed her eyes, repentant in the face of her self-righteousness.

"Patience," she prayed when dealing with Leila Hummingbird.

Leila tossed a lock of luxuriant hair over her shoulder. "What are you mumbling about?"

Although Leila's mother died in the act of bringing Leila into the world, Sarah Jane's mother only succumbed to pleurisy of the lungs a few years back. And Sarah's mother had spent as much time on her knees for the motherless, little Cherokee girl as for Sarah Jane.

For the sake of her dearly departed mother, Sarah Jane held her tongue and held fast to her temper when Leila Hummingbird's irritating presence drove her out of sheer exasperation to the throne of her Consolation.

Carriage wheels rattled on the gravel path. She and Leila, for once in total harmony, both flung their ladylike endeavors to the side and rushed for the window overlooking the circular drive.

Sarah Jane steepled her hands under her chin. "Blessed be God."

Leila clapped her hands together, the red and green tartan ribbons bobbing in her hair. "Finally . . ." Her face fell. "Oh. Your father came alone. Wonder where the new doctor is?"

At the sight of the brown parcel clutched in his hand, Leila squealed and darted on the tips of her patent leather shoes to the entrance hall. She flung open the door before the Hummingbird's Negro butler, Samson, could grasp the door handle. Sarah Jane followed more sedately—something *she'd* learned in the two-year Moravian finishing school.

Glimpsing Sarah, her papa paused on the wide veranda, his whiskered cheeks breaking into a smile. Leila seized the parcel and ripped into the brown paper. He winked at his daughter over Leila's head. Leila dashed into the house with her prize, eager to escape the biting cold.

Sarah Jane's arms encircled his ample girth. "Welcome back, Papa."

He kissed the top of her head. "Thought we'd ride home alone together. Give the young doc a chance to catch his breath after the long journey into our mountain wilderness."

"And spare him fresh off the boat from New York an untoward encounter with the likes of Leila Hummingbird?"

He laughed and patted her shoulder. "Remember charity, my Sarah Jane. And, kindness."

She rested her cheek against the smooth brocade of his vest. "I speak the truth."

"But dost you speak the truth in love?" His words remonstrated, but his eyes twinkled. "Have you no curiosity about the gift I have for you, my daughter?"

He hugged her close. "A gift of a new laborer unto the harvest of souls in our mountain fold." He tugged playfully at a strand of her strawberry blonde hair.

"Is he nice?"

What she wanted to ask was if he were handsome.

Her father's face wreathed into a broad smile. "An interesting travel companion. A worthy sort with whom to while away a winter's evening. Especially, I think, to a young lady, such as yourself."

Anticipation filled Sarah Jane with a certainty that something far better than silk awaited her at home.

Today might just provide the first entry into her journal . . . An inexplicable feeling arose.

Sarah Jane put a hand to her throat. Perhaps a milestone along the journey of the rest of her life.

3

2018—Cartridge Cove

I don't see why the tribe hired that white, big-city woman to promote what's supposed to be a Cherokee event. Why not one of us?"

Walker yanked open the door of his gunmetal gray F-150 and slid in beside his uncle. Cranking the engine, he slammed the dinging door shut.

Hawk-faced, Ross narrowed his eyes. "Because she's Marvela Campbell's granddaughter, and the Campbells *are* one of us."

Walker shoved the gearshift into reverse, gravel spraying as he backed out of the temporary lodgings his uncle rented. "White Appalachian, Indian wannabes—"

"The Campbells are good people. Marvela may be white, but she understands The People."

His uncle Ross had gone ramrod stiff, his spine as straight as the career soldier he'd been before retirement last year. "Their roots are as deep in this town as ours. Preachers, doctors, teachers the lot of them." He cocked an eye Walker's way. "She could teach you a thing or two about community service."

Walker shot Ross a suspicious look. "Sounds like you know her. And I thought her name was Birchfield." The truck rattled over the wooden trestle bridge that straddled Singing Creek.

Ross gazed out the window. "Born a Campbell. Her daddy and granddaddy preached at the old church on Meetinghouse Road. After she left Cartridge Cove, she married a Birchfield."

"Part of them Birchfields up Asheville way?" Walker crinkled his nose. "The timber people who almost stripped the mountains bare a hundred years ago?"

Ross glared. "You and your trees."

"The Birchfields," Walker gritted his teeth, "who hobnobbed with the Vanderbilts at the turn of the century."

Walker threw up his hand to wave at Calvin Ledford closing the co-op craft gallery, probably on the way home to feed his belly. Too early in the year for many tourists—not that Cartridge Cove being so far off the beaten path exactly crawled with tourists even in the height of the season. Which was just how Walker liked it.

The peaceful mountain life he'd dreamed of while soldiering in the hot sands of Afghanistan would be irrevocably destroyed if his mother, the tribal council, and Marvela Birchfield had their way.

Walker grimaced. "She married the Birchfield who became a U.S. Congressman, didn't she? What did she want to come back here for, you reckon?"

Ross averted his gaze. "Maybe she wanted to come home. After your aunt Bonita passed . . ." He sighed. "Maybe Marvela, like me after all my wanderings across the earth, just wanted to come home."

Walker glanced over at the strange expression on his uncle's face. A man who'd fought in Vietnam, Desert Storm, and every twentieth-century military conflict in-between. "You know her?" At Ross's shrug, Walker prodded. "Know her well?"

Ross cleared his throat. "Knew her. A long time ago."

Walker negotiated a curve, calculating his uncle's age and Marvela Birchfield's.

"Things were different then." Ross folded his hands in his lap. "Summer after we graduated, Marvela and I met at the community gospel sing in Robbinsville. Dinner on the grounds. The one time Cherokee and non-Indians got together every year. Still do. She'd been reading that book by C. S. Lewis they made into a movie."

"And?"

Ross shuffled his feet in the floorboard of the pickup. "I've always loved a good book."

Walker raised his eyebrows, waiting for the rest of the story.

"She let me borrow it. Next week, the singing was held in her pappy's church. Between singing groups, we talked about the book. The symbolism. The metaphors for life. The trials the children faced, and how in the end they triumphed over their own individual weaknesses to become the person Aslan knew they could be all along. You ever read *The Chronicles of Narnia*, boy? It's a classic."

"I saw the movie." Walker clenched his hands around the steering wheel. "At the base."

Feeling his uncle's eyes on him, Walker dared not turn his head and witness the compassion he'd find there. If anyone would understand the kind of things you endured in the face of enemy fire, Uncle Ross would. But sympathy often undid him since he'd finished his tour and come home for good. And Walker was tired of being the object of everyone's well-meaning pity.

The old man laid a gentle hand on Walker's shoulder. "I don't fault you, son. If anyone's earned the right to live the rest of their life in peace, it's a veteran."

Ross smiled. The wrinkles around his hooded dark eyes deepened. Wrinkles earned over a lifetime of scanning distant desert and jungle horizons. And, juggling the responsibility of the lives under his command. "You've made your mom so happy since you've come home, come to the altar and been baptized a new man."

"The old Walker wasn't so great. Figured it was long past time for a change. Of heart. In direction. In everything."

His uncle's cheeks lifted. "Had a talk with God myself in a jungle in 'Nam. Until then, a more stupid, foolish young man you've never met in all your born days."

"You, Uncle Ross?"

"Me." Ross thumped his chest. "Don't make the mistakes I did. Don't try to run or," he nudged Walker with his elbow, "hide in those trees of yours from life, love, and what God knows you can be."

Walker stiffened. "Mom's been blabbing to you, too, hasn't she? About the Sheriff's offer? He's concerned over the vandalism and the attack on the Center. Hotheads on our side are threatening retaliation, too. But I told her and I'm telling you, I'm done with violence. Give me those trees and a clean mountain breeze any day."

"Love's so wasted on the young and foolish." His uncle's lip curled. "Those trees. Don't you find bark a little rough for cozying up to sometimes? Especially when it's cold outside?"

Walker rolled his eyes. Just what he needed. A lecture on love from his elderly uncle. "Did the committee bother to investigate this Birchfield granddaughter's credentials?"

"Sure. We've got her résumé on file. Considered the references she provided."

"Notoriously unreliable. Did you run a background check or—?"

Ross's bushy eyebrows furrowed. "You talking a criminal background check?"

"Yes, I am. What do you know about this woman?"

Ross drummed his fingers along the armrest. "Graduated from UVA with a communications degree. Worked for a New York City firm for three years before leaving and returning to Raleigh to start her own PR company."

Walker pivoted. "Why'd she leave? Fired?"

"You read the papers lately?" Ross sniffed. "Oh, I forgot. Your generation only gets its news from the Internet. Laid off in a sluggish economy, not fired."

"Laid off? You know that for sure?"

"Her former boss spoke highly of her work ethic and character. We examined her portfolio and the ad campaigns she created. Not that we needed those other references. Marvela Birchfield's was plenty."

Walker resolved to do a Google search on this Birchfield granddaughter as soon as he got home.

"Do you know Marvela Campbell, boy?"

Walker cut his eyes over to his uncle at the wistful note in his voice. "Just in passing. From church. She's only been back a few months, but keeping the local carpenters in business remodeling that house of hers."

"She's still a stunner, I'll bet."

Walker shrugged. "I guess. She's old."

Ross punched him in the muscle of his arm.

"Ow!" Walker took one hand off the wheel long enough to rub his arm.

"I repeat, love and I don't know what-all," Ross's nostrils flared. "Is so wasted on the young."

Passing the Mercantile and his mother's quilt shop, Walker veered onto a side street that jutted off Main and into a recently blacktopped driveway. He stopped the truck beside the shaded, deep porch that ran the length of the three-story Victorian home.

Walker shifted the gearstick into park. "Yeah, it's the 'what-all' that gets me every time." He opened the door and thrust his jean-clad legs over the side.

"Don't you dare . . ." Ross growled.

Walker swiveled.

Ross's face flushed to an interesting shade of apoplectic purple.

A sudden sympathy for the Vietcong caught in one of his uncle's crosshairs surfaced in Walker's mind.

Ross stalked over to the driver's side—pretty good for a man of his advanced sixty-plus years, Walker reckoned—and jabbed a pointy brown finger in the region of Walker's ribs.

Walker inhaled. Sharply.

"Don't you dare, young man, embarrass me in front of Marvela Campbell. You hear?"

What in the Snowbird had gotten into the old guy?

"I hear."

But he didn't have to like it.

◆

"Sarah Jane, the daughter of a medical missionary to the Cherokee . . ." Linden flipped back a few pages and huddled closer to the late afternoon sunshine streaming through the attic window. Dust motes danced in the air.

"Uh-huh." Marvela rummaged in the trunk.

"She mentions a green trunk." Linden raised her head. "Like the one you're determined to excavate today. But it says here," she tapped Sarah Jane's journal with her finger. "The trunk, if it's the same one, belonged to a Cherokee girl named Leila Hummingbird."

Marvela's penciled brows inverted into a V. "Never heard of her. And I assure you, neither the Campbells nor the Birchfields have a drop of Cherokee blood in them, although not for lack . . ."

Crouching once again, Marvela plunged the upper half of her body inside the trunk and emerged with several sepia-toned daguerreotypes in one hand.

Linden smiled. "Wouldn't it be something if there was a false bottom to the trunk and more treasures yet to be revealed?"

She returned to her perusal of the journal. "Sarah Jane drew a picture of the quilt she mentions in the diary. A pattern called Carolina Lily."

Marvela foraged around, one hand inside the depths of the trunk's confines. "Old North Carolina pattern. With the local connection you've discovered, maybe we should include that pattern alongside the others planned for the Cherokee Quilt Barn Trail."

"Wait . . ." Marvela grunted. "Found . . . something . . ."

Linden scanned the drawing. "I like the quilt guild's idea to paint local barns with quilt squares. And featuring patterns associated with this part of North Carolina and the Cherokee is even better."

Marvela set her jaw as she thrust both hands around the perimeter of the trunk bottom. "Irene Crowe's spearheaded that committee."

Linden thumbed through the book. "Here's another quilt of a Cherokee Rose pattern. The Campbells or Birchfields own any quilts, Gram?"

"Only the ones my granny stitched during the Depression. Not a Carolina Lily or a Cherokee Rose among them. I've given a Sunbonnet Sue to Quincy for the display on white Appalachian history in Cartridge Cove. Hope it wasn't damaged in the attack."

Linden glanced at her watch. "Don't forget that ga-gadoo—"

"Ga-doo-gee is an old custom. The Cartridge Cove Community Development Club has embraced *gadugi* as part of its mission to foster a Cherokee spirit of goodwill. They chop firewood in the fall for the elderly. Help the needy. Raise money for the volunteer fire department and local athletic teams."

Marvela's once pristine French-manicured nails scrabbled across the trunk upholstery. "Irene's son, Walker, rotated into club leadership this year. He'll supervise the actual painting of the barns if, between the two of you, you can get those stubborn old coots—Cherokee and non-Indian alike—up the mountain to agree to having the quilt billboards affixed to their property. Almost . . ." She heaved and pried. "Almost . . ."

"Shouldn't we wrap it up here?" Linden frowned at the current state of her own appearance. "It's going on four now. But you know me with a book . . . I lost track of time. You, too, once another adventure has gotten hold of you, Gram."

A ripping sound.

"We're on Cherokee time here, darlin', not like New York." Marvela fell back upon her designer-clad haunches. But in her hand she gripped a small, oval portrait of a beautiful Cherokee woman.

"Ta-da!" she crowed. "Maybe that Leila Hummingbird you mentioned?"

Laying the journal aside, Linden caught the sound of a vehicle door slamming. She scooted closer to examine the oil painting.

She whistled in admiration. "Sarah Jane was right. If this was Leila Hummingbird, she wasn't only beautiful, she was drop-dead gorgeous. Would you look at those cheekbones?"

Marvela wasn't listening, though. She'd returned to her trunk diving. "And what do we have here?"

Clutching a wad of cotton batiste, she rose, one hand gripping Linden's arm for support. "These knees aren't as young as they used to be, my darlin' girl."

Marvela unfolded the yellowed fabric. Two silk ribbons dangled. "A bonnet?"

Linden's fingertips brushed the once-starched cap.

"Oh." Marvela's eyes widened. "It's—" She jerked the tiny hat behind her back.

At a sudden, quick memory, the familiar weight settled upon Linden's chest. A smothering ache. She tried, like all the other times, to swallow past the lump. But she swayed against the attic wall, the breath knocked from her lungs.

Her grandmother's strangled voice filtered through her suffocating grief. "Linden, honey, I would've never pulled it out if I'd known . . ."

Linden inhaled and exhaled, fighting past yet another trigger, struggling to execute the breathing exercises her father swore in his considerable medical experience would help. But despite long years of counseling and medication, they never did.

"I-I can't—" Linden dodged her grandmother's outstretched hand. "I can't stay here. Why did I think I could do this? Do anything ever again?"

Marvela blanched, as ashen as she'd been while prying Linden's fingers off the sides of the hospital bassinet with its IV lines and electronic monitors. "Linden, don't . . . You've come so far. Made so much progress."

Linden darted for the stairs. "I need some air. I need to—"

If she didn't escape, she'd either retch or hyperventilate. Her feet pounded down the steps and onto the second floor landing. The mauve tones her grandmother adored—aka Barbara Cartland gone American Victorian—blurred as she lurched toward an exit.

Recalling the incessant beeping in the neonatal ICU, Linden clapped her hands over her ears as she stumbled down the main staircase toward the ground floor. Images flooded her mind. And the final, droning flatline of her nightmares.

As long as she worked until she collapsed into bed each night, as long as she filled her days with New York's subway sounds or the blaring horns of Raleigh's rush-hour traffic, the white noise held those other sounds at bay. Preserving for Linden whatever sanity yet remained.

Why had she come to this godforsaken place with nothing but the chirping of birds to drown out what she'd spent ten years trying to forget? Why Cartridge Cove, where nothing but the wind moaned? With nothing but reminders of those desolate days after the small coffin had been lowered into the ground. Reminders of a lost time when no one could console her.

Dashing through the foyer, she stifled a sob. Who was she kidding? She was the godforsaken one.

Hot tears burned. Everything her fault . . .

White-knuckled, she grabbed the brass handle on the oak door, flinging it wide. And in her near-panic, she hurtled across the threshold and smack into a mountain whose hand was upraised in the motion of knocking.

Linden bounced off him and into the doorframe. She screamed and the mountain yelled in surprised unison. Clutching her racing heart, she took a swift look at the scowling, immovable obstacle in her path.

A Snowbird Cherokee mountain.

4

January 1838

Sarah Jane stretched her arms skyward, billowing the sheet over the clothesline on the first, moderately mild day since Old Christmas. She reveled in the warmth of the sun on her cheeks beneath her woolen bonnet. And, she sensed his gaze out the window upon her. A smile flitted across her lips.

His tiny cubicle in her father's surgery overlooked the kettle where she boiled the linens over the fire outside the house. She often encountered his scrutiny as she tended to her papa's household while her father gave Pierce a crash course in herbal remedies he'd gleaned from his Cherokee friends and incorporated into his own practice.

And what was it her papa said yesterday, a teasing glint in his blue eyes?

That Sarah Jane's domicile had never looked so well kept and scrubbed? How ". . . not a streak of dirt dared rear its ugly head amidst such dedicated daily ministrations."

She blushed at the memory. Her papa knew her too well.

Had it only been a month since Pierce arrived? She felt she'd known him forever.

"Sarah!" Her father's voice called from inside the house.

Her head snapped up as a blur of movement around the corner of the house snared her attention. Straightening, she wiped her hands on the faded blue calico she wore on washdays. Hurrying forward, Sarah observed a tall, Cherokee man and his older companion leaning against the wood-framed farmhouse. The younger man wore fringed, deerskin leggings.

Sighting Sarah, he scowled. He crossed his arms over the loose-fitting ribbon shirt most Cherokee favored. His thick mane of dark hair unbound and blowing in the slight breeze, he moved to bar her path to the door.

Taken aback by the undisguised hostility on his face, Sarah faltered. She put a hand to her hair. Her fingers shook as she tucked an unruly tendril inside the bonnet.

What ailed this young man? But everyone was tense these days. Soldiers swarmed over the valley settlements erecting stockades and recording names in some military census.

She squared her shoulders. This wasn't the frontier any more, although the copper-skinned man looked like a throwback to more primitive times.

As if he had his druthers, he'd just as soon scalp her.

She reminded herself the Cherokee were one of the Five Civilized Tribes and gathered her courage. "Excuse me, please."

He stood unmoving, rock solid in her path.

Clearing her throat, she tried again. "Did you bring a patient?"

Towering over her, he peered down his long nose at her, adept at the silence game the Cherokee often employed.

Flustered, she felt the heat rise beneath her collar. One of the curses of her redheaded, Scots-Irish heritage. "My father called . . . He requires my assistance . . . If you'd just . . ."

Maybe, like many of the Cherokee especially those with farms high in the mountain hollows, he spoke no English.

His eyes darkened. One lip raised in a sneer, he muttered something in Cherokee. She reared back as much at the malice in his tone as the stinging, vulgar word he'd used. The old man made a motion of protest, halted by a sibilant hiss from the younger man.

She bit back the reply that rose to her lips, reminding herself of her father's admonition—also from Scripture—that a gentle answer turned away wrath. An inexplicable wrath on this young man's part.

"Nv-wa-do-hi-ya-dv." Lifting her chin, she met his stare head on. But she took care to maintain a soft, even tone. "Peace. No harm," she repeated.

An uncharitable feeling of satisfaction bubbled in her chest as his smoldering eyes widened in confused surprise. He had the grace, if not the manners, to flush.

Few whites, truth to tell, spoke the intricate, tonal Cherokee language, but Papa made sure Sarah Jane did as part of their mission. Along with his training of Cherokee convert laypersons, he believed to minister fully to the Cherokee's body and soul, one must understand them. And speaking their language was a first step toward understanding.

The back door squeaked open. Pierce, his starched collar open at the neck and his sleeves rolled to his elbows ready for doctoring, emerged into the sunlight. A muscle twitching in his cheek, he inserted himself between Sarah Jane and the Cherokee. Forcing her to peer over Pierce's broad shoulder.

Pierce jutted his jaw. "Is there a problem here, Miss Hopkins?" His gaze never left the Cherokee's face.

Miss Hopkins. Sarah swallowed an inward sigh. Pierce, always so formal and correct on the surface. But his cornflower blue eyes often danced merry as he teased her over dinner at the end of a busy day.

Caught in her perpetual daydreaming, she'd been too slow to respond, Sarah realized, as Pierce angled toward her, concern etched across his features.

"Sarah?" His eyes did not dance with amusement at this moment. Something else, fiercer and protective, however, shone.

"I'm fine. I was just about to help Papa but . . ." Her gaze sharpened past Pierce's chiseled New England features to where the Indian glowered.

Pierce clamped his hand upon Sarah's arm. "Your father has a female patient." Veering around the Cherokee as one would an annoying wasp, he advanced toward the steps, pulling her along behind him.

Something flickered in the Cherokee's face. He sidestepped a pace, allowing her and Pierce access to the porch. But with another murmured epithet, the Cherokee screwed his face and spat, releasing a wad of saliva and tobacco, which landed square on the toe of Pierce's shoe.

Gasping, she grabbed Pierce to prevent him surging forward to answer the Cherokee's disrespect.

His pale face engorged with blood fury. "What did he call me, Sarah Jane?" Pierce hissed between thin, fine lips.

She fought to hold on to him as Pierce and the Cherokee strained toward the other like cocks at a fight. "Nothing. Ignore him."

The older man jerked the younger's sleeve. He repeated Sarah Jane's earlier salutation of peace. "Nuh-wah-doe-he-yah-duh."

In rapid-fire Cherokee, the old man reminded the younger man of his grandmother's condition. The old man sent Sarah Jane an imploring look.

"U-lo-gi-dv," the old one remonstrated.

His grandson stalked away toward the front of the house. She released a ragged breath.

U-lo-gi-dv? So the hostile one's name was . . . Touch the Clouds.

The old man lifted his hands. "Excuse . . ." He shook his head at his broken attempt at English. "Young men . . ." He raised one shoulder and let it drop in resignation. "Angry these days."

Pierce shrugged free of her grip. He extended his hand toward the old man. "Nuh-wah-doe-he-yah-duh," glancing at her to make sure he'd pronounced it correctly. "Peace to you and to your family in the name of our Lord and Savior, Jesus Christ."

The old man narrowed his eyes at his reference to the Lord, but accepted Pierce's hand. Pierce, Papa had remarked for her ears only, possessed great medical expertise, head knowledge, and religious zeal.

Practical application? Her father had shaken his head. Not so much. Not yet.

She tugged at Pierce to follow her into the house. "Better to show him our Christ first through our medicine and compassion."

"We'll take good care of your wife," she told the old man in his own language.

The old man, like his grandson, would prefer to remain in the habitat he knew best.

Yielding, Pierce allowed the door to bang shut. His lanky beanpole posture stiffened as his nose wrinkled. "Not sure why the Doctor feels it necessary to soil your fair hands in such professional matters."

Untying her bonnet, she strode toward the washbasin and pitcher on the kitchen table and resisted the urge to roll her eyes. "Speaking of soiled . . ."

Papa had found Pierce an apt and able assistant. He predicted a bright future for Pierce in furthering God's kingdom among the *Tsalgi* or Principal People, as they called themselves.

Just as soon, Papa had added, as God took down the young doctor and his notions a peg or two first.

"You said the patient was a woman. An old woman?" She scrubbed the lye soap against her skin all the way to her elbows. Another one of Papa's medical protocols Pierce found inexplicable, but followed under Dr. Hopkins's tutelage.

Grabbing a dishtowel, she wiped her hands and made room for Pierce. She poised the water pitcher over the bowl.

A mutinous expression on his face, he pushed his lips forward.

"Papa will insist you wash again."

Grimacing, he thrust his hands over the basin, and she poured a steady stream of water over his hands as he lathered his hands and arms once more.

She tried her best to prevent her eyes from lingering too long on the corded muscles of his forearms. "The Cherokee, most of them anyway, even after Papa's labor among them all these years, prefer their own shamans to treat their ills."

He snorted.

She ignored his outburst. "The shamans are powerful figures, especially among the Snowbird Cherokee, less so in Georgia or—"

"The more civilized parts of the Cherokee Nation."

"In the more prosperous regions, I was going to say." She handed another towel to him. "Once it's gotten beyond the shaman's skills or enough fear for the injured has had time to set in, they will—with trepidation—seek out the white man's medicine. The women and children usually prefer another female on hand during diagnosis and treatment."

He flicked water droplets over the pan. "Yes, she's an old woman. A bad cut on her leg from a misaimed axe stroke now infected, your father surmised from his questioning of her. In Cherokee."

Pierce threw Sarah Jane a pointed glance. "I've almost finished my study of the herbs. Maybe . . . ?" He twisted the cloth around his hands.

Such strong, long-fingered hands.

A surgeon's hands, Papa said. Her insides aquiver, Sarah Jane drew her gaze out the window. A mockingbird sang in the winter-bare branches of a dogwood tree.

"You want I should teach you the language?" she whispered. She kept her gaze averted to spare his male dignity the indignity of seeking help from a member of the fairer sex.

Pierce maintained such inconvenient ideas of what was proper and what was not she reflected, not for the first time in their short acquaintance.

Ideas—Papa had commented with a wry twist of his lips when Pierce objected to her attendance over a child's broken arm—of which necessity would soon disabuse him.

Pinching his lips together, Pierce folded the towel in exact thirds, draping it over the ladder-backed kitchen chair. "If it led to the greater efficacy of my mission, I'd . . ." His eyes fell to the puncheon wood floor.

Efficacy. Pierce and his words. Must be how folks talked in the North.

Sarah Jane wouldn't know. She'd been born and reared in these smoky blue hills, home to the Cherokee for millennia.

A sunbeam made its way through the glass pane, highlighting the curly, close-cropped blond locks on his head. A ping went through her. She ran her gaze over the angular line of his strong jaw.

Blessed be God. She'd never met a handsomer man.

Not white, leastways. And though she suspected her father schemed for someday Pierce to take over the mission—and perhaps wed his daughter—Sarah Jane, plain as she was, realized the possibility of Pierce ever thinking of her in that light was slim to none.

But she wouldn't pass on a chance to spend more time with him.

Her heart hammered.

"I'd be happy to instruct you in the rudimentary elements of the Cherokee language. Perhaps a lesson every night after dinner?"

He raised his eyes to hers. A slight smile quivered on those oh-so-fine lips. "Perhaps over the washing and drying of the supper dishes. I've been told I'm quite handy when it comes to cleaning up."

She returned his smile. There might be hope yet for Dr. Pierce if he was willing to disgrace himself with menial, womanly chores. "You have yourself a deal." She extended her hand and then retracted it. "I'd shake your hand, but then we'd both have to wash again."

He grinned, shuffling his feet. And being the lovesick creature she was, she grinned back at him.

"Sarah Jane! Pierce!" her father bellowed down the hall.

Pierce blinked and Sarah Jane jolted.

"Coming, Papa!" she yelled in her not-so-ladylike nurse voice.

Plucking a clean, white pinafore off the hook on the wall, she hurried to assist him. She schooled her heart, as she had a thousand times this last month, to pay better attention to her patients.

And, blessed be God, not to the handsome object of her affections.

5

2018—Cartridge Cove

That had gone well.

Walker threw his uncle, poised on the wide-planked step, an exasperated look. The council had hired a nut job in this Birchfield woman. The petite woman backed into an ivy-draped urn.

He steadied the urn, wobbling on the stone-columned pedestal, at the same instant the Birchfield woman had the same idea. As his hand mounded over hers, her eyes widened. She snatched her hand free.

Stung, he retreated a step.

Right. Add paranoid to the list. Prickly as . . .

She glared at him as if he was a serial killer. Her eyes as blue as . . . He gulped.

As blue as the April sky over the ridge of his farm this morning.

Shoes clattering down the staircase, Marvela Birchfield hurried out. "Honey, are you . . . ? I thought I heard . . ."

Her granddaughter crossed her arms, her face one big scowl at the object of her displeasure—him. Marvela's gaze flicked between her granddaughter's taut features and his.

The old woman looped a conciliatory arm around her granddaughter's waist. "I see you've already introduced yourself to Walker Crowe, Linden."

Linden? He frowned. "Like a tree?"

Her head tilted, the Tree jabbed her finger at him. "That's Irene's son? The one I'm supposed to—?"

"A linden tree? And Birchfield, too?"

He flushed. That sounded even more stupid out loud.

Marvela's granddaughter bristled. "Yeah. So what?" Strands of light brown hair tumbled out of a clumsy attempt at a topknot on her head. "Linden Birchfield—a tree in a field of other trees. Ha. Ha. Ha."

He'd know in the future to leave her name alone. This woman possessed enough emotional baggage to fill the cargo hold of a plane.

Ross cleared his throat. "Marvela?"

Marvela peered around Walker and gasped. She put her hand over her mouth.

Ross came level with them. He stopped inches from Marvela. "Still as beautiful as the day the Ford Modeling Agency snapped you up."

Walker and Linden, relegated to outsider status, exchanged puzzled glances. He let his shoulders rise and drop in response to the unspoken query in Linden's eyes.

Ross's face softened. "Marvela the Marvelous as marvelous as ever."

Marvela Birchfield glowed as pretty as the last rose of summer. She smiled, her eyes turning into half-moons. She clasped her hands in front of her. "And you've not changed a bit either, Ross Wachacha."

It was Ross's turn to pink. "You're being gracious." He touched a finger to the white hair above his ear Walker believed gave his uncle a distinguished, authoritative air. "Didn't know if you'd remember—"

"Ross the Resolute." Breathless, her eyes swept over his uncle's weathered face. She touched his arm. "And I never forgot."

Something passed in the air between his uncle and Marvela Birchfield.

Walker sighed, for the first time in a long while, feeling his aloneness.

Linden moved toward the door, breaking the spell in which their elders seemed mesmerized. "It's getting cold out here." She wrapped her bare arms around herself.

A hand over her heart, Marvela stepped into the interior of the house. "Where are my manners? Ross, Walker . . ." She gestured. "Come inside and let me fix coffee for everyone."

Ross, as sure-footed as any mountain goat, stumbled across the threshold. Stumbled, probably because it was awful hard to walk and keep your eyes on a moving object like Marvela at the same time.

He reached out to steady his uncle. But Ross threw off his arm and surged after Marvela. Walker bit back a smile.

Old love? First love? He'd enjoy worming this story out of his uncle later.

He crossed into the spacious oak-floored foyer. Of Linden there was no sign. Marvela led the way into a Victorian nightmare of a parlor. At her insistence, he settled behind a mahogany coffee table onto a stiff pink silk settee. The springs and his backside groaned at the effort.

Ross eased into a chintz-covered easy chair. "Marvela, you've done wonders with this place."

Walker took a moment to absorb the ambience. Trained to observe and absorb details at a glance, he noted the mantel with its hand-carved Cherokee Rose finials. The silver candlesticks. A Seth Thomas clock. The Tabriz carpet at his feet. Rosewood end tables.

Something the tourists would eat up.

Marvela craned her head in the direction of the foyer. "I don't know where that girl has got to." She shook her head. "This generation . . ."

Ross shot Walker a less-than-friendly look. "Self-absorbed—"

"Hey," Walker protested. "I resent that remark."

Ross arched his eyebrow. "You resemble that remark."

Marvela laughed. "Sounds like my Linden and Walker will get on fine."

Ross stroked his chin. "Like a forest on fire."

Walker winced. "No need to bring the trees into it."

A floorboard creaked. "What is it with you and trees?"

He jerked at the sound of Linden's voice. She'd changed into more businesslike attire—navy blue slacks and a white linen blouse. The smudges of dirt erased from her face, she'd restored her hair to its uptight, updo.

Carrying a sheaf of folders, she plopped them onto the coffee table. "Excuse me, please."

Blocked on the other side by Marvela and Ross, she scooted between him and the table. Too late, he realized he could've slid farther down and saved her the trouble.

A whiff of roses floated past his nostrils as she edged past. Like the old roses his now deceased grandmother had once grown in her front yard. The large, fragrant kind in keeping with this Victorian decor.

Marvela clapped her hands together. "Why don't I make the coffee while you two get acquainted?"

Ross stood. "I'll help."

Marvela gave a cheery wave as they disappeared toward the back of the house. Linden inched away from him, leaving Walker feeling like a pariah.

Not the usual reaction he received from the ladies. He didn't bite, after all. But if he did, Walker wouldn't have touched Linden Birchfield with a ten-foot pole.

So not his type, if he had a type. Whatever her problem, nothing to do with him. He had his trees, his team, and his family. And no interest in the romantic complications, which came part and parcel with women—no matter their ethnic heritage.

He shot another surreptitious look in her direction. This lady, he sensed in his gut, was full of snaring entanglements.

Good thing, he'd sworn off women since Afghanistan.

She opened the folder and fanned out its contents.

He allowed himself one more sneak peek. A pretty woman. Petite like a ballerina. His gaze traveled from her eyes to the curve of her neck and back to the blue of her eyes.

Which narrowed.

"If you're done sizing me up, I'd like to show you what the committee and I have planned." A frown hollowed the space between her brows.

He chewed the inside of his cheek. Pretty, yeah, but that mouth of hers?

A woman, he got the distinct impression, who didn't smile much. He wondered what it'd take to make her smile.

Pondered what he could do to make those rosebud lips smile. He swallowed.

She handed him a paper. "I've created ads for various media outlets, print, online, and television."

He leaned forward to get a better look-see.

"Area churches are coordinating the gospel singing. The Jaycees are handling the kickoff parade. Local artisans are renting vendor booths. I'm coordinating my efforts with Dr. Sawyer and the grand opening of the Trail of Tears Interpretive Center—"

His knee brushed against her leg.

She stopped. Her fingers fondled the silver locket at her throat. Silence ticked between them.

His heart thudded, and he searched desperately for something—anything—to say to this sophisticated career woman who stirred his senses. She stared at him, as if waiting.

Waiting for what?

His gaze locked onto hers. And something flickered in her sky blue eyes. His pulse rocketed.

If the cool Linden Birchfield could affect him so, maybe his mom was right. Maybe it was time to get out more.

Time to find a nice, Christian Cherokee girl. Farm the land. Have kids of his own . . .

"Are you listening to me, Mr. Crowe?"

"Uh-huh . . ."

Gulping, he dragged his eyes away from her accusing ones.

Keep it cool, Crowe. Businesslike.

He took a breath. "You've accomplished a lot. How long have you been in town?"

Better.

She shuffled some papers. "Just a week, but I've been working with the committee via email since January." Lining up the edges of the papers, she rapped them against the table, straightened a few unruly corners and racked them together again.

Her slim piano fingers seemed incapable of remaining motionless. He wondered if he made her as nervous as she made him. Though why the high-strung city lady . . .

Get a grip, he scolded.

Army specialists didn't—shouldn't—get intimidated. And certainly not by some slip of a woman, no bigger than one of the willow trees down by Singing Creek. But the correlation of the graceful, bending trees and Linden Birchfield wouldn't leave his mind. His gaze flitted to her hands again.

Ringless fingers . . .

"The quilt patterns will be painted onto wooden blocks and installed on the barns, which meander along the historic Cherokee Trail. Other quilt barn trails around the Blue Ridge Parkway have proven to be a draw for tourists." Her mouth pursed. "Your mother's selected patterns with definite Cherokee significance, but some of the barn owners are proving difficult to convince."

Remembering his own opposition to the festival, he clenched his fists. "'Cause giving up their privacy and splendid isolation isn't worth the tourist invasion."

"Hardly an invasion. I've seen the numbers, Mr. Crowe." She made an expansive gesture. "Cartridge Cove. Western North Carolina. The high unemployment. I've been up the road to see what Cherokee town offers. Tourists are the bread and butter of your entire tribe."

She slammed the folder shut. "So what exactly is your problem? It's not like anyone's asked you to paint your barn."

He gritted his teeth. "My problem is you have no idea what you're unleashing upon this town. You do your work, get paid, and then leave. The rest of us have to live with the changes you bring."

She leaned into his space. "I've done my research, Mr. Crowe."

He broadened his chest. "Head knowledge. You don't understand a thing about The People, Miz Birchfield."

"Is that what this is about?" She jabbed a finger. "Reverse discrimination because I'm not Native American?"

"Cherokee."

"What?"

He pointed to her and then to himself. "You and I both are native Americans. As is anyone born on U.S. soil. We prefer non-Indians call us American Indian or even better, by our tribe affiliation—Navajo, Lumbee, Cherokee."

Walker mirrored her body language, inches from her face. "Just one example of what you don't understand." He shook his head. "Not discrimination."

Her eyes flitted to the swishing motion of his ponytail. Her lips parted.

Walker's heart jackhammered at the blue flicker in the depths of her orbs.

Exhaling, she raised both hands, palms up. "I need this account, Mr. Crowe. The Snowbird Cherokee need this festival. Sure, it's about revenue, but it's also about restoring a lost heritage. A symbolic reunification of the tribes separated by an inhumane event."

Her shoulders slumped. "I don't understand your people, but I'd like to. I want to do the best job I can and represent your people and my clients the best way I'm able."

She turned those eyes of blue sky on him. "You could help me to understand. I'm willing to learn if you'll show me." She angled her knees toward him.

"And," she whispered. "It's Miss Birchfield, not Ms."

His mouth went dry. Walker broke eye contact and scanned the empty foyer. Where were his uncle and Marvela Birchfield with the coffee?

Linden placed her hand on top of his on the settee. "Would you help me?"

The scent of roses wafted around him. Reminding him of his grandmother?

Not.

Was it hot in here? He tugged at the collar of his shirt. Or was it just him?

Linden moistened her lips. "Would you help me to understand what it means to be Cherokee?"

Good thing he'd sworn off women. Especially uppity, wound too-tight, non-Indian women.

She reclined against the silk upholstery and crossed her ankles. "You're not afraid for some reason, are you?"

His eyes jerked to her face. She cocked her head and smiled.

Perfect, white teeth. He'd have expected no less with her Birchfield blood.

"I'm not afraid of anything." Or you, he added to himself.

A strange, sad look clouded her eyes. Her lips quivered. "How fortunate for you."

She stirred and donned the aloof, brittle smile she wore like a cloak. She extended a hand. "Do we have a deal? Will you help me?"

He gripped her hand, and they shook on it. But he did so against his better judgment. And with a sudden lurch of his stomach, he wondered what he—Mr. Noncommitment—had gotten himself into.

Linden's fingers tingled as his hand clasped hers. This was about the job, she reminded herself. And second chances. Her professional future depended on this festival being an outstanding success and enhancing her portfolio.

The pleasing aroma emanating from the man teased her senses. A clean scent she couldn't identify. Something that reminded her of . . . Christmas?

"Well," Marvela swept in. Two steps behind, Ross carried a mahogany tray with coffee cups and a silver pot. "It looks like the children are playing nicely together after all, Ross."

Her hand still gripped Walker's. Or was it the other way around?

She blushed.

He dropped her hand. And his eyes to the toe of his dark leather boot. "What took you so long?" he growled.

"Well-mannered, too, this generation." Ross set the tray down. "I apologize on behalf of my nephew. Holed up in his mountain aerie, he doesn't get out much."

She stole a look at Walker's face. A pulse ticked in his jaw. A handsome jaw.

Not that she was in the market for a face, handsome or otherwise.

Maybe not handsome exactly, she amended her mental perusal. But interesting, with his raven black hair skimmed out of his broad face into a band at the back of his head. Unlike the usual corporate guys of her acquaintance. Unlike The Jerk and his cloned horde of frat brothers, who took clean cut—if not respectable—to a new level.

Then again, being so different from The Jerk and his ilk could only be a point in Crowe's favor.

Ross handed a cup to Marvela. "Just catchin' up. The time got away from us."

Marvela giggled.

Giggled?

She raised her eyebrows at her grandmother, which Marvela— being Marvela—ignored.

Marvela gripped the coffee pot. "Do you still take your coffee black, Ross?" The "r" elongated in the air, Miss Ophelia-style.

Linden's gaze sharpened on her grandmother. She probed the look exchanged between Gram and Walker Crowe's uncle as Marvela passed the old gent his cup.

Marvela thrust the china plate stacked with her famous Cinnamon Delights at Linden. "Pass the cookies around, Linden. And what about you, Walker, darlin'?"

Linden nudged Walker with the plate. Guests first, but her mouth watered, anticipating the cinnamon chips melting against her tongue.

It was the cookie she craved, wasn't it?

"Uh . . ." Walker tore his eyes from her face—again—and took the plate from her hand.

What was with him? Did she have snakes coiling around her head? After the heavy lifting in the attic today, she didn't look her best, but really?

And he wasn't exactly a big talker. Although after the smooth-talking, full of you-know-what kind of eloquence from The Jerk, silence could be golden.

"Cr-Cream," Mr. Big Communicator stuttered.

His eyes, the blackest she'd ever seen in real life, fell to the plate in his hand. He shoved a whole cinnamon-studded cookie into his mouth. A wide, full-lipped mouth.

"Sugar, hon?"

Linden shot Marvela a suspicious glance. What was this Hostess-with-the-Mostest routine? The B & B didn't open for another six weeks. Why the Martha Stewart practice session?

"No shuggg . . ." Walker said around a mouthful of cookie. His big hand wrapped around the delicate porcelain plate.

Long, strong brown fingers. She made a conscious effort to peel her eyes off Walker Crowe. And failed.

Because despite the red flannel shirt and cell phone affixed to the pocket of his blue jeans—all of which he filled out so well—there was something wild and untamed about him. Exciting and scary, all at the same instant. And it was so not fair a man possessed those cheekbones.

What was wrong with her today?

Marvela reached for the cream pitcher. "Linden likes a little coffee with her cream. I keep pouring till she tells me to stop."

Linden shook herself from her contemplation of the Cherokee enigma beside her. "Till it's the color of beech trees in winter."

He choked.

Linden grabbed his plate as he hunched. She pounded him on the back with her other hand. And, after his snarky remarks moments earlier, none too gently.

Sputtering, he clamped a hand over his mouth to prevent cookie crumbs from splattering her grandmother's refurbished parlor. His face, a naturally dusky color, turned an unhealthy shade of red. His eyes watered.

Ross set aside his cup and started to his feet.

For pity's sake.

"Here," Linden handed Walker a napkin. "Arms up," she commanded. "Over your head. Did your mama never teach you what to do when you're choking?"

She hauled him to his feet. "Don't make me do the Heimlich on you."

Confusion, humiliation, and distress crisscrossed his stoic features, but she used the voice her dad utilized with first-year med students. And the six-foot plus Cherokee obeyed, coughing and towering over her. He shoved his long arms toward the ceiling like a teller in a bank holdup. His broad shoulders tapered to a narrow waist above his jeans.

Her mind wandered for a second, illogically wondering what it'd be like to wrap her arms around his sturdy frame—and from her up close and personal vantage point—well-defined middle.

Marvela thrust a glass of water in Walker's hand. "My son, Linden's dad, teaches at the hospital in Chapel Hill." She squeezed Linden's shoulder. "Guess you absorbed something over the years, huh?"

Wrinkling her forehead, Linden sniffed the air. "Gram? What's that smell—are you frying chicken?"

Marvela clamped a hand over her mouth. "Ross."

Again with the r-r-r-r's?

Ross sprinted out of the parlor with Marvela hot on his heels.

"It's my contribution to the Indian dinner being held at the church tonight," Marvela called over her shoulder.

Walker gulped down three-quarters of the water.

Between the rattling of pans in the kitchen and Walker's noisy attempts to regain his composure, Linden wrung her hands. "Do you need my help, Gram?"

"No," bellowed Marvela from the kitchen. "Ross and I have it under control. Just in time . . ."

"What's an . . ." Linden lowered the decibel of her voice and faced Walker dabbing at his eyes with the mauve-colored napkin. "What's an Indian dinner?"

He set the glass on the table with a ping. "Lesson number one." He scowled.

Good to know the belligerence as well as his dignity had been restored.

"An Indian dinner sells plates of food to the public to raise money for hospital bills, pay for local team uniforms, or to support the volunteer Cartridge Cove Fire Department. This one's put on by the church your grandmother, my mother, Irene Crowe, and I attend."

She quirked an eyebrow. "You attend church?"

A comment that earned her another scowl.

"You don't?"

Two could play this porcupine game.

"Not if I can help it."

He set his jaw. "Like I said, if you want to understand the Cherokee you've got to understand their heart. And a large part of their Snowbird heart revolves around community and church. It might just behoove you, Miz Birchfield," he drawled. "To join your grandmother tonight for a worthy cause and get to know some of the people you're supposed to be serving."

She pushed back her shoulders. "Well, maybe I will, but not because you think you can boss me around. You're not the boss of me, Walker Crowe. Nobody is."

He threw the napkin on the table as Marvela and Ross rejoined them. "Which, I suspect, lies at the heart of *your* personal problems."

Walker wheeled past his uncle. "I should've already picked up Emmaline by now."

So he'd assigned a field trip for her—a church field trip from the sounds of it—while Snowbird's gift to womankind gallivanted all over the county with a date? She hadn't realized it was possible for someone's blood to boil as hers did now. She'd have to remember to ask her dad about it later.

Ross stared between the two of them. "So soon?"

Marvela laid a restraining arm on Ross's shoulder. "Can't we—?"

Linden sidestepped Ross and Marvela, beating Walker to the entrance. She swung the front door wide. "Best be on your way. Wouldn't want Mr. Crowe to miss his . . ." She jutted her jaw. "His . . . appointment."

6

Mid-January 1838

Miss Hopkins! Slow down, I beg you."

Sarah Jane swiveled in the saddle. She peered over her shoulder at Pierce who clutched his hat atop his head with one hand and held the reins in a death grip with the other.

Clicking her tongue against her teeth, she eased the mare to a gentler pace, allowing Pierce time to catch up. "Papa said to hurry. The children seemed sure their mother was in a desperate way."

He blew out a breath, which hung like fog in the crisp winter air. "Most improper it is, I fear, Miss Hopkins, for us to be out riding unchaperoned." He fell in alongside Sarah.

She leaned over and plucked an errant pine needle from the curls at his ear. "Things are different here, Pierce. It's not New England. Same rules don't apply. We do what we have to do. And Papa already had his hands full with Mrs. Corn Tassel's baby on the way, too."

At the word, "baby," he flushed as scarlet as the cardinal *cheer-cheer-ing* over their heads on a branch of a tulip poplar. "Again, Miss Hopkins, most irregular and inappropriate for a young lady such as yourself . . ."

He swallowed. "A maiden lady to witness, much less participate—" The red patches on his windblown cheeks deepened.

She tried not to laugh as he realized his own unfortunate choice of words.

He floundered. "I mean, assist in such a delicate matter as—"

"Cows and horses."

She dug her heels into the mare's side and motioned him to follow.

"I beg your pardon, Miss Hopkins?"

One look at his dear, befuddled face, and she surrendered to the impulse to laugh this time. "In these parts, my papa's often called upon to tend livestock as well."

"But-but he's a medical practitioner. Of humans."

She rocked in rhythm with her horse, glad she'd worn her serviceable if ratty jacket over her striped, wool homespun on this brisk ride into the hills. "He does whatever it takes to get his foot in the cabin door. If he manages to bring their only source of milk unscathed through the birthing process—"

His eyebrows ascended almost to his hairline. "Miss Hopkins."

"The Cherokee will often bestow a measure of trust on him the next time one of their family members needs medical attention."

"But to involve his own daughter . . ."

She gave him a sidelong glance. His concern for her sensibilities was real, if unwarranted. "Things are different here," she reiterated for the thousandth time. "Society's rules don't apply. We do what we must. The women feel more comfortable with me present. And Papa needs my help since Mam died."

Reaching over the gap between their two horses as they picked their way across the mountain meadow, she took his hand in her gloved one. He appeared startled at first, but he wove his fingers into hers.

A shiver of something delicious warmed her.

He squeezed her hand. "I'm just concerned for your well-being, Sarah Jane." His earnest blue eyes stared into hers.

A gaze, she reckoned, in which she could lose herself forever. Like in the expanse of a blue sky.

She swallowed past the lump forming in her throat. "It'll be all right, Pierce. Like the apostle instructed, we must try to be all we can to all the people we can while we have the opportunity."

He favored her with a sweet smile. "Your faith and courage shame me at times, Sarah Jane Hopkins. I fear I have more to learn than I realized, and not only Cherokee words or herbs."

A beam of light from high over the forest haloed the manes of their horses. Kind of like how her heart felt, full of light these past weeks. Sighing, she noticed he hadn't let go of her hand as their mounts plodded side-by-side down the well-beaten hunting trail.

"The Cherokee believe they have a great responsibility to the earth and to each other. They're committed to caring for their elders as well as their youth. They're actually quite humorous—"

He snorted at that, his horse whuffling in response.

"No, really. I'll grant you, it's a dry humor. But they often employ it to diffuse a potential conflict with each other and to preserve harmony."

"You talk of pagan people with such admiration, Miss Hopkins."

"They possess many admirable qualities, Pierce. Not the least of which is how they regard each day as a gift unto itself."

"And the converts in the services." He shook his head as if to erase inner doubts. "It's so foreign to how we worship."

"They love the songs. And when they speak, they speak long in prayer." She shrugged. "Not so different from us."

His brow creased. "But the dances, Sarah Jane?"

"They dance to honor the Creator. Not our way, but flowing out of as sincere a heart toward God as any believer you'll ever meet, I promise you."

Fear he'd always feel out of place lanced her insides. Fear niggled that one day he'd pack up and leave the mountains, the Cherokee. And her.

"I'll be right there with you, Pierce. I'll help you any way I can. Oh," She reluctantly extracted her hand from his. "Looks as if we've arrived."

She swept aside an evergreen branch to reveal the crude, little cabin nestled in the mountain hollow up and over the creek from her father's surgery. Smoke billowed from the stone chimney over the top of the wood shake roof. Chickens squawked and pecked at the frozen ground. At the clip-clop sound of the horses, two children, who summoned her papa this morning at the break of dawn, scampered around the corner of the house.

Low moans issued from the interior.

He threw her a sardonic look. "From the sounds of it, Miss Hopkins, I'd say so."

A man, she'd seen him once at the Mercantile, emerged onto the sagging wooden porch. A Mr. Kingfisher Jameson. He twisted a cloth in his hands.

She held up her hand and called a traditional Cherokee greeting. "Osiyo! Hallo to the house."

At the porch railing, Sarah Jane dismounted. She heaved off her saddlebag, bulging with items she might need during this medical emergency. Pierce joined her on the porch beside Mr. Jameson. The children grabbed the horses' reins and led them to the barn.

"Oh-say-oh," Pierce intoned.

Mr. Jameson flicked a glance her way and motioned them within.

"Well done," she mouthed. Pierce flushed with pleasure at her approval.

Say what you would about Pierce and his big city ways, but when he committed himself to a venture—like learning the difficult Cherokee—he committed all the way.

Hanks of spun cotton hung from the rafters inside the log home. A spinning wheel and loom rested upon a packed, dirt floor. The fireplace of wood and clay dominated another wall. Mr. Jameson, speaking a broken mixture of English and Cherokee, communicated his wife had never suffered through childbirth like this before, and he'd grown tired of the potions of the shaman, which made his wife retch and did little to alleviate her pain.

Sarah noted with pride she only had to interpret for Pierce in two instances during Pierce's examination of the bedridden woman. And per Papa's precise protocol, Pierce directed the children, hovering in the doorway, to fetch a basin of water for his hands before he began the exam.

"Breech." Pierce searched Sarah's face. "You and Mr. Jameson," who listened closer at the sound of his name, "are going to have to hold her down while I turn the baby. No pushing . . ." He admonished the woman whose uncomprehending, terrified eyes met his.

"Uh, Sarah. Maybe we better concentrate on Cherokee medical words from now on."

She nodded and gave Pierce a small, reassuring smile. "Right. Pushing." She grasped the woman's arm and gestured for Mr. Jameson to do the same on the other side of the corn-stuffed mattress.

"No pushing," she commanded the woman in Cherokee. "Not till Doctor say yes."

Pierce's forehead glistened with beads of sweat. "A prayer might be in order, if you please, Miss Hopkins."

"Our Father, Heaven's Dweller—O-gi-do-da ga-lv-la-di he-hi," she began.

With a muttered apology for the discomfort he was about to inflict, he bent to the task.

The woman moaned.

"Ga-lv-quo-di-yu ge-se-s-di de-tsa-do-v-i" Sarah Jane recited. "My loving will be to Thy name."

Writhing, the woman struggled against the restraining bonds of Sarah and her husband's hands.

"Tsa-gv-wi-yu-hi ge-sv wi-ga-na-nu-go-i—"

Pierce clenched his teeth together. "Thy Kingdom come, I'm guessing, Sarah Jane? Almost . . ."

She studied Jameson as blood flowed from between his wife's bent knees at the foot of the cot. His tanned face resembled the color of chalk in a schoolroom. Would he pass out?

"A-ni e-tsa-hi wi-ni-ga-li-s-da ha-do-nv-tse-s-gv-i. Here upon earth let happen what You think."

The man wobbled.

"Deep breaths in and out," she advised.

A wrenching cry from the woman.

Pierce looked up, his eyes shining. "It's done. We—God—did it." Rivulets of perspiration and blood stained the front of his white, starched shirt.

"Na-s-gi-ya ga-lv-la-di tsi-ni-ga-li-s-di-ha," she exhaled. "The same as in heaven is done. God be praised."

The woman slumped in momentary relief. Sarah Jane reclined her against the flat pillow.

Mr. Jameson gripped his wife's hand. "Baby?" he murmured. "Usdi?"

Sarah handed Pierce a clean cloth.

Pierce straightened and wiped his hands. He clamped a hand on the man's shoulder. "Oos-dee. Baby soon."

The man huddled over his wife with words of encouragement.

Sarah Jane moved to a side table to fill a tin cup with water for the patient. "He must love her a great deal." Returning, she filled another and handed it to Pierce.

"Why's that?" He gulped the liquid.

"Cherokee men consider it beneath their dignity to attend the births of their children."

Pierce smoothed a tangled strand of hair from her face. "Love? Or just scared to death like me?" He gifted her with a wry, one-sided smile.

Her skin burned from the feel of his hand, strong and warm. "You did fine. As I knew you would."

Pierce took another long swig of water. "We're not done yet, Sarah Jane. We've only begun, in fact."

She darted a look to make sure the patient still rested comfortably.

Pierce downed the rest of the water in a single swallow, tossing back his head. A thrill of sheer pleasure at the sight of his tight, yellow curls shot through Sarah.

Thrusting the cup into her hands, he winked. "But we do make a right fine team, don't you think?"

She grinned, feeling the closest she'd ever come to being as pretty as one of the red lilies that grew on the mountain. "Mighty fine indeed, Doctor."

And three hours later, all was truly fine as the patient delivered without further complication her third son into the Cherokee Nation.

It was late afternoon by the time they approached the Hopkins dwelling and surgery located down the road from the mission meetinghouse.

"Papa may still be at the Corn Tassel's. I'll fix us a quick, if cold, supper."

He eyed the jouncing chicken he'd tied to his saddle-pack. "Just so long as you promise tomorrow you'll redeem Mr. Jameson's payment for our house call with some fried chicken . . ." He smacked his lips together. "Some potatoes . . ."

A swirl of anticipation melted her insides. "Is that all you're wanting?"

Lord-a mercy, she clapped a hand over her mouth.

What had come over her suddenly bold tongue? That sounded like something Leila Hummingbird would say.

But Pierce, for all his proper poses, apparently thought nothing untoward about it. "Well, now you mention it, some cobbler—apple from your orchard—would hit the spot right nice."

She laughed. The clipped, nasal Yankee speech of his was slowly but surely giving way to a gentler drawl. "You stay here long enough, and we'll have you sounding like a real Snowbird Mountain boy."

Her high, good humor plummeted once she sighted who awaited them on a bench beneath the redbud tree. Sarah's lips tightened.

Leila, in a red velvet overcoat, sprang to her feet. In a matching bonnet trimmed with a sprig of holly berries, Leila waved a small lace handkerchief in their direction.

As if anyone with eyes in their head could avoid seeing Leila Hummingbird decked out in her plumage.

Sarah Jane felt, as well as heard, Pierce's short explosive breath when he caught sight of the exquisite Cherokee maiden. His boots hit the hard-packed earth with a thud. She swung her leg over the horse's back and allowed herself to slide slowly toward the ground.

His hat clasped against his chest, he advanced across the lawn. Leila met him halfway, skirts rustling. Her big eyes beckoned and perused the young doctor. Sarah Jane did a halting stutter step until she reached Pierce's side. She crossed her arms over her worn overcoat.

Leila twisted her face toward Sarah, her features sharp as a vulture. Her dark eyes glinted at Sarah and slid away to Pierce. "Why, Sarah Jane, how dare you keep this handsome young man to yourself?"

She'd tried to avoid this moment for weeks.

Leila fluttered the handkerchief in the scant space between her body and his. A whiff of the expensive musky scent Leila's father shipped from Charleston permeated the air.

Sarah Jane cut her eyes at Pierce. His eyes transfixed, he breathed in and out with rapid, shallow breaths.

Her heart began an undulating, death spiral to the region of her toes.

"Well," Leila stamped her foot. Prettily, of course. "Aren't you going to introduce us?" She leaned toward him, swaying willow-like in the wind.

Pierce quivered like the string on a tightly strung bow.

Leila brushed her shoulder against his black suit coat. "Or, will I be forced to fling convention to the side and perform the introductions myself?"

As Leila lifted her hand, Pierce pressed his lips against her fingers.

Leila cast a predatory gleam of triumph at Sarah Jane. Sarah's fists curled into a ball as a sick feeling welled.

And Sarah Jane—this afternoon a one-time lily—faded to drab Sarah once again.

7

2018—Cartridge Cove

Linden steered her Toyota compact into the graveled parking lot of the white clapboard church. "What's going on with you and Ross Wachacha, Gram?"

Marvela fingered one of the pearl buttons lining her pink cashmere twinset, her best attempt—after five discarded tries—to replicate the casual, outdoorsy wear preferred in the mountain community. She yanked down the visor and peered into the mirror. "You sure I look okay?"

"When don't you look more than okay, Gram? And stop trying to change the subject."

Marvela snapped the visor closed. "There's nothing 'going on,' as you so decorously phrased it, between Ross and me."

Linden aimed the car into an empty slot between a Ford Focus, and a mud-splattered, gun-toting, wide-body pickup that'd seen better days. A two-flag sporting pickup—reflecting the owner's dual citizenship: Dixie and America.

"Haven't seen the man since the summer we graduated from high school." Marvela reached for the door. "And *I* have no intention, Smarty Pants, of telling you how long ago that's been."

"And you'd no idea he just returned to Cartridge Cove like you?"

Marvela flung the door open. "Pop the trunk, Honey Girl, so I can get the box of chicken. And I do not pretend to know what has got into you, Linden Birchfield. Such unspeakable rudeness to our guests this afternoon. You embarrassed the life out of me in front of my old *friend*, Ross."

The undulating r-r-r-'s. Linden gritted her teeth. Subject evaded again.

She joined her grandmother at the open trunk. "I'll get it, Gram." She handed Marvela her keys.

Linden heaved the cardboard box lined with aluminum foil out of the trunk. The mouthwatering aroma of fried chicken permeated the air as the setting sun cast long shadows across the bustling parking lot.

Marvela slammed the trunk shut, and pressing a button, locked the Toyota with a beep. "This way."

She followed as Marvela wove her way among the cars coming and going out of the church parking lot. Their progress slowed as Marvela introduced her "Honey Girl" granddaughter to old friends.

"This box isn't getting any lighter," Linden protested after the tenth such introduction. "And I thought this was a Cherokee event. You know," she whispered in Marvela's ear. "An Indian dinner."

Marvela held the side door for Linden to pass first. "That's what we call it because of the menu. Take out or eat in. But it's always well patronized by every segment of Cartridge Cove society. Especially for a bi-ethnic cause like this one."

"The volunteer fire department?"

Marvela nodded. "The firemen are frying trout caught right out of Singing Creek for the fundraiser, too. I bought supper plates for both of us. We'll eat here so I can take my turn on the serving line." She smiled. "It's good to be part of a caring, close-knit community again. All the Cartridge Cove's churches are helping out."

Her grandmother called greetings to various female members of the Baptist, Methodist, and Hallelujah Community churches manning the stovetop and serving line.

"Imagine that," Linden muttered to the boxed chicken. "All *three* of them."

What she wouldn't give for a little civilization right now?

A Starbucks. A mall. Linden sighed.

Marvela tied a navy blue chef's apron around her svelte form. The apron read, **Blue Mountain Majesties—God Bless America and Snowbird**. The volunteer waiters sported similar kitchen attire in various red, white, and blue combinations. "Grab a plate, Linden. Go ahead and eat. Time for me to dish out the cherry cobbler."

Eat? Alone? Surrounded by all these people she didn't know?

Marvela deserted her for the long dessert table on the far end of the fellowship hall.

Linden picked up a tray, a white Styrofoam plate, cup and napkin-rolled bundle of plastic utensils. This was going to be about as much fun as a . . . ?

A case of indigestion.

She curled her lip as she glanced over the aluminum pans. One of the "helpers" slopped a serving of hominy onto her extended plate. Another added a piece of fatback.

"Don't worry, Miz Birchfield . . ."

At the taunting familiar voice, she swiveled.

Walker Crowe leaned his elbows on the other side of the galley counter. "You look like you could use a little more fat on that Madison Avenue figure of yours." Smiling, he straightened to his full height, looping his thumb into his jean pocket.

Had he just complimented her? Or insulted her?

She glared at him to be on the safe side. But she'd misjudged his evening assignation. He wasn't on a date. He'd come to volunteer like Gram.

He held out a ladle filled with boiled potatoes. "I'd offer you some potatoes, but I think you have enough starch in your system." Mischief gleamed from his eyes.

Pasting a fake smile on her face, she glanced from side to side to see if anyone was watching before she stuck her tongue out at him.

He chuckled. "Glad to see you took my advice and came tonight."

She rolled back her shoulders. "I didn't take your advice."

He raised an eyebrow into a question mark.

"I-I," her hands gripped the cafeteria-style tray. "I simply accompanied my grandmother."

He rolled his tongue in his cheek.

She clenched her teeth, wondering what it'd take to wipe that arrogant, patronizing smirk off his face. But mesmerized by his sensuous mouth, she licked her lips at the same moment the most obvious solution to accomplish such a feat occurred to her. Her breath hitched.

Although that might lead to more than she bargained for. She flushed. He laughed out loud.

Could he read her mind? Or just her body language?

He pointed to the hunk of bread. "Bean bread. Lesson number two. Corn meal cooked with pinto beans and then wrapped with cornhusks to boil like a dumpling. Produces a solid cake."

She levied her tray against the counter and dropped the "biscuit" with a resounding thud onto the plate.

Walker gave her a lopsided smile. "Most people season this Cherokee staple with grease."

"The fatback, I'm presuming?"

He folded his arms across his chest, lowering his eyes to half-mast.

"An acquired taste, too, I'm assuming?"

He grinned. "Kind of like me. We Cherokee grow on you once you get to know us." He rested one hip against the counter separating them.

Was he . . . flirting . . . with her?

Flustered, she tilted the tray, causing the plastic utensils to slide forward. She made a wild grab for them but knocked her empty cup into the pan of creamed corn. She sighed.

Leaning closer, he fished the cup out of the corn. "Or maybe just me you might grow fond of."

She quirked an eyebrow to indicate the likelihood of that happening. He handed her a new cup.

Linden pointed at a pan of greens. "What's that?"

"Something we call ramps. A wild spring onion."

"O-k-aa-ay." She extended her tray to him.

Walker shook his head. "Because I like you and you're new around here, and because we have to work together this week, I'm going to steer you away from this traditional favorite."

He liked her?

She felt the pink working its way from beneath her denim jacket. A quivery feeling had taken hold of her kneecaps.

"You eat this and everybody in a five-mile radius will know it for the next day or so."

"Oh." That's what he'd meant.

Feeling like a fool, Linden half-turned to go. "Right. Thanks for the tip, Mr. Crowe."

His face fell. "I didn't mean . . ."

She picked up the tray.

"I was just teas—Wait."

She paused midstep.

He swallowed. "I thought we could do some fieldwork on the mountain after church tomorrow. No need to put it off."

Linden's neck burned. You'd think she'd been born a redhead. "Good idea. Get it over with."

His cheeks puffed, splotching. "I didn't mean—" He raked a hand over the top of his head.

"Now you're going to have to wash your hands again, Crowe." She gave him her best Madison Avenue smile. "Lesson number three? Two o'clock?"

A glint of something sharpened in the fathomless depths of his dark eyes. "Lesson three. Two o'clock. You got yourself a date, Miz Birchfield."

She sniffed and moved toward the table loaded with tea pitchers. His mocking laugh echoed behind her.

With a great deal of relief, she spotted Quincy—newly PhD-endowed Dr. Sawyer, an American Indianist anthropologist—chomping on a chicken thigh. Hips swinging—she so hoped that obnoxiously-pleased-with-himself Walker Crowe was watching—she flounced over to Quincy.

Flounced? She crinkled her nose. This was what a week keeping company with Marvela and by extension, Miss Ophelia, produced.

She plunked her plate on the laminate tabletop. "Quince."

A goofy smile lit his face at the sight of her.

Some of her ruffled female feathers settled. At least one man appreciated her finer qualities.

Not that she cared if Walker Crowe appreciated her qualities. "How's your head?"

Museum curator by day, avid downhill skier in season. He'd admitted the proximity of the ski slopes north of Asheville as much as anything had enticed him to the area.

Quincy shrugged. "I'll live. Proves what Mom said all along about my hard head."

"I see you replaced your glasses, too." She reached for her shoulder bag and withdrew a manila folder. "Look what I found in this diary from 1838."

His baby blue eyes almost bugged out from behind his retro black, horn-rimmed glasses. "A diary? Let me see . . ."

"Didn't bring it with me."

His shoulders slumped.

"I'm reading through it when I get the chance. I'll pass it on soon as I'm done. I wondered with your ancestry database if you could find some info about the people I've run across in the diary."

Out of the corner of her eye, she watched his doctoral candidate assistant—on loan from the Western Carolina Archaeology Department's satellite office in Cherokee—stroll over to the counter Walker worked and . . .

Her eyes widened as the tawny-complexioned Emmaline threw her arms around Walker Crowe's neck. Comprehension dawned. The Emmaline, her stomach clenching, he'd spoken of being late to pick up.

Linden's fingers clawed the folder.

"Careful, Lin. You're going to crush whatever you wanted to show me," Quincy warned.

She thrust the packet at him and cut her eyes around the room. No one but her seemed to think it unusual Emmaline Whatever-Her-Name-Was had just . . . just . . .

Whatever you called that sort of public—and totally inappropriate in her opinion—display of affection.

Quincy removed the daguerreotype. "Wow."

Everyone continued with their own conversations as if such carryings-on were commonplace with the likes of Walker Crowe and his . . . girlfriends.

Which perhaps, for all Linden knew, they were.

Not that she cared.

Not that his relationships were any of her business.

Maybe he *was* like The Jerk.

"These are great, Lin. Have you identified the people yet?"

She tore her gaze from Crowe and his paramour.

Paramour?

She grimaced. Maybe Gram was right. Maybe she did need to get out more if all she could do for entertainment was immerse herself in the nineteenth century world of a long-dead woman whose love life modeled her own.

As in lack thereof.

She bent over the picture of the family. The man she could tell even from the faded photograph was fair-haired and handsome, although his face wore a stern countenance. "From their clothing, I'd guess mid-nineteenth century."

Quincy nodded. "Circa 1850s or pre-Civil War, for sure."

. She flipped the photo in his hand and pointed to the spidery, inked documentation on the back. "'Home of Dr. Horace Hopkins,'" she read aloud. "The little boys are labeled—Gram thinks they range in age from eleven to four—Ethan, Caleb, Johnathan, and David. The man's identified as Pierce."

A trace of excitement laced her voice. "The diary talks about a Dr. Horace Hopkins, medical missionary to the Cherokee at the time of the Removal and his daughter, Sarah Jane. Maybe the woman in the photo is Sarah Jane."

He whipped his iPhone out of his shirt pocket. "Horace Hopkins, you say." He typed in the name. "Sarah Jane Hopkins what? You think she married this Pierce guy? Is that his first or last name?" He glanced at the photos on the table between their plates. "Doesn't look too happy, does she?"

The sadness on the woman's face pricked at Linden's heart. About as happy as she'd look if she'd married The Jerk. For the first time, Linden thanked God she'd been spared that on top of everything else.

"I don't know whether it's his first or last name, although I do know that like Dr. Hopkins, he was a medical missionary, too." She gave Quincy a brief recap of the story she'd gleaned thus far.

She examined the picture under the florescent lighting of the church hall. The photo depicted Pierce on a striped settee in an old-fashioned frock coat, vest, and starched cuffs. "At this point in my reading, I'm not even sure Sarah Jane ultimately marries this Pierce or not. The woman may or may not be Sarah Jane Hopkins."

On either side of Pierce sat two of the younger boys—clothed in knickers and wide shirt collars. Behind the sofa, a boy leaned against the armrest. Another, the oldest boy, had his arm draped around the woman's shoulders.

The woman's hair parted in the middle of her scalp and pulled to the nape of her neck in the severe style Linden recognized from the antebellum era. The woman gazed into the camera, her beringed left hand resting atop the carved back of the settee. Her eyes caught at Linden, their expression wide, round, and . . .

Vulnerable? Or was Linden projecting her own sensibilities upon the woman?

"I'll see what I can learn and get back to you." He tucked the photo into the folder, handing it to her. "What's your interest in this?"

She placed the folder into her purse and smiled. "You know me and one of history's mysteries."

He laughed.

"I'll try to run that next donation to you tomorrow afternoon before my . . ." she grimaced, ". . . appointment if you think you'll be there on a Sunday."

He chewed his lip. "I'll be there all right. Trying to erase the graffiti. Cleaning up the mess. Sheriff has no leads on what he calls a racial hate crime."

"Who does he think is behind it?"

"Lot of mixed feelings on both sides about the changes the festival's bringing."

She frowned. "But you said skinheads. Surely not the Cherokee?"

"For political, tribal reasons, not everyone in the Cherokee Nation wants this reunification of the Eastern and Western bands. Nor are the descendants of the Appalachian land grabbers eager to revisit a dark time in the town's history."

An echo of Walker's earlier words at Gram's. Maybe this so-called partnership with Crowe wasn't such a good idea. What did she really know about him, other than he was Ross Wachacha's nephew?

Glancing around, she discovered Walker had disappeared from the fellowship hall while she and Quincy had their heads doubled over the daguerreotype.

Linden squared her shoulders, pushing down her apprehensions about Walker for the moment. This account with the town of Cartridge Cove was too important for her future to allow anyone to ruin the festival. "What's the sheriff doing about it?"

"Everything he can. He's understaffed. Extra patrols around the Center. But it's a big county with lots of rough terrain. Even if they acquired a lead, fugitives have been known to evade capture for years."

Her lips curved. "Snowbird Cherokee hiding from the federal soldiers, case in point."

"Exactly." Quincy gave her an adorable, boyish grin. "So I've reconciled myself to live at the Center 24/7."

She nudged him with her shoulder. "Till the—"

"Excuse me, Dr. Sawyer?"

Linden looked up to find Emmaline glaring daggers at her over Quincy's short-cropped straw-colored head.

Emmaline bared her teeth. "You must be Miss Marvela's granddaughter. The PR woman who's not from around here."

Which, in Southern speak, sometimes translated to "not welcome around here, either."

Linden pursed her lips. What did this girl have against her?

Quincy blinked owlishly at the curvaceous co-ed—displaying her charms in Nike shorts, running shoes, and a skintight t-shirt reading: **Cherokee and Proud of It.**

"Why, Emm—maa," he stuttered and cleared his throat. His Nordiclike features shadowed in confusion. "I almost didn't recognize you."

Emmaline crossed her arms over her "pride," and glowered at Linden.

His lack of recognition Linden's fault? Go figure.

Uncrossing her arms, Emmaline pushed out her chest—on the off-chance Quincy, Walker, and every other male in the room hadn't noticed already?—and jutted her hip. "Didn't you mention you needed my help this evening cataloguing some recently donated items to the Center?"

"I-I," His gaze ping-ponged between the women. "I did?"

Emmaline's mouth flattened. "You did." She slitted her eyes in Linden's direction.

Linden shrugged. Whatever this girl's problem was, next move Quincy.

He scraped back his chair. "Well, sure, Emma. If you say so." He reached for the remains of his dinner. "I guess I'll see you tomorrow, Linden." Emmaline inserted her arm through the crook of his elbow.

Linden fiddled with the paper band encasing the napkins and plastic utensils. "Sure, Quince. Tomorrow."

As Emmaline propelled him to the nearest trashcan, Quincy mounted one more feeble protest. "You know the Department won't spring for overtime, Em."

"No worries." Emmaline tilted her head. "Working at the Center has other compensations, Dr. Sawyer." She clutched Quincy's arm tighter.

He furrowed his brow before nodding. "I understand. I guess."

Biting back a smile, Linden somehow doubted he did.

8

Mid-February 1838

Perhaps Pierce isn't as well suited to minister to our Cherokee flock as I once believed."

Horace placed his pipe onto the side table. The pipe, a hickory-carved replica of a beaver, a gift of appreciation from one of his first Cherokee converts.

"A word to the Board and he'd be transferred to another mission outpost," Horace snapped his fingers. "Like that."

Sarah Jane raised her eyes from hand-quilting the Carolina Lily. "No, Papa."

Why she bothered to complete it, she didn't know. Because if ever she'd intended the quilt for her "hope chest," it was a futile endeavor now. But the rocking rhythm of the needle in and out of the fabric soothed the sore places of her heart.

"That wouldn't be right. Pierce has made a place for himself among The People."

Her father's nostrils flared. "A place for himself these last weeks, cavorting around the countryside with the likes of that trol—"

"Papa."

He clamped his lips shut, but his fiery gaze didn't abate. Once Leila Hummingbird's most valiant defender, she'd at last done the unpardonable. Hurt his beloved daughter. Now Leila

Hummingbird wasn't the only one struggling with the Spirit's fruits.

Restless, she laid her hooped quilt aside. Sarah peered out the window at February's milky excuse for sunshine. "I just don't understand what I ever did for Leila to hate me so." She rested her forehead leaning against the frosted glass pane.

The chair groaned as her father lumbered to his feet. The winter played havoc on his joints. He came alongside, placing an arm around her shoulders.

"Because you have everything she's never had, my girl."

Sarah swiveled. "Me?" She gathered the folds of her shawl closer around her frame. "Leila's had everything her heart ever desired."

He shook his head. "She's had everything Ambrose could buy her in exchange for what he didn't have within him or was too busy to give. And you know how Leila loved your mother. As for Pierce?"

The doctor clenched his fists. "I placed such high hopes in that lad. When I think about how he led you on—both of us . . ."

She reached for his hand. "Don't, Papa. Pierce never spoke a word of promise to me."

And at the foot of her bed each night when she poured out her tears to the God of her consolation, she prayed—with her hurt pride and splintered feelings—Pierce would never glean what impossible dreams she'd constructed out of wishful thinking. Her mouth twisted.

Seeing her pain, Horace growled. "What good sense that boy ever possessed has apparently left his brain and traveled to the more nether regions of his—"

"What God means to be, will be." She tightened her grip on the sleeve of his coat.

He released his anger with a great gust of breath. "You're a credit to your blessed mother." He rubbed at his white-whiskered cheeks. "Loving your enemies and praying for those who persecute you . . ."

She gave him a brittle smile and huddled closer to the comforting warmth of the hearth. "Easier said than lived, Papa."

At the rattle of carriage wheels on the drive, Horace parted the curtain. "It's the Reverend Endicott and Preacher Tobias."

She rose, grateful for a distraction from less pleasant conversations revolving around Pierce. "I'll bring coffee and cake."

Making her way to the kitchen, she heard the murmur of male voices in the entrance hall as her father welcomed his spiritual colleagues into their home.

The Reverend hailed from a tiny Baptist mission on the other side of the Unicoi range. Tobias, a young Methodist evangelist, had recently been expelled from riding his circuit in volatile Georgia, where gold lust and land fever had driven the state government and white settlers near mad with an unquenchable thirst for Cherokee holdings.

And Tobias had been lucky—no, that was wrong. She offered a repentant plea to the kitchen ceiling. He'd been blessed and guarded by God.

Which led Sarah to another theological conundrum as to why God had seen fit to allow other brethren to suffer beatings and prison for daring to defend the rights of The People God had placed in their care.

She hurried into the front room to find the men standing around the fire, hands extended to its warmth. As Pierce expressed B.L.H.—before Leila Hummingbird—ecumenical unity was one good thing to emerge from this crisis. A constitutional crisis, Papa maintained, of American citizens like Mr. Tobias for the freedom of speech and worship.

As well the miscarriage of justice regarding the Cherokee rights to life, liberty, and happiness, same as any human being. Pastor Endicott's face contorted as he recounted yet another degradation perpetrated upon a member of his Cherokee flock.

Tobias glanced up as she entered with the tray. He favored her with an admiring smile as she handed him a plate of applesauce cake. Her father, a speculative gleam in his mild blue eyes, didn't miss it, either.

Biting her lip, she eyeballed her father and gave a slight shake of her head. Which he ignored. Papa being Papa.

Sarah offered cake to Endicott who waved the plate away in his zeal to expound upon their present predicament. "Some of my people have already left. Voluntarily enrolled and headed west."

"Wonderful cake, Miss Hopkins," Tobias murmured.

Glee fairly radiated off her papa. And truth be told, Tobias's unabashed admiration did take the edge off Pierce's stinging rejection of her so-called womanly charms. Sarah set about pouring the coffee. These men came often enough to confer with her father that she knew which way they preferred their brew.

The aromatic steam seeped into the air. "Sugar with cream, Mr. Tobias." She handed over the cup and saucer. "Just the way you like it, I think."

A surprised look crossed the young man's otherwise ordinary face. "Why, thank you, Miss Hopkins. I can't believe you remembered." He flashed her a shy smile, which offset slightly crooked teeth.

Not overly handsome. Unlike Pierce's—

She dropped her eyes to the tray, her hand not quite steady as she poured a cup for the Reverend Endicott, black the way he preferred. And one for Papa.

Would she spend the rest of her life comparing every potential suitor—as if beggars could afford to be choosers—against the masculine perfection of a certain perfidious New Englander?

". . . heard Jackson refused to give an audience last year to Junaluska," Endicott continued.

With effort, she dragged her attention to the conversation.

Her father's eyes rounded over the rim of his cup. "Didn't Junaluska save *General* Andrew Jackson's life some years back against the Seminole during the Battle of Horseshoe Bend?"

Tobias's shaggy mane wobbled in agreement.

Endicott frowned. "Chief Ross is still in Washington negotiating. He's convinced he can get President Van Buren to change his mind—"

"Van Buren's a mere toady for that Indian hater, Jackson." Her father pursed his lips.

"Or, at least, negotiate more favorable terms per eventual removal." Endicott took a quick swallow. "Good coffee, Miss Hopkins." He wrapped his hands around the fragile Delft cup—a china set Sarah Jane's Mam had only used for company.

"Welcome on such a cold, winter day." Tobias presented another timid smile in Sarah Jane's direction.

Tracing her finger along the rim of her saucer, she wondered how the life of a circuit rider's wife compared to a medical missionary's. She blushed and at the lifting of the corners of Zeke Tobias's mouth knew he'd drawn a completely erroneous conclusion of her feelings.

Horace sighed. "Ross has his representatives riding hither and yon through these valleys and hollows counseling The People to be patient, to maintain the faith."

"Faith?" Endicott's bushy eyebrows rose. "In what?"

Tobias shook his head. "In his assurances of an eleventh-hour compromise." He gestured out the window. "Farmers are making plans to sow corn, come spring, they may not be here to harvest."

Horace knit his brows together. "Shouldn't he urge them to prepare? Mentally. Emotionally. Put their affairs in order?"

Endicott gazed out the window at the cloud-covered sky. "We may get more snow tonight." He rubbed his palm along the side of his trousers. "Some of the men won't go so peacefully, despite Ross's admonitions to offer no resistance to the soldiers. It's going to get worse before it gets better. Georgia alone is a powder keg waiting to blow."

Tobias grimaced. "The stockade at Fort Butler is complete, I heard. And in my new circuit, I've ridden past Fort Lindsay and Fort Hembrie." He ticked off the fingers of one hand. "Fort Montgomery and Fort Delaney all this side of the Carolina border. The soldiers have etched out a road at Tatham Gap to connect the forts. A network of forts to aid in the removal."

"And you, my brothers," Horace darted a glance at Sarah as well. "What will be your stand when the soldiers come?"

Endicott's eyes took on a faraway look. A look that reminded her of illustrations she'd seen in Papa's big Bible of the saints before the lions. "I'll stand—and go—with my flock to the Indian Territory if need be. There'll be a need for spiritual guidance."

"And medical attention." Horace fixed his hand palm down in the air above the tea table. "As will I."

Gulping past the lump in her throat, she reposed her hand on top of her papa's liver-spotted hand. Endicott, his gray eyes welling, followed suit.

Tobias laid his hand over theirs. "General Wool asked Brother Evan Jones to help him persuade the Cherokee to disarm when the May twenty-fourth deadline arrives. He refused, and he's been arrested."

Would spring see her father imprisoned, too?

She shivered, her arms prickling with more than the cold. The impending deadline hovered over their hearts. Outside, a crow's sharp caw broke the silence.

"To The People." Her father raised his eyes to heaven. "And to our God be praise forever."

9

2018—Cartridge Cove

For the second time in less than twenty-four hours, Linden found herself strong-armed—courtesy of Marvela—into a church. She couldn't remember the last time she'd been in a church sanctuary.

That wasn't true. She did remember. Massaging her temple, she willed her brain to eradicate the images of that last time.

In the vestibule, a jean-clad usher handed her grandmother a bulletin. Linden stiffened. She didn't care if she embarrassed Gram in front of all of Cartridge Cove. She'd bolt if lilies adorned the altar.

Sprays of white lilies had dotted the altar that day so long ago. Grouped on the floor, covering the steps to the platform, the lilies draped the tiny casket. And their cloying fragrance haunted her dreams still.

Cautious, she sniffed the air as Gram pulled her further inside. And to her relief, her eyes landed on a homegrown arrangement of sunny bright daffodils. She released the gust of air she hadn't realized she'd been holding.

Marvela steered her into an empty pew and thrust a green hymnal at Linden as the organ began a rousing rendition of "I'll Fly Away."

Grabbing the other side of the book, she kept her mouth closed. There'd been no victory for her in places like this. Only defeat and death.

Marvela sang with enough gusto for the both of them.

The preacher greeted the congregation. In tonal Cherokee. And then, in English.

Taken aback, she darted a few glances around, noting for the first time the large preponderance of Snowbird Cherokee. And a substantial number of white Appalachian families, too.

In church? Together? The last bastion of the racial divide?

Marvela and the congregation stood once more. At a displeased downward tilt of her grandmother's lips, Linden jumped to her feet, not realizing in her abstraction the preacher had called for the singing of another hymn, "Amazing Grace."

This time, the hymn was sung in Cherokee only.

Bewildered, she clutched the hymnal as her grandmother hummed the familiar tune. All around them—the Snowbird, at least—rendered the song in the lilting tones of their native tongue.

Amazing, indeed. And, Linden chewed her lip, scrutinizing the English words in the hymnal, amazingly beautiful.

Too soon—most surprising of all—the congregation came to the end of the four stanzas. The hickory-carved pews creaking, the worshippers eased down.

Marvela grasped the hymnal and leaned over. "A particular favorite of The People. Since the time of the Removal," she whispered as the preacher strode forward, his hands gripping the sides of the pulpit.

His kind face shone with something that touched a chord in Linden's long dormant heart. Peace? Contentment?

"Friends, today I have a special treat for you." He flashed a smile at someone behind her. "I've convinced—"

A loud, throat-clearing cough from the vestibule.

The preacher laughed.

At the sound of shoes scuffling the carpet, Linden half-turned and beheld a grinning Ross Wachacha and others striding down the aisle toward the front.

The preacher gestured as Ross mounted the platform. "Okay, I coerced Ross and company into giving us a preview of their version of a song I know y'all love."

Marvela squeezed Linden's arm.

"Gram," she hissed. "You're—"

But when Marvela faced her, her periwinkle-colored eyes shone bright. "I'd forgotten what a wonderful singer, Ross was. Is."

She smiled and let go her death grip on Linden. "The Cherokee love to sing and embraced the shape-note style of the early missionaries."

Her grandmother wriggled, like a schoolgirl, in the pew. She patted Linden's hand and put her finger to her lips. "Now hush and listen."

Me? Linden mouthed.

Gram ignored her as the trio grouped around a lone microphone—Ross, Walker's mom, Irene, Emmaline . . .

Linden's eyes widened at the Cherokee girl even more beautiful in a simple, knee-length lavender dress. A furtive look to the right revealed Quincy three pews ahead, in suit-coat and tie, edged forward in his seat, his eyes intent. His elbows rested on his knees, and his hands formed a steeple underneath his chin.

From a side door behind the platform, she watched Walker join his mother, uncle, and Emmaline. Her mouth hung open in an O, Linden stared.

And couldn't, for the life of her, stop.

With his blue Oxford shirt open at the collar and tucked into his slacks—she hadn't realized until now he knew how to tuck a shirt into a pair of pants—Walker Crowe gave a whole new definition to Sunday best.

Lord-a mercy. She blushed, twisting her hands in her lap.

"Old friends who need no introduction . . ."

Linden marshaled her thoughts.

What was wrong with her?

She was in a church, for heaven's sake.

Walker gave Emmaline a playful nudge with his hip. Emmaline leaned on tiptoe to whisper something in his ear, bringing to his face a swift, eye-blinding flash of strong, even white teeth.

Linden's gut did a curious rolling, clenching, seething nosedive.

" . . . A song they've also chosen to sing at the upcoming commemoration in memory of all those who suffered and overcame before us . . ."

Linden squirmed. The nerve of that Emmaline. In church, no less.

". . . 'Guide Us, O Thou Great Jehovah.'" With a nod to Ross, the preacher sat down behind the pulpit. Marvela forced the bulletin into Linden's hand and jabbed at the English words.

She knew the exact minute Walker Crowe spotted her amidst the sea of faces in the congregation. The smile faded. His eyes sharpened. He clamped his lips together.

His gaze shifted over her head. At something—or someone?—beyond her.

The pianist hit one note and Ross opened the song. In Cherokee, his deep bass mixed and mingled with his niece Irene's contralto. The pure sweet vowels of Emmaline's soprano and Walker's baritone floated upon the undercurrent of their harmony. Their voices soared toward the wood-hewn rafters, transcending time.

Linden's eyes welled despite herself. Despite her best efforts to wrap the tattered cords of her impenetrable self-control around her heart. Or, did she mean her soul?

Her eyes traveled to the bulletin she clutched in her hand. To the words of the song sung on the Trail as a bewildered, but resolute people left everything they'd ever known and went forth into the unknown.

Guide me, O thou great Jehovah,
Pilgrim through this barren land;

I am weak, but thou art mighty,
Hold me with thy powerful hand;
Bread of heaven, bread of heaven
Feed me till I want no more;
Feed me till I want no more.

Open now the crystal fountain
Whence the healing stream doth flow;
Let the fire and cloudy pillar
Lead me all my journey through:
Strong deliverer, strong deliverer;
Be thou still my strength and shield;
Be thou still my strength and shield.

She needed a strong deliverer. But where had God been that day when she'd needed strength the most? Linden longed for a shield from the ravaging emotions that had crippled and paralyzed her for a decade. But to do so meant relinquishing the anger. And the anger kept Linden on her feet.

Was she ready to give it over? Exchange it for something better? She thirsted for the peace reflected in her grandmother's face. And in the face of Walker Crowe.

Ross motioned for the congregation to join them. Marvela stood as the congregation switched to English. With an overwhelming desire to be free of grief's shackles, she rose also. Gripping the pew in front of her, the words blurred, but Linden sang, her voice rusty from disuse.

When I tread the verge of Jordan,
Bid my anxious fears subside;
Death of death and hell's destruction
Land me safe on Canaan's side:
Songs of praises, songs of praises,
I will ever give to thee;
I will ever give to thee.

Marvela's lips trembled. Tears streaked, ruining Marvela's perfect Bobbi Brown foundation. She patted Linden's hand as they sat down. Head bent, Marvela fumbled in her Gucci purse for a tissue.

Linden leaned against the hard wood of the pew and took an exploratory breath.

No trumpets sounded or lightning crashed. Nothing miraculous had occurred.

Or had it?

After the service, Walker slipped away as quickly as he slipped in. She and her grandmother were delayed by well-wishers welcoming Linden to their Cartridge Cove fellowship. The preacher stopped her at the door, and clasping both her hands in his, mentioned he'd love to talk with her some time if she liked.

Maybe, she said.

Soon, he encouraged.

They were also delayed when Irene complimented Linden for finding "those authentic heirloom Cartridge Cove quilt patterns."

Linden shot a look at Marvela, who smiled and shrugged her shoulders.

"The Cherokee Rose pattern in particular," Irene leaned in. "Might be the thing to change Dottie Swimmer's mind about us painting her barn." She gave Linden a broad wink. "Same thing with our other problem old-timer, Fred Alexander. Maybe you and Walker could try that idea on for size with those two when you meet with them."

"Speaking of Walker . . ." Marvela tugged at Linden's sleeve. "Got to go, Rennie. The children have a—" She paused at the frown Linden threw her way. "An appointment. With each other."

Linden sucked in a disapproving breath.

"Conferencing this afternoon about the festival, I'm sure." Marvela winked, and Irene chuckled. Linden stalked toward the car.

With her grandmother "about cooked out" after the Indian dinner, she put together a quick, Southern favorite for lunch. Mashed bananas mixed with peanut butter. And a dash—or three—of sugar. On slices of thick, homemade sourdough slathered with mayonnaise.

Marvela took a bite and closed her eyes in ecstasy. "Dar-ar-arlin' . . . Almost as good as the way your Granddad used to make 'em."

"Granddad?" She laughed around a swallow of sweet tea. "In the kitchen?"

Marvela wiped her lips with a napkin. "Not often, I'll grant you. But one of the first—and most successful—ways he attempted to woo my exiled Southern heart."

Exiled? An interesting way to phrase it.

With Marvela promising to wash up, Linden gathered the box of vintage clothing they'd unearthed in the attic and headed to her car. If she hurried, she'd have time to drop this off at the Center and be back in time for Walker.

Driving down Main Street past the bank, library, and gas station, she quickly arrived on the other side of town. Which sounded grand until you realized you were talking about Cartridge Cove. The two-story brick Center had recently been certified as an official interpretive site on the historic Trail of Tears. And somebody had been busy erasing all traces of the graffiti and vandalism.

No sign of Quincy's red VW, she started to turn around and go home but on second thought figured she'd leave the box at the front for him to find later. She didn't relish entering through the forest-shrouded back entrance anytime soon. Her good intentions were halted at the front door by none other than Emmaline.

"What do you want, Birchfield?"

Linden juggled the box in her arms and struggled to maintain the light feelings she'd experienced since the morning service. She pushed the box in Emmaline's direction. Emmaline's lips disappeared into a straight line.

"I promised Quince—" What was with this girl? "—I'd drop this off today."

Patience . . . Linden pursed her lips. Her first real prayer in a long time. Self-control . . .

Emmaline stepped away, leaving Linden to follow her into the high-ceilinged entrance hall. "Leave it inside the door. Quincy and I will deal with it. Now you can leave." Her foot tapped a staccato beat on the golden toned oak floor as if marking her territory.

Did this girl lay claim to every male in the village? Quincy *and* Walker . . .

Emmaline went round-eyed.

Linden went rigid. The box hit the floor with a dull thud. She hadn't said that out loud, had she?

Emmaline bent over double, clutching her sides.

Apparently, Linden had.

Linden closed her eyes and willed herself to breathe. Could she die now, Lord, now she and He were on speaking terms again? Die of mortification?

"You think . . ." Emmaline jabbed her finger in Linden's direction, "that Walker . . . ?"

Linden palpitated the strap of her shoulder bag.

" . . . that he and I . . . ?"

Linden's hand tightened. Hee, hee, hee. It was all fun and games until someone got a fist in their mouth.

She glanced at the coved ceiling. *Sorry, God.*

Emmaline leaned for support against the cantilevered staircase. "Oh, Linden." She turned bright eyes upon Linden. "May I call you, Linden?"

Linden retreated a step. This girl was nutty. From hostility to BFF all in one instant.

Emmaline took a deep, shuddering breath, struggling to regain her composure. "That's so precious. So rich. I didn't realize . . . I thought you and Quincy . . ."

Linden groped behind her, unable to remember if the crazy Cherokee girl had shut the door. Her gaze flickered toward the rooms on either side of the hallway for an alternate escape route. She licked her lips. "Wh—where's Quincy, by the way?" in what she hoped was a casual voice.

Emmaline squared her shoulders. "I sent him on an errand to the Walmart in Murphy for supplies. I wanted us to have a little chat." She stepped toward Linden.

Linden pressed her back against the hard grain of the door. Traffic hummed from the road outside. How to—?

"But that's before I realized you liked Walker."

Linden's head snapped up. "I do not."

Emmaline flipped her blue-black hair over her shoulder. "Oh, yes. You do."

"I don't."

"You do," Emmaline insisted, nodding.

Linden stamped her foot. "I absolutely do not. We've just met, and I'm only in town—"

"I'm thrilled to pieces now I understand." Emmaline smiled. "And I can tell he likes you, too."

"Huh?" She sympathized with how Alice must've felt sliding down the rabbit hole.

"You are all he talked about when he picked me up for our rotation at the dinner—and believe me when I tell you Walker uses words like he has to pay for each one." Emmaline smacked her lips. "Exactly what my cousin needs—despite his protests to the contrary—a woman in his life."

Linden shook her head and seized on the most vital piece of information Emmaline let drop. "Walker Crowe? You and he are . . . cousins?"

Emmaline blinked. "Yeah. My dad and Aunt Irene are brother and sister. Ross is our great-uncle."

And the penny dropped. Wachacha. Her name was Emmaline Wachacha.

"Oh. I see." Linden let go of her grip on her purse. And suddenly, Emmaline's inexplicable hostility made a whole lot more sense. "You like Quincy Sawyer."

Before her eyes, Emmaline wilted, becoming less De-Leila-like. She dropped to the first stair, becoming more Sarah-Jane-like. "Quincy doesn't know I'm alive."

Emmaline lifted her large, chocolate brown eyes to Linden. "I've known him since we met as undergrads at Carolina. You wouldn't believe the hordes of women over the years I've fended off him."

Hordes? The goofy professor? Linden bit back a smile, allowing Quince did possess a haphazard, boyish charm.

Emmaline's mouth trembled. "But we're just friends. I hate that word . . . if only I could be . . . like you . . ."

Linden plopped down beside her. "Me?"

Emmaline fingered the hem of the lacy white tank top. "You're so put together."

Linden placed her hand over Emmaline's fingers fretting the edges of her shirt. "You have more going for you than I ever did at your age."

She gave Emmaline the once-over. Outside, a motorcycle roared. "You're trying a new tactic to get him to notice you, aren't you?"

Emmaline grimaced. "A change from my usual jeans and flannel. But what is it with guys? The only thing Quincy can see is my brain."

The absurdity of that remark struck them both at the same time. They'd collapsed in near-hysterical laughter on each other's shoulders when Walker thrust open the door and charged inside. He scowled.

Maybe his face didn't do smiling around her.

"So, I've finally managed to track you down."

"Walker." Linden jumped to her feet, smoothing her jeans. "I lost track of time. I meant to make a quick run to Quincy and return before—"

"Save it," he barked. "You can leave your car here if you can pull yourself away from your boyfriend—"

"Chill, cuz." Emmaline inserted herself between them. "Stop being such a jerk."

Linden swiveled. "He's not a . . . it's my fault. I should've . . ."

Walker went stone-faced.

Emmaline stepped aside. "Quincy will give you a call later about the stuff he's discovered regarding your quest. Enjoy your ride."

Walker stalked out to the portico.

Enjoy her what?

The mischievous look returned to Emmaline's face.

She gave Emmaline a swift hug. "Hang in there." Linden gave her a thumbs-up.

"You, too. No, what I really mean to say is," A laugh—semi-wicked—drifted out from Emmaline's full lips. "Hang on."

Pivoting on her heel, Linden came to a dead stop when she sighted Walker, arms folded across his chest, waiting for her in the parking lot.

Leaning against a Harley.

10

Early March 1838

Easy come. Easy went—the devotion of Leila Hummingbird.

Several weeks ago, Pierce returned to the mission clinic, bewildered and angry. He'd been turned away by Kweti at the Hummingbird door.

Being Pierce, he persisted. To no avail.

Sarah Jane should've rejoiced at this entirely predictable—to anyone who understood Leila—turn of events. But with his handsome face melancholy, she lacked the heart to gloat over his misfortune. Because thanks to him and Leila, she knew all too well the pain of rejection.

After a week of moping—and inadvertently mixing up an herbal tincture for a patient—Papa shouted at him. She'd never before heard her father raise his voice.

To anyone.

"You've acted the fool for a lacy bit of petticoat," Papa yelled. "And for what result?" He'd slammed something onto the examining table. "You either pull yourself together or go home. Because at present, you're no good to me, your God, or these people."

Pierce promised to do better and spent the better part of the afternoon in the chapel at the meetinghouse. He'd emerged wan-faced, but with a martyrlike air of new determination drawn like a fine cape about him.

At the rumble of carriage wheels, Sarah Jane peeked out the dimpled glass window. With trepidation—and not a little anger—she watched Leila hand the reins to Kweti as the carriage rolled to a stop. Leila descended, her skirts swooshing. Tight-lipped, Sarah met her at the door.

"What do you want, Leila?"

Leila's eyes darkened under her blue velvet bonnet. "That's a fine greeting from my dearest friend."

Sarah Jane—God help her—rolled her eyes. "We're not friends. I think the events of the last month have more than proven that." She deposited her hands on her hips.

Leila gazed past her. "Aren't you going to invite me in?" She pretended to shiver.

Pretended because after one of the harshest Februarys any old-timer recalled, spring arrived at last with the welcome unfurling of the chartreuse willow trees by the crick.

Sarah Jane stood her ground, filling the doorframe. "Why should I?"

Thank God Pierce and her father were out on a sick call. No telling the fit her normally mild-mannered papa would've thrown at the sight of this Miss. And, Sarah Jane sighed at the thought, she lacked the stomach for any more of Pierce's wretched groveling to this creature.

"What do you want?"

Leila pushed out her lip. "Why do you think I've come because I want something? It's been so long since we—"

"Because you always want something." Sarah crossed her arms over her pinafore, stained with the removal of ashes from the hearth this morning. "Just get on with it so you can be on your way, and I can finish my chores."

Leila dropped her eyes to study the toe of her boot. "I-I . . ." She swallowed. "Something's happened, Sarah, and I need your help."

"I knew it."

Leila raised her gaze, her black eyes pleading. "Please. I need your help. I don't know where else to turn." Her lower lip trembled.

"You can save the histrionics for the male of our species, Leila Hummingbird. Your tricks don't work on me."

"I'm not playacting." Leila's face twisted. "Father's being completely unreasonable. He won't listen. He doesn't understand if he won't give us permission to marry, I'm going to die."

Sarah dropped her arms. "Marry?" Her breath hitched. "You and Pierce? Is that what this is about?" Her fists clenched in the sides of her calico. Her heartbeat accelerated.

Leila frowned. "No, not Pierce." She waved a hand. "You're more than welcome to him. You and he are a match made in heaven with your boring talk about God and church."

Sarah slumped against the door. "I don't understand."

Lifting her chin, Leila edged past her. "If you'd let me in, I'd explain." She minced into the parlor, leaving Sarah Jane to follow.

She found Leila studying the Carolina Lily quilt she'd left draped over the arm of the wingback. "You've almost finished." Leila pivoted, smiling. "Just the binding left to attach and you're done."

"Whom do you want to marry?" Sarah Jane inserted herself between Leila and the quilt lest Leila's next statement be a criticism of her stitches.

Leila made a slow, three hundred and sixty degree turn, taking in the humble furnishings. "I always imagine when I come into this room your mother will be sitting . . ." Her voice quavered, but she squared her shoulders and faced Sarah Jane. "I've fallen in love."

Sarah Jane allowed her eyebrows to rise. "Again?"

"No, really fallen in love this time." Leila sighed. "I've never met anyone like him before. He's . . ." She studied the ceiling as if searching for the right words. "He's different. And exciting. And wild."

Sarah racked her brain to make sense of it all. "Wild?"

One of those hotheaded Georgian Cherokee south of here? A white planter from Charleston? Though on second thought, she doubted Ambrose Hummingbird would take issue with that.

"Who, Leila? Who's this mystery man?"

"I met him about a month ago when he arrived with the messenger from Chief Ross about our temporary difficulties."

Only center-of-the-universe Leila. Not so much a hummingbird regarding world events as an ostrich.

"He disagrees with my father and the other old men about what should be done in response to the deadline."

A sneaking suspicion crept up Sarah's Jane's arms. "What's his name?"

The girl tossed her head. "I doubt you know him. He comes from over the mountain."

"Leila . . ."

"Touch the Clouds."

Sarah groaned and sank into the chair. "Your father's right."

"My father is wrong." Leila's eyes flashed. "Father says we're not suited for each other."

Sarah pursed her lips. "You're *not* suited for each other. You'd end up making each other miserable."

"With him, I'll never be miserable again. He loves me. He, unlike you pious saints," her lips protruded, "understands me. The me that longs to be as free as him. The me you Bible-thumping Pharisees have tried to extinguish."

Sarah Jane bolted to her feet. She'd repent over James, chapter 3, later. "Touch the Clouds is more than just 'wild' as you so aptly put it. He's conservative and traditional. And you are . . ." She jabbed her finger at Leila. "You know what you are."

Leila stamped her foot. "Well, I want him, and he wants me. I came here hoping you'd speak to your father and he'd speak a word to mine."

Sarah hardened her heart and locked gazes with Leila. "I will do no such thing and neither will my father, especially not after the stunt you've pulled with his apprentice."

Leila threw up her hands. "Oh, for mercy's sake. Will you both—and as I've told that weaned-on-a-sour-pickle Pierce—get over what amounted to nothing more than a harmless flirtation? It meant nothing."

Sarah gritted her teeth. "It meant everything to Pierce."

Leila's mouth thinned. "He'll get over it."

Sarah Jane prayed every night he would. "Seeing as how you don't speak a word of Cherokee, I can't imagine how you managed to fall in love much less converse with that . . ."

Leila gave her a pointed look. "Oh, he speaks English as well as you or I." She flipped a curl over her shoulder. "When he chooses to."

"Forget it, Leila. It's a path straight to disaster. Don't do something reckless you'll regret."

"So you won't help me?"

"Absolutely not."

Unused to being defied, Leila's eyes narrowed into rattlesnake slits. Sarah Jane took a step back.

"If you won't help me, then I'll have to help myself. My way won't be as pretty, but it'll accomplish the same purpose."

A flicker of fear knotted Sarah's belly. "Don't be rash, Leila." She laid a restraining hand on Leila's sleeve. "What're you planning?"

Leila shrugged her off. "Never you mind. You had your chance to make a difference. But make no mistake." She poked a finger at Sarah's face. Sarah flinched.

"Any and all consequences will be on your head. Not mine." Leila whirled.

The slamming of the door punctuated her words, leaving Sarah with a sick, uncertain feeling of dread.

In April, triumphant in purple silk, Leila stood before the altar at the meetinghouse. Sarah Jane had been coerced into becoming her reluctant bridesmaid.

Furious, Ambrose Hummingbird, as grim as Death, acted as the other witness. Preacher Jones—released from General Wool's custody and ordered to quit the state—united the headstrong girl in holy matrimony with Touch the Clouds, whose face resembled granite.

Leila Hummingbird was with child. Probably by six weeks to Sarah Jane's best reckoning, recalling her last conversation with Leila.

To remove him as far as possible from the ceremony, Dr. Hopkins sent a distraught Pierce clear to Buffalo Town to visit patients.

When Pierce first learned of Leila's "shotgun" nuptials, he'd gone a little crazy. And Sarah Jane was glad their humble home sported neither strong drink nor weaponry. Her father had restrained Pierce from rushing over to Chestnut Hill and making a bad situation worse.

Although in her opinion, it couldn't have been much worse.

Which just showed how little Sarah Jane Hopkins knew.

11

2018—Cartridge Cove

He'd managed to make a right mess of things with Linden Birchfield.

But something cold and hot had gone through Walker when he spotted her and Quincy Sawyer huddled at the dinner last night. And the fact she stood him up to visit Sawyer at the museum . . .

If he wasn't a Christian man . . . who'd sworn off violence the rest of his days . . .

But upon every sighting of her, he opened his mouth and inserted more than just his foot.

She made him nervous. That's what it was, Walker decided. Strange, because not many people did.

Not the Taliban, not singing in front of folks at church, not fighting fire. But one look at the city-smart woman, and he became stupid.

And he didn't like it. Not one little bit.

Walker thrust a motorcycle helmet at Linden. "Prefer 'em young, Miz Birchfield?"

Her brows, as delicate as butterfly wings, rose. "You're referring to Quince?"

Walker's lip curled. "What's that saying? Get 'em young, train 'em right."

"Not quite a jerk." She shoved the black helmet at his stomach. Walker let out a whoosh of air. "But you are an idiot."

He moved far enough away to swing his leg over the Harley. And, stop breathing the fruity rose fragrance she wore.

Straddling the bike, he jammed his own helmet onto his head, striving for a nonchalance he didn't feel. "Not that it's any of my business."

Linden tucked her bun into her helmet. She leaned forward—in case he needed to read her lips.

As if he'd hadn't had a hard enough time over the last few days forgetting her lips . . .

"Quince and I are just friends. Not that it's any of your business." Her feet planted in a wide stance, she crossed her arms.

Tearing his eyes away from hers, he fumbled for the dangling straps of the helmet and clicked them closed underneath her chin. "There."

It was all he could do to withdraw his fingers from lingering at the tempting softness of her skin.

He swallowed. "Are we good?"

Why didn't she say something? Or did she enjoy watching him drown in the blue of her eyes?

"To go, I mean?"

"Lesson three, you said?" Her voice quavered as she contemplated his road hog.

Walker motioned toward the Snowbird range west of town. "Best way to catch a glimpse of the Cherokee soul is to see it from the eagle's point of view."

He'd show her his definition of freedom—a wide, open space far removed from her skyscraper world. Real freedom.

She placed her hand on the sleeve of his leather jacket. "Crows fly there, too?"

"This Crowe does."

She smiled as she mounted the bike behind him.

"Glad to see you wore a jacket," he called over his shoulder. "'Cause where we going—as fast as we're going to fly—it's liable to get a mite chilly."

Walker lifted the kickstand with his boot. He balanced the bike, planting both feet on the ground. Wobbling, she immediately wrapped both arms around his waist.

As he knew she would when he planned this little outing.

Facing forward, he allowed a grin to break the contours of his face. Who'd call him stupid now?

Past Lake Santeetlah, Walker caught 143 West, also known as the Cherohala Skyway, a biker's dream with its hairpin curves. Lush forests of blooming rhododendron and mountain laurel covered the range on their right, and nothing but a thin guardrail stood between them and a sheer drop-off to their left. Deep gorges studded with dark timber revealed the flashing silver of rushing streams below.

Giving it the gas, he wound higher and higher, faster and faster. The exhilaration of the wind slapping at his exposed cheeks and the pushing back of the earth's stranglehold always made him feel more alive than anywhere else on the globe. Sent his heart into overdrive.

Kind of like how Walker felt the first time he ran into Linden Birchfield on her grandmother's porch.

He eased his hand on the throttle, slowing. He'd probably scared the—

"Faster," she shouted, her mouth pressed against the side of his helmet. "Go. Go. Go." She bounced on the seat.

"Linden," he bellowed.

Next thing you know, this crazy white woman would throw her hands skyward as if she rode a roller-coaster.

"Hold on. Don't . . . let . . . go."

Linden's untapped aura of recklessness excited and frightened him.

Her arms tightened around his rib cage. "I'm not planning on letting go," she yelled into the wind.

Despite the momentary fear seizing his gut, delight threaded through his heart.

"Okay," he shouted, revving the engine and surging forward. "You asked for it."

She buried her face in the soft leather of his back. Her laughter bubbled against him. Over the few days he'd known her, he'd gotten the distinct impression she wasn't a woman given to smiling, much less laughter.

Walker embraced the joy of the day—the blue sky and this alluring, not like anybody he'd ever known before, woman. Celebrated the gift of today from the Creator Himself. Because Walker had lived long enough—and hard enough—to understand such days were fleeting. Rare and worthy of great praise.

An hour or so later, he steered onto a pull-off overlooking the vastness of the valley. He let the engine idle while he propped the kickstand in place with his boot. She released his waist, and he regretted the loss of her warmth right away.

The bike tilted to one side. She scooted backward and dismounted. Unstrapping his helmet, he swung his leg over and, with a snap, unclasped her helmet as well.

She pulled the helmet off her head and handed it to him. With a self-conscious smile, she reached behind the crown of her head, her fingers tucking and winding at her disheveled hair.

He licked his wind-chapped lips. "Better let it all the way down." He set the helmets on the seat. "The Cherohala doesn't do much for hairdos."

"You first."

Rolling his eyes, he slipped off the leather band and tucked it in his pocket. Brushing the hair out of his eyes, he edged toward a granite outcropping the Department of Transportation had seen fit to leave at this kingly view of Creation. Undulating misty blue hills folded one upon the other.

She joined him, fiddling with loose tendrils of hair.

A tremor of desire forced him to stuff his hands into the pockets of his jeans lest he give in to the urge to "help" her. "Your turn."

She tilted her head, an ambiguous smile on her face. "Never much cared for any man with hair prettier than mine." She laughed. "Oh, well."

With a simple twist, she loosed her pent-up hair. Its light brown waves fell in a silky cascade down her shoulders, past her shoulder blades and to the small of her back.

His eyes widened. He'd not realized her hair was that long. He gulped.

Or that lovely.

"Y-you've nothing to fear on that score," he stammered, reduced once again to a blathering idiot.

She took a deep breath of the crisp, clean air. "It's beautiful here."

His knees feeling shaky, he lowered himself to a sitting position, the boulder at his back. With nothing but space and Linden Birchfield between him and God.

She slid down beside him, and there remained nothing between them but God.

He gathered whatever wits he still possessed and tried to focus on his purpose for bringing her here in the first place. Lesson number three . . .

"The Cherokee believe there are three worlds. The world we walk upon, the world above on top of the Sky Vault, and the world below. We also recognize seven directions.

She looked at him. "North, South, East, West. What else?"

"Up, down," he pointed at the earth. "And here."

She nodded.

"Death lies always to the west. That's the direction the traditional Cherokee believed the soul traveled after departing the body."

She sighed. "So when the government ordered the Cherokee west to Indian Territory . . . ?"

"The spiritual aspect linked with the fear of the unknown."

He gazed across the skyline at wave upon rolling wave of hills and ridges until the defined lines of the horizon receded leaving a blending of mountain and sky. "There are seven traditional clans from which we, especially the Snowbird Cherokee, trace our lineage."

"Matrilineally."

"Yes. The Bird, to which I belong," he pointed at himself. "The Deer, the—"

"The Wolf, Long Hair, Wild Potato, Red Paint, and Blue Paint." She gave him the pleased smile of an expectant child who'd recited her letters perfectly to the teacher.

"You *have* done some homework," he chuckled and as a sharp wind whistled, placed his arm around her shoulders.

So she wouldn't get chilled, of course.

His other hand swept the ridges and valleys. "All you see once belonged to the Cherokee. Where the Creator placed us."

The silkiness of her hair brushed against the hollow of his throat.

His pulse leaped. "We'd been told since colonial days if we settled onto farms, dressed like the white man, talked like the white man, and stopped our heathen ways—"

"Some of you," she unfolded her legs and stretched them out in front beside his, "would have a harder time with that than others."

He brushed his lips across her hair to hide his smile. "With or without Harleys?"

She nestled like a robin in her nest. "My point, I believe."

"Anyway . . ." His heart thudded, but despite his misgivings, he took a chance and draped both arms around her.

He allowed himself to fantasize if he bent his head . . . and if she leaned forward another few inches . . . would her lips taste as sweet as she smelled?

Linden angled, her eyes catching hold of his. Her breath whispered across his cheek. Her mouth compelled him.

When her lips parted, he decided to stop imagining. His lips feathered against hers and lingered.

At her sudden intake of breath, Walker sensed himself on the threshold of territory he'd sworn to never revisit. But instead of pulling away, she molded her mouth to his.

Walker's gut twisted. It'd be so easy to lose himself in the moment. And he didn't know what he feared most.

That she'd prove to be like the others?

Or that she wouldn't?

Breaking contact, he drew back. A flicker of confusion dotted her face. He turned, cooling his cheek against the hard stone of the boulder.

She cleared her throat. "I'm guessing the Cherokee stab at civilization didn't amount to much in the face of gold fever and land hunger."

Grateful, he seized on the topic and raked his hand over the top of his head. "You got that right. But you've heard the stories of how the North Carolina Cherokee were able to hide and remain. In the end, nobody much wanted our Snowbird Mountain land. Except for us. Too isolated and rugged. Therefore of all the Cherokee, we've remained the most traditional, the most closely knit. The highest percentage of pure Cherokee spoken in the counties around the Snowbird range."

She sniffed. "Civilization's overrated anyway."

Keep it light, Crowe.

"Seriously?" He cocked his head. "Says the poster child for Starbucks and Madison Avenue?"

Linden slapped at his sleeve. "Shows what you know." She blushed. "This place kinda grows on you after a while."

"Oh, really?"

He wished he could show Linden the Great Smokies. The People called the mountains of the blue smoke, Shaconage. Would she be around come autumn to see the in-your-face glorious display of russet red, saffron yellow, and lit-from-within orange mountain peaks? Or would she leave after the festival ended in late July?

Cartridge Cove, without Linden Birchfield, seemed suddenly an empty, hollow place.

She gave him a searching look, sending his heart into fast forward. "Really."

What had become of his self-sufficiency? His serene enjoyment of his self-imposed splendid isolation?

"A splendid isolation," he whispered the words, reminding himself of his opposition to what she represented.

Doubt ate away at his stomach. He already liked her more than he should.

What further damage could she yet do to his way of life and his heart?

Linden closed her eyes. The tease of the wind pulled at the long strands of her hair. On top of the mountain, only the caw of a bird and the rustling of the wind among the treetops broke the silence. And yet here—with him—it was good.

If only she could forever capture this place out of time, distill everything through the filter of slow motion to rewind and replay later. She breathed in this moment of serenity and relished its clarity, made possible by the man sitting beside her. She soaked in his warmth.

"What's this quest thing Em mentioned?"

She filled him in on the journal she'd found in the attic.

"Hummingbirds? Hopkins?" The wind ruffled his raven black hair. "A few Hummingbirds escaped the Removal. Their descendants are scattered between here and Cherokee town. Painttown. A few in Yellow Hill. Never heard of any Hopkins. But the Snowbird tend to stick to their own communities, and the white Appalachians stick to theirs. Works well for everybody."

She threw him a sharp look. Flirty one minute. Withdrawing into that private Cherokee enclave the next.

"Do you think we have enough daylight left for Lesson Number Four before we head back to town?"

His breath blew against a tendril of her hair. "Sure."

"A lesson explaining a certain tree-hugger, motorcycling enthusiast named Walker Crowe?"

"I do not hug trees. I grow them."

Her mouth lifted at the corners. "I didn't know that. See . . ." She tugged at the zipper on his coat. "I've learned something about you already."

She nudged his shoulder. "I get the feeling there's lots more."

With her cheek pressed against his jacket, she felt him tense.

Okay . . . awkward.

"Forget it. You don't have to tell me anything."

He sloped back, distancing himself. "What do you want to know?"

"I've met your mom, Irene—"

"My dad was a professional hunter. He took groups of week-end enthusiasts on deer hunts in season. He taught me to take only what is needed and to live in harmony with nature. To smell the earth. To see its beauty. To be quiet long enough to appreciate my place in it. To be still and hear the Creator as He walks among the trees."

Walker sighed. "But he died when I was sixteen. A hunting accident."

"I'm sorry."

He gazed at the horizon. "Life happens. So does death."

She flinched.

His brow wrinkled. Questions clouded his face. To her relief, for now he let off the asking. "My older brother and sister live in Asheville and have their own families. After I got out of service, I went to—"

"You were in the military? What branch?"

His lips tightened. "Army. Same as Uncle Ross. Anyway, I went to North Carolina State and studied—"

"My brother Royce is in the Marines. How long ago were you in the army? Where were you stationed?"

A muscle pulsated in his cheek. He jerked to his feet, dumping her into the gravel. "Is this an interrogation?"

Okay . . . good to know.

The army was a closed topic with Walker Crowe. He didn't appear the dishonorable or disorderly type. But what did she know about men?

Past experience only served to illustrate what an abysmal failure she was at making those sorts of judgment calls.

"Sorry, journalism background before I switched majors. Gram says I'm the nosiest—"

"I shouldn't have barked." He offered her a hand.

Sprawled on her butt, she accepted. And like every other time her skin made contact with his, the familiar tingle sizzled her nerve endings. A jolt of fire and ice.

He pursed his lips as he hauled her to her feet. "What made you decide to leave your high-powered job for North Carolina?"

She blew a strand of hair out of her face. "Is *this* an interrogation, Crowe?"

He leaned against the boulder, the long length of him stretched out. "I studied agribusiness at State, graduated, and came home. End of my story. A boring story, I imagine, compared to your jet-set life." He crossed his ankles. "Now your turn."

She pointed to herself. "Me? Jet set? Hardly."

"I've done a little research on your background."

Her eyes widened. "You Googled me?" A sliver of fear lanced her heart at the thought of what one could unearth these days on the Internet.

"You spent a lot of time traveling with your parents as a child on medical missions. Bosnia. Zaire. India."

He wanted to know about her parents?

She let a trickle of air escape from between her lips. "Right. War-torn and famine-starved. Those places the very definition of glamour. My folks are medical mission adrenaline junkies. Any catastrophe on the planet, and you can bet my parents will be on the next plane out."

"Your dad's a doctor, right? Sounds as if he uses his skills to help the less fortunate."

"And my mother's a surgical nurse." She sighed. "Don't get me wrong, they're wonderful. How could any son of Marvela and Fraser Birchfield not be warm and fascinating? It's just . . ."

"It's just not easy for children spending birthdays and Christmas with their grandparents instead of mom and dad."

"How'd you guess?"

"Family is everything to the Snowbird." His arm swept the expanse around them. "And roots."

"That's been part of my trouble. The lack of roots, I mean."

"So who was the wandering star? Your dad or mom?"

"Both, I think."

"Where is home for you, Linden?"

She dropped her eyes. "Wherever my next client takes me. And Gram."

"At the risk of incurring your wrath again, dare I ask one more time why they named you after, and I quote, 'a tree in the midst of a field of other trees'? End-quote."

Her mouth quirked. "If you knew the grief my name caused in junior high . . . My mother is from the Cotswolds."

Walker raised his brows. "England? Like I said, I continue to be amazed at your international background."

Linden rolled her eyes. "She grew up in a lovely golden stone house at the end of a lane of linden trees. When she was pregnant with me, she and Dad ministered in the middle of a hot, dry savanna in Africa."

"Treeless?"

She laughed. "Yeah. Your idea of hell, huh?"

He smiled. "And hers?"

"Something like that. She says she dreamed every night about trees, especially the linden trees that grew outside the window of her girlhood home, Linden Hall."

"Were you named after the trees or her home?"

She stared at him. "I-I don't know. I never thought of it like that, and I've never asked."

He cast a long look at the fading light of the mountain sunset. "We better hit the road." He ambled toward the bike. "And maybe you should. Ask, I mean."

Walker handed her the helmet. "Was it greenery she longed for? Or home?"

12

June 12, 1838

At the timid knock on the back door, Sarah Jane found the Hummingbird's housekeeper, and Samson's common-law wife, on the stoop twisting her apron. "Come in, come in, Yolanda. What brings you here so early?"

Yolanda bobbed a curtsy at Sarah's father who'd risen from his place at the kitchen table. "Dr. Hopkins, Miss Leila done sent me to get some medicine since she's been feeling so poorly."

Dr. Hopkins folded his napkin under his plate. "Poorly? I'm sorry to hear that. A catarrh? A cold?"

Yolanda's green head rag shook from side to side. "No, sir. It's the sickness that comes upon females sometimes in their confinements . . ." She blushed.

Dr. Hopkins nodded. "In the morning, is it?"

Yolanda rolled her eyes. "Morning, noon, and night. Although with both of my babies, I never—" Yolanda swallowed. "Miss Leila says she feels like she's going to vomit all the time, but doesn't. She thinks she'd feel better if she could."

"That Kweti." Yolanda's mouth did a fair imitation of turning inside out. "She's done tried her heathen magic on Miss Leila, and Miss Leila's 'bout done with all that, so she sneaked me out of the house first thing this morning."

Sarah Jane glanced out the window. "You came all this way by yourself?"

Yolanda jabbed her finger toward the front of the house. "Samson's waiting for me with the rig. Miss is in a hurry for a cure."

Dr. Hopkins plodded toward his surgery where he kept his herbal remedies under lock and key. "No cure for what ails her but childbirth and delivery."

He paused. "Let me get this straight. Leila wants me to give her an emetic to induce vomiting?"

Yolanda shrugged.

"Humph. Emetics are for real sick people. Might harm the baby. She'll get ginger root like the rest of the pregnant mothers. I'll write out the instructions for the preparation." His footsteps echoed down the hall.

Sarah Jane reached for the coffee pot warming on the stove. "Want some coffee while we wait, Yolanda?"

Yolanda gave Sarah an uncertain look. "I don't rightly know about that, Miss."

"We could bring a cup to Samson, too. I'm sure your day started long before this, with chores and cooking for everybody else."

Sarah gestured to a chair. "Sit and rest a minute."

Yolanda's mouth hung open. "At your table? With you? Wouldn't be fittin'."

Sarah touched the woman's ragged sleeve. "You wouldn't let me drink alone, would you? It would be rude while you had nothing."

Yolanda, at the pressure from Sarah's hand, allowed herself to sink into one of the chairs. "Well, when you put it that way, Miss Sarah."

Sarah doctored the brew and joined her at the table.

The woman, scant years older than Sarah, took a cautious sip, her coffee bean eyes wide over the brim. "Miss Leila also wanted me to ask if you'd visit with her a spell."

"No." Sarah set her mug down with a clatter. "I don't think so, Yolanda."

"Miss Leila's powerful lonely at her pa's house these days."

Sarah frowned. "How long has Leila been at Chestnut Hill?"

Yolanda's eyes darted out the window at the sound of a robin's cheery greeting. "'Bout two weeks, I 'spect."

"Two weeks? What about her husband?"

"He's not come. She said she got to feeling bad and needed Kweti. Needed to come home for a while."

Sarah Jane arched a brow.

"All she's done is stay in bed with Kweti fussin' over her. But we ain't seen hide nor hair of that husband of hers."

Yolanda placed her cup upon the red-checked cloth. "She seems to be right blue. A visit from you would sure cheer her up."

"I don't know if I can, Yolanda." Sarah scraped back her chair to fill a cup for Samson. She'd spent the better part of two months asking for divine help in forgiving the unrepentant Leila.

Was this God's way of asking her to put her will where her prayers were?

"How does Samson favor his coffee, Yolanda?"

Yolanda drifted alongside her. "Black as his skin." She laughed. "You're a fine Christian lady to think about us'uns, Miss Sarah."

Sarah winced, unsure if her attitude toward Leila Hummingbird qualified her for that bit of undeserved praise. "You said both your babies, Yolanda. I didn't know you had children."

With great care, Yolanda trundled the chairs to their proper positions around the table. "Had babies."

Sarah stilled.

"Before." Yolanda's voice quivered. "Before Mr. Hummingbird bought me in Charleston. I don't plan on repeating that mistake with Samson."

Dr. Hopkins emerged with a brown bag in his hand.

And as it turned out, Sarah did accompany Yolanda and Samson to Chestnut Hill when her father was called out by one of the soldiers bivouacked in the crossroads adjacent to the mercantile. As for Pierce? He'd taken to riding out at the crack of dawn to make Dr. Hopkins's follow-up rounds.

Which was just as well.

She found Leila ensconced on a chaise lounge in her upstairs bedroom. At the sight of Sarah, Leila jolted to her feet. She'd never seen the Cherokee girl so pale.

Only a small bulge beneath her navy cotton skirt betrayed Leila's condition. She threw her arms around Sarah's gone-stiff figure. "Oh, Sarah. You've come."

"I so hoped you would." Leila laughed. "Almost prayed on it." She gripped Sarah's arm. "Now don't give me that sourpuss look. I've missed you, Sarah Jane."

And Leila's eyes pooled. "It's not been what I envisioned . . ." She swayed. "Do you think I'm going to die like my mama?"

Sarah wrapped an arm around Leila's shoulders and led her back to the chaise. "Yolanda and Kweti are working on the medicine. It should help alleviate the nausea some. You're going to be fine. You're strong and in otherwise good health. You need to think of the baby. Of the joy that's to come."

Leila swallowed. She gestured toward the green trunk at the foot of the bed. "Look what I've been working on."

Sarah strolled over to the bed, laying a soft hand upon the turkey red and saffron yellow quilt. "You finished the Cherokee Rose. It's beautiful." She stroked the inset white blossoms.

"Not that," Leila waggled her hand. "In the trunk."

Sarah drew the lid and lifted out a pink and blue crocheted blanket. "Oh, Leila. How lovely."

"Unwrap it."

Spreading the blanket on top of the quilt, she uncovered a baby's bonnet and gown. Her breath caught.

"Yolanda worked as a ladies' maid in Charleston. She taught me how to tat the lace on the edges. I'm thinking of knitting booties and a sweater next." Leila's eyes twinkled. "I may even ask your father to christen him or her when the time comes."

"Really?" Sarah eyed Leila. "How will Touch the Clouds feel about that?"

A mulish look crossed Leila's face. "If he's around to care."

117

Sarah rewrapped the baby clothes and rejoined Leila on the chaise. "Have you parted ways with your husband so soon, Leila? Why are you here at Chestnut Hill?"

Unhappiness flitted across Leila's face. "He told me not to come. That it was safer to remain in the mountains away from town with the soldiers prowling around. But he wouldn't allow Kweti to live with us."

Her full lips trembled. "Kweti's been with me since my mama died. With my mother when she was a little girl, too. And that shack he and his grandparents call home . . ."

Leila gulped. "It's so primitive. You can see the ground between the floor planks. No windows. We slept in the loft and his grandparents on the pallets downstairs."

"His people aren't as wealthy as your father, Leila. Surely, you understood that. You must've known that."

Leila glared. "I believed we'd live here at Chestnut Hill. Father offered him a position running the plantation, but he refused to live this close to town." Her voice hardened. "Refused to abandon his traditions and his grandparents and the wilderness he calls home."

"But to leave him, Leila . . ."

Leila crossed her arms. "That bossy grandmother expected me to work dawn to dusk. 'Sweep the floor, Leila.'" Her voice took on a singsong quality in imitation of the elderly woman. "'Peel the potatoes. Grind the corn.'"

Exasperation flickered across the Cherokee girl's face. "Me? Leila Hummingbird doing the work of a field hand? I think not."

"And what did Touch the Clouds say to this?"

Leila flopped onto the cushions. "Who do you think translated his grandmother's Cherokee to English?" She twirled a long strand around her finger. "So I showed him."

"By flouncing home in a snit like a child throwing a tantrum?"

Leila's lips bulged. "If all you can do is preach, Sarah Jane Hopkins, feel free to go home." She swept her arm toward the door.

"What about your vows? What about your baby? Every baby needs his father."

Leila collapsed against the chaise. "He'll come around eventually. This is just part and parcel of our ongoing negotiations."

"Marriage isn't a game, Leila. Nor a skirmish in a war."

Leila tossed her head. "And you'd be an expert on relations between a man and a woman how, Sarah Jane?"

Sarah flushed. She should've known coming here would only lead to insults and hurt feelings.

Hers. Sarah rose.

Leila grabbed her arm. "I'm sorry, Sarah. That carried more sting than I meant." Shadows smudged her eyes.

Sarah yanked her sleeve free. "I think you said exactly what you meant. And if Touch the Clouds means no more to you than—"

"Don't read more into it than it is, a test of wills. Touch the Clouds is a strong man, and he wouldn't respect me if I didn't from time to time take a strong stand on certain things."

Her face was as serious as Sarah had ever beheld her. "I'm not forsaking my husband, Sarah, rest assured." Leila shook her head. "We understand one another. Father was wrong about us in the ways that count. We *are* suited to each other. He is to me," Leila's frame quivered. "Like a consuming fire."

More like a moth to the flame.

"That description's reserved for God, Leila. A consuming fire, jealous for those who belong to Him."

Leila squared her shoulders. "Well, since I've never belonged to Him in the first place, what business is it of His what I do or feel?"

Sarah gasped. "You blaspheme, Leila Hummingbird. You've belonged to Him since the day He gave you breath, but God will not be mocked—"

A pounding sounded from the front door downstairs. Shouts. She and Leila exchanged puzzled looks at the sound of scuffling.

"Miss Leila!" Kweti burst into the room, her red turban slipping sideways over one eye. "The soldiers. They've come."

13

2018—Cartridge Cove

Descending the mountain proved a much quicker trip than ascending. And on the return trip to collect her car at the Center, Linden pondered Walker's mixed signals on the mountain.

Walker stowed her helmet in a compartment on the Harley. "I'll follow you to Miss Marvela's."

She fished her keys out of her jean jacket. "Don't bother. It's not far."

His gaze darted toward the woods behind the Center. "It's not a bother. And I'd feel better if I saw you safe and sound inside your grandmother's house. It's getting late and after the trouble you've already encountered surrounding this festival, I insist."

Linden scanned the darkened interior of the Center. She hoped wherever Quincy spent his evening, it included Emmaline. She glanced over to Walker, balancing the motorcycle on the balls of his feet.

Truth be told, since the skinhead incident the mountains gave her the willies. "Aren't you the Southern gentleman?"

He grinned. "Southern chivalry at its finest here in Snowbird. We pride ourselves on curbside, door-to-door service."

The effect of the deep dimples bracketing both sides of his mouth almost sent her into cardiac arrest.

Linden drew a draught of air into her lungs to steady her pulse and yielded to an impulse. "What is it you long for, Walker?"

His smile froze.

The wrong question. Again. Trying to get behind that oh-so-polite wall of his, an endeavor fraught with emotional landmines.

His hands curled around the handlebars. "Not much. Best not to expect too much because life has a way of disappointing."

She cocked her head. "How has life disappointed you, Walker?"

Horizontal lines plowed across his forehead. "Hasn't life ever disappointed you?"

Linden dodged his question as adroitly as he'd dodged hers. "Interesting perspective from a church man."

"I struggle with the faith to believe—not in God or His goodness—but the faith to believe in me and a future I know I don't deserve."

Linden nodded. "For me, His goodness is where I stumble."

He studied her face. "Maybe some time we can trade war stories. When you feel I've earned enough of your trust to share."

The way he said it left her feeling as if he'd laid down an emotional gauntlet. "Maybe." Moistening her lips, she slid into the Toyota.

On the short drive to her grandmother's, she scolded herself for acting like a teenager on the mountain. It'd be too easy to get used to the lazy smiles Walker threw her way. To come to expect and depend on it.

She reminded herself of why that wouldn't be a good idea. Why she wasn't ever going to be the marrying kind. Marriage led to ramifications she didn't ever intend to put herself through again.

Pulling into the driveway, he rolled his motorcycle to a stop behind her car. She caught the glint of glass reflecting off the deep-fronted porch. A shape moved in one of the wicker rockers.

Walker swung off his bike and tucked his helmet under his arm.

Heavy-lidded, he leaned against the hood of her Toyota. "What do you long for, Linden?"

Is that what he'd been thinking about as they caravanned to Gram's?

He'd lose all respect for her if she told Walker about what she'd done and who she really was. How the repercussions of those adolescent decisions marked her for the rest of her days.

And reduced viable options for her future.

She hedged, shuttering her emotions. "For my business to—"

"No, I mean what *you* want. For you. Not your work."

She tapped her fingers on the car roof. "A house of my own. Maybe a dog someday when I don't travel so much."

Walker edged closer. "Sounds lonely so far."

Her fingers rapped a staccato beat. "Alone works best for me. From all appearances, works for you, too."

"Me? I've got plenty in my life. Don't you want a husband and children some day?" He wrapped his hand around her restless fingers and stilled them.

Her eyes darted to the verandah. "I don't need to be in a relationship to be happy."

"You don't like children?"

She flinched. "Children and I . . ." She swallowed. "Not in the cards. Wouldn't work out."

His mouth tightening, Walker released her hand. At his expression, her eyes welled. Linden blinked back the moisture. This same upfront and honest conversation stalled every relationship she'd ever attempted since The Jerk.

She hated feeling this way. She hated watching what a family man like Walker must think of her. How his condemnation played out across his face. But it couldn't be helped. Save both of them heartache in the long run if he knew where she stood on this all-important issue.

The phone buzzed in her jacket pocket. Linden welcomed the distraction. "From Quincy." She made a feeble attempt to smile. "Wants to know if I'm—and you, too—are available to join him and Emmaline for pizza."

She raised her eyes to Walker's to find a thundercloud darkening the broad planes of his features. He stomped over to the bike. "What's wrong?"

He swung his leg over the seat. "Emmaline has no business giving that man any encouragement."

"Why not? Quince is a great guy. They've been friends for ages. She likes him. She and I are both hoping he'll like her back."

He thrust the kickstand up with his boot. "Friends are one thing. Anything else is out of the question."

She grabbed the sleeve of his jacket. "But why not Quincy and—?"

"Because Emmaline," Walker threw off her hand. "She's a Wachacha and a Snowbird Cherokee," he growled. "Did you learn nothing from the redneck vandalism?"

"What are you talking about?"

He turned the key, engaging the engine. "Look beneath the surface of our public Cherokee makes-nice-for-the-tourists face." He revved the motor. "The Snowbird has the largest percentage of full-bloods than any other Cherokee community. Cherokee is the true American language around here. It's English that's foreign."

"You mean because Emmaline's Cherokee and Quincy is . . ."

"Is not." Walker grimaced. "Here's a freebie, an inside tip on why Cartridge Cove works. Sure, we mingle in town. Go to school with each other and one or two like your grandmother attend our churches. But basically we stick with our kind, and they stick with theirs. Why mess with something that's worked for both groups for 180 years?"

"Your churches?" Linden sneered. "My bad. I thought it was Jesus' church."

He flushed.

"What about what just happened?" Linden jabbed an arm toward the mountains. "Are you telling me this afternoon was you having a little fun? Getting some kind of flirt on, but because I'm non-Indian nothing else could ever . . ."

She narrowed her eyes. "I'm sorry if I did or said something that gave you that impression of me. That I was the kind of—"

"Like you'd ever consider making this hick town your permanent home? We were both just stepping across the divide to see how the other half lives."

He jammed the helmet onto his head. "No harm. No foul. Nothing serious. Nothing could be serious between you and me. Two people who've absolutely nothing in common. All in the interest of whiling away a boring Sunday afternoon."

She crossed her arms. "That's the most racist hogwash I've ever heard. Like the imbeciles who wrote those slurs on the walls of the Center."

His nostrils flared. "I'm not racist. We're the last bastion of pure-blood Cherokee, thanks to your infamous Removal Act. Not Cherokee town. Not Oklahoma. The Snowbird."

"My Removal Act?" Her voice ended on a high note.

"Ever wonder why this town's called Cartridge Cove, Linden?" His decibel level rose. "Let me give you another historical factoid. Think boxes of paper cartridges. And Colt rifles with bayonets fixed, rounding up the area's indigenous people. My people. And then herding them like cattle to the rendezvous point over the mountain."

Her nose crinkled. "And you, Walker Crowe, have got the nerve to accuse me of having personal issues?"

Walker flipped the visor down veiling his eyes. "Much as I'd love to stand here all night in a shouting match with you, I have better things to do."

"Fine. Me, too. Sorry to have wasted your afternoon and your gasoline. Emmaline's right. You are a jerk."

Maybe the king of jerks. Could Linden pick 'em or what?

His only reply was to do a three-sixty and gun it as the back tire hit street level.

"Idiot," she yelled at the disappearing red taillight.

She grabbed her purse out of the trunk where she'd stored it when she'd been dumb enough to take a motorcycle ride with a raving lunatic. She slammed the lid shut.

"Creep." She stalked up the sidewalk between the driveway and porch. "Loser."

She took the three steps in a single bound to find her grandmother seated in a rocker and drinking sweet tea out of a crystal goblet.

Gram gave Linden a cat-swallowed-the-cream smile. "My, my, darlin'. What you two must have gotten up to this afternoon to put such a fear inside that young man?"

"Me?" Linden lobbed her purse at the door. "I guess you heard all that." She waved her arm behind her.

Gram set the glass with a tiny ping onto the side table. "Honey Girl, half of Cartridge Cove heard 'all that' just now."

Linden frowned as her grandmother's words registered. "Scared? Him? What're you talking about?"

Marvela patted the armrest. "Got too close would be my guess."

Linden obliged and perched. "Somebody ought to knock some sense into that man's head."

"Typical of a Wachacha." Her grandmother snorted. "Typical of the male of our entire species, if you ask me. Red, white, black, or purple—if such a male existed."

Linden squirmed. "If you're implying he and I . . . ? Give me some credit, Gram." She tossed her head. "He's a moron."

Marvela laughed, the sound like a bird trilling across the deepening twilight. "Has there ever been anything more irresistible on this earth, Honey Girl, than a man who doesn't think he needs a woman?"

He'd said stupid things. Things he didn't really believe. Walker wouldn't have blamed Linden if she'd bopped him upside the head.

It certainly wasn't any of his business with whom his adult cousin chose to spend her time. But he used Emmaline as an object lesson to derail the direction he and Linden seemed to be taking.

This thing with Linden hit him out of left field. She triggered something inside him that had launched Walker into full panic mode.

On call at the fire station, he busied himself this morning cleaning up around the firehouse. Anything to take his mind off his altercation with Linden the night before.

As if he'd been able to take his mind off her.

Linden left him feeling out of control. And out of control soldiers, he'd learned the hard way, made terrible mistakes. Better to squash this . . . whatever it was . . . this you've-taken-leave-of-your-senses chemistry before he made another horrible, life-altering mistake.

Because he wasn't ever setting foot off this mountain while he had breath in his body, and Linden Birchfield sure wouldn't ever surrender access to haute cuisine and Neiman Marcus.

So he'd tried to play off everything they'd shared as if Linden meant nothing to him. As if he was one of those good-time guys with nothing more on their minds than love in the afternoon. Like Walker didn't have the sense to know she wasn't that kind of girl.

Linden was an all or nothing. Serious was her middle name.

The marrying kind.

Not his type at all.

Out of the open bay of the fire station as he hosed down the truck, he watched her drive down Main and park outside the Blueberry Hill Diner. Getting out of the car, she waved to someone seated in a booth at the front window.

He wondered who she was meeting so early on a Monday. Walker also realized it was none of his business. Especially not after the way he'd behaved.

She was right. He was a jerk.

And he'd been getting funny looks all morning. Lots of folks stopping by the station to shoot the breeze. He and Linden had provided the Cartridge Cove grapevine more to chew on than in the previous three months.

But what shamed Walker the most was the thought of what the struggling-to-believe Linden must think of his Christ.

Not one of his finer moments last night. He peered at the vaulted ceiling of the station.

"Not going to get any peace of mind, am I, God, until I march over and apologize?"

Silence, except for the whistling of the wind in the leafed-out crape myrtles lining Main.

Answer enough for him. If you understood how to listen versus opening your mouth and verbalizing something moronic.

He sighed, calculating the strides it'd take before he reached the diner.

This was going to be about as much fun as . . . a middle school dance.

"Okay, God." He threw down the shammy in his hand as a buddy entered with a disposable tray of donuts and lattes from the diner. "Time to eat some . . ." He grimaced.

"Crowe."

❖

Linden scooted into the booth opposite Quincy and readjusted the folds of her teal skirt. The smell of fried everything—bacon, sausage, eggs, and hash browns—permeated the cafe.

His eyes, behind the horn-rimmed glasses, lit.

She toyed with the laminated menu stuffed between the salt and pepper shakers. "Sorry I didn't make it for pizza last night."

"Em's got this great idea to organize a group to hike the Heritage Trail over the mountains and follow the water route before rendezvousing and returning to Cartridge Cove with the Oklahoma delegation. What an adventure, huh? The brain on that lady never stops working." Quincy signaled for the waitress. "Another coffee, Marge?"

Linden smiled. Quince, despite what that imbecile named Crowe contended, seemed to be fitting in nicely within the community.

Quincy pushed a folder across the table. "For your eyes only, Linden Birchfield." His baby blues twinkled.

He swept his hand across his brow, pushing away his tangle of blond curls. His version of rakish? Try instead, cute as a puppy.

"All right, James Bond, what did you find out for me?"

Marge set a cup and saucer in front of Linden. She murmured her thanks.

Quincy reached beyond the plastic red carnations and handed Linden some creamer packets. "Just what you said, Lin. I photocopied the names of the people in the census the army conducted before the Removal deadline."

He opened the folder. "Hummingbird, Ambrose. Daughter, Leila. Servant named Kweti. And the slaves he listed."

Taking a quick sip, she leaned forward to get a better look. She made a face. Needed more cream. "That's right. The date before Leila got married. I don't suppose you've run across any Cherokee of a certain age named Touch the Clouds?"

He shook his head. "He'll be hard to trace, if not impossible, since I understand from your reading he refused to take an English surname."

She underscored one of the names with her index finger. "Samson? Check. Yolanda? Check. Kinda funny strange how an oppressed people like the Cherokee owned slaves themselves, huh?"

Linden skimmed the remainder of the list. "Just as Sarah Jane explained in the journal."

He gave her hand a quick squeeze. "Only history nerds like us would get so excited about something like this, but yeah, Lin, it gave me a thrill, too. Especially . . ."

Releasing her hand, he flipped to the next document in the folder. "When I found a survey from 1838 showing the outlines of the Hummingbird plantation. And it's right outside the modern town limits of Cartridge Cove. I included a recent survey of town boundaries and overlaid the surveys so if you want to—"

"A field trip?" She laughed and relaxed against the cracked green vinyl upholstery. "I love it. And what about Sarah Jane?"

"No joy yet on Sarah Jane. I did run across an archive connected with the American Mission Board referencing a Horace Hopkins. If only we knew the last name of the guy in the photo."

She sighed. "Or Sarah Jane's married name."

"You're convinced the woman in the picture is Sarah Jane?"

She recalled something Sarah had mentioned in the diary. "How about checking out another missionary by the name of Zeke—maybe Ezekiel—Tobias? He seems to have had a romantic interest in Sarah Jane Hopkins. Perhaps that's who she married."

"You say they pledged to follow the Cherokee? Maybe I should run the names through the Oklahoma records and see if we get any matches."

"Good idea. You're the expert." She took a sip after doctoring her brew. "Speaking of Em . . ."

He furrowed his brow. "Were we? Speaking of Em?"

She contemplated kicking Quincy under the table just for practice. Talk about oblivious . . . his IQ dropped ten points in her estimation.

"What else do you and Em have to do to get the Center ready?"

He perked. "A lot. The council approved funds to build a tree walk that leads to the remnant of the Trail the Cherokee walked to the fort. A company from Asheville's coming to install those push button boxes, giving our visitors factoids about the Snowbird."

Factoids? She frowned. What was it with men and factoids?

She realized Quincy had asked a question. She lugged her attention back to the coffee shop and away from other jerks of her acquaintance. "What? I'm sorry, what did you say?"

". . . . Em's cousin, the tree guy." He laughed, a trifle nervously. "That big guy I get the feeling doesn't approve of me for some reason."

She mentally raised his IQ five points upward for possessing good instincts. "What about him?"

"The technicians will be here by the end of the week to install the boxes on the trees he planted last year. And Em had another good idea . . ."

Something in his voice caused Linden to narrow her eyes.

"Em and I do boring, academic writing. We need someone with experience writing scripts to make the walk more fun and interesting to people of all ages and—"

"Why do I get the feeling a whole lot of extra work is about to get dumped in my lap?"

He gave her a shamefaced grin. "Em mentioned to Irene—that's the tree guy's mom—"

"I know who Irene Crowe is, Quince. We're working together on the quilt barns."

"Exactly." He nodded. "It was those quilts and the stories you discovered in Sarah Jane's journal that inspired Em."

Taking a deep breath, he plunged in. "Reminded her of what the Holocaust Museum in D.C. has done with one family's story." At Linden's blank look, "That we could do the same with Sarah Jane's story."

He lined up his gaze to meet hers. "The white Appalachian experience coupled with the Hummingbirds' story. Take snippets of it to record on the audio boxes. Represent both points of view."

Quincy speeded up his pitch at the speculative look she pasted on her face. ". . . so people could more easily relate to them. Wrap their minds around the impact of the Removal on real people, not so different from themselves, with similar hopes and dreams and fears." He finished with a rush.

"Humph."

Quincy pushed back the bridge of his glasses with his finger and smiled again.

Despite herself, she did think it was a great idea. And, a publicist's dream to promote.

"O-kaay . . ."

He jumped from his seat and scurried to her side of the booth. He threw his arms around her neck as a tall shape cast a shadow from the sidewalk outside. Afraid Em might happen upon them and get the wrong idea, she pushed Quincy gently away.

And glimpsed the back of a navy blue t-shirt emblazoned with the CCVFD logo disappear around the corner.

Her hand quivering, she smoothed her hair into the tight bun. And told herself she didn't care what he or anybody, except for Em, thought in this whole hillbilly town. Her heart thudded. No doubt he'd assume the worst.

When Quincy grabbed hold of the tab, she let him. She rustled in her handbag for her lipstick, dotted her lips, and pressed them together. What had she committed herself to with Quincy and the talking boxes?

Grabbing her purse, she slid across the booth, joining Quincy at the register. Sudden fury over the obtuseness of the entire male species rose in her chest. She couldn't get out of this one-stoplight town fast enough.

But while she was here she might as well further someone else's chance for a happily-ever-after.

Quincy held the door as they strolled onto the sidewalk. "Thanks, Lin. The Center, the barns, and the local Trail connection are going to put Cartridge Cove on the map."

"Plus Em's brilliant idea about the boxes." She removed the key ring from her purse and with a click, popped the lock open. "She's one in a million."

Linden patted the downy fuzz, which passed for Quincy's beard shadow. "Whatever will you do without her once the festival's over and she returns to her real life?"

Quincy reeled as if she'd struck him. "Her real life?"

His eyes flickered. "This is her real life. Her family's here."

She gave him a kind, indulgent look. "This is work. Her professional life."

Linden fluttered a hand in her best imitation of Marvela Does Beauty Pageant. "After adding this festival and her work at the

Center to her vitae, I'm sure the job offers will pour in from across the nation. And, of course, she'll move away . . . get married at some point."

His eyes behind the thick frames grew owl-like.

Linden laughed. Wicked, with a trace of saccharine. "But not right away, I'm sure."

He exhaled.

"You've probably got her at least for the rest of the summer."

He tensed.

She opened the car door, edging her body half-in, half-out. "But I'm thinking she'll move on to greener pastures, sooner rather than later."

A dull splotch crept up his neck and a muscle ticked in his jaw. "What did she say? H-how do you know this?"

Linden plopped into the seat and shut the door. Turning the key in the ignition, she rolled down the window and Quincy leaned in. "Just something us girls know."

She shifted the gearshift to drive. He rocked back as the car lurched a few inches, scraping the curb.

"About Em . . . Are you sure . . . ?"

Ignoring him, she checked the street before pulling out into the leisurely vehicular stroll Cartridge Cove liked to refer to as morning traffic. Leaving him on the curb, his mouth opening and closing like a snared trout, she gave a final call as she pulled onto Main. "You and Em, y'all have a good day now, you hear?"

She allowed herself a small smile as she merged. Because the way she stretched out the one syllable word of "y'all"? Linden figured she'd done every female graduate of Miss Ophelia's proud.

14

June 12, 1838

When the May 24th deadline came and went with nary any trouble from the soldiers, Sarah Jane, her father, and the Cherokee breathed a sigh of relief. As she faced the lieutenant on the steps of Ambrose Hummingbird's mansion, her relief had been premature.

The lieutenant waved the paper in Hummingbird's red-splotched face. He threw Sarah Jane an apologetic look. "I've got my orders, Miss Hopkins."

Ambrose snatched the paper from the young man's hand.

Leila leaned against the banister of the cantilevered staircase. "What does this mean, Father?" Kweti hovered like a mama bird. Samson and Yolanda stood silent in the hall.

The lieutenant's brow lowered. "It means you've got one hour to gather your things before my men and I," he glanced over his shoulder into the yard as if to assure himself they remained, "escort you into town where the others are being rounded—"

"Like cattle?" Ambrose flung the papers at the soldier.

Sarah watched the pages flutter, like dragonfly wings, to the floor.

The lieutenant flushed. "You knew this was coming, old man."

Ambrose's face contorted.

Unconsciously—or not—the lieutenant placed a hand on the holster at his hip. "You've had two years—"

133

"An hour?" She inserted herself between the men. "To pack the entirety of a man's lifework?"

For the first time, gazing beyond the lieutenant, she spotted a rustle of men, perhaps twenty, at the edge of the woods. Straining forward like rapacious wolves. The hair rose on the nape of Sarah's neck.

The lieutenant swallowed. "Please, Miss Hopkins. My men and I want no trouble. Every place we've been those roughnecks have followed. An hour is the most I can guarantee before they become impatient and . . ."

"Looters." Ambrose clenched his fist and advanced. Leila cried out.

Sarah caught hold of him. "Mr. Hummingbird, don't. They are so many, and we are so few. Do you want Leila to watch while they—?" Her voice trembled.

Ambrose went still.

"My father was called to town. Let's follow the lieutenant there and see what Papa has to say about what can be done."

Without taking his eyes off the looters, Ambrose called for Samson. "Hitch the carriage. Tell the field hands to gather what belongings they can carry."

"Yessir. How about the wagon and the oxen? The cows? You could—"

Ambrose pivoted on his heel. "Oh, I don't think we'll have need of those."

"What should we pack then?" wailed Leila.

A dazed look crisscrossed Ambrose's broad-planed features. "Don't you worry your head, Leila Mae. Dr. Horace and I will soon put this young man and his commander right, and we'll be back in time for supper."

"For supper?" Leila staggered to his side. "You heard what the man said? What about them?" She gestured at the looters creeping closer.

Hummingbird swiped a hand across the beads of sweat dotting his brow. "Run along, child. I'm going to get my pipe and a bag of tobacco. Maybe one suitcase," he allowed as a second thought. "Kweti will help you choose a pretty dress to take."

"But Father! The soldiers—"

Ambrose turned on her, his expression fierce. "I've got important work to get done before we gallivant off to town. Bring all the fripperies you want, but I have to . . ." His shoulders slumped. "I have to . . ." He disappeared toward his study leaving Leila staring dumbfounded after him.

"Has the world gone crazy?" Leila placed a hand to her head. "Is he right? Will we really be home by supper?"

Sarah Jane had a bad feeling Leila and her father would never return to this home again.

Yolanda cleared her throat. "What should we do, Miss Sarah? What should we bring?"

Sarah eyed the shamefaced lieutenant shuffling his feet and the wisecracking militia guarding his flank in the yard, oblivious to the family's distress. She squeezed Yolanda's hand.

"Go ahead, Samson, and hitch the wagon and oxen, too. Yolanda, gather the pots and other cooking utensils. Kweti?"

The old woman remained frozen on the bottom step of the staircase, transfixed at the sight of the mob on the periphery of the property.

"We'll need to bring all the bed linen we can find, Kweti." She moved to the woman's side. "And you'll need to help Miss Leila put in everything that green trunk can hold."

Sarah darted her eyes toward the expensive silver in the dining room, the family portraits that lined the walls of the entrance hall, the grandfather clock ticking down the minutes of their hour.

Not enough room to carry everything in the wagon.

"If your father has any money stowed away, Leila . . ."

Leila's head snapped up.

"You'd better bring it, too. And, anything else you can't bear to part with."

Coming to herself, Leila insisted Samson saddle the horses and fill their saddlebags with as much as they could carry of the food supplies. "Could we borrow your barn, Sarah Jane? Until Father gets this sorted out? You could ride one horse home. Samson another. I can drive the buggy, if Yolanda drives the wagon."

At Sarah's nod, Leila waved Kweti upstairs. "Be sure and pack my dresses, shoes, shawls and what-all in the trunk." From the space underneath the stairs, she withdrew a small, carpet-covered case.

"The candlesticks, Sarah Jane."

Sarah halted midstep. "What?"

"My mother's silver candlesticks. And the clock on the mantle. Father bought that in Boston. Yolanda," Leila called down the hall. "We'd better pack a bag for Father. He's like a child," she murmured as she swept into the parlor. Sarah followed on her heels. "Never packed a bag for himself in his life."

Where she pointed, Sarah Jane plucked and dumped in the soon bulging bag. In typical Leila fashion, no books were claimed off the shelves. She wondered if she'd been in Leila's shoes, what she wouldn't have wanted to live without.

Books would've headed her list of necessities.

"Perhaps you should help Yolanda gather the coffee, flour and other essentials," Sarah suggested.

Leila's face sagged as she realized the scope of what she'd never be able to fit inside one valise. "Why is this happening to us, Sarah Jane? Why?"

"I don't know." Sarah placed an arm around the quivering girl. "I don't know."

"Where's the justice of your God?"

"He *is* just and good, Leila. It's His creation that often fails to be either, not Him."

As Leila scurried from the room at Kweti's insistent summons, Sarah Jane spotted the small portrait of Leila painted by an itinerant painter last summer. With a sigh, she stuffed the framed cameo amidst the other detritus of Leila's life.

When the clock chimed the hour, the lieutenant escorted a belligerent Ambrose, crystal decanter clutched in hand, from the study and into the waiting carriage. Ambrose seemed well on his way toward inebriation, Sarah noted with concern.

The rest, including Sarah, took their places on horses or in the wagon as Leila instructed. A ragtag group of slaves formed a single line behind the wagon to walk to town on foot. Leila emerged from the house last. In her arms, she clasped the prized Cherokee Rose quilt.

Her eyes shone with unshed tears, but Sarah knew Leila would die before showing any sign of weakness in front of the soldiers. Leila faltered on the steps, casting one glance of farewell at the house before straightening her shoulders.

Beside her father in the carriage, Leila took the reins from Kweti. Her gaze focused ahead, refusing to acknowledge the cat-calls of the bearded vermin, emboldened by their removal. With a click of her tongue against her teeth, she slapped the reins across the back of the sorrel mare. As the horse surged forward, the circle of men were forced to part. Leila headed the buggy between the rows of cedars toward town.

Samson gestured for Yolanda to follow next. She and the field hands ate the dust Leila's fury churned beneath the carriage wheels. With a narrowed look at the empty sacks slung over the ruffians' shoulders, he nodded for Sarah to follow with one of the Hummingbird stallions. He slipped into place with his own mount beside her, leaving the lieutenant and his men to bring up the rear.

The sound of coarse shouts and breaking glass shattered the air behind them. A shiver crawled up Sarah's arms. She prayed the noise wouldn't reach the ears of the Hummingbirds.

When the caravan arrived at the mercantile crossroads, they entered a scene of utter chaos. Shouldering rifles, soldiers barked orders, and herded weeping Cherokee women from army-issued wagons into the center of town. Crying, terror-stricken children clutched the skirts of their mothers. In the midst of the mayhem, she spotted Pierce racing from one group to the other, patching cuts and offering ointment to bruises that'd be shiners come the morrow.

Not all, it appeared, had obeyed Chief Ross's injunction to offer no resistance.

"Pierce." She steered her horse ahead of their group. "Are you all right? What's happening? Where's Papa?"

Dripping with sweat, his blond curls had darkened to near brown under the heat of June's noonday sun. "I was at the Jameson's when the soldiers arrived."

He swiveled, searching the crowd. "Your father." He pointed toward the mercantile. "Over there with the major. These idiots plan to march the people to Fort Butler today. In this heat without any supplies of fresh water or food."

"That's over eight miles," she protested.

But she'd lost his attention.

His handsome face underwent a transformation the minute Leila's buggy drew near.

Pierce stepped around Sarah's horse and laid his hand upon the wheel of the carriage. "Leila, are you all right?"

Glaring at the lieutenant who sidled his horse next to the Hummingbird carriage, Pierce's mouth tightened. "Did they hurt you? Lay hands on you?"

Handing the reins to Kweti, Leila flung herself out of the carriage and into his arms. "Oh, Pierce." She buried her face into his shirt. "Chestnut Hill . . ."

Leila pounded her fists upon his chest. "Don't let them take me, Pierce. I want to stay here with you."

Sarah gasped.

His black eyes full of pity, Samson reached for Sarah's bridle and helped her dismount.

Pierce sneered at the unfortunate lieutenant. "My father is well-connected with West Point, sir. I'll have your name and the names of every man in your detachment. I'll—"

"You'll take your hands off my wife, white man."

At the unmistakable menace in Touch the Clouds's voice, Pierce dropped his hands and Leila sprang back. Her gaze scudded between the two men.

Pierce clenched and unclenched his fists. He bounced on the balls of his feet as if he weighed the odds of challenging the hardened outdoorsman.

As still as the granite mountains and as impervious, Touch the Clouds's face betrayed no indecision or fear. Only a calm and immense resolve.

Sarah Jane tugged at Pierce's arm. "He's right. She is—"

Touch the Clouds laid his hand on Leila's shoulder.

"Pierce," Leila whispered, her face white with an unhealthy pallor.

"She belongs here." Pierce stood his ground, but his voice quavered.

An ugly smile twisted the Cherokee's mouth. "She belongs with her people. And, her husband."

He pulled Leila toward him and lifted her chin with the tip of his finger. "Just think, my love, how life has a way of coming full circle. If you'd married this white man in the first place, you'd be safe from the Removal and serving tea in your father's parlor as we speak."

Touch the Clouds caught Leila's upraised hand seconds before it made contact with his face. They stared at each other, a long, smoldering moment. Her chest heaving, she yanked her hand free and wheeled toward Kweti in the carriage.

"Or, perhaps you'd be swabbing wounds and handing out Bible tracts in the backwoods with your missionary husband?" Touch the Clouds shouted to her retreating back.

Sarah Jane stepped between the men, both gazing after the Cherokee girl. Unable to bear looking into what she'd see in Pierce's face, she focused on Touch the Clouds, studying him in his buckskin and ribbon shirt.

But instead of finding anger as she'd expected, she glimpsed such raw pain that when he became aware of her scrutiny, he quickly masked it behind a show of bravado. Pierce slouched off as someone called for a doctor.

She sighed. "Leila's good at leaving a mountain of carnage wherever she goes, isn't she?"

Touch the Clouds shot her a sharp look, but said nothing.

"I figured they'd never bring you in."

"They didn't bring me in." From his six-foot plus height, he tilted his head at her. "But when they herded my grandparents to town in a predawn raid, I followed and surrendered myself." His lips tightened.

Leila had been right about one thing. Touch the Clouds spoke better English than either she or Sarah Jane. English in a well-modulated baritone that overlaid the slight accent of his mother tongue.

Sarah answered him in his own language. "A man who follows the Cherokee way directs his course for the good of The People. Your strength will be needed."

His enigmatic eyes never left her face, but a surprised gleam flickered in their obsidian depths. "Strength and weakness. Balance and harmony." He pushed back his shoulders, speaking to her in the tongue of the Principal People. "Love and hate. You understand the Cherokee way."

Touch the Clouds's craggy face shadowed.

"Better, I think, than my Cherokee wife."

15

2018—Cartridge Cove

Linden spent the entire week finalizing the quilt barn designs with Irene and the Cartridge Cove Quilters. She wrote the talking trees script and helped Marvela clear out the last of the Birchfield/Campbell junk from the attic so the contractors could begin the final phase of the remodel next week.

What she didn't do was see Walker Crowe.

Grapevine news—courtesy of Marvela—maintained he'd holed up—again—on his farm doing, Linden assumed, farm stuff.

Which suited her fine.

On Friday, Irene invited her to come by the quilt shop to view the full-size drawings the *gadugi* crew would transfer to the wooden blocks, paint, and then affix to the top of the barns.

At the tinkling of the bell, fifteen heads snapped up. Wide smiles deepened life-sketched wrinkles on Cherokee and non-Indian faces alike, their welcome warm and immediate. Irene gave her a hug.

Linden gazed at the sample quilts above the fabric shelves. Many of the quilts on display had been made by the guild in honor of the commemoration.

Irene pointed out the different designs. "That one's a crazy quilt. The Upcountry Cherokee in South Carolina made a lot of those I'm told because it used scrap pieces and reminded them of the Cherokee rag-cloths of their grandmothers."

Taking Linden's arm, Irene pulled her farther into the shop. "The missionaries brought quilt making to the Cherokee in the late eighteenth and early nineteenth centuries."

"Like maybe Sarah Jane's deceased mother?"

Once again, thanks to the small-town grapevine, everyone knew about the diary.

"Maybe so. Let me give you a tour." Irene paused in front of a wall hanging. Its many colorful pieces reminded Linden of a kaleidoscope.

"The Cherokee Star." Irene's finger counted the points on the perimeter. "Seven points like the Cherokee Nation tribal flag. Seven colors used to create each point. Seven because—"

"Seven is a special number to the Cherokee. Seven-sided council house, seven clans, and seven directions." Linden blushed at Irene's surprised grin.

"I see you've been doing your homework."

Linden feigned a sudden interest in the pale pink polish on the tips of her toes, peeking out from her sandals. "Sort of."

"Good to know my son has been doing something besides making trouble."

Her eyes flew to Irene's face, whose cheekbones broadened even further with amusement. Irene named off the other quilts. "Bear Claw for the black bears in the Great Smokies. Cherokee Sunburst. Turkey Tracks. Log Cabin," she rattled off rapid fire. "Our quilt barns will feature traditional Cherokee *and* Appalachian patterns."

Irene nudged her to the space behind the cash register. "For the pièce de résistance—the quilt that will be raffled and the funds used for the Center. The Road to Soco quilt we renamed The Trail of Tears is based on a pattern created by Cherokee women in the 1930s."

Linden peered at the intricate stitching. The cut shapes sewn together resembled mountain vistas and meandering trails.

She ventured to a paper rendering of Leila's Cherokee Rose quilt propped against a basket of fabric squares. She traced her finger around the shape of the penciled petals. "I wish I could've seen the original quilt. I'll bet it was glorious."

Irene cocked her head like a pert raisin-eyed robin. "You could make one of your own."

"Me? I can't thread a needle. And appliqué?" Linden shook her head. "I'd never get the hang of it."

"Nonsense. Ever hear of an invention called a rotary cutter and a sewing machine?" Irene snapped her fingers. "With instruction, you could whip up a crib-size version in no time."

Linden sucked in a breath so hard she staggered.

Irene grabbed hold of her arm. "What's wrong?"

She broke free of Irene's hand. "I-I need to go."

The rushing sound of a thousand, thunderous waters pounded inside her head. She needed air. Now. Flinging her hands against the door, she shoved. She needed to get out before—

"Wait, Linden." Irene jogged after her onto the sidewalk. "Should I call a doctor? Why don't you let me drive you home?"

Quivering like an aspen leaf, Linden rummaged in her voluminous purse for her keys. Her fingers closed over them, but she dropped them on the concrete.

"Here." Irene held up the keys. "Let me take you home."

"No, I can't go home." Her hands palm up in front of her, she backed away. "I just need to get some air. No need to worry Gram. I'll be fine."

Irene said nothing more, but her face softened. "How about I take you to my house to see the pottery studio and give you a chance to regroup?"

Still feeling shaky, with a reluctant nod, she allowed Irene to drive the Toyota to a small ranch-style house at the edge of town. Irene parked beside a large, barnlike building.

"The kiln's over there," Irene gestured. "I'll show you my finished pieces and take you through the traditional Cherokee process."

Once inside, Linden marveled at the beautiful, geometric patterns on the glazed pots, stored on wooden shelves near the entrance. Skylights and floor-to-ceiling windows flooded the space with plenty of natural light.

"These are fabulous." Linden smiled. "Are you including your studio on the Cartridge Cove tour?"

Irene shrugged, glancing at the dusty, clay-daubed floor and walls. "I'd be forced to clean up my mess if I did. The Ledford gallery consigns my work and the big Co-op in Cherokee rents me space, too. Between the quilt shop and the collector commissions, I've got all the work I can handle."

"Where do you get your clay? Wholesale?"

Irene's eyes gleamed. "No, always did love to play in the mud. I've got my own source. I dig my clay from a spot by one of the cricks. A secret spot."

Linden smiled. "And if you told me, you'd have to kill me?"

Irene laughed. "Something like that." She pointed to a pot in process on her workbench. "The Cherokee use a coiled rope method. Here, let me show you."

Sitting on a stool, she flicked her long hair behind her shoulder. Irene reached into a plastic-lined bucket and removed a glob of wet, gray clay. She demonstrated a quick coiling technique.

"Wow," breathed Linden, watching the pot take shape.

Irene picked up a sharp, chopstick-shaped wooden stylus. "Then, after I flatten and smooth the coils into a uniform shape with this, I stamp traditional Cherokee designs on the exterior." She pointed to a white oak basket filled with assorted corncobs and peach pits.

"And another Irene Crowe masterpiece."

Irene bustled over to the porcelain farmer's sink and cleaned the clay residue off her hands. "Or something like that. Wanna get a sandwich before heading back?"

"Aren't I keeping you from the store?"

"Nope." Irene dried her hands on a cloth. "I usually run home for lunch."

She followed Irene across the grassy yard and stepped through the sliding glass door.

Opening the refrigerator, Irene held up a container of pimento cheese. "This suit you?"

"Love it. One of Gram's go-to meals. Dare I ask if you've also got sweet tea?"

Irene propped the refrigerator door with her hip. "Reach in and grab that pitcher for me. This may be the Cherokee Nation, hon. But we're still in the South." She nudged her chin toward the pine-paneled cabinets. "Glasses there. And you know where to find the ice."

Linden paused to examine a collection of photos on the fridge. Two adorable Cherokee children who probably belonged to Walker's married siblings. Another photo of Ross and an attractive Cherokee woman arm in arm against the great backdrop of the Grand Canyon.

"Ross and his wife, Bonita." Irene scooted around her, placing napkins and plates on the kitchen table. "She died a few years ago."

"No children?" Linden whispered.

Irene threw her a funny look at the strangled sound in Linden's voice. "He says he always felt like he could share mine."

Linden studied the final snapshot in the tableau of photos. A much younger and close-cropped edition of Walker—courtesy of Uncle Sam—in desert-colored fatigues.

Was there a more handsome sight on earth than a man in uniform?

Irene's lips curved. "He is a handsome boy, if I do say so myself."

Linden jerked, knocking the ice cube tray into the sink.

Had she verbalized—once again—her thoughts out loud?

Hoping to lessen the redness in her cheeks, Linden took a welcome swig of tea. Irene offered her a plate of chocolate chip cookies.

She helped herself to one. "Thanks."

"Don't thank me. I'm a working mother. Thank Nabisco."

"That must've been hard raising three children on your own."

Irene folded her napkin in her lap. "Walker tell you about his dad?"

"Yes, ma'am."

A smile flitted at the corners of Irene's mouth. "I do love a child with manners." Her eyes slid downward to the tabletop. "Walker's not been the same since he returned from Afghanistan. He never used to have a temper. Wild, yes. Temper, no."

Irene raised her eyes from her plate. "Maybe a symptom of PTSD. What do you think?"

Linden cut her eyes at the door. As the virtual queen of post-traumatic stress, not a discussion she wanted to have. "I'm sure I wouldn't know, Mrs. Crowe."

"Irene," she corrected. "Walker snapped at everyone when he first came home. Then, the Lord got a hold of him, and he's been so much better." Irene reached across the table and snagged Linden's hand. "I want you to know he tries."

Linden nodded.

"I'm sure he sounded like some sort of crazy person . . ."

Remembering the scene she'd made in the quilt store, Linden shifted. She removed her hand from Irene's. "There's all kinds of crazy, Mrs.—Irene. Don't worry about it."

". . . but he hasn't had a fit like that in a long time."

"Maybe," Linden knotted her fingers. "I bring out the worst in him."

Irene pushed out her lips. "Absolutely not. He usually goes so glacial, so remote. At least he felt safe enough with you he dared to let it all hang out, as they say."

She gave Linden a mocking smile. "Lucky you to be on the receiving end."

Linden couldn't help but smile back.

"I've been telling him for months if he would talk about what happened he'd feel better."

Linden shook her head. "I'm not sure talking is the answer."

Irene sighed. "His father's death hit him hard, too. With Uncle Ross flitting all over the globe, he didn't have much in the way of male influence. After 9/11, Walker couldn't wait to graduate from high school and join up like his great-uncle Ross. But he's learned it's a tricky business being fully American and fully Cherokee."

Linden played with a potato chip on her plate. "What do you mean?"

"Our dilemma is to balance our modern American life with our traditional Cherokee values." Irene swallowed a sip of tea. "You'll find no more patriotic Americans than Snowbird Cherokee. Cherokee fought on both sides of the War Between the States—"

"You mean," Linden pitched her voice in Marvela's inimitable gravelly style, "the War of Northern Aggression?"

Irene grinned. "You got your own characters in that non-Indian family of yours."

"Amen." Linden reached for her glass. "But go on. Sorry for the interruption."

"The island-hopping World War Two Navajo—those media hogs—get all the good press, but did you know the Cherokee were the original code talkers during the First World War?"

Linden shook her head.

"The Cherokee have fought bravely and proudly at every American military engagement from the beginning. You'll find no American loves their country more than a Cherokee."

"You were the first Americans."

"But the government?" Irene quirked an eye in Linden's direction. "The government's another story. This festival illustrates how the government hasn't always acted in our best interests."

Linden tilted her head. "So you've got mixed feelings?"

"Specially our boys—and girls now—in fatigues. Walker just about worshipped his father. They went hunting every chance either of them got."

Linden wasn't sure she understood the connection between Walker's military service and his father.

"That's why he was chosen. What his commander attributed to his high kill rate."

Linden straightened. "His what?"

"His outdoorsy upbringing. The stealth required in hunting expeditions. That keen eye."

Linden stared at her.

Irene opened and closed her mouth. "Oh." She fiddled with her napkin. "I thought he'd told you that, too. It's not like it's a secret."

"Told me what, Irene?"

"Walker was an Army Ranger." Irene inhaled. "And a highly trained sniper."

Leaving Linden to wonder why he'd felt the need to leave that essential element out of his bio.

When Linden returned to Gram's, she found Marvela digging her bare toes into a freshly furrowed patch of ground.

And gyrating.

Jutting her skinny right hip out. Then, her left. Her hands in front of her, as if she held imaginary tea glasses, swinging in rhythm to music only Marvela could hear. Bending and bouncing, her kneecaps flashed from underneath her white cotton dress. Throwing her head from side to side.

Doing the Watusi.

Yes, Linden leaned against the porch railing and crossed her arms. The Watusi. She spotted two condensation-beaded, empty glasses on the garden bench.

Ross Wachacha strikes again.

"It's all fun and games until somebody breaks a hip, Gram," she called, cupping her hand around her mouth.

Gram, never one to care whether the neighbors observed her antics or not—an interesting attitude for a former politician's wife—shouted back, "But if I die, I'll die happy." Marvela strode unfazed to the porch steps.

"Irene's neighbor plowed the ground so we can plant our squash, beans, and corn. The Three Sisters, Ross called them."

Linden adjusted a portion of Marvela's sleeve, which bunched during her dance craze.

Yep, thinking on Irene's revelation, there were all kinds of crazy here in Cartridge Cove. Including . . . herself.

" . . . And I'm planting a perimeter of sunflowers around the patch. So pretty for the guests to look out their windows and see." Marvela made a frame with her hands, encouraging Linden to grasp her vision. "Zinnias and dahlias."

Marvela clasped her hands together in a rapt pose. "I do *love* zinnias. Do you love zinnias, Linden?"

She tugged at Linden's arm. "Come on, Honey Girl. You haven't lived until you've scrunched your toes through Cartridge Cove dirt."

"Ah, no thanks. Not right now,"

Only Marvela would garden in a Sunday dress. And, not look the worse for wear.

"Well, darlin'," Marvela collapsed into one of the wrought iron chairs. "Good thing you've come to Cartridge Cove so we can remedy your sadly neglected education."

"And I see you've been entertaining a gentleman caller while I was out this morning." She gave her grandmother and the tea glasses a quelling look.

"Lord-a mercy, Linden." Marvela tossed an imaginary boa over her shoulder. The air in the seat cushion whooshed. "You make it sound like I'm running a bordello."

"Gram."

"Don't look so outraged. Miss Ophelia, bless her dear, departed soul, isn't around to hear us."

"When did you decide to return to Cartridge Cove and open a B & B, Gram? Before or after the infamous Cartridge Cove grapevine informed you the widowed Colonel Ross Wachacha had decided to retire to his mountain homeland?"

And to Linden's great surprise, the unflappable Marvela Campbell Birchfield rosied up as pretty as a schoolgirl.

Linden planted a fist on her hip. "Exactly what I suspected."

Marvela lifted her chin. "And who died, may I ask, and made you my mother?"

"Pay back, shall we say, for a certain junior-senior dance at Stonebriar High?"

Marvela sniffed. "As I recall, I acted, as your granddad phrased it, in *loco parentis* while your parents were in . . . ?" Her penciled eyebrows drew together. "I forget where Cam and Vanessa were that year."

Linden waved a hand. "I forget, too. But speaking of Granddad . . ."

Marvela chewed her lower lip. "I want you to know I loved your grandfather dearly, Linden. Never forget that."

"What happened with Ross Wachacha, Gram?"

Marvela slumped upon the cushions. "We met like I told you that summer. The Cherokee and the rest of us didn't mix as much as we do today. People kept to themselves."

"Like Walker said," Linden added with a sinking heart, uncertain she wanted to hear the rest of her grandmother's story.

Marvela toyed with the end of the black belt encircling her waist. "We fell in love. Spent every minute we could sneak together."

"Didn't your family like him? Was the prejudice against the Cherokee so bad even then?"

"Not my family, Honey Girl. His."

Linden reached for Marvela's cool, blue-veined hand. "Oh, Gram, I'm sorry."

"Things are different now. But Cartridge Cove is still so deeply isolated in the Snowbird. Times and attitudes change more slowly here."

"Like a glacier melting?" Linden smirked.

"But you never know what rapid changes a little global warming can bring."

Linden rolled her eyes.

"And Walker and his people have been hurt by our kind before."

"Our kind? Not you, too, Gram. That was almost two hundred years ago." She made an impatient gesture. "And I thought we were talking about you and Ross Wachacha."

"Were we just, darlin' girl?"

"Gram . . ."

"You got to know," Marvela's eyes took on a faraway look. "There'd only been one." She held up her index finger. "One interracial marriage in the whole county at that time. The Civil Rights Movement was all over television. Political assassinations. Vietnam. The world seemed to be going to hell in a bushel basket. And lots of folks circled their metaphorical wagons."

Linden watched a single tear, like a raindrop sliding down a windowpane, plow its way across her grandmother's cheek.

"Family and tribe always come first. The Cherokee call it 'the right way,' to seek balance and harmony. It's at the core of their spiritual DNA. To be in balance is to be responsible for one's actions and uphold the good of the whole—family, tribe, and earth."

Marvela's face drooped. "Ross was too honorable to continue to see me after his family made their wishes known. They advised him to forget me and marry a nice local Cherokee girl. But instead, he drove to Asheville and enlisted. I never saw him again until a week ago."

"What did you do when he left?"

Her mouth trembled. "I ran away, too. Not to Vietnam," she gave a hoarse laugh. "But to New York City and the Ford Modeling Agency. Didn't take even a year for that world to show this country girl she wasn't meant for that lifestyle. So I ran again. This time to Raleigh and met Fraser Stanton Birchfield the Fourth."

Marvela sighed. "And the rest is my history." She squared her thin shoulder blades. "And yours, too."

Her grandmother leaned forward, her palms flat against the table. "But I didn't mean to imply I wasn't happy before coming home to Cartridge Cove. Because Fraser was the man I needed. And in forty years of marriage, what a blast we had . . ." Her voice quavered.

"But you never forgot Ross Wachacha."

"No, Honey Girl." Her grandmother gazed at the fading light over the mountains. "I did not."

She and her grandmother sat in silence. Amid the quiet beauty of the garden, they listened to the late afternoon birdcalls and the thrumming of the cicadas.

"You can never go too far or become too old, for God's love not to reach you, darlin'."

At the pensive note in her voice, Linden glanced at her grandmother.

Marvela lifted her face to the slanted rays of the sun and closed her eyes. "Blessed be God for second chances."

Blessed be God . . . a strange echo of Sarah Jane.

Marvela swung toward Linden. "Don't waste your chances, Honey Girl, I beg you. Don't reject God's love for you."

Linden gripped the arms of the chair. Her grandmother and Ross Wachacha. They deserved a second chance.

Her?

Not so much.

"Well, then." Linden released a gust of air. "I trust, Gram, you invited your 'young' man to dinner."

16

June 1838—Fort Butler, NC

The stockade, built as a temporary holding facility, had proven completely inadequate for housing the hundreds of Cherokee men, women and children garrisoned there. Sarah Jane ran a grimy hand across her sweating brow. Shielding her eyes against the blazing sun, she prayed for a quick end to the drought.

According to the old-timers, the hottest summer in living memory. Sweltering heat. No privacy in the overcrowded fort. Sanitation and the drinking water had long since been compromised.

She, Pierce, and her father spent the last few weeks combating a raging outbreak of whooping cough. Between the dysentery and the sense of hopelessness, scores of the North Carolina Cherokee finally found a permanent home in shallow graves beside the river.

With handkerchiefs wrapped around the lower half of their faces to avoid infection and the stench of rotting death, soldiers carried a litter of bloated corpses for yet another burial. Leaning against one of the wooden palisades, she spotted a human vulture bargaining away the last earthly treasure from a Cherokee she recognized from Buffalo Town. For a vastly inflated measure of flour and corn.

"Sarah. Sarah Jane?" Her father, whiter-haired than she remembered before June, searched the enclosure for her.

Wiping her hands on her apron, she lurched forward.

He gave her a slight smile, like her possessing not enough energy, to do more. "The smallpox vaccines arrived. Since the whooping cough has hopefully run its course, I don't want to take any chances on a smallpox outbreak."

She followed him into the paltry shade underneath the white canvas tent they'd erected as a makeshift hospital. Pierce's glazed eyes flitted up, acknowledging her arrival, before returning to his ministrations of the old man.

Her breath hitched as she noticed the muscular form of Touch the Clouds at the foot of his grandfather's cot. She hurried forward, retrieving a basin of water and a cloth. She paused to lay a comforting hand atop his grandmother's shoulder.

The old woman slumped almost lifeless on a stool. The woman's dark, birdlike eyes never wavered from the too-still form of her husband.

Sarah swabbed the old man's feverish brow, raising her eyes to Pierce's dull gaze. "How is he?"

Pierce pressed his lips together and gave a tiny shake of his head.

Her eyes darted to Touch the Clouds. A spasm of pain rippled across his features before he resumed the mask the Cherokee were so careful to keep in place before non-Indians. He unwound himself like a coiled spring to where her father, shuffling from one patient to another, attempted to ease the stinging throes of ignominious death.

As death drew closer and exile imminent, many abandoned the old ways, declaring their old gods either nonexistent or uncaring. After a lifetime of laboring among The People, Tobias and Endicott baptized more Cherokee in the last two weeks than in the previous twenty years of her father's tenure in the Snowbird Mountains. Her father had been too busy wresting the sick from death's door to participate in the nightly revival meetings within the fort.

Touch the Clouds blocked Dr. Hopkins's plodding path. "Did the major say what time we move out next week?" He spoke in Cherokee.

Pierce stiffened at the exclusionary insult, but continued checking the old man's vital signs.

Her father straightened as if startled at the sound of an actual human voice, still living, still speaking Cherokee. "After we reach Tennessee, Chief Ross has requested the army delay moving more pris—" He swallowed. "—Cherokee until this heat wave breaks. And General Scott has agreed for humanitarian reasons."

Dr. Hopkins moistened his lips. "Too little, too late in my opinion. Though in fairness, Scott and the army had no idea of the logistics of gathering and moving this many people between here and the Indian Territory."

Touch the Clouds shot an angry glance in the direction of his grandmother who'd closed her eyes. "Fairness is a luxury my people can't afford."

Part of Sarah Jane was surprised anyone still had the strength to be angry. But if anyone had the emotional fortitude to remain angry, it would be Touch the Clouds, who wore his anger as if a shield.

Where, Sarah gritted her teeth, had Leila gotten herself off to? Her place should be here, with her husband and his ailing grandparents.

Dr. Hopkins laid a restraining hand on Touch the Clouds's arm. "Many of your people will refuse the smallpox vaccination unless someone like you leads the way and shows everyone how it will save lives."

Touch the Clouds tightened his lips and stared at the doctor's liver-spotted hand on his copper-hued arm until the doctor removed his hand.

"White man medicine is not helping my grandfather. Why should I tell my people to allow themselves to be poked by your potions?"

Moving alongside them, she felt Pierce's eyes on her back. "Your grandfather has a disease we cannot treat. Smallpox we can. Those immunizations will save countless lives in the weeks ahead. Men, women, and children."

"There must be balance." She held her hands, palms up on either side of her body as if weighing a scale, endeavoring to help him to see with words to which a Cherokee could relate.

"Women balance men in the equilibrium of the cosmos. Death and life. Sickness and wholeness. I think it's time for wholeness to weigh in so that The People can emerge on the other end of this journey with the strength to rebuild, to start over, to not cease the fight to survive."

She balled her hand into a fist and shook it in his face. "You cannot allow the forces against you to win."

Amusement glinted his eyes. He covered her fist with his larger one. An instrument clanged on a metal tray. Pierce appeared at her elbow.

Touch the Clouds kept his eyes trained on Sarah, but his other hand fingered the knife at his belt.

"Pierce . . ." Her father grabbed his apprentice's sleeve.

She didn't want to know how Touch the Clouds had managed to sneak the weapon past the soldiers, but she released the breath she'd been holding when Touch the Clouds relinquished his grip on the hilt of his knife. Her father planted himself between the two men as Touch the Clouds cupped her hand in his.

He gently pried open her fingers until her hand lay flat atop his. "I think you have a Cherokee heart. Like one of the beloved women who followed the warriors to battle in the old days."

Dropping her hand, Touch the Clouds turned toward the doctor. "Because your daughter speaks wisdom, if this will help The People, I will do as you ask."

His grandfather died the next day.

"You need to go home," Horace insisted later that week in the midst of packing empty boxes Pierce toted to the wagon.

"I'm going wherever you go, Papa."

Her father shook his head. "This is no place for a woman."

She set her jaw. "I made a vow to The People same as you, Tobias, and Endicott." She tucked a loose strand of her hair underneath her bonnet. "Besides, I promised Leila. She needs me."

Horace frowned.

"You need me. Pierce—"

Horace rounded on her. "How much of this pigheaded stubbornness is about ministry, and how much is about Pierce?" He threw his hands in the air. "I rue the day I ever brought that fickle-hearted young man into your life."

Sarah touched her finger to his lips. "Hush, Papa." She jerked her head at the tent entrance. "He'll hear you. He's worked as hard as you to save The People. Be honest and admit you couldn't have done what you have without him. Or me."

Her father hunkered against the wooden table. "It's going to get a lot worse, Sarah Jane. I don't want you to live the rest of your life with those memories in your head."

Too late.

But she didn't say those words out loud. It would serve no purpose and only hurt her father. She'd done what needed to be done.

It was decided, in light of her growing concern over the waning of her father's health, Pierce would travel the fifteen miles home to restock medical supplies and other necessities from their larder. She desperately longed to accompany him, but for once, her father put his foot down.

"Not appropriate," Horace thundered. "An unmarried young lady alone for several days in the company of an unmarried man."

He did task her with the job of making a list of the supplies Pierce should retrieve and plead from neighbors. Neighbors who watched over her neglected garden and empty house, but who were also sympathetic to the plight of the Cherokee with whom they'd lived peaceably for so many years.

She composed the list in her journal as a first draft before copying it again onto a torn scrap of paper for Pierce.

—Castor oil, manganese, cayenne pepper, extract
of licorice, and cream of tartar.
—Quinine, wormseed oil, whiskey, coffee, and tea.
—Ammonia water, anti-bilious pills, Epsom salts,
borat of soda, and laudanum.
—Thumb lancets, syringes, vials, tin cups, and
buckets.

She examined her penmanship for legibility and decided the
Moravian ladies at the Salem Academy would've been pleased
with her efforts. She paused, the list in her hand, and wondered,
like the Cherokee, if she'd ever see her home again.

Tobias begged a ride from Pierce to restock his supplies, too.
Only as the wagon disappeared over the hill, did Sarah think of a
dozen personal items she wished she'd remembered to add to the
list. But she blushed, glad for the oversight upon reflection. Her
heart beat treacherously at the prospect of Pierce's hands riffling
through her personal garments.

When she turned, she barreled into the solid form of Touch
the Clouds.

"My grandmother."

She nodded. "I'll see what I can do." She edged past him to the
makeshift shelter he'd constructed to protect his family from the
heat and rain. Leila preferred the palleted comforts of her father's
wagon.

Touch the Clouds followed Sarah into the shade of the lean-to.
"She won't eat since E-du-di flew to the Beyond."

He looked away from where Sarah squatted, brushing strands
of gray white hair from his grandmother's feverish forehead. "She
wishes to fly away, too, I fear."

"I'll stay." Sarah's eyes caught his. "I promise." She flicked the
ever-present flies away from his grandmother's face.

He knelt, and the loincloth he wore over his leggings swept
the dirt. "Do you know the story the Cherokee tell of the hummingbird and crane, Sarah?"

The corners of her mouth curved at the way the sound of her name emerged from his lips. The "s" slurred into the sibilant lilt he placed at the end.

"No, tell me." She hoped to divert his worry over his *aginisi*. Born storytellers, most Cherokee didn't need much encouragement. Just a listening ear.

"It is said long ago among The People there was a woman . . ."

"A beautiful woman, no doubt."

He bit back a smile. "Of course. And she found herself in love with a hummingbird who was also beautiful. But a crane loved the woman, too, so he challenged the hummingbird to a race around the world for the maiden's hand in marriage."

She dropped her eyes to her soiled apron. "Cranes are not beautiful creatures, Touch the Clouds. I think I can guess the end of this story."

"You listen to the rest, Sarah." He grabbed hold of her hand.

Sarah's eyes widened.

"The hummingbird flew all day in a zigzag like this." He used her index finger to draw a jagged line in the dirt. A flash of lightning. "The crane flew a straight line to the edge of the world and beyond."

Over the zigzag, he caused her finger to trace a long, straight line with an arrow's point at the end. "The hummingbird was fast that first day. The crane, not so much. But as night fell, the hummingbird lay down to sleep."

He gazed at her, solemn as a tombstone, as her eyebrows quirked upward. He touched her finger to the straight line again. "The crane, Sarah."

She lifted both shoulders and let them drop. "What about the crane?"

"Through the greater strength of his wings, the crane was able to fly all night. And so it continued for four days and nights. Until at last, the crane reached the woman's dwelling place beside the creek from which they'd begun their journey. The hummingbird was much surprised when he arrived later to find the crane had won the race."

Her hand warmed in his palm. She jerked free and twisted both hands into the folds of her pinafore. She bolted to her feet. "She chose the hummingbird, anyway."

Rising also, he pursed his lips. "True. The hummingbird is still renowned to The People for its beauty and charm, but the crane is revered for its wisdom."

He wiped the earth clean of the zigzagged line with his moccasin. "She made a poor choice. Which she lived to regret."

She shifted, wondering whom he'd cast as the woman and the crane. Of the identity of the hummingbird, there could be no doubt.

"Are you trying to make some sort of statement about Pierce? Because I fear his choice has already been made."

Sarah cocked her head at a sudden realization. "Or is this about you?"

"All of us play many different roles in the course of a lifetime." He moved to the curtain flap he'd fashioned over the entrance to the lean-to. "Think on which outlasts them all. Don't be misled as Pierce and I—" He bit off his words.

"It's too late," she whispered. "I love him."

The words felt good on her tongue. It was the first time she'd allowed herself to utter them. But the barrenness of the words stabbed at her heart.

He gave Sarah a deliberate look. "Then I fear you have set for yourself a wearisome journey."

Touch the Clouds sighed. The sound trickled from between his lips. "An unrelenting, unrequited pain. Like The People will face till the end of our days. As we forever long for that which we can never possess."

160

Pierce and Tobias returned, the wagon loaded with produce and nonperishables culled from generous neighbors. Maybe some from the guilty consciences of those who'd plucked this same produce from empty Cherokee fields.

He related news of the settlement the locals now referred to as Cartridge Cove.

Pierce went round to the driver's seat and pulled out a bundle of something tied into a bed sheet. "I know how hard you worked on this last year."

He glanced around at the myriad campfires winking within the confines of the fort. "The nights will get cooler once we're over the mountain."

She undid the knots. "Pierce . . ."

Her eyes grew wide at the Carolina Lily quilt she'd once dreamed of covering her marriage bed.

In Pierce's eyes, a flicker of regret. "You brought your Bible with you, but I thought this might be a comfort to you, too, Sarah Jane."

She swallowed past the sudden lump in her throat.

"Blessed be God." She traced one of the appliqued red lily petals. "Thank you, Pierce."

She squeezed his arm. How had he known its significance to her?

For one too-brief moment, he laid his hand over hers.

"Sarah, I . . ." His voice tremored, and he clamped his lips together. Pierce veered toward the medical tent. "I'd best see if your father needs my assistance."

But a tiny spark of hope flared in her spirit. He did see her, Sarah reassured herself. He understood her heart, at least a little.

And clutching the quilt to her chest, for tonight, it was enough.

17

2018—Cartridge Cove

Standing in the bed of the pickup, Walker handed paint cans over the side to his stickball crew. Ross leaned against the truck, arms crossed, waiting for Walker to join him.

Just what he needed.

One more lecture. Walker knew he needed to make his peace with Linden. He'd been on his way to do just that when he spied her and that—

His lips tightened. Who'd have thought that egghead Sawyer would prove such a ladies' man? If not working his magic on Emmaline, then sparking with Linden.

Delaying the confrontation with Ross, who'd appointed himself Walker's tribal conscience, Walker paused to survey today's *gadugi* crew. The handful of men, including his stickball guys, were already hard at work. Scaffolding covered the front facade of the Moser barn from the ground to the peaked roof.

The artists among them had transferred the design graph from the quilt guild to the squared wooden pallet. Now, steady painter hands would bring the block patterns to vibrant life. Once the blocks dried, still more men, with no acrophobia issues, would affix the quilt block to the barn's cornice. Barring rain, if the crew knocked out a quilt barn every Saturday they'd be finished by June.

Ross cleared his throat. Walker glanced at the tailgate to see his uncle waiting, his booted foot tapping the ground. "Word with you, son?"

Here it comes.

Walker jumped to the ground, heaving a sigh, and landed lightly on the balls of his sneakers.

"Hadn't seen much of you this week," Ross observed.

The opening volley.

He flicked a glance at his uncle's unreadable face, the color of a tanned deer hide.

"Been busy on the farm."

Two could play at this imitation of a cigar-store Indian.

He could almost visualize the wheels turning in his uncle's mind. Reassessing, regrouping, repositioning.

Both turned at the sound of tires on gravel. Linden's Toyota barreled to a stop behind the conglomeration of vehicles in the Moser yard.

Ross clamped a stem of grass between his teeth. "I've got one word of advice for you, if you'll allow me."

"As if I could stop you . . ." Walker muttered. Under his breath.

Because in more ways than just the army, Ross outranked him. He was a tribal elder, after all.

Linden emerged from the driver's side, her hair in its usual updo, wearing a pale pink cotton blouse and denim capris.

"If you ever want to get a woman, boy," Ross twirled the stem between his thumb and forefinger. "You got to learn to talk more."

"Who says I'm looking for a woman?"

Ignoring him, Ross chawed down on the end of the stem. "And once you get one, then you've got to learn to hush again."

Walker drew his brows together.

Linden waved to the elderly Mosers on their screened porch.

Ross threw the blade of grass to his feet and ground it in the dust with his heel. "You get my meaning, boy?"

He resisted the urge to salute. "Loud and clear, Colonel." Walker watched Linden remove a foil-wrapped platter from the backseat of her Toyota.

"Well then, my work's done here." Ross wiped his palms down the front of his Carhartt overalls. "I best be on my way."

"You're not staying to help?"

"'Fraid not. I promised Marvela I'd help her plant her garden today."

"I do so admire that sacrificial servant heart of yours, Uncle Ross."

With a wry grin, Ross clapped a heavy hand on his shoulder. "You know me, son, I'm nothing if not all about *gadugi* helpfulness."

He propelled Walker toward Linden weaving through the parked cars. "Now you go and do likewise."

The shove sent Walker on a collision course into her path, made worse when he tripped over his own feet. With a slight gasp, she clutched the platter and sidestepped. He caught himself, palms down and face planted, on the front grille of a Buick.

"Clumsy long, Crowe?"

Suppressing an inward groan, he righted himself. "I'm s-sorry—"

"You got that right."

"I meant . . . I wondered . . ."

Her eyebrows arched, waiting for him to finish a coherent thought.

Could he complete any thought while in her presence? The likelihood of that, he was beginning to believe, fading fast.

"If we could talk . . ."

She thrust the platter into his chest. "So talk." She crossed her arms.

He glanced from left to right. "Not here." He gestured at the work crew whose ears even one hundred feet distant he imagined were straining from the effort to eavesdrop. "Alone."

A wary look flashed across her face. "I'm not sure that's a good idea. If you've got something to say . . ."

He lifted his nose and sniffed the air like one of his dad's old bird dogs on the scent of quarry. "What's that smell?"

"You mean the biscuits? I made them for the crew. That's why I'm late." She peeled back the top layer of foil. Aromatic yeasty steam arose.

His mouth watered. The banana he'd eaten on the way to Robbinsville for paint had long since digested. He noted the glass jar she'd wedged in the middle of the towering pile of flaky buttermilk biscuits. "Strawberry jam?"

"From a lady at church. Marvela wants to make her own soon." She rolled her eyes. "My grandmother. Martha Stewart gone rustic."

He leaned over and inhaled.

She removed a biscuit from the topmost stack. "You want one?"

He reached and then drew back, scrubbing the side of his neck. "You made these?"

"Why?" She narrowed her eyes. "Afraid I've added poison?"

"Probably what I deserve." But he opened his hand anyway.

Linden deposited a warm biscuit onto his palm. "You probably do. But I'm the merciful sort."

She set the tray on the hood of the Buick. "Here. I was going to put these on the picnic table. But since you can't wait . . ." She unscrewed the gingham-covered lid of the Mason jar.

From the confines of the purse slung over her shoulder, she retrieved a blunt butter knife. "Be still while I slice open the bread and spread on some jam."

He tensed as she placed her hand under his to steady it. Tingles frolicked like the wisp of dragonfly wings against his skin.

"What's the matter?" Linden smirked, the butter knife poised in her other hand. "Afraid I'll go for the jugular?"

Actually, not what had crossed his mind. He chewed the inside of his cheek.

But she smiled. "Trust me and don't move."

"I trust you."

Do you? her eyes challenged.

Leaving him to eat his biscuit, she ambled toward a suddenly ravenous—and nosy—cluster of workers. He glowered as his boys—Matt, Jake, and Eli—used their best adolescent pickup lines on Linden.

She dodged their sophomoric attempts with a gentle laugh and a few artfully placed words, leaving their dignity intact.

He wiped his hands on a napkin. "Out of your league, boys."

Like he wasn't?

Striding across the barnyard with his shirttail flapping in the wake of his own breeze, he grabbed two of them by the scruff of their necks. Matt, as usual, proved too fast to be caught. "Back to work, guys. Quit sampling the merchandise."

Linden gave him a funny look as the crew erupted into sarcastic laughter.

He raked a hand over his head and tightened the leather band holding back his hair. With a flurry of jeers, the men and his boys resumed their former tasks.

Figuring he ought to heed his own advice, Walker stripped off his long-sleeved shirt down to the grubby, grease-streaked Henley he saved for messy work. Scanning around for a place to hang it, he became aware of Linden's intent gaze, fastened upon him.

Her cheeks flushed a becoming shade of rose pink when he caught her eye. Sensing her attraction, relief washed through him she didn't hate him after last week.

"I'll put it in your truck." She glanced away. "I'm assuming, unlike Raleigh, nobody in this town bothers to lock their vehicles."

"You got that right." His lips quirking, he handed her the shirt. "Lot of things different—and better—between Raleigh and here."

She tugged at the shirt. He held on to one end.

Linden moistened her lips with her tongue. "Of that, I have no doubt."

When he let go, she staggered a few steps.

"Thanks for the biscuit."

"You're welcome."

Walker glanced skyward. "Crew's knocking off about three."

Her eyebrows rose. "Everybody got a hot date?"

"Not me. Unless," his heart pounded in his ears. "You'd go someplace with me so I could give you a proper apology for last Sunday."

"A proper apology?" She gazed at him with those big sky eyes of hers. "Huh . . . that sounds enlightening. Lesson number four or five? I forget." She sidled closer, draping his shirt over her arm. "I might could be persuaded."

The tight feeling he'd carried in his chest since last weekend loosened a notch. He smiled and stuck out his hand. "Friends?"

Linden studied him long enough for his breath to hitch again in fear she'd changed her mind, but finally, she stuck out her hand in return. "Friends, I can do. Besides, you always take me to the most interesting places."

As she strolled over to the bevy of vehicles with his shirt clutched in her hand, he reflected the same thing might just as equally be applied to the places she took his heart.

If she lived to be a hundred, Linden reckoned she'd never forget her first sight of Walker's farm. Or the trees.

He'd paused his truck at the crest of the hill on the one-lane road that led to nowhere. Nowhere except to the glory of Walker's rustic, two-story farmhouse. And beyond the furrowed field behind the cabin, acres and acres of trees swelled as far as the eye could see.

Christmas trees.

The memory of her up close and personal encounter with Walker on her grandmother's porch resurfaced. She'd been right to think of Christmas when they met. The tangy, pleasing fragrance of evergreen.

She swiveled, taking in the mountain views. Walker hunkered forward in the seat. His hands gripped the steering wheel.

At the sight of several corralled horses eating grass in a meadow, she sighed. "Splendid, indeed."

He rotated toward her, his lower lip caught in his teeth, and she smiled.

"Like you said once. A splendid isolation." She gave a low whistle. "I bet the Blue Ridge Parkway itself would be hard pressed to compete with this." Her arm swept the landscape. "Especially come autumn."

Some of the tension oozed out of his shoulders. His hands relaxed and uncurled from the wheel. And his face, usually as maddeningly remote as this farmhouse, looked as proud as if he'd conjured all this himself.

Just for her.

"Are you going to dangle this morsel in front of my nose, or do I get to see the rest?"

His face broke into a broad grin. The dimples bracketed his mouth, lifting his cheeks, like a glacier calving.

She usually got scowling from Walker Crowe. He'd not favored her with this side of himself before. The transformation—and the contrast—was startling.

Mind blowing. Pulse leaping. Knee . . .

Sucking in a breath, she strove for nonchalance she didn't feel. "Lead on."

Men this handsome ought to come with warning labels. As in hazardous to your heart and good sense.

"Okay . . ." He shifted into drive, and the truck coasted the last few yards onto his farm.

Jumping out of the cab, she stopped at the wooden porch that spanned the front of the log cabin. "Did you build this yourself?" She rubbed her hand along the railing of the wide-planked steps.

He shrugged. "On top of an old stone foundation. Nothing else remained but a stone chimney I also reworked. Nobody had lived here for a long time. I bought the property, which backs up to the national forest."

"You've been busy."

He rocked on his heels, sticking his hands inside his jean pockets. "I have."

She jerked her head toward the walls. "Hand-chinked?"

He nodded. "And sturdy. Keeps out the wind and the snow."

Again, that look on his face. The self-deprecating, yet proud, tone in his voice.

He gestured around toward the back. "Come see."

Taking her arm, he pulled her toward the fields. "Strawberries will be ready for the public next week." He nudged her with his shoulder. "I'll give Marvela and her assistant a call when they're ripe."

She gave him a pointed look. "Thanks a lot, Crowe. I thought you said we were going to be friends."

The corners of his mouth twitched, but he gazed over his fields as if into his future. "Blueberries will be ripe for picking this summer. Pumpkins in autumn."

Her eyes grew round, imagining the orange balls lining the fields. "A real working, year-round farm."

She sighted an old tobacco barn and the rusted wagon moldering beside it. "You could have school groups visit. Offer hayrides. The pack house will need restoration, but you could sell mountain handicrafts and baked goods from the produce of the farm there. Create a petting zoo. Build a corn maze." She laughed. "M-a-z-e not m-a-i-z-e."

"I get it." He plunged one hand in the pockets of his baggy faded jeans. The jagged tears above both knees hadn't been put there by some designer but from hard work. He fished out a business card and handed it to her.

She peered at the block-style print. "Have you got brochures to go along with this? Ads? Website and video trailers?"

"Whoa there, PR lady." He held up both hands. "This is a one-man operation. I don't work as fast as you can think of the ideas. I've still got my main crop of trees to harvest."

"The trees?" She bounced on her toes. "Can I see?"

He laughed. "Sure." He led her up an incline to the rows of Fraser fir that stretched in parallel lines across the horizon.

"Welcome," he threw out his hands. "To Christmas."

"You should have an open house. And a party." She pirouetted, taking in the sight and lovely smells of the firs. She whirled to a stop, both feet planted. "I can picture it now."

He folded his arms across his chest. "I just bet you can."

"A Cartridge Cove Christmas." She drew an imaginary banner across the space between them. "You ought to use that in your advertising. Reels 'em in every time."

She gave him a knowing look. "Marketing, Walker. It's all about the marketing."

"I'll take your word for it." He tapped the pine needle mulch under the base of a tree with the side of his sneaker. "The trees have been seven years in the growing. This year will be our first harvest. Mainly wholesale flatlander clients, but I'm hoping for local retail sales, too."

"Seven years?" She laughed. "Of course. What else could it be here in the land of the Cherokee?" She leaned over a branch to take a pungent whiff. "I love Christmas."

His eyes crinkled at the edges. "I can tell that."

"Wait till you see how Gram decorates for Christmas. She puts more Dickens into Christmas than Dickens himself." She sighed.

Bird songs filtered through the surrounding forest. Peaceful.

Walker shuffled his feet, his eyes downcast. "I'm sorry, Linden. I didn't mean those things I said the other day. I've been wanting to apologize, but it took me a good week to screw up the courage and . . ." His raised his eyes, his expression regretful.

His hands found their way once more into the front pocket of those ragged jeans. "I'm caught between wanting the environment and The People to remain as they always have versus everybody's economic need to survive. Things are changing around here. And I don't always change as gracefully with the times as I should."

"Maybe the changes won't be as bad as you fear." She squeezed his arm. "And like I said before. I'm the merciful sort."

He peered at her out of those unfathomable, bottomless eyes of his. "Thank you, Linden. I'll try to keep my personal neuroses in check in the future."

She laughed. "You and me both. Good luck with that."

And with a playful punch on his bicep, she darted behind a tree, calling behind her, "Tag. And you're it, Walker Crowe."

Startled, he dropped his arms and took a step toward her. "Oh, yeah? We'll see who's it." A sardonic smile allayed the dangerous glint in his eyes.

"Got to catch me first," she yelled.

Feeling six years old again, Linden took off running up the hill. She zigzagged between the rows with Walker hot on her heels. Panting in the higher elevation, she paused behind a tree to regain her breath. She rested her hands on her knees.

"Give it, up, babe," Walker taunted. "You can't hide from me. I've got recon skills . . . stealth training . . ." His voice drifted away.

Silence.

Only the ripple of the wind in the trees. Her breath seemed loud by comparison. She strained to hear his footsteps.

An arm shot out from around the tree.

Squealing in feigned terror, Linden allowed herself to be caught as he grabbed hold of her shirttail and trundled her into a headlock.

"Gotcha. As I knew I would." Releasing his hold around her neck, he grasped her shoulders and spun her around.

Linden's heart pounded. "I knew you would, too."

His breath came in ragged gasps. Walker gave her a lopsided smile. "Are you trying to vamp me, Linden Birchfield?"

Such an old-fashioned word. Such a surprising man.

He brushed the tips of his fingers across her cheek. She'd wanted him to touch her. But afraid of herself, she gave a nervous laugh and stepped away.

"Why, Walker Crowe, I do believe I am."

Linden's eyes dropped to her shoes. "You seem to bring that out in me." Her gaze flew up. "Sorry."

He encircled her waist with his arm and hauled her against him. "Don't be." His voice roughened, hollowing into the marrow of her bones.

She struggled to remember why she'd been mad with him. Did this man have only to quirk his little finger and all of her common sense flew away? "Friends, you say?"

Walker bent his head. Her lips parted.

His lips skimmed across hers. Tasting. Testing. Exploratory. "Friends with limited fringe benefits maybe?" he whispered.

"Who is vamping whom, Walker Crowe?"

"Does it matter?"

She bit back a smile. "No, I suppose not, if we're negotiating terms."

Walker unsnapped the barrette holding her hair in place, sending her hair cascading down her back.

His hands lifted and fanned her hair over her shoulders, letting the mountain breeze take hold of it. "You might be surprised how agreeable a guy like me can be." He cupped her face in his palms.

Linden's stomach did a funny lurch, yet at the same time she fought to hold on to her plans for the future. She wouldn't be here when winter covered the Snowbird like a blanket. She wouldn't be around to see the blue-white reflection of the sky upon the snow and ice. She dared not stay and allow Walker to show her crisp, starry nights, the likes of which she'd only found in her dreams.

"Summer only," she cautioned.

Linden felt the beating of his heart through his ribbed cotton tee.

Walker's eyes probed and measured her. "I can handle that. If you can."

Unsettled, she nodded and breathed a tiny sigh of relief. A sensible, let's take it slow attitude. Not much commitment required. Nothing wrong with putting a fence and boundaries around expectations.

Hers and his.

"There's a few more views I reckon I could show you in these mountains."

From where she stood gazing up at him, this view alone well worth any other considerations.

She'd have other clients to attend to once the festival ended, God willing. In Raleigh. But for now?

Grabbing fistfuls of his shirt, she yanked Walker and his mouth closer. "Are you going to kiss me or what?"

He smiled, gathering the folds of her hair, rooting through it until he held both hands on either side of her head. "If you're done negotiating." He lowered his mouth the rest of the way.

And stopped.

Teasing. Tantalizing.

Distracted by his nearness, she drank in the scent of him. The essence of Walker filled her senses and tugged at her heart.

His breath feathered her cheek. "Are you?"

Linden's pulse skyrocketed.

"Am I what?" She kneaded her hands on his hard-muscled shoulders.

He gave her a long, slow smile, infuriating her with his deliberateness. "Finished hedging your bets."

She nodded and locked her hands behind his head.

"Impatient much, Birchfield?"

Why did Mr. Pay for Each Word have to go all wordy on her now?

She made a sound in the back of her throat. If he didn't go ahead and kiss her . . . Linden thought she might fall out.

And when he did?

She thought she might fall out anyway.

First, a sweetness and something that reminded her of the taste of cinnamon red gum. Then, the growing pressure of his mouth on hers. An insatiable hunger. A latent wildness. A consuming passion that left them both gasping for breath when he broke contact.

They stared wide-eyed, chests heaving, at each other.

He took a deep, steadying breath. "That answers that question." His hands cradled the nape of her neck.

"W-what question?"

He didn't answer, but his eyes traveled to the region of her mouth. His eyes full of her, he moved as if to kiss her again. But halfway there, with a sigh, he released her.

"Limited fringe benefits," he murmured more to himself than to her.

Instead, his thumb fondled her lips and trailed a caress across her jaw line. He gave her earlobe a playful tug and dropped his hand.

Breaking off a cedar twig, he tucked it behind her ear, his hand lingering for a moment. He gave Linden a crooked half-smile. "Want to see the cabin?"

She twined her fingers into his and let him lead her down the slope toward the house.

He slowed as they approached. "Just remember. I'm a farmer. Not a decorator. I spend most of my time outdoors." He ushered Linden into a sleek, modern kitchen.

"Nice job, Crowe." She admired the rack of copper pans hanging over the wooden butcher block island. "You cook, too?"

He shrugged. "Or starve up here by myself." He gave her the ten-cent tour of the large living area at the front and escorted her to the three bedroom dormer-storied loft upstairs. He showed her his "office" and she quirked her brows at his laptop.

"You've got Internet?"

"Contrary to popular opinion, I do enjoy some of the perks of twenty-first century civilization."

"Bet it cost you a boatload of money to get it out here, though."

He grimaced. "One of the hidden costs of trying to run a business."

Downstairs again, she surveyed the dormitory cast-off look of his furnishings. "Lots of potential. Lots of natural light and views all the way to Tennessee, I bet."

A stack of cordwood lay next to the deep-throated hearth. She ran her hand over the smooth creek stones that composed the fireplace. "Lots of character." She shot him a look out of the corner of her eye. "Like its builder."

But at her words, his face drooped. "Come sit with me on the porch, Linden. And I'll tell you about my character." He swallowed, averting his eyes. "And about what I did in Afghanistan."

18

October 1838—Blythe's Ferry, Tennessee

If she lived to be a hundred years old—a slim possibility the way her bones ached from too many nights sleeping on the ground—Sarah Jane would never forget the eighty-mile trek over the mountains into Tennessee. Nor the first sight of the internment camp at Fort Cass. They'd arrived footsore and weary.

The drought broke at the end of September. Everyone—Cherokee and white—raised their faces into the pelting rain, allowing the liquid to saturate their hair and clothing.

Faced with the stark reality of the Removal and the demise of his people if conditions continued unchanged, Chief Ross prevailed upon the government to allow him and the Council to organize the remaining logistics involved in moving over twelve thousand people one thousand miles to Indian Territory.

In return for his promise as Principal Chief to ensure the Cherokee went without further resistance, President Van Buren had agreed.

The Cherokee were divided into sixteen detachments of twelve hundred persons each. Ross appointed Reverend Endicott as one of the leaders of the detachment composed mainly of the Carolina Cherokee. Endicott enlisted Dr. Hopkins and Pierce as the detachment's medical attachés.

One by one, the detachments crossed the river and headed west. Endicott's departure was scheduled for today. At noon, a bugle sounded.

"Move out!" rang the cry of the sergeant at the head of the wagon column.

Sarah Jane, along with scores of the Principal People, lifted their eyes for one last glimpse of the mountains of home. An ear-splitting crash of thunder jolted her attention toward the west. An ominous black cloud hung suspended across heaven's canopy in the direction into which they were to travel. She shuddered.

Tobias with his strong baritone initiated the hymn, "Guide Me O Thou Great Jehovah" in the minor key the Cherokee preferred. The wheels of the first wagon entered the water.

At the river's edge, the shaman—who'd assigned himself to this group—offered his ash-smeared face to the sky. Wailing women and children hung back at the sight of the dark, rushing water. Rattling the ceremonial gourd, the shaman began a guttural, pulsating chant to rid the water of *Uktena*, the water-serpent.

"What pagan superstition is this?" Pierce halted his horse alongside the medical wagon Sarah drove.

"The Cherokee believe the underworld lies beneath water. He's praying for safe passage for his people to the other side."

Shading her eyes, she peered over the continuous column of wagons, horses and people, which stretched for three miles behind her. "The traditional ones won't set foot in that water until he removes the curse."

His fine, thin lips tightened. "You believe such nonsense?"

She sighed.

How could she make him understand the heart of The People?

"Of course not. But *they* believe, and they're afraid." She tied the bonnet strings under her chin. "We're here to help. To lift their eyes to the hills and the One True God from whence their real comfort will come."

He ground his teeth. "Are you still so sure God can comfort them? That He's even there?" His arm swept the lopsided wooden stakes lashed together into crude crosses atop grave mounds he'd helped dig before the start of the morning's march.

"Pierce." Reaching, she grasped his arm. "This is not of His making."

His fist knotted in the reins. "He's done nothing to stop it, either."

She straightened on the buckboard. A breeze ruffled her hair under the bonnet. "Don't tell me in addition to apostasy you've also become a Calvinist?"

He swiveled in the saddle. "What?"

And then, the corners of his blue eyes quirked, the crow's feet formed from too many days scanning the heaps of sick lying on the ground underneath a blazing summer sky.

Pierce leaned forward on the saddle horn. A smile, the first she'd seen him don in days, replaced his scowl. "No, not that."

He laughed, rusty sounding but a laugh. "All right, Sarah Jane, in appealing to my dogmatism, you've convinced me to stay for now in the Free Will fold."

She swiped at her forehead with the back of her hand in a mock sigh of relief. "Whew! Another soul snatched from the flames of fire." She sobered. "But seriously, Pierce, I have questions, too. Doubts."

"You always seem so strong. So unflinching." He gazed at her until she flushed, self-conscious under his scrutiny. "When my strength begins to flag, I see you soothing a child. Holding the hand of one awaiting death. Encouraging the forlorn. And it gives me strength to do the next thing. And the next."

Her lips trembled. "I'm not as strong as you think, Pierce."

A pulse beat in the hollow of his throat. "Sarah Jane, if I could—" He stared at her, a mixture of longing and regret darkening his face.

"All I know is we must be there for The People," she whispered.

"If we lose heart," she strengthened her voice. "If we lose faith, what will we have to offer them when their time comes? What good would we be? What truth would we block them from receiving when they—and us—have most need of consolation?"

"Will any of them or us be able to live after this?" He gestured. "To reach this place beyond the mountains and the river and across the plains?"

The driver in the wagon ahead snapped the reins on his double-row of oxen and surged forward hollering "Ho."

"Some of us will, Pierce." She picked up the reins as her turn came to follow. "God is in control despite what we can see. He's able to make all of this work for our good." Hers and Pierce's, too, she prayed nightly, as well as the prayers she lifted on behalf of The People. "If we surrender our fears and our plans to Him."

It took two and a half days before the last of their detachment crossed the river. The unbroken monotony of ten miles on a productive day followed day upon day. Camp life achieved a rhythm of sorts, albeit a foreign, hardscrabble existence wrested from the increasingly bitter elements as winter approached without mercy.

At first, the pitted, dirt roads jarred the teeth, but chill autumn rains soon transformed the roads into mud pits. Ensnaring the wagons, the oceans of mud often broke the wheels. Or if not yet broken, the backbreaking labor—an immeasurable cost—to pry the wheel free resulted in half-day delays in reaching their projected nightly destination

Relentless and remorseless, the wind hammered the unwanted outcasts of a burgeoning nation determined to achieve—at any cost—its destiny.

Either drunk or sick most days on his pallet, Ambrose gazed out of the wagon at the diminishing sight of the blue-gray hills as if he waited for death. Near term, Leila shifted with Kweti to the Hopkins wagon. And commandeered the Lily quilt. Sarah and her father slept underneath the wagon.

Pierce shuffled off each night to Tobias and Endicott's wagon. Sarah wondered, when she wasn't too run off her feet to fall asleep right away, if desire explained the nature of Pierce's feelings for

Leila Hummingbird. An obsessive urge to obtain—as Touch the Clouds phrased it—what you could never possess?

Cherokee scouts traveled ahead to search for campsites. They searched for meadows adjacent to a fresh supply of water. Some in the detachment were assigned the task of gathering firewood. Others took on the splitting of the cords. Sanitation requirements for twelve hundred people each day were of tremendous concern, too. Trenches had to be dug. And those same trenches covered when the detachment moved on.

Pierce rode ahead to set up a medical ward, often commandeering a schoolhouse or a church.

Touch the Clouds ventured into the Tennessee woods and later into the Kentucky pines with the other hunters to trap as much food as they could find. The army would not rearm them. So they caught what they could the traditional way, the old time Cherokee way before the whites had come and given them muskets.

Women and children scoured the forests for herbs and plants, at this time of year, few and farther between. Stronger youth hauled water to individual family encampments. Hygiene was a luxury. The cleaning of plates and utensils proved difficult enough. The same dishcloths had to be used over and over. She asked her father if such practices accounted for the outbreak of dysentery on the Trail.

His chin dropping, he'd said he didn't know. Sarah worried about her father. He appeared listless. Except when the wagons rolled to a stop and he proceeded to tend the patients who would let him.

So many still preferred the shaman. His deathbed crooning over yet another one of The People drove her to distraction and Pierce to muttered curses for the shaman to get out of his way.

The soldiers kept to themselves. Some of them, younger than Sarah, cradled their rifles in their arms, shame written over their faces at what they'd been tasked to do. Others . . .

Pierce positioned her behind him when the others swarmed through camp or his clinic. They preyed upon the weak, the sick, and the old. Pawing through what scant possessions had been snatched from home.

Tempers flared on both sides. When one woman heavy with child refused to move fast enough to suit the brigands, one of them bayoneted her. She and the child died, their blood staining the ground.

Leila shrank against the canvas cover of the wagon. Touch the Clouds surged forward.

Sarah Jane grabbed his arm, halting his forward motion. "Be still. Think of your family."

Pierce glared at her from atop his horse, with a pointed look at her hand wrapped around Touch the Clouds's arm.

Mutterings were heard across the encampment that night. Dr. Hopkins spent long hours counseling Touch the Clouds. His band itched to retaliate. Her father urged them to stay their hand for the sake of the weaker upon whom army vengeance would most certainly be wreaked.

Junaluska and about fifty Cherokee made a play for freedom. But he was captured and brought back in chains. Some, however, escaped the army's clutches. She prayed the end of their journey found them at home within the Snowbird.

Worry prickled within her at a certain, calculating look she'd encounter in Touch the Clouds's eyes when he returned from the hunt with a rabbit or a fish.

"No squirrel for Leila," he explained, only half-joking. "Might cause the baby to go up instead of down."

"Like the squirrel in the tree," she agreed at his small attempt at humor.

Incapacitated most of the time, Ambrose succumbed to the curse of the whiskey. Leila sold the field hands to a sympathetic adventurer on his way to Texas.

"Don't try it," Sarah Jane warned Touch the Clouds one evening in Illinois.

His head snapped up and his eyes, black in the darkness of the night, narrowed. "You think you can read my mind? Does your

God give you—" He tapped the side of his temple. "Special powers to see inside my head?"

"Your grandmother's too weak." She stirred the broth bubbling in the black iron pot over the bonfire. "Leila's too close to the baby arriving. She'd never make it." Sarah let the metal ladle clang against the side of the pot. "You were going to take her with you, weren't you?"

He tore off a hunk of bread with his teeth. "You think me the kind of man who'd abandon his child?"

She heaved a sigh of relief before she realized what he hadn't said.

The next day, somewhere before they reached the great river, his grandmother breathed her last. One final phlegmy cough and she flew away. In the drizzling rain, Touch the Clouds refused all offers of help and retreated to dig a quick, shallow grave in a bend of trees off the road. Sarah followed him anyway.

His bearing erect, he thrust the shovel into the hard-packed winter ground like a sword. His strong arms vibrated from the effort. "I don't need your help."

"I promised I'd stay with her. That you wouldn't be alone. I keep my promises."

He stopped scraping the earth and leaned upon the handle. His eyes traveled to the bunch of red berries she clutched in her hands.

"It was all I could find this time of year." She bit her lip. "They're not edible so I thought . . ."

Something quivered in his face—as if he'd become unused to human kindness—before he clamped all emotion into the pitiless void he maintained.

He returned to his digging. "Your mother died when you were a girl, didn't she?"

Sarah nodded. She didn't resemble that girl anymore. She felt old, death and disease hanging like a mantle upon her shoulders.

"My grandmother once spoke of your mother. She said she wasn't just a good white woman." He favored Sarah with a flash of strong teeth. "But a good woman."

He bent his head to the task, averting his face. "Much like her daughter has become, I think."

Sarah shook her head. "I'm not really—"

"Your God is real in you."

She swallowed, her heart beating faster.

He cocked his head toward the soldiers lounging by one of the fires. "Not the God they speak of in one breath and curse us with the next. If you and I had been different people in a different time . . ."

She caught her breath as if she stood on the edge of a precipice.

"I would've liked to get to know more about this God you serve."

He lifted the body of his grandmother, wrapped in an old bed sheet by Sarah and Kweti, from the back of a horse he'd borrowed. After mounding dirt over the slight depression where she lay—all he'd been able to hew out of the frozen ground—he stood silent beside Sarah.

"C-Could I speak a few words on her behalf?"

He nodded. A bleak expression entered his eyes. "She liked you," he whispered. "Your God intrigued her, too."

She recited the twenty-third Psalm as tears rolled down her cheeks. Touch the Clouds remained motionless and mute. She left the sprigs of berries atop the soil where his grandmother's hands rested, folded underneath the earth.

Without a backward glance, he leaped onto the horse's bare back. Leaning over, he extended his hand to Sarah. She stared at him a moment before grasping his arm. With a sudden whoosh of her calico skirts, he swung her onto the horse. She perched sidesaddle. His arms reached around her and tugged at the reins.

"You deserve someone more worthy than—" He used the derogatory name he'd taken to calling Pierce. A Cherokee name not understood except by Cherokee speakers.

She made a motion of protest.

"You must find someone with the mighty spirit of your father," he continued, weaving the horse among the various campsites. "Tobias is a good man. For a white man."

She swiveled so suddenly only his arms tight around her waist prevented her from unseating herself.

He jerked the reins, bringing the horse to a standstill.

Sarah frowned at him, her face inches from his darker one. "Are you trying to—?"

"Get your filthy hands off Miss Hopkins, savage."

She and Touch the Clouds both reared at the murderous sound in Pierce's voice. He stood, hands upon his hips. They'd arrived at the wood-framed church that had thrown open its doors to the refugees for the night.

"Pierce," she gasped.

In a lunge, he strode toward them and pulled at Sarah. For a moment, Touch the Clouds's arms refused to let go. But with a muttered disdain, he slackened his grip and she slid off the horse and into Pierce's arms.

"You misunderstand, Pierce."

He shot a look over her head at Touch the Clouds. "Oh, I don't think I do. What? You think to possess them both?"

Touch the Clouds yanked at the reins, turning the horse. "Do you?"

"Possession? Is that what everything boils down to for you?" She shoved away from Pierce as Touch the Clouds disappeared from sight. "You make me sound like a piece of meat."

Shaking with rage, she stalked away.

Only to have him catch at her sleeve.

"Sarah Jane."

"Get away from me." She flung him off. "Where's my father?"

"I was looking for you. Sarah . . ." Something in his voice halted Sarah in her tracks.

She wheeled so quickly the earth tilted. "What's happened?" She put a hand to her throat.

"He collapsed, Sarah." Concern shone out of his eyes. Pierce took her hand. "And Ambrose Hummingbird died a few hours ago. Leila's distraught. I fear she'll go into labor too soon."

Sarah snatched her hand away. She should've known. Sarah was sick of his obsession.

Always and ever about Leila Hummingbird.

"Where's my father?"

Pierce took a step back. "In your wagon. I transferred Leila to her own wagon since her father . . ."

She pivoted toward her wagon, parked under the shade of a basswood tree.

"Wait, Sarah. Where're you going?"

She didn't turn around. "To my father."

"But what—but what about Leila?"

She didn't slacken her stride. "Let her find solace in the comforting arms of her husband."

19

2018—Cartridge Cove

What he was about to tell Linden pretty much assured their budding, tentative on-again, off-again relationship wouldn't outlast the summer. Maybe not even this visit to his tree farm. Walker gestured for her to take one of the Adirondack chairs on the porch overlooking the Snowbird Mountain range.

He sank into an adjacent chair. "I wanted to be a true warrior. I had a lot to prove. To my family. To The People. To myself."

She said nothing, but stared over the smoky-smudged peaks and allowed him tell his story in his own way.

"I caught the attention of one of the sergeants on the firing range. He suggested I consider making my MOS—"

She angled toward him.

"Military Occupational Specialty—sniping. So I attended Infantry School, made it through the Marine Corps Sniper School at Camp Lejeune . . ."

Walker grunted. "Carefully calculated hell on earth. Designed to break every sniper hopeful. Challenges that rewire the brain and help you survive in the field. Lots of psychological and physical testing to determine how susceptible you are to anxiety." He sighed. "Or remorse."

"How'd you get through?"

"Sheer pigheaded Cherokee willpower not to give in, not to let them drive me away. To prove myself better."

"I think I've glimpsed some of that pigheadedness you're talking about." She smiled. "What happened next?"

He settled against the backrest. "I volunteered as part of my ongoing training for Ranger School and eventually was assigned as a sniper to a special ops team."

Walker studied his hands. "No recoil. No remorse. And once you're in the middle of that military mindset and culture . . ." He blew out a breath. "I did a lot of things that I'm not proud of—and I'm not just talking about missions, but in my free time, too, on leave with the guys."

His voice dropped. "The guys and me," he swallowed. "We painted a big swath through Germany . . . Italy . . . And after one mission involving a drug cartel outside Bogotá . . . ?" He shook his head, wishing he could as easily shake off the memories.

What she must think of him . . .

He shriveled inside himself. "I was raised to know better."

"So was I," she whispered.

A sheen of tears glimmered in her eyes. But instead of condemnation, he was relieved to find an honest understanding and a shared sense of regret. She drew one of his hands alongside hers on the armrest.

"What exactly," she moistened her lips and changed topic. "Do snipers do?"

He didn't shy away from meeting her gaze this time. "Hollywood would have you believe we're glorified assassins. But despite our 'one shot, one kill' motto, our main job is recon. We're experts in stealth, camouflage, infiltration, and observation. We sneak behind enemy lines and provide intel to Command on the enemy's size, strength, and location."

Linden wove her fingers through his.

"Sometimes in Afghanistan, my spotter and I—" He broke off at the upward tilt of her eyebrow. "A sniper works in a two-man team. The spotter is a kind of . . ."

He squinted his eyes in thought. ". . . an apprentice sniper. We take turns using the high-powered scope during a surveillance that often lasts for days. He carries an M-16, a much more useful asset than my bolt action—"

"English, please." She laughed.

"Once fired, I had to clear the rifle of its shell casing and load another round before I could get off a shot. A real handicap when you're in a hurry to get your butt out of range after the enemy's located your position."

She gave him a mock salute with one hand. "Got it." But she held onto him with her other hand. "And your spotter?"

"One of his main jobs is to watch the vapor trail left by the bullet's trajectory I've fired and give advice on readjusting my aim or position if I miss."

She cocked her head. "Do you miss?"

"Just once. And for me?" He skittered away from that particular cliff's edge. "I decided it was time to hang up my rifle and come home after I finished the tour."

"Were you and your spotter close?"

He relaxed, appreciating once more her willingness not to push. "Yeah. We had nicknames on the team. They called me . . ." He darted a glance to make sure he had her attention. "They called me Injun."

A deadpan expression on her face. "And they lived to tell about it?"

The corners of his mouth curved. "Boyd's from Wyoming." He waited for the coin to drop and the bubblegum to roll out.

"Don't tell me. Cowboy and Injun?"

He bent over, laughing at the incredulous look on her face.

She sobered. "Is-is Cowboy okay?"

He nodded. "Took my vacated position. Finished his enlistment and went home to marry his high school sweetheart. He's running his dad's cattle ranch, and I've got a standing invitation to come visit. He's also got three kids under the age of five."

This time she glanced away at a distant point on the Snowbird horizon. "Every guy's dream."

He cut his eyes at her and frowned. "Sometimes we'd be ordered to destroy material targets like a generator or transmitter or fuel supplies behind enemy lines. We usually traveled under the cover of darkness from the drop-off point, established a camouflaged position, and learned to remain motionless for hours on end to avoid detection. And whatever mission we were tasked with, we always established our escape route first thing. A place to fall back to."

She gave him a shrewd look. "This place with the trees is your fallback."

A shiver pricked his arms at how she got him. Scary in a pleasurable mixed with gut-clenching fear kind of way how much Linden Birchfield seemed to know him. The him he camouflaged.

"Why the trees, Walker?"

An honest question deserved an honest answer.

"Iraq and Afghanistan were shades of brown and tan. Open space. Jagged mountains like sandblasted rock fangs. A savage beauty all its own, but not what I was used to. Always left me on edge, exposed, vulnerable. I longed for the comforting greenness of summer. The riot of autumn. The rolling, gentleness of these old mountains. The Appalachian spine that cradles The People."

"And like an exile, you eventually found your way home." A pain Walker didn't understand flitted over her features.

What he longed for most right now was to penetrate the heavy cloak of mourning she clutched around her. "Have you found your home yet, Linden?"

"No," she answered him in a clipped voice, her face tense. Nothing if not a straight shooter, she'd fired a warning shot telling him not to trespass on forbidden emotional terrain.

The silence deepened.

"Mostly we waited."

She exhaled as if she'd feared he wouldn't respect her **No Trespassing** signs. "Waited for what?"

"The right moment to take the shot." Timing—a fact that most definitely applied to the woman sitting beside him—was everything.

"When we weren't on assignment, we tried to stay on good terms with the locals. More than once, one of the friendlies would give up a key piece of overheard conversation. Some of the guys organized impromptu soccer games with the kids. I formed a stickball team to initiate them into America's oldest sport."

Now, for the hard part. He took a deep, steadying breath.

Would she still speak to him once he finished telling her about that last fatal mission?

"Nothing nice or pretty about what I did. But yes, we concentrated on hunting key people. Take out one lynchpin terrorist and save thousands of innocents. A carefully placed shot out of nowhere often enough to break the terrorist cell's ability to fight."

"How'd that feel? Taking a life?"

Because he was beginning to understand what made Linden Birchfield tick—though not as well as he'd like—he believed her question wasn't borne out of morbid curiosity but out of a genuine concern for his well-being. An attempt to know him better.

He gazed off, thinking analytically, to give her the best, non-sugarcoated answer he could. "A sniper stalks his prey for days. You get to know a person in great clarity through the scope. Details of their personal lives and relationships become up close and personal. You learn to keep an emotional distance to protect yourself."

Walls not so easy to shed once you returned to civilian life.

"It's a strange feeling. Weird to see someone on the ground and know they'll never laugh again, make love to their wife again, kiss their children again because of you."

He shook his head, trying to clear the memories of the first kill he'd recorded in Ramadi. From a nearby rooftop, he'd watched the figure, garbed in a head scarf and full-length black *abaya*, hurry toward a squad he'd been assigned to overwatch.

"Something about the woman seemed off. Iraqis don't hurry unless they're dodging bullets. Something about the way she swung her hips . . . her eyes never wavered from the squad. I had two seconds to make the decision to shoot a woman. I decided to be safe and not sorry. I took the shot."

Later inspection revealed the dead woman was actually a male suicide bomber. He'd made the right choice and saved his buddies' lives as well as the lives of countless innocent bystanders.

"You did what you had to do."

He gave a shaky laugh. "You must think I'm some sort of . . ." He gulped. "Monstrous, unfeeling machine." He tried pulling his hand away.

She was having none of it. She held on. Tight. Refusing to let go.

But he hadn't told her the worst of it.

Lots of missions he'd never tell her about—or any other living soul. Things with which he wouldn't taint her soul's innocence.

She inched her chair closer until her shoulder pressed his. Comforting, championing.

"Cowboy and I were tasked in Afghanistan," he plunged in. "With taking out a suspected bomber after we received info the Taliban planned to salt our main supply route with IEDs. Cowboy and I watched him move around the village. Noted each time someone new arrived to conference with him. Kept tabs on his coming and going. And then one day, a dusty sedan pulled up outside his house. One of the men gave him a wrapped, cylindrical device."

"Where were you and Cowboy?"

"Second floor of an abandoned building. The village had been built around an Afghan version of an industrial zone on the outskirts of Kabul. The man unwrapped two artillery shells primed with wires hanging out. Not an IED but worse."

"Did you shoot them?"

He shook his head. "Command said to let the men in the sedan go free. In-country operatives were following them to bigger fish.

The sedan left. The bomber rewrapped the shells and laid the package in the front seat of his own vehicle while he took one last smoke. A lucky break for Cowboy and me."

Walker shrugged. "All he had to do was move the shells to the road, hook them up to a battery and detonate at will. And of course, village life continued on around us. Women with plastic water jugs headed for the communal well. A lady in the adjacent apartment block hung laundry over her balcony. The little guys kicked around what they called a soccer ball."

"I adjusted the angle of the shot. Took into account the range of about one thousand meters." His chest heaved as he struggled with the last bit of the retelling. "I don't know what set the guy off. Sometimes the hunted . . ."

He clenched his fist inside Linden's palm. "Sometimes it's as if they know. They sense something is off. Some primeval instinct for survival warns them."

She covered his fist with both of her hands, her touch warm, life-sustaining.

"As I pulled the trigger, he grabbed one of the kids as a shield." His voice choked. "One of my kids. The bullet entered the boy's skull where I placed all my shots."

"He never knew what hit him." Walker swallowed past the bile that rose in his throat.

"What happened to the bomber? Did he get away?" Her voice with its compassion and cool sanity brought him back to his porch overlooking his mountains.

"No." His lips flattened. "After I cleared the chamber, I took him out through the back windshield as he drove away."

"The kid? It bothered me. I won't deny it. Worried at the back of my mind while I finished that tour. Woke me up at night, but I coped. I had the guys and the whole military apparatus supporting me, justifying what we did—what I did."

"Collateral damage." He gritted his teeth. "I hate that phrase."

"But when the commander wanted to recommend me for a citation, I balked. He congratulated me on my team's successful disposal of our thirtieth kill in a month."

Her soft intake of breath lanced his heart.

"Yeah." He scrunched his face. "The count for just that month."

She nuzzled her cheek against his shoulder.

"The commander said I was a natural-born killer." He flinched at the remembered words. "I decided I didn't want to be anyone's killer ever again. I believed my troubles would be over if I could just get home, but returning to normal society proved harder than I thought."

"What did you do?"

"Preacher Bushyhead, a vet himself, spent a lot of time talking to me. He introduced me to a sniper support group over the mountain." He laughed without mirth. "Who knew there'd be enough of us to form something like that? But between the preacher and the guys, I discovered my faith had been misplaced."

"What do you mean?"

"My faith in these mountains. In myself. In everything that had no power in and of itself to cleanse and heal."

"Walker . . ."

His eyes traveled over to a bank of billowing clouds on the distant horizon. "Look," he pointed. "The Magic Lake."

"The what?"

"Traditionalists believed high above the mountains of the Sky People resided a lake in the clouds to which bears or any who were injured could go to receive wholeness and healing."

She gazed into the distance, a pensive look on her face. "How did someone reach that sacred place?"

"Ah . . . there's a question for the ages."

"Have you reached such a place, Walker Crowe?"

He nodded, slow. "After a long and painful journey, I think I have."

Linden drew her knees to her chin. "But where did it begin for you, Walker? The healing and the wholeness?"

"Same as it must for all who truly come seeking." He fixed his eyes on her. "At the foot of the cross."

He'd spent the better part of an endless night reliving every expression on her face, every nuance in her voice. Walker tasted her lips in his mind over and over again.

Berry flavor, Walker concluded about two A.M.

"She's gone?"

Later that morning standing in the aisle of the church, his voice rose in pitch as he gaped at his uncle. "Just like that? She left?"

"Steady, son." Ross pulled him into an alcove. "You look like you've been sideswiped."

Walker took a ragged breath and scrubbed his hand over his jaw. He'd spooked her. Dropping his hand to his slacks, he clenched and unclenched his fist.

He'd feared telling her about his past, afraid the ugliness would sever any hope of a relationship with her. But the way they'd left it when he dropped her off at her grandmother's house, he believed he'd survived the baring of his soul.

But with her trust issues, she possessed walls higher than his. He should've never told her about what he'd done, what he'd been trained to do in the name of his country. He should've known she wouldn't understand, couldn't understand.

He didn't half understand it himself.

Walker deflated against the wall, a whirring in his head. Images flashed of her hair blowing wild and free on the Skyway. And the picture he'd tucked into his heart of her twirling on her toes, her eyes rapt upon his trees.

She'd gone.

Ross jostled his shoulder. "Are you listening to me, boy?"

"W-What?"

"I said she called her mother in Haiti. And her mother told Linden she'd be on the next flight to RDU."

"Wait." His brow furrowed. "Her mother? What's going on?"

Ross shrugged. "Marvela encouraged Linden to meet her mother, Vanessa, at the airport. Said it was a conversation ten years and many prayers in the making between Linden and her folks." He tilted his head. "What did you say to Linden yesterday that brought this on?"

Walker shook his head, his eyes wide. "I took her to see my trees and told her about my last mission."

"Hallelujah!" The undemonstrative, spit-and-polish old man raised a hand toward heaven. "The walls of his mountain fortress breached at last."

A conversation between Linden and her far-flung mother prompted her departure? He struggled to wrap his mind around his uncle's words.

Not his fault, but the fact remained, she was still gone. Slumping, he stuffed his hands into his khaki trousers.

Ross squeezed his shoulder. "Linden said to tell you she'd see you at the *gadugi* barn painting next Saturday."

Walker straightened, his mouth as dry as desert sand. "She said that? She's coming back?"

Ross looked at him like he'd grown horns. "Well, yeah. Duh? The festival."

And maybe returning on behalf of Walker Crowe, too? He allowed himself a small flicker of hope.

The organist banged out a foot-tapping prelude. Ross grasped his arm. "Marvela's waving us over. We'd better sit down. Oh, and Walker?"

He nudged Walker down the aisle. "Linden also said she'd email you when she got to Raleigh."

Walker went rigid. "You waited to the last to tell me that part?" He threw his hitherto beloved uncle an exasperated look and pivoted on his heel. Behind him, he heard Ross laugh and Marvela ask why Walker was heading the wrong way.

"Gone to check his laptop, I expect." And another laugh.

His uncle's words registered, barely, as Walker bolted past the startled ushers, offering plates in hand. The laptop was a good thirty minutes up the mountain at his cabin. He leaped off the concrete steps in a single bound.

As the splendid isolation of his private sanctuary rapidly lost some of its charm.

20

December 1838—Illinois

Waiting beside the ice-swollen Mississippi proved another chapter in the continuing nightmare, which plagued Sarah and The People. They waited for the ice floes in the river to thaw and render it crossable. The privations had grown harder. The conditions, harsher.

Many, now shoeless, left bloody footprints in the falling snow before they set camp beside the river. Amidst the howling wind and driving sleet, the detachments bunched again. At this point in the miserable, inexorable tread toward Death, the soldiers didn't much mind what The People did. As long as they didn't try to duck out for good, The People wandered at will among the detachments in relative freedom.

Some families were reunited. Parents found lost children who'd been playing in the woods when the rest of the family had been rousted from putting breakfast on the table. Captured and sent to Fort Delaney or Fort Montgomery, husbands dragged from cornfields and wives visiting a neighbor on that fateful morning in June, fell into each other's arms again.

The deaths continued. From starvation. From exposure to the elements. One woman carried around her dead baby for three days before Sarah and Pierce convinced her to let them bury him. The woman didn't survive the night.

Over the next few days, conversely, the weather turned, becoming almost balmy. The soldiers urged the wagons forward onto the flatboats charged—at Cherokee expense—to ferry the forsaken across. The transition took three, long, exhausting days. But the weather held.

On the other side of the river, Leila's water broke. Pierce had ridden ahead to look for the coming night's shelter of his patients. Touch the Clouds had gone somewhere to secure food. Sarah's father had sunk into a delirium.

Neither, she, Yolanda, nor Kweti were strong enough to lift Leila into the wagon. Samson had been sent to find water, buckets of it, and to heat it. Calling Leila to the courage of her ancestors, Kweti spread a coarse woolen blanket under the Hummingbird wagon. And there, in the dirt and squalor, rending the air with curses to Sarah's God and Kweti's, Leila gave birth to Touch the Clouds's daughter.

Exhausted from the birthing and in grief over her father's passing, Leila consented to hold the baby only long enough for Kweti to retrieve the Cherokee Rose quilt from her trunk inside the wagon. Yolanda draped Sarah's Lily quilt over Leila's knees. As she did so, Sarah spotted unfamiliar squiggles drawn on the back.

It was thus when Touch the Clouds returned from the hunt, he found his daughter crying in Sarah's arms.

"Nunahi-Duna-Dlo-Hillu-I." He took the baby from Sarah. "Born crying onto the Trail Where They Cried." His daughter quieted and gazed deep into her father's dark, hooded eyes. His lips rested on the newborn, and he whispered into her ear.

Kweti bustled about, entreating her beloved to take a sip of water or have a nourishing bite to eat. Leila twisted her face in the direction from which they'd come and refused. Unease niggled Sarah.

Something wasn't right with Leila. Sarah wished her father were here. He would've known what to do. She'd done her best, but Leila had lost a lot of blood in the birth process and her depression hung like a palpable cloud over the campsite.

"What do you want to call your daughter, Leila?" Sarah tucked the quilt over her one-time friend. Her question merited no response from Leila.

Sarah recalled with a slight shudder how the army dealt with one old man who'd not responded to an order to move along. They'd shot the old man, deaf since birth.

"Leila?" Sarah gently shook her, to nudge Leila out of her apathy.

Touch the Clouds pointed his chin toward the quilt covering his wife, but his gaze traveled to Sarah. "She shall be called A-ma-ye-du-hi."

Sarah thrust her hands deep within the pockets of her pinafore. "Water lily." She glanced at the sluggish river alongside the campsite. "Appropriate."

"And," he stroked the quilt in which Lily was wrapped. "Tsistunagiska. A wild rose. Seven leaves for the seven clans. The gold center for the treasure taken from her father's home. White petals for each of her mother's tears."

Sarah repeated the names in Cherokee. And in English. "LilyRose." She smiled at him, the corners of her mouth lifting. "A fine name, indeed."

But not by so much as a flicker of an eyelash did Leila indicate she'd heard.

Or cared.

Due to sickness among the soldiers, the party rested beside the Mississippi for a week. Sarah busied herself tending to Leila and LilyRose. Her father, his strength if not his faith broken by the Trail, grew steadily worse.

Avoiding the new baby—or perhaps what she represented— Pierce spent several days in the company of the soldiers, tending to their needs.

Five more babies were born along the river. Four of them died within hours of their birth. Touch the Clouds made himself scarce as well.

Sarah often fell asleep in the middle of her prayers. In a weak moment, after the fourth baby died in her arms, she pondered whose company she missed the most. Pierce, who'd given her little comfort over the course of this long passage? Or the solid, common sense of Touch the Clouds?

On the evening of their fifth day in the same campsite, Touch the Clouds joined her once more around the campfire. They'd journeyed together on the Trail now for two and a half months. He warmed his hands over the blaze, his black eyes reflecting the shooting tongues of the flame. He'd spent a long time in Leila's wagon that day, LilyRose hanging in the snug, deerskin papoose he fashioned for her.

"I wanted to thank you, Sarah," his eyes bored into hers. "For what you and your father have done for The People. For me, my family. My wife and my daughter."

She realized he was telling her good-bye.

"You mustn't." Sarah laid a hand on his coat. "Not now. Leila's too weak, and LilyRose is too young. It's too cold. Wait and try in the spring."

He covered her hand with his own. "Spring will be too late. Too far. If we die, we'll die on our journey toward home. Surrounded by everything that makes us who we are. Who the Creator meant us to be."

"No, don't—"

"Do not trouble yourself. You will awake one morning to find us gone." He swallowed hard. "I would covet your prayers on our behalf. For the journey we take."

Tears clouded her eyes. "May the Creator hold you and yours from this day and forever in the palm of His hand."

He smiled, a faint glint of his old self returning. "Be it as you pray, Sarah Jane Hopkins."

Rising as if an old man, he dropped a twig from the sacred cedar tree into the fire. Inhaling the aroma, he watched the smoke, like incense, spiral upward in the night sky. "May your steps be guided, and may your days be filled with laughter in the land of the living until you fly to your true home at last in the great Beyond."

She awoke in the early hours of dawn to an utter stillness. Not a bird called. Not a sound broke the silence hanging in the air.

As if The People and creation held their breath.

She shrugged off the blanket she slept under. With shaking hands, she smoothed her gingham dress.

Gunfire blasted her from the wagon.

She dashed toward the sound of screaming. Toward Kweti's guttural cries.

On the bluff overlooking the river, the sight that met her eyes robbed Sarah of words. In the middle of the watery chasm floated a raft of logs lashed together with the reeds that grew along the banks. Touch the Clouds's head bobbed above the water as he and several other men dog-paddled the raft toward the other side and freedom.

Atop the raft, a dazed Leila clutched the papoose to her breast. Another woman hugged a young girl of about sixteen. Two other women helped the men with the concerted, broad stokes of a paddle against the strong current of the river.

Sarah found her voice. "Shut up, Kweti." She pondered how much of the old woman's screeching had to do with Leila's danger and how much involved the separation from her beloved.

The soldiers, standing on the water's edge, continued to fire into the river, aiming for the men swimming below the raft. The People gathered beside Sarah. With muttered exclamations, they cheered their comrades on toward Home.

Pierce shoved his way toward the front. He cursed Touch the Clouds for his obsession and his foolishness.

An exercise rich in irony.

One of the bullets found its mark. Sarah stifled a cry and craned her neck to discern the man's identity. The man sank beneath the surface.

She prayed, her hands clasped under her chin, as she'd never prayed before as another bullet struck its intended target. A pool of red ebbed in concentric circles from the raft. At the increasing distance, she wasn't able to make out who lived or who had died.

The soldiers shifted their focus.

One of the women atop the raft jerked as blood spurted from her chest. She toppled into the water. When the young girl's mother fell, the raft overturned, dumping her daughter, Leila, the other paddler, and the baby into the dark, icy river.

There were cries from the women in the murky water. An infant's piteous screams. Pierce wriggled out of his overcoat, loosened his cravat, threw off his hat.

He dove, headfirst, into the churning depths. She held her breath until his tight, blond curls emerged moments later. He treaded water and dove again, searching. He wobbled to the surface sputtering, calling Leila's name.

A few of the Cherokee started for the water to assist him, but afraid of an insurrection, the soldiers warned them back with a volley of gunfire. Tobias jumped in. And Reverend Endicott swam out as far as he dared, pulling one of the women's bodies to shore.

Scanning the shoreline, Sarah scrutinized the current for a scrap of deerskin, a flash of the blue ribbon Kweti had laced into the drawstrings. There. Sarah's heart pounded. In the reeds.

The papoose with LilyRose floated right side up, caught like Baby Moses, among the bulrushes this side of the river. The baby wailed, but she was alive.

Sarah plunged into the river, the breath knocked from her lungs as the icy water saturated her woolen stockings. Straining forward, her efforts were hampered by the weight of her skirts, dragging her downward.

Reaching LilyRose, she struggled to release the baby from the reeds. Her feet knifed through the water as she went under again, scrambling for a foothold. But she couldn't find the bottom.

Brackish water filled her nostrils. The light receded. Suffocating darkness deepened. Sounds muted.

She pushed upward against the water, surging to the surface, and gulped a great draught of air. Cutting her fingers on the knife-sharp cane, she treaded as best she could while she tugged to free LilyRose from her bonds. Panic rose as she descended. Again.

"Let me help you, Sarah."

She beat ineffectively at the water and found Tobias beside her. He stationed one arm around her waist to keep her buoyant. With his other hand, he yanked the baby free.

He shoved the papoose across the water like a tiny flatboat, rippling the surface ahead of them. LilyRose continued to cry, a droning, whimpering sound. Spent and exhausted, she could do little to help Tobias as he towed her and LilyRose to safety.

On shore, Pierce hunched over Leila. Leila's big eyes darted wild and fearful around the cluster of people who surrounded her. Sarah attempted to pass LilyRose to her mother, but Leila shunted away, her gaze directed at the river.

"Touch the Clouds," she moaned. "He's dead. Everyone dies and leaves me." She closed her eyes, the color draining from her face.

"Give the baby to me," Kweti murmured.

Sarah handed the child over to Leila's nurse.

The old woman fastened the papoose to her back. "Get up, Leila Hummingbird," she commanded in a voice unlike any Sarah had ever heard from the old Cherokee woman. "You will get up now."

And Leila got up.

Kweti trundled Pierce aside and grasped Leila's arm. "We find the quilts," she promised. "Wrap you and the baby." She hustled Leila toward their wagon.

The other bodies snatched from the river were identified. The Teesateskie mother. White Owl, her husband. One of the women paddlers. Soldiers were sent to scout the riverbanks for any bodies, which had floated downstream.

Sarah shut her mind to the image of Touch the Clouds's body, left for the fish to feed upon. Instead, she flooded her thoughts with the memory of him as he'd been that long ago day outside her father's surgery. Strong, defiant, proud.

As he'd died.

They moved out the next day. Kweti allowed none but herself to care for LilyRose. She was a good baby, content in the old woman's arms.

Sometimes she was so quiet it was easy to forget the baby was even there. Sarah wondered if Leila had forgotten. But Kweti removed the baby from the papoose, an ever-present reminder of her father's tragedy, and bundled LilyRose in the Cherokee Rose quilt. Kweti carried the baby in her arms each painstaking step farther toward her new home.

Encased in the folds of the Lily quilt, Leila had taken to wandering among the detachments, asking the weary travelers in the caravan behind them if they'd seen Touch the Clouds. If the soldiers had found him.

The Lily quilt represented something to Leila. The happy days before the Removal? The whiteness of the non-Indian world to which all her livelong life she'd sought?

Sarah didn't know, but she hadn't the heart to take its small measure of comfort from Leila.

An outbreak of dysentery claimed the wee Jameson infant Sarah and Pierce had brought into the world in that spring a lifetime ago. The babies and the old suffered the most as winter descended in its fury upon them again.

Sarah stole moments between nursing to check on her father. Yolanda took over his care, freeing Sarah to give succor to the dying. Her clothes now hung off her frame.

"Thin as a broomstick," Yolanda fussed.

Beyond exhaustion, at the first sign of dizziness, Sarah learned to simply lie down beside her latest patient and catch a few hours of sleep before her buckling knees sent her crashing to the ground. Of Pierce, she caught only scattered glimpses of his drawn, beard-shadowed face.

Leila's primal cry summoned Sarah and Pierce from the sickbeds toward the sound of her wrenching sobs. Shivers oozing to her boots, Sarah hurtled past the wagons rolling ever forward west. Pierce outstripped her without a backward glance.

A crazed look upon her face, Leila huddled over Kweti where she lay in the dirt of the road. Leila rocked the old woman's lifeless form in her arms. "No, no, no."

Sarah placed her hands on Leila's shoulders. "Leila?"

Pierce's chin dropped. "Starvation." He closed Kweti's eyes with the palm of his hand. "Her heart finally gave out."

He attempted to pry Leila's arms from her hold around the dead woman. Leila's eyes grew overlarge. She bolted to her feet and shoved him aside.

"My baby," Leila screamed, gripping Sarah. "Where is my baby?"

Sarah's mouth trembled. "LilyRose? I thought she was . . ." She swiveled from side to side. "Oh, Pierce, where is she?"

No papoose. No baby in Kweti's arms. LilyRose was gone.

When Leila collapsed, Pierce and Yolanda carried her to the Hummingbird wagon. Samson flicked the long whip over the team of oxen and jolted forward.

Ever forward.

Prodded by the soldiers not to hold up the line. Couldn't stop. Couldn't rest until they reached . . . Wherever it was they were supposed to land.

A sick dread clenched Sarah's stomach into knots as she searched on foot. She made her way from campsite to campsite, given over to the driving need to find LilyRose, Touch the Clouds's daughter. But no one knew anything. No one had seen the baby as they hunkered sick and weary over January campfires, sharing pots and cooking utensils.

Leila, when she awoke, cursed Pierce for keeping her sedated, wasting valuable time in looking for her child.

If Leila searched in one direction, Sarah took the other to cover more ground. Leila shouted until her throat grew hoarse and raspy. Leila called for her baby.

And for her dead father.

Perhaps a passing settler, on the way to California or Texas, had found the child in the dead woman's arms and carried her off in an act of mercy, Sarah speculated. She bent her knees calling upon God's mercy to cover LilyRose wherever she happened to be.

At the end of a fortnight, one day Leila Hummingbird disappeared. No more to be found. Simply no longer There.

Distraught, Pierce combed the detachments for her.

But she, along with the Lily quilt, appeared to have vanished like LilyRose, from the face of the earth.

21

2018—Cartridge Cove

It was no accident Walker purchased the paint for the Tahquittee barn Friday night. Although, he knew full well there was no way Linden could drive six hours from Raleigh, even if she left at the crack of dawn, and still get to Cartridge Cove before lunch.

But a guy could hope. And dream. Which was about all he'd done as one week turned into two.

They exchanged emails and texted sometimes three times a day. He lived for those messages. And, the oft-remembered feel of Linden Birchfield in his arms. He was a big man and unlike her statuesque grandmother, Linden was a small woman. Sometimes he feared through the intensity of his feelings, he'd end up breaking Linden.

If he ever got the chance to put his arms around her again.

First, the endless four-day blackout of communication when Linden and her mother traveled to Charlottesville. Back in Raleigh, she updated Walker on her recent activities. Like the Tuesday hot dog special at Snoopy's he remembered from his own North Carolina State days. Enough to make his mouth water.

And not just for hot dogs and ice cream.

He glanced through the cloud cover toward the sun, calculating her approximate location on the highway at this moment.

A daub of paint flicked across his cheek.

"Hey." Walker spun around. He clenched the paint stick in his hand like a tomahawk.

"Better not mess with Crowe, Colonel Wachacha." Jake, one of his boys, backed away from Ross who gripped the incriminating paintbrush.

Ross grinned that evil Cheshire smile of his. "Is that right?"

Jake rubbed a shoulder. "He took out his lovesickness on us at practice yesterday. Like a grouchy, black bear."

Ross chuckled. "Gotta go." He waved at Walker. "Marvela wants my help picking your blueberries today."

"You got no room to laugh, old man." Walker sized up his uncle. "Not so much the tomcat warrior any more. You're more like a domesticated lap kitty now." He made sure his uncle observed his lip curl.

Ross jutted his jaw and aimed the brush at Walker's chest. "Takes one, I reckon, to recognize one."

Walker's attention wandered as a Toyota parked under the shade of a grove of willows. His pulse skyrocketed. Walker thrust the paint stick at his uncle and strove to maintain a sedate, leisured pace in a straight trajectory toward Linden's car. His heart hammered out a staccato drumbeat.

Linden stepped out of the driver's seat. She smiled. "Hey, stranger."

Songbirds never sounded sweeter to Walker's ears.

Yeah, by now he'd figured out he had it bad.

Across the width of the Toyota, Walker rested the palms of his hands on the roof of the car. "Hey, yourself. Good to have you home."

Her eyes clouded.

"Good to be back," Linden corrected. She balanced a green and white box in her arms.

Walker's eyes widened. "Is that . . . Krispy Kreme?"

Linden laughed. "Bought them on Peace Street first thing this morning when the hot sign came on."

She pushed the box over the top of the car toward him.

Lifting the lid, he closed his eyes and inhaled. Nothing like the aroma of fried dough and sugar to jumpstart a man's heart.

At least, a Southern man's heart.

Not to mention what the sight of Linden in a lime green t-shirt and khaki shorts did to his heart.

He crammed half the donut in his mouth.

"Slow down, Injun man." She sidled over to his side of the car. "Or you're going to choke. Again."

Linden reached for the box. His hand covered hers.

"Aren't you going to share with the guys?"

He swallowed and grabbed her by the belt loops on her shorts. "Not feeling in a sharing mood today."

Pulling her closer, he bent his head. "Thought you said you bought them for me."

Giving him a sideways glance, she pointed at his face. "You've got sugar on your mouth."

Tightening his hold on her, his lips parted. "Why don't you take care of it for me?"

And to his delight, she did.

"I've got a surprise for you."

She cut her eyes over the truck cab to Walker.

Lord-a mercy, she'd almost forgotten what the sight of him did to a person's heart.

Almost . . .

Linden's lips curved. "What surprise?" She wasn't above admitting to a growing fondness for trucks with dirt on the floor.

"We're going on a field trip. To a place where cars can't go. Where you can only travel by wing or on foot. We're going horse-back riding into the Snowbird backcountry this afternoon." He frowned. "You ride, don't you?"

Using her forefinger, Linden smoothed out the furrow at the bridge of his nose. "Anybody ever tell you, you scowl too much? And yes, summers with Gram in Raleigh involved horse camp."

He loosened his grip on the wheel. "That's a relief. I've already set it up to talk with Mrs. Swimmer and figured horseback was a more scenic route to her house."

Linden nodded. "Good. If the painters are following the Quilt Trail loop, we need to get her permission to paint her barn as soon as possible. Thanks for taking care of that while I was gone."

"I didn't take care of much. She called me."

"That's a switch. I got the impression from your mom Mrs. Swimmer was much opposed to the commemoration. Like you." She elbowed him as she scooted toward the center of the seat.

Walker pressed his shoulder against hers. "Like I was. After the publicity in the *Advocate* about the diary you found, she said she'd changed her mind and had something to tell us."

"Huh . . ." Linden tilted her head. "You think she knows something about Sarah Jane or Leila?"

Walker laid his arm along the length of the seat and leaned closer. "I'm sure we'll know soon enough." His lips moved across the curve of her neck and nibbled.

Ignoring the tingle that reached all the way to her toes, she grasped both his shoulders. "I'll take a rain check on that." She smiled at his expression. "But business first."

He slumped but with an amused grimace. "Me and my big mouth."

She helped him saddle the horses. Clicking his tongue, he swung his horse toward the perimeter of his property where it abutted the national park. She followed alongside him across the high mountain meadow until they came to a forest trail, nothing more than a narrow, faded footpath.

He led the way, and her horse clip-clopped behind. The thick, green canopy of trees soon cut off most of the sunlight. The temperature—and for this she was grateful—also dropped five degrees. A startled white-tailed deer crashed away through the brush.

"Stay with me," Walker called. "Don't let Daisy wander off the trail. This time of year no telling what you'd encounter in these woods. Black bear, wild boar, bobcat. Better stay close to your guide."

Linden made sure he saw her roll her eyes at him.

He directed the horses around enormous trunks belonging to trees so immense she strained back in the saddle to peer to where their leafy tops pressed upward toward the sliver of blue sky.

"This wilderness area is an old-growth forest," he gestured. "Like the Joyce Kilmer Memorial Forest. Eighty percent of the virgin forests were lost in the Smokies and Blue Ridge before the Forest Service bought these tracts and saved them from the timber companies."

"Companies like the Birchfield's?"

"I wasn't trying to—"

"No worries." She waved a hand. "Since hanging out with you, I'm getting more eco-friendly every day."

They grinned at each other.

She lifted her face, allowing a ray of light piercing the canopy to warm her cheeks. "That Kilmer guy was a poet and soldier from the First World War, wasn't he?" A chittering squirrel scolded the intruders from a nearby branch.

Walker negotiated around a tree trunk that dwarfed them. "That's right. And as to be expected, author of my favorite poem, 'Trees'." He threw her a teasing glance over his shoulder.

She steered Daisy over one of the fallen timbers that littered the forest floor. "'I think that I shall never see a poem lovely as a tree.'"

He swiveled in the saddle. "Very good, Miss Birchfield."

She batted her eyes at him. "I memorized it when I realized what a tree nut you were."

"I appreciate the backhanded compliment." He cocked his head. "I think."

His horse, Old Blue, picked its way among the kelly-green moss, past mushrooms and gnarled gray lichen.

She followed him past a lush carpet of spring violets, a bank of ferns, and a whimsical jack-in-the-pulpit. "These trees are like giants."

The faint sound of songbirds filtered through the rafters of forest branches. Their songs of courtship and nesting echoed around the wood.

"My people called these giants Standing People and had great respect for the blessings they shared with us." Walker glanced around. "To me this place has its own mystical magic. And some-times when I come to the mountain to pray, I feel the great Creator closer here in this green cathedral than in the white-steepled cre-ation of man's worship in the valley below."

Flushing, he lowered his eyes to his boots. "That sounds crazy, doesn't it?"

Linden shook her head, leaning to pat Daisy's neck. "I get what you mean. And for the record, sanity may be overrated."

"Some of these trees are over four hundred years old. Here when De Soto encountered The People for the first time." Walker pointed out the different species as they passed.

Tulip poplar. Oaks. The flowering dogwood and beech under-story. Carolina silverbells. The decaying, splintered stumps of the once-proud chestnuts before a blight decimated them along the Appalachians.

"We're still fighting an infestation of aphids and beetles among the hemlocks and pines." Walker sighed. "It's not only man who takes a toll on these beauties. Speaking of beauties?"

He wheeled his horse and stopped beside one small sapling. "A basswood that has found sanctuary in our mountains, too."

As she pulled alongside him, Walker plucked one triangular shaped leaf and tucked it behind her ear. Rising in the stirrups, he reached forward and unclasped the clip that held her hair in place.

Linden threw him an exasperated look, but she tossed her head, letting her hair fall free down her back. "Might as well not bother fixing it every morning with you around."

"Might as well not." Walker curled a strand of her hair around his finger. "I'll bring you back to see the bright yellow blossoms this tree will sprout in about a month."

She fidgeted in the saddle. Timetables made her antsy. "What's so great about this little tree compared to these other titans?" A scarlet tanager darted from its perch to a safer distance.

He smiled. "Little trees need our guardianship most of all. To be protected and nourished so they can attain the full measure of their God-given potential."

She blew out a breath at a gnat hovering in her face.

Both hands on the saddle horn, he planted a kiss on her mouth, seizing the opportunity she'd presented. "Besides," Walker sat back. "This little tree has become my new all-time favorite."

She scrutinized the tree whose leaves just topped her head. "Really?"

"Yeah." He favored her with a lopsided smile. "'Cause the basswood is also called the linden tree."

Her heart whooshed. Who knew tree talk could be so romantic? Or this pay-for-every-word Cherokee?

"I'll bet you bring all your girlfriends here to brag about the trees."

His eyes sparking, Walker placed his thumb and forefinger on her chin. He tugged her mouth closer and traced the line of her jaw with his lips. "Just the ones named Linden."

Awhile later, they emerged from the shelter of the trees at the top of a ridge. He pointed out the white clapboard farmhouse and adjacent red-roofed barn in the grassy meadow. As they drew near, they skirted a vegetable garden, a squawking chicken pen, and an orchard.

Shading her eyes with her hand, she glanced at a bald knob high above the bluff overlooking the farmyard. "This barn's on the Quilt Trail?"

"We came the long, scenic way." He nudged his head toward the house. "The road branches right off Highway 143 and Cartridge Cove, I promise."

He called a greeting to a bundle of clothes waiting for them on the back porch. The bundle of clothes shifted, and Linden's eyes widened at the sight of the shriveled old woman. Possibly the oldest human being she'd ever seen.

Walker halted Old Blue outside the barn. Swinging his leg over, he looped the reins into a loose knot over a fence post. He held Daisy steady while Linden kicked free of the stirrups and slid to the ground.

"That's Mrs. Swimmer? She looks ancient."

He secured Daisy. "Think she may have known your Sarah Jane?"

Linden took a minute to calculate that possibility as he laughed. "Okay." She punched Walker in the arm. "Not possible, I guess."

"Mrs. Swimmer is in her nineties, though." Stepping inside the barn, he filled two plastic buckets with water from the spigot outside the barn door.

"What do you think she wants to tell us?" She fed Daisy a bunch of hay. "At her age, do you think she's . . . ?" Linden swallowed, unsure how to phrase this delicately.

He tossed handfuls of hay on the ground for Old Blue. "Mrs. Swimmer's a spring chicken compared to many Cherokee women 'round here. Her mama was one hundred and five and, like Mrs. Swimmer, lived alone on this farm with only her great-grandsons coming by on Saturdays to help."

Looping Linden's arm through the crook of his elbow, he strolled over to the old woman.

"One hundred and five?" Linden whispered in his ear.

"Good, clean mountain air. Strong, Cherokee blood. What better combination for a long life? You should try it."

She still pondered that pseudo-invitation when he threw out his hand. "Thanks for the invite, Mrs. Swimmer."

The old woman beckoned them into the house. "Been expecting you." Her aged face bore the crisscrossing signs of a life long lived. Her cheekbones were high like Walker's, but the contours of her face more hollow-cheeked. Sharp, birdlike eyes sparkled with the promise of years yet of vitality and energy.

Walker performed the introductions.

"Let me get you some refreshment after your long ride." Mrs. Swimmer squinted into their faces. "You're looking a mite peckish, Walker Crowe. This girlfriend of yours not feeding you?"

He laughed. "She feeds me fine." He placed his arm around Linden's waist.

If you counted Krispy Kreme donuts.

But Linden broke away from Walker and followed Mrs. Swimmer into the linoleum-tiled kitchen. "Oh, Mrs. Swimmer, don't bother with—"

He snagged her arm in passing. "Some liquid refreshment would hit the spot, Mrs. Swimmer. And any dessert you think might go bad before you get around to eating it, we'd be glad to help with, too."

Linden rounded her eyes at him. "I don't—"

He squeezed Linden's hand.

"Not a bother." Mrs. Swimmer flitted a blue-veined hand. "Don't get as much company as I'd like." She opened a Frigidaire Linden suspected came off the assembly line circa 1960. "Take a seat at the table. Most folks seem to gather in the kitchen anyways. Saves me a few steps. I've made blueberry pie. I'm assuming you still like blueberry pie, Walker Crowe?"

He lugged Linden to a seat at the Formica-topped table. "Sure do, ma'am."

"But—"

"Sit, Linden," he hissed in her ear. "What's the rush? Consider this lesson five or six."

Linden sank into the chair across from Walker.

With a crackle of ice cubes from the blue tray in the freezer, Mrs. Swimmer poured them each a glass of tea. Sweet tea, of course.

"Thank you, Auntie." He took a sip.

"Auntie?" Linden mouthed. "I didn't realize—"

He gave a tiny shake of his head. "Term of respect for elders," he answered *sotto voce*.

"I must say," Mrs. Swimmer sliced the pie into quadrants. "This girl may be too pretty for the likes of a rascal like you, Walker Crowe. I assume you want Cool Whip on top, boy?" Topping the pie with a dollop of cream, she handed the plate over.

Linden laughed at the expression on Walker's face and warmed to the old woman.

Sheepish, he cut into his pie with the edge of his fork. "I expect you've figured right as usual, Auntie."

The old woman cackled and settled herself into a seat between the pair. Linden waited for the niceties of Cherokee—and Southern—hospitality to be completed. Mrs. Swimmer offered seconds, which Walker declined. Of course, Mrs. Swimmer had to offer again, to be sure her guest was sincere and not just being polite. Patting his stomach, Walker declined once more.

Satisfied the customs that held society together had been overseen, Mrs. Swimmer laid her hands upon the table. "I wasn't in favor of dredging up the past for the festival in Cartridge Cove." She crinkled her eyes Linden's way. "You finished reading that old diary?"

"No, ma'am. I keep thinking I will, but," Linden smiled at Walker. "I keep so busy here in Cartridge Cove, I've only had odd moments to read an entry or two at a time. I'm working on it, though."

"Good. I'd like to hear sometime the rest of that Sarah Jane's journey. I think I can add a few pieces of the puzzle for you today . . ." Mrs. Swimmer's voice trailed off as if visualizing some long ago event or person.

Linden had the sense to be still. She'd observed, since coming to the Snowbird, the Cherokee told their stories as if they'd happened yesterday. Recalling an emotional pain that lingered, too.

"But when the article came out last week about how you and that young lady, Marvela found an old diary . . ."

Linden fought not to look at Walker lest her twitching lips betray her into a full-fledged laugh. Though on second thought, she guessed to someone Mrs. Swimmer's age, Gram was a young one. Maybe Gram was right. Age was only a matter of perspective.

". . . I got to thinking about the members of my own family who escaped from federal custody and made their way home from the Trail."

Linden wrinkled her forehead. "Some of the Cherokee returned?"

Walker nodded. "Junaluska led two escape attempts. The first time he and the others were caught. Twenty or so escaped capture. After a few years in Oklahoma, he walked all the way home."

"Folks round here," Mrs. Swimmer poked her chin toward the mountains beyond the window. "All got their own family stories handed down. Some slipped away over in Tennessee. Some crossed the great river west and yet still managed to find their way home. My great-granddaddy, great-grandmother, and auntie were three who did just that."

The old woman propped her elbows on the chipped tabletop. "'Course that was ages before my time, but my great-grandmother lived a long, long time, well over a hundred years. The auntie who came back," she tapped her finger against her head. "Never was quite right afterward. My grandmother told me the stories. About the hardships they endured. It changed them. Marked them forever."

Mrs. Swimmer reclined in her chair. "Sad old lady, that auntie who returned. Wandered if you didn't watch her. Not much use for farm work, but my great-grandmother was a pure saint, according to my granny, the way she took care of the auntie. My great-grandmother's name was Miriam—Miry my great-grandfather called her. She and he walked all the way back, cleared this land and farmed till he joined Thomas's Legion."

Walker set down his glass. "The Legion?" he breathed. "Really?"

Mrs. Swimmer snaked a look at him, a pleased smile on her face. "I see you've studied your Cherokee history and have heard tell of them."

Linden gave Walker a quizzical look.

He nodded. "Confederate regiment raised by Will Thomas, a white man adopted by the Cherokee. The force consisted of both white Appalachians and Cherokee. Fought all over the Tennessee and Virginia theater. The last Confederate troops to surrender, after Appomattox, not far from here near Waynesville. Fierce fighters . . ."

Walker coughed into his hand. ". . . took a few Yankee scalps, I understand, before Thomas strongly encouraged them to cease and desist."

Mrs. Swimmer's eyes twinkled. "My great-grandfather—the one who returned from the Trail—died in one of the last skirmishes near Bryson City. But when I read your story in the paper, Linden, I realized it was time the truth was told about the Trail. And sometimes there's nothing to beat a physical object in bringing home the truth to generations so greatly removed from the tragedy of the Removal."

"I don't understand, Mrs. Swimmer."

The old woman heaved herself to her feet. Walker scooted his chair back to offer a hand, which she waved away. "Land sakes, boy, you're making me feel old."

She tottered toward a hallway. "Be right back. I got it out of Miry's trunk when I knew you'd be coming today."

Bursting with anticipation, Linden sighed at Walker. He shrugged his shoulders. "Patience," he urged.

Accompanied by creaking floorboards, Mrs. Swimmer emerged with a folded quilt in her arms. The background had once,

Linden guessed, been snowy white, but over time had faded to a cream color. Brownish squiggles marked the backside.

Mrs. Swimmer draped it over her chair and unfolded the quilt top to reveal red flowers and green stems.

Linden gasped. "A Carolina Lily." She reached out a tentative hand and drew back.

Mrs. Swimmer patted the quilt. "It's okay to touch, honey. This old quilt's been through the march, the woods, war, depression, and I don't know what-all. It won't dissolve today."

"Is it?" Linden gulped. "It couldn't possibly be the same—"

"The very same one that Sarah Jane of your'n made." With a gnarled, shaky hand, Mrs. Swimmer flipped a corner of the quilt. "Right here. Initials S. J. H. Dated," her finger pointed. "1838." She glanced up. "Sarah Jane took it with her on that mission of mercy with the dislocated Cherokee, didn't she?"

Linden's eyes shone. "Oh, Mrs. Swimmer. What a treasure."

To think Sarah Jane's hands had touched this same fabric so long ago.

Mrs. Swimmer caressed the quilt with her work-worn palm. "Been in my family so long, it has its own story, just as important to tell. I reckon if you twist my arm, I'd be willing to loan it to the museum in Cartridge Cove." She traced the muted red petal of a lily. "Leastways for the duration of the festival."

"How?" Linden reminded herself to breathe. "How did it come into your family's . . ." She paused, careful to choose the right word. "Stewardship?"

Walker lifted the back of the quilt to the overhead light. "What's on the backside, Auntie? Looks like . . ." His finger stroked the pointed tip of what resembled a mountain.

Several mountain peaks and the passes in between.

"Passed to me by my auntie." The old woman clapped Walker on the shoulder. "It's a map drawn with whatever natural resources were along the Trail. Sarah Jane or somebody drew this map to guide those who could escape toward home."

Mrs. Swimmer placed a hand on Linden's arm. "And my great-grandfather took Miry's family name as he possessed no other. Teesateskie. My maiden name."

The old woman took a deep breath. "But I believe, Linden, you know him better by his Cherokee name. Touch the Clouds."

22

Pierce had become a wreck of his former self, and as Sarah's father approached his final days on earth.

"I'm taking my father home to die."

That penetrated the malaise into which Pierce had descended. He frowned. "You can't. It's too far. You're just a woman."

She tightened her lips. "I can and I will. He deserves to lie beside my mother. And while I've breath in my body, I will see that he does."

Pierce shook his head. "It's too dangerous." For the first time in weeks, genuine concern for her shone out of his eyes.

It was of little comfort to Sarah that at last, after so much, for once he finally seemed to see her.

But go she would, despite his repeated attempts to change her mind.

The first thing she did in preparation for leaving was to create manumission papers for Yolanda and Samson. Then, she forged Leila Hummingbird's signature and added her father's, Dr. Horace Hopkins, to the bottom. She didn't know if the papers would pass intense scrutiny, Sarah told Samson, but she'd tried to make them look as official as possible.

Yolanda twisted her hands. "Lord-a mercy, why you do this, Miss Sarah?"

"Because it's the right thing to do. Head north," she cautioned Samson. She gave him what supplies she could spare.

Samson shifted Leila's trunk and the last remaining Hummingbird possessions into Sarah's wagon.

"You could trade those candlesticks," she argued with him. "That clock is worth money. None of the Hummingbirds are left to care anyhow."

"I care, Miss Sarah." He lifted his chin. "Folks will be suspicious enough with two black 'uns like us in possession of the wagon and oxen."

Stunned, Yolanda examined the papers. "You know I can't read or write, Miss Sarah. But I thank you." She pressed Sarah's arm. "God bless you and yours for all eternity."

The soldiers offered no resistance when they saw the white doctor's daughter drive her wagon out of the line, followed by Samson and Yolanda in the other wagon. Their job was to herd the Cherokee. Not detain American citizens like Sarah Jane Hopkins and her servants. The wagons parted at the ferry landing.

Sarah steered her wagon eastward, retracing the painful trek of earlier weeks. The wagon wheels rolled through the same rutted grooves of the Trail. Away from exile. Toward home.

Milking each ounce of daylight, she drove the team as hard as she could.

The earth awakened once more as the wheels wended east. Sarah barely noticed the increasing warmth as February moved aside for March. She kept herself alert on the driver's seat by rewriting in her mind everyone's personal histories to her own satisfaction. That Touch the Clouds had survived drowning. That it was he who'd taken LilyRose.

And, spirited LilyRose's mother away to the Magic Lake high above the mountaintops. Where all hurts healed.

Fantasy, but it soothed a tiny bit of the raw, aching part of Sarah's heart. In Tennessee, Pierce appeared as out of nowhere one day.

He tied his horse to the back of the wagon and slid onto the seat next to her. "I thought . . ." He swallowed and kept his eyes downcast. "It was time . . . to go home."

She studied him. His face brooked no questions. Pierce would've searched until there remained no hope of finding Leila alive in the winter blizzards of the Plains.

"Please, Sarah." He clenched his fists in his lap. "I'm sorry for so many things." Uncertainty quivered in his voice. "Could we go back together to Cartridge Cove?"

And she resolved to never speak Leila Hummingbird's name in his presence again. She handed Pierce the reins. He clucked his tongue under his teeth and headed the team over the mountains. A week later, they returned to Cartridge Cove, slipping back to the home place under the cover of night.

Pierce carried her father into his bedroom. She made her father as comfortable as she could. Pierce left them to their privacy.

His eyes weak, her father attempted a smile. Holding his hand, Sarah recited the twenty-third Psalm, a sorrowful reminder of how she'd done the same for Touch the Clouds's grandmother. Willing herself not to cry, Sarah sang the song that had become the strength of many along the Trail, "Guide Me O Thou Great Jehovah."

Tears could wait. And she prayed out loud over her father that Jehovah Himself would guide His ever-faithful servant, Horace Hopkins, in his final journey to the Beyond.

As the rays of first light shattered the night sky, her beloved papa turned his head for one last look out the window—perchance to see where he was headed—and breathed his last.

In the hours that followed, Pierce summoned the neighbors. They attended to the necessary preparations for the burial. After the funeral, Pierce found Sarah, alone in the surgery, alone in her grief for her father.

He cleared his throat. "What plans have you, Sarah Jane, now your father has passed to his reward? Have you family to take you in?"

She shook her head.

He tugged at the knot in his tie. "It isn't proper you should stay here." Pierce flushed. "Alone with me."

She stilled the restless fretting of her fingers at the fringed hem of her shawl.

"I'm proposing to continue your father's life mission to keep this clinic alive. To doctor the needs of this community he so faithfully served."

Sarah lowered her lashes. "He would've wanted that." She'd need to find a new place to settle. "Perhaps the Board would appoint me as a teacher to one of the other mission schools on the frontier."

Pierce let out a prolonged sigh. "I did not explain myself well." He went down on one knee. Sarah's eyes widened.

"I'm asking if you'd marry me, Miss Hopkins. That if you'd consent to be my wife, we could build a life here."

Her hand flew to her throat. The irony of all she'd longed for gifted to her at this moment struck her, and she fought the urge to laugh. Because Sarah feared the sound that would emerge from her lips might be on the hysterical side.

And that once she started, she might not be able to stop until Pierce would be forced to lock her in her room for her own safety.

He must have noted the dubious look in her eyes for he took both of Sarah's hands and held them in his. "I'd be the best husband I could be to you, Sarah Jane. You'd never suffer from want as you have these last months."

Sarah withdrew her hand and waved that concern away. But Pierce captured her hand and brought it to his mouth, which trembled on the delicate skin of her wrist. "Sarah . . ." His voice deepened.

Craving the touch of his lips upon hers, Sarah shivered as she gazed at his head bent over her hand. At the tight, blond curls she'd always ached to run her fingers through.

As his wife, surely she dared.

The weakness within her for Pierce resurfaced fierce and tempestuous. Her love for him flared as strong as it ever had.

And she accepted his invitation.

Mrs. Simkins at the Mercantile helped Sarah into her best brown-checked frock for the ceremony. "You two were ever the pair. And after all you've been through together."

The morning after her wedding night, Sarah awoke to find her marriage bed empty of her groom. Throwing back the coverlet, she resolved to create a brand new quilt honoring the bliss of this most longed-for union between her and Pierce. Stretching in her nightgown, she marveled at the love she felt for her husband. At the love possible between a husband and wife.

She'd never imagined such joy. Sarah hugged herself on the cool, spring mountain morning. Oh, she prayed, that she might be the helpmate her husband desired. On bare feet, she tiptoed to the mullioned window at the sound of a strangled cry from outside.

Her gaze locked onto Pierce, his nightshirt stuffed into trousers. Leaning over the wood block, he flung the axe to the ground. Sinking to his knees, he buried his face into his hands and wept. His shoulders shook.

And then Sarah knew, though they'd never speak her name, that the shadow of Leila would always hover between them. That neither time nor Sarah Jane Hopkins would ever erase Leila from Pierce's heart.

She recalled the cautionary tale Touch the Clouds shared with her of the beautiful woman and the choice of wisdom or beauty. And understood at last his warning to beware of longing for that which she could never possess. Because in her foolishness, she'd chosen—like others before her—the hummingbird.

But, the hummingbird did not want her.

Sarah put away her wedding dress and pushed Leila's green trunk into a corner in her old room. Donning a serviceable work dress, she gave her husband time to recover his dignity. She set about making breakfast, planning how she'd sow the garden this year, scrub the house from top to bottom today.

And keep doing what needed to be done.

But she struggled with the deep well of grief for all she'd experienced, all she'd lost, and all she'd never have with Pierce. And for the first time in her memory, Sarah was unable to find any peace at the throne of her Consolation.

Often morose, Pierce nonetheless fulfilled his marital duty to her. Unlike her father, however, Pierce catered his business toward the white citizens of Cartridge Cove. As if he was unable to bear the sight of another Cherokee face.

Because soon after, word began to circulate some of The People had hidden deep in the mountains from the soldiers. Few trusted the Cartridge Cove citizens enough to venture into town. The white Appalachians by mutual consent with the Snowbird Cherokee each kept themselves to themselves.

In May, her womb quickened with life. And concurrently, her spirit stirred to life, too. Especially as June brought the flickering light of the fireflies and tuned her heart to the One True Light. In the chirping of the crickets on a summer evening, Sarah heard His voice calling her name.

Her joy returned in full measure when the first snow laced the Snowbird. As she held her dear Johnathan in her arms, her grief eroded. The baby assuaged her soul. Her Consolation had not forsaken her or left her outcast.

For in His mercy, He'd provided another type of solace for those bereft by man.

23

2018—Cartridge Cove

Quincy pushed his glasses farther onto the bridge of his nose. "Lucky for us the Civil War regimental rosters are so well-documented. Like Thomas's Legion of Cherokees and Highlanders, Mountaineers 69th North Carolina."

He squinted at the computer and frowned. "Except for Companies C and D Cherokee Battalion." He groaned. "No known roster exists of the Cherokee recruits of those companies."

Linden slumped. "Oh."

"But as I recall . . ." He clicked the cursor. "Company A and B rejoined Thomas and the rest of the Legion for the final days of the war. Maybe, just maybe, Touch the Clouds was a member of one of those."

She held her breath. Her hands twisted into knots.

He spun his chair around. "Voila!"

Coming full circle, he pointed at the name on the screen. "Company A, Touch the Clouds Teesateskie. Mustered in as a sergeant at Quallatown on April 9, 1862."

Linden peered over his shoulder at the computer screen. "He's real." She shook her head. "Until Mrs. Swimmer showed me the Carolina Lily quilt, I was almost at the point of believing Sarah Jane had tried her hand at fiction."

Quincy grinned. "A truth stranger than fiction. Try this on. The last surviving Union army widow died in 2003. Her husband fought against Thomas's Legion." He underscored the line item containing Touch the Clouds Teesateskie's name. "He's real, all right."

"But we still don't know how Sarah Jane's quilt came to be in his possession."

Carrying a sheaf of papers, Emmaline ambled into Quincy's office. "That quilt, and him, certainly walked a long way home."

Linden liked the way Quincy's face transformed at the sight of the Cherokee girl.

"How went the recording of Leila's story for the talking trees, Em?"

Emmaline smiled. "Fine. As did Quincy's rendition of Pierce." She drifted over to the filing cabinet. "Still working on getting Walker to agree to do the voice-over for Touch the Clouds."

With amusement, Linden noted how Quincy followed Emmaline's movement around the tiny cubicle.

Emmaline slammed the cabinet drawer shut. "Walker's being difficult as usual. Claims he's too shy."

Both women snorted in unison at the likelihood of that.

Emmaline flopped into an overstuffed leather armchair. "Taciturn maybe?"

"Stubborn and contrary more like it." Linden leaned against the desk. "Speaking of finding Pierce, Quince . . ."

"Boy genius having a slow day?" Emmaline bit the inside of her cheek. "Chop, chop, Dr. Sawyer."

With an effort, Quincy tore his gaze from Emmaline and scrolled through the rest of the names in the Thomas Legion. He muttered something uncomplimentary under his breath about stubborn females.

Linden perched her hip on the corner of his desk, her foot dangling. "What are y'all up to tonight?"

"Quince and I thought we'd do a quick supper at the diner and then go to Asheville for some nightlife." Em cocked her head. "Why don't you and Walker come with us? It'd be—"

The boy genius emitted a growl.

Linden laughed. "Or not. Four can be such a crowd." She shrugged. "Walker's got his shift at the fire station, anyway. Maybe next time."

Quincy jabbed at the screen. "I've found him."

Linden wended her way around the desk. "What did you find?"

Quincy flashed a triumphant grin. "And you'll never guess who the mysterious Pierce has turned out to be related to."

Her brows constricted. "Who?"

"You."

Linden's eyes widened. "Me?"

Emmaline joined them as all three scrutinized the faded ink of the original document from the state archives on the monitor. Her hand squeezed Linden's arm. "Birchfield, Pierce. Doctor assigned to the 69th. Mustered in September 30, 1862, Quallatown." She high-fived Linden.

Quincy typed furiously into the search engine. "I have an idea." A newspaper clipping from the Waynesville Mountaineer emerged onto the screen.

"Just as I thought. Dr. Pierce Birchfield attended the thirtieth anniversary Battalion reunion." Quincy pulled up an indistinct black and white image of a group of old men—Cherokee and white Appalachian—arranged around a tattered Confederate flag. "There. That's your Pierce Birchfield."

Linden swallowed past the lump in her throat. It was indeed an older version of the young man in the daguerreotype. Which meant the young woman—his bride—had to have been Sarah Jane.

Swiveling in the chair, Quincy drew Emmaline onto the armrest and encircled her waist. "If you'd give me a little more time, I think I could dig up some census records now we know their surnames." Em snuggled into the crook of his arm.

Linden resisted the urge to smile. She could take a hint. Time to get lost and leave these two to their evening. Besides, she couldn't wait to get back to Gram's and finish reading the diary. She was close, very close now, to the end of Sarah Jane's story.

She grabbed her purse. "Have fun tonight." She winked.

Emmaline's cheeks reddened, but Quincy gestured toward the door. "Good-bye, Linden."

She was still laughing when she drove out of the Center parking lot and headed for her grandmother's house. Passing Walker's truck at the fire station, she resisted the urge to stop. She really needed to get a handle on her emotions.

The festival would come in less than a month and go—along with her. No matter how much she enjoyed Walker's company, no matter how much he haunted her every waking thought, this thing between them was temporary. A summer romance.

Nothing more. Linden didn't do more, couldn't allow more, than casual liaisons. Wasn't fair to the guy. Not in her bucket list for life.

So she liked him.

Okay, she liked him a lot. Maybe more than anyone she'd ever known.

But that other "L" word wasn't going to happen. Not in her vocabulary. She'd discovered the hard, painful way physicality was the least of what it took to make a relationship work. Although, Linden flushed, she and Walker possessed that in spades.

What counted in the end was common interests, common goals, a common faith. She frowned. Why did it always have to come back to God? She'd thrown away her chance long ago for that sort of happily-ever-after.

So, she'd readjusted her goals into the only purpose that served to get her out of bed in those terrible days past. She couldn't undo the choices she'd made. Walker deserved better than she could give.

And that, plus God, Linden knew on some instinctive level, would be a deal breaker for Walker Crowe.

From the church portico, Walker allowed himself the pleasure of watching Linden emerge from her grandmother's Caddy. The sunlight danced across hitherto undisclosed reddish highlights in her light brown hair. Worn in her usual topknot.

His lips tweaked upward. He'd get that sorted out soon enough. His gaze traveled to the simple strand of pearls at her throat to the sleeveless, belted pink linen dress she wore.

A surge of doubt pierced his heart.

What was someone like Linden Birchfield doing in a place like Cartridge Cove? He stuffed his hands in his pockets. What was someone like her doing with someone like him?

And how long before she wised up or grew restless and moved on from both Cartridge Cove and him?

Marvela gave him a strong hug. "Where's that handsome uncle of yours, Walker?"

Linden's eyes lit at the sight of him, and some of the tension that had built inside him loosened. But purplish shadows bruised the fragile skin underneath her eyes.

As if she'd worried or fretted all night over something.

She reached for his hand. He caught it and threaded his fingers through hers.

A fleeting smile crossed her pale features as she cut her eyes at Marvela. "Really Gram? What about 'Hi, Walker. How are you? Beautiful morning, isn't it?'"

"I'm sure the boy knows what I meant, Honey Girl." Marvela peered from under the brim of her garden party hat, crowned with delicate silk violets. For a congregation that favored blue jeans and boots even on the Lord's Day.

And only Marvela could pull it off.

"You understand." Marvela tapped his arm. "Don't you, son?"

"Front and center, Miss Marvela. He's conferring with the good pastor about the gospel singing scheduled for the festival."

Marvela nodded, and with a significant glance toward Linden, left them to their own devices.

"You okay today?"

Linden shot him a look.

"You seem . . . Kind of . . ."

She rounded her eyes at him, arching a brow.

Open mouth, insert horse.

She pulled away, smoothing her dress. "Right as rain. Isn't that the expression?"

Right only if it wasn't raining on the Fourth of July or your birthday.

She moved toward the portico. "Shall we go inside?"

"Mom's asked me to lend a pair of arms to the Sunday school effort. Feel like helping out, too?"

"Sure. Lead the way."

And he got the distinct impression she was relieved not to have to deal with the sermon. As he pushed open the door, a blast of air conditioning and the raucous sounds of thirty of so rambunctious children held in captivity on a bright June day filled the air.

She flinched.

"Mom's doing double duty teaching the combined third and fourth grade."

Walker pondered Linden's uncharacteristic silence, but continued along the mural-splashed hallway to the nursery. "I thought you might prefer to assist Mrs. Swimmer who volunteers here every . . ."

Linden's face had gone ashen.

Walker opened the door. Baby smells, mostly pleasant like lotion and shampoo, permeated the air.

Mrs. Swimmer, seated in a maple rocker, bounced a baby to the child's delight on her knee. "Glad you decided to drop by, son. Could use a hand. Must be something in the Singing Creek water. Everywhere you look, babies, babies, babies."

Striding forward, he cranked the handle of the baby swing, setting another tiny tot into motion once more. "Sure thing."

He rescued a toddler who'd managed to hoist himself to a standing position but clung to the wall unable to sit down again.

One of the babies, her thick black hair scrunched into a ponytail on the top of her head, saw her chance to escape and took it.

Linden shrank against the doorframe.

"Quick, Linden," he gestured. "Come in and shut the door. The inmates are rioting."

When she didn't move, Walker inserted himself between the baby girl and the door. He tugged Linden inside.

"Here." Scooping the baby girl out of harm's way, he handed Linden the baby and reached past her to shut the door behind them.

Linden went rigid.

Squatting on the matted floor, Walker distracted the toddler with a set of foam blocks.

"I-I can't . . ."

He looked up at the raspy note in Linden's voice. She held the infant away from her as if the child were toxic.

"What's wrong?"

"I d-don't . . ." Linden's chest rose and fell, her breathing labored. "I-I c-can't do this . . ."

He half-rose.

"Don't m-make m-me . . ." Her voice hitched in a smothered sob.

Hearing the anxiety in Linden's voice, the baby girl wailed. Linden swayed like a river reed in the wind.

"Walker, take the baby from her now." He met Mrs. Swimmer's concerned eyes. "Do it."

Taking the child from Linden, he cradled the baby.

Linden sagged against the wall, her hand over her mouth. "I'm sorry. I'd hoped . . . I've prayed, but it never gets . . ."

She gagged, her face turning a sickly green as Marvela burst through the nursery door. Linden's grandmother, for once, looked her age, the wrinkles unusually pronounced.

Marvela reached for Linden. "I came as soon as I realized."

Linden flung off Marvela's arm and raced for the door. Walker, the baby in his arms, started after her.

Marvela caught his sleeve. "No. Let me go."

Through the plate glass window that overlooked the playground, he watched Linden stagger toward the wooded lot and drop to her knees. She retched over and over into the pine needles.

A dreadful uncertainty squeezed his insides. "What's going on, Miss Marvela? Is she sick?"

Tears shimmered like dewdrops in Marvela's eyes. "Some days are better than others."

Fear stabbed at his heart. The worst thing Walker could imagine popped into his mind. "Does she have—?"

Marvela shook her head. "No, honey." She swallowed. "She's just feeling poorly today." She patted the baby Walker held. "I'll take her home."

She patted his cheek, too, as if he, like the baby, had need of comfort. "Try not to worry, son. But she sure could use your prayers."

As if he wouldn't do both. "Can I call her later . . . to make sure . . . ?"

Marvela headed for the door. "Better let her call you."

Disquieted, he watched Marvela help Linden to her feet. Linden shook with dry heaves. And resembling a sad, rag doll, she sagged against her grandmother.

"How much do you like her, Walker Crowe?"

Walker had almost forgotten Mrs. Swimmer's presence. "What do you mean?"

Mrs. Swimmer hummed a lullaby. Her foot tapped out a beat as she rocked forward and backward. Forward and backward.

"I think you know what I mean."

His eyes darted around the nursery, out the window to where Marvela guided Linden to the parking lot. His stomach clenched.

"I like her a lot."

The old woman stopped crooning, but the rhythm of the glider continued. "Still not ready to commit yourself to that other word yet, are you?" She brushed her lips across the blond fuzz of the infant's head.

She gazed at him, her raisin eyes sharp as flint. "You're right to count the cost first. Because with every precious gift of love from the Creator, there is always a price to pay."

"I don't understand."

"A cost. Of independence. A willingness to share the pain of deep wounds. A sacrifice of dreams on the altar of another's good."

Forward and backward. Backward and forward, she rocked.

"Pray," she advised him. "Pray and count it well. For your own sake and hers."

24

1863-1900—Cartridge Cove

Joy upon joy followed upon the heels of Johnathan's birth. Sarah Jane birthed David Horace a year later. Ethan the next year. Her stair-step babies. And Caleb, when she believed her childbearing days to be over, arrived when Ethan was seven years old.

Like sorghum on biscuits, she slathered them with the love their father spurned. And she fed them on tales of heroic wielders of the gospel like their grandfather and the brave, quietest People in adversity she'd ever seen.

David came home one afternoon, spouting tales of an Indian princess who prowled the ruins of Chestnut Hill. He'd heard the ghost story at school from one of the boys whose family claimed the land surrounding the plantation after the house burned that fateful day of the Removal. Sarah shushed him and told him to stop speaking nonsense before his father came out of the surgery.

In those busy years, she reckoned Pierce made good on his promise to her—to be the best husband he could be. What she hadn't understood was how little he'd left of himself to give. He made sure, though, she and the boys never wanted. He tore down the little mission house, expanded it to two large stories plus an attic and built a porch, which wrapped the entire exterior.

"For you, Sarah Jane." An unusual twinkle sparked in his sky blue eyes. "So that you may hear those crickets, frogs, and bird-calls as many fine evenings as you like."

And she accepted his gift and the affection, if not love, which inspired it. Fine furniture filled the rooms. Her armoire held dresses, as Leila's once had, of satin and silk. They rode in a grand carriage to town.

Pierce, however, lost his faith somewhere along the Trail, another tragedy of the Removal. He refused to accompany her to the Meetinghouse services. But he loved her boys. Their boys . . .

When Johnathan, the wise one, quoted something profound, or David, the witty one, made some outlandish statement that sent them into gales of laughter—Pierce would look at her and smile. A real smile. The smiles Sarah remembered him wearing as easily as he'd worn his youth when he first came to study under her father.

And in that smile, she caught glimpses, not just of who he'd been, but of who he could yet be. Sarah savored his contentment at such moments, which revealed the depths of his feelings for her and their family. Feelings he wasn't ready to acknowledge.

But perhaps . . . one day.

Sarah prayed the burden of bitterness would release Pierce from its grip and he'd be free to fully embrace the love she had for him and the love she knew he could feel for her if he'd allow himself. In the meanwhile, she practiced what she'd learned from the Cherokee and from her God, persistence and perseverance.

Dinner became an increasing strain as Pierce and the boys debated the political situation as the threat of war loomed. A just recompense upon the young nation, a curse incurred by its despicable treatment of the Negroes and Indians. Laconic David became impassioned on the subject of abolition. Johnathan agreed in theory, but maintained Home must be defended.

Pierce threw down his napkin. "I, for one, am hoping this war will bypass us in Cartridge Cove."

But Sarah awoke one morning to find that David had departed over the mountains to Kentucky to follow his conscience and enlist in the Union Army. Johnathan announced his intention to travel to Quallatown and enlist in the rebel regiment white Cherokee businessman, Will Thomas, organized for the defense of the western home counties.

"He's recruiting Cherokee and mountaineers," Johnathan told her with pride. "The hunters. The sharpshooters. The toughest. The best of the best."

"I don't know if I can bear two of my sons going off to war." Her lips trembled. "Shooting at each other. Pierce, tell him he can't go."

Pierce shook his head. "He's a grown man. He, like David, must follow his conscience or be unable to live with himself." He gazed out the window upon the rows of sunflowers edging her garden. "And that I'd wish upon no man."

To her horror, Pierce declared he'd offer his services as an adjunct surgeon to the regiment. "I'll keep one eye out on our son, Sarah Jane," he consoled. "And one eye on my patients."

"And when you've employed both eyes and have no more to spare," she sniffed. "Who will keep an eye on you?"

Ethan, of course, demanded to be allowed to join his father and brother. But Pierce tasked him with keeping his mother and little brother protected through the dark days ahead.

After a month of rifle drills, Sarah wanted to visit Quallatown before her men shipped out to battle. But instead, Pierce came home. Holding himself aloof, she caught him staring at her. A furtive, secretive look creased his face. And a cold feeling settled in her chest, colder than any since that morning after their wedding day.

The regiment, she learned through the mountain grapevine, was sent over the mountains to Tennessee. With Ethan and Caleb, she scoured the woods as summer evolved into autumn and her garden played out. With food scarce, she taught the boys to look for the roots and plants the Cherokee had shown her on the Trail.

Ethan baffled her. Unable or unwilling to commune with the Creator, more often than not, Ethan narrowed his eyes at the giant trees. "How much you think a timber company would pay for lumber to rebuild the country after the war, Mother?"

Sarah gaped at him. But despite her best efforts to help Ethan listen to the call of the blue jay, to appreciate the reddish Cherokee lilies on the mountainside, within Ethan the mountain only inspired dollar signs.

Marauders on both sides preyed upon the isolated homesteads. But when the federal troops marched into town, they chose Sarah's home as their base. She and the boys retreated to the attic.

The Yankee colonel hand-delivered to Sarah a folded Stars and Stripes. And with the flag, a letter from a general's wife of the Ladies Sanitary Commission, who tended Union soldiers in battlefield hospitals. The letter, couched in sympathy, informed Sarah that on September 1, her second-born son had died of wounds suffered in battle.

Sarah crushed the letter to her chest. Her sweet David had flown, like the others she'd loved, to the Beyond. Heartbroken, she found some solace with her Consolation. She placed David's flag in the trunk.

Ethan chafed, angry he wasn't doing his part. Arguing folks called him a coward behind his back. That if he didn't up and join, the Union would conscript him or the marauders would take him and he'd have no choice in the matter.

"Please, Ma, let me go to Papa and John. It's not right Papa doesn't know about Davy. Let me go."

That dried her tears and moved Sarah into conceding to his pleas. Pierce deserved to know about his son. Perhaps when he heard, he'd . . .

Sarah wasn't sure what she hoped for at this point with Pierce.

Before dawn, Ethan crossed the enemy lines around Cartridge Cove. She held her breath and prayed, expecting any hour to see him dragged back by Union patrols. Or worse, his body returned for burial. But the days passed into weeks, the weeks into months.

Knee-deep inside hostile rebel territory, the enemy occupiers treated the mother of a fallen Union comrade with respect.

One day with Caleb busy chopping wood, Sarah ventured alone into the cemetery behind the Meetinghouse. In her arms, she carried a bouquet of the wild Cherokee lilies David had so loved. A twig snapped as she arranged the flowers upon his grave. A hand at her throat, she wheeled.

An old Cherokee man approached, a finger to his lips. His eyes cast around for eavesdroppers. Seeing none, he beckoned her to the edge of the forest and withdrew from his tattered butternut coat, another flag. The Stars and Bars of Dixie.

Folded like David's.

"No, God. Please . . ."

Sarah dropped the flowers, scattering them over a multiplicity of Hopkins and Birchfield graves.

Images of Pierce, Johnathan, and Ethan stabbed.

Her knees buckled. "Which one?"

The old man grasped her arm and held her upright. "Your young man, Johnathan."

Sarah clamped her hand over her mouth. The anguish gutted her. But she couldn't scream or yell lest she bring the Yankee invaders upon this soldier's head.

He eased her to the ground beside David's lilies.

"I knew your father." The man shuffled his feet. His toes poked through his shoes. "I'm sorry to bring this news to you, Miss Hopkins."

Her head jerked. A long time since she'd been Miss Hopkins. Now Sarah was nothing more than a forlorn mother who'd lost yet another son.

"I've never forgotten your father's kindness to The People," he stumbled on. "I promised your husband I'd bring you the news."

"Pierce?" She choked back a sob. "He was there with Johnathan?"

Agony ripped through her soul. Oh, God, her precious joy, her firstborn joy, gone.

Sarah gripped his sleeve. "But Pierce and Ethan? Do they still live?"

He nodded.

A rustling in the brush, probably no more than a squirrel, set his limbs aquiver. "I'd best be off afore the Yankees . . ."

Through her tears Sarah thanked him and watched him dart into the trees. He disappeared from sight as quickly as he'd appeared.

Sarah fell face down upon the lilies, their petal softness like a caress as she wailed alone upon the ground. There'd be another headstone to carve.

In May of '65, Pierce's regiment were the last to surrender in Waynesville, once the news of Lee's surrender caught up to them. Ethan returned home alone, his heart further hardened by the war. When several weeks passed with no sign of Pierce, she and the boys feared he'd died in the last fierce thrust of the Confederacy along the Blue Ridge.

One afternoon in late June, she had the house to herself. The Yankees relocated to Waynesville at the news of the surrender. Ethan had driven the buckboard to town for news of his father among the veterans who trickled through Cartridge Cove. Now a young man, Caleb roamed the woods, communing with his God. He'd taken over the pulpit at the Meetinghouse when old Preacher Thompson passed.

With her house chores complete, Sarah sat on the front porch with her mending. Laying aside for a moment the heaviness in her heart, she reveled in the bright sunshine. She breathed deep of the crisp, mountain air.

The birdcalls quieted. The thrumming of the flying bugs ceased. And at the sudden hush, Sarah glanced up from her needles to find a bedraggled, old man standing stock still at the foot of the steps. She jerked.

He wore a uniform. Gray, Sarah thought, its original color. Or maybe, on second thought, from the mud and dust of the road.

The old man's face lay shadowed beneath the stubble of his beard and the brim of his hat. Disconcerted at the unwavering focus of his eyes, she tensed. Sarah laid aside her knitting, all except for one needle she kept close just in case.

"Could I offer you some water?" She half-rose. "Some food before you're off on your journey home again?" Never before had she felt her home's isolation more.

He twisted his battered hat in his hands. The old man's eyes traveled over her dress, her hair, probing her face. Sarah clenched the knitting needle in her fist and wished she'd thought to bring the squirrel gun outside with her. These were troubled times.

Taking a step forward, his cracked lips parted. "S-Sarah. Sarah J-Jane . . ."

Her breath hitched as recognition dawned. "Pierce . . . ?"

Sarah's hand spasmed. The metal needle fell to the planked step with a clatter. "Pierce? Is it you?"

He swayed and leaned upon the railing for support.

In a flash, her skirts rustling, Sarah was at his side, holding him upright with her arm around his waist.

Pierce shied away from her touch. "Lice, Sarah Jane. I'm-I'm filthy . . . unclean . . ." Tears ran down his face, leaving wet trails of dirt. "More than you can imagine."

She slipped his arm around her shoulders. "Blessed be to God, Pierce. You've come home."

He collapsed onto the step. On his knees, he pillowed his face in the hem of her skirt and wept.

As she'd not seen him cry since that first morning after their wedding day.

"Pierce . . ."

Her hands flew up in the air, hovering above his bent head. Longing, yet not daring, to touch him. Yearning to comfort him in the grief that assailed him.

Gathering his tattered emotions, Pierce searched her face. "I'm so sorry, Sarah Jane." He captured her hand. "For all the hurt.

How I held myself apart from what you offered. I beg for your forgiveness for not telling you."

She cupped his jaw with her hand. "Pierce, what is it?"

Pierce averted his eyes. "He lived, Sarah Jane. We met again when we both enlisted in the Legion. But I was afraid . . ."

His lips quivered. "I was afraid if I told you, I'd lose you. Lose your love forever. Lose the only love that kept me anchored, kept me from drowning in despair. So I forbade you to visit us at Quallatown."

Sarah frowned, remembering Pierce's brooding silence in those days before he went to war. "What are you talking about? Who lives?"

"Touch the Clouds." At her sharp inhalation, Pierce positioned her hand over his heart. "I watched you when you were with him. I recognized the feelings you'd never admit to yourself."

A roaring like the waterfalls high in the Snowbird filled Sarah's head. "H-he lives?"

"No more . . ." Pierce trembled. "He took a bullet—"

Raw pain sliced open an old wound of which Sarah had believed herself long ago healed.

Pierce drew a deep breath. "Despite the years, until the end, we remained as always like oil and water."

Her eyes flitted to the Snowbird. "A balance in the cosmos," she whispered.

"What?"

She shook her head and swallowed past the lump in her throat.

Pierce dropped his chin, unable to meet her gaze. "He appointed himself protector over his son and mine."

A son? Her heart fluttered. Strange to think him so close all these years. And yet so far the divide that separated them.

She withdrew her hand and knotted her fingers into her apron. "How?"

"The Yankees broke through our lines. He appeared at the medical tent and told me I had to leave at once. That he'd buy me all the time he could afford."

Pierce's eyes took on a distant look. "I refused to leave the patients. Only one wagon. I couldn't take them all, you see. He insisted the Yankees would treat them well as prisoners of war, that the war was almost over, and they'd probably receive better food and more medicine under Yankee care."

He reached for her hand.

She shrank against the railing.

Pierce let his hand fall to his side. "Touch the Clouds said to tell you he'd been too late to save Johnathan from the artillery, but he wouldn't allow you to lose your husband, too."

Sarah tightened her grip on her dress, making a strangled noise in the back of her throat.

"He joined me on the wagon, returning fire, holding off the patrol until . . . one shot . . . severed his carotid artery, Sarah Jane."

She closed her eyes against the burning, stinging tears.

Pierce released a slow trickle of breath. "He told me to drive, to keep on driving until I reached rebel lines. Once out of range, I tried to stem the blood flow as best I could with what supplies I'd managed to grab."

She flinched. The carotid artery. Touch the Clouds would've had minutes before he bled out.

"He said . . ."

She opened her eyes at the ragged thread of Pierce's voice.

Pierce chewed the inside of his cheek. "Touch the Clouds told me he'd loved, only loved, two women in his life. The mother of his second family and . . ."

Sarah fought the urge to clap her hands over her ears lest she hear Pierce say the name neither of them had uttered in over twenty-five years. But he, and Touch the Clouds, surprised Sarah.

"Two women. The mother of his children. And you." Pierce touched her sleeve. "He loved *you*, Sarah Jane Hopkins."

Pierce brushed his hand over hers bunched in her skirt. "That what he felt for anyone else he'd come to realize had been something else, something other than love. He asked me," Pierce's voice wobbled. "If I'd stopped being a fool."

She pulled away.

"Touch the Clouds sent you . . ." Pierce pressed his lips together. "He sent you, Sarah, his 'esteemed regards'."

Draping her arms around herself, Sarah drew her knees to her chin. "You took him home?" Sarah's voice convulsed. "You brought him back to his mountains, didn't you?"

"His son and I . . ." Pierce gestured toward the ridge. "We brought his body to his wife, a Christian woman. And met his four children."

Sarah lifted her eyes. "He had other children." The corners of her mouth curved.

And hope quivered in her heart, a deeper hope than what Pierce supposed.

"His wife is a Christian, you say?"

Perhaps her prayers for Touch the Clouds had come true. Perhaps at the end, he'd no longer been a stranger to God.

"I brought Touch the Clouds home to everyone who resided there." Pierce choked. "And I've stopped being a fool, Sarah Jane."

His gaze went skyward. "God forgive me, I have."

Pierce buried his face in the folds of her apron. "I love you, Sarah, despite how I've acted, I always have. Loved you for your strength, your gentleness, your soul . . ."

His hot, scalding tears soaked her skirts until the coil of bitterness loosened, until the weight of the world rolled off his shoulders. As Pierce surrendered before God and Sarah Jane the pain of the years the locusts had eaten.

Sarah's hands hovered like a hummingbird's wings above his bent head, his blond curls plastered with grime. Her temples pounded with the fear once again of rejection.

Wisdom or folly?

But something broke in her heart at Pierce's need of her. Quieting her doubts, she wove her fingers into his hair. And when he stilled at her touch, she drew his head upward between her hands.

To the welcoming hello kiss of her mouth.

His face alight, he stroked her hair. "My beloved wife. Oh, Sarah . . ."

She shivered at the sound of her name upon his lips and closed her eyes as his finger traced the pattern of her features. He wrapped his arms around her neck, his weight toppling them backward on the porch. Then both of them laughed at the absurdity of it all.

Joyous, hope shining, he kissed Sarah with the fire and passion of which she'd dreamed for so long.

And at last, he became in the years that followed, the man she'd always known he could be. Compassionate physician, devoted husband and lover, fervent in faith and the Holy Spirit. The latter twenty years eclipsed the sorrow of the first as if they'd never been.

Now an old woman, Sarah sat beside the grave of her beloved husband. Who'd departed, flown to the Beyond. "I'll join you ere long," she whispered, propping a jar of red lilies beside his gravestone.

She opened her journal, begun a lifetime of hurts and triumphs ago. Sarah strolled through the pages, remembering, grieving, giving thanks. The journal had become a memorial.

A testament to God's love and faithfulness to her, Sarah Jane Hopkins Birchfield, in this land of the Snowbird in which she'd sojourned.

God in His mercy, Sarah wrote in her final entry, *unchanging*. Always her Consolation in her hour of greatest need. And beyond.
Blessed be God.

25

2018—Cartridge Cove

Her weakness exposed, Linden lay low at Gram's for the better part of a week. But every afternoon at precisely two o'clock—because Walker Crowe was nothing if not precise—he telephoned her grandmother's house.

And when each afternoon her grandmother suggested Linden pick up the phone, she refused. Linden, once a coward always a coward, hid her shame from the world. Or at least from the good people of Cartridge Cove, who no doubt considered her a deranged idiot.

"This is getting ridiculous," Marvela nagged, night and day.

Linden fluffed her hair over her ears to shut out the sound.

"It's not the end of the world. Time to get on with life. You can't hide from the past or the future forever."

The only visitor Linden deigned to admit into her self-imposed hermitage was Quincy. And only him because he came bearing gifts. He'd located the gravestones of the Birchfields, and he promised to bring photocopies of every census until their deaths if she let him into the house.

Which she did. And like he'd single-handedly raised Lazarus from the dead, Marvela insisted Quincy stay for lunch and feted him as if it were Thanksgiving and not just another unseasonably humid day in June.

Quincy, between bites of turkey sandwich and sips of sweet tea, assured Linden nobody in town was talking about her. She didn't believe him, understanding how the grapevine worked.

He implored her to return to the Center. Emmaline was worried about her—he coughed—and he was worried about getting the Center ready for opening day of the festival.

She told him she didn't care. Quincy raised his eyebrows at Marvela. He switched to a different tack.

"Well, if you don't care about yourself or your friends," he drawled, pushing the glasses up the bridge of his nose. "Think about what you're doing to your grandmother."

Linden darted a glance at her grandmother whose face remained impassive. The longer Marvela stayed here, Linden reflected sourly, the closer she came to resembling these stone-faced Cherokees. But she took the bait.

"What do you mean?"

He crinkled his forehead. "The recluse of Cartridge Cove's only B & B can't exactly be good for Miss Marvela's bottom line or her love life, either."

Linden sniffed. "I never said the Colonel wasn't welcome. Of course, he's welcome." She gathered the papers scattered on the tabletop. "How about I go back to Raleigh and then no one will have to worry about me?"

Quincy narrowed his eyes. "How about I go tell that Cherokee mountain boyfriend of yours you need an attitude adjustment and see what he wants to do about it?"

She poked out her chest. "You wouldn't dare. Besides, he's not really . . ." Flushing, Linden shuffled the papers into a folder. "Gram wouldn't allow him to . . . to . . ."

Marvela placed her hand atop Quincy's shoulder. "Watch me fling open the door, Honey Girl."

"Humph." Flipping her hair—which could stand to be washed—over her shoulder, the folder clutched to her Carolina Girl sweatshirt, Linden did her best imitation of Marvela flouncing out of a room.

In the safety of her room, Linden spread the papers across the bedspread. Down below, the front door creaked open and banged shut. Voices—Marvela and Quincy's—murmured on the verandah and moments later, she heard the crank of Quincy's Mini Cooper engine.

Round one—she licked her finger and scored the air—Linden.

She pored over the documents, noting the overlay map Quince superimposed on the oldest part of the church graveyard on Meetinghouse Road. The Community Church had been built on the stone foundations of the original mission house.

Great. She'd have to return to the scene of her humiliation if she wanted to get a look at Sarah Jane's grave. She tucked the map alongside the location of Chestnut Hill into the recesses of her purse. She jumped as the phone vibrated on the nightstand.

Had Quincy made good his threat? Was it Walk—? She breathed in relief after scanning caller ID.

Not him. But Dottie Swimmer? Other than Walker, the person she most didn't want to talk to.

Linden flung the phone onto the bed. The vibrating stopped. She heaved a sigh, wondering if she tiptoed down the back stairs if she could snag the last carton of Rocky Road without encountering one of Marvela's always-on-a-diet reproachful looks.

The phone vibrated again, jolting and jiggling across the counterpane. Linden ignored it and examined her reflection in the mirror. She smoothed a hand over the bushiness of her hair and rubbed at the dark circles under her eyes.

Not one of her most attractive days. Another reason not to see Walker anytime soon. Linden might be depressed, but her vanity remained intact. People just needed to let her work out her angst in her own way.

The cell jerked and bounced.

Linden padded over to the bed. "Lord-a mercy." Would it never stop?

She pressed Talk. "Hello already. What do you want?"

A lengthy silence.

She had the grace to blush. "I'm sorry, Mrs. Swimmer. I shouldn't have barked at you. I haven't been my—"

"I wanted to let you know," the old woman cut in, "if you want that Carolina Lily quilt created by Sarah Jane Birchfield featured at the Center you better come get it yourself, and I mean within the next hour."

Her eyes widened at the inflexible tone in the old woman's voice. "What?"

"You heard me. You've got one hour to get here or all deals are off."

"But Mrs. Swimmer, we've already done the publicity and planned an entire exhibit around this aspect of—"

"Am I speaking English or what, Miss Birchfield?" The iron thread in her voice flaked like chips of flint. "'Cause I could've sworn I wasn't speaking Cherokee."

"But Mrs. Swimmer . . ."

Quincy would kill Linden if she didn't secure that quilt for the show. Not to mention that Sarah Jane Hopkins Birchfield, second fiddle to everyone in her own lifetime, deserved her own moment of fame, no matter how after the fact.

"You want it. You come get it. Now."

Sputtering with righteous indignation, Linden nonetheless assured Dottie Swimmer she'd be there within the hour. As soon as, with another dismal look in the mirror, she washed her hair and got dressed. For the first time in a week.

As she pulled the phone away from her ear, Linden could've sworn the old lady murmured something about "tough love." Scowling, Linden clicked off and reached for the shampoo.

Twenty minutes later while toweling her hair, tires screeched to a halt outside her window. Shuffling over, Linden hugged the wall and peeked around the window frame. Walker catapulted out of his truck and slammed the door for good measure.

He stalked up the steps, lost to her view. Squeezing the handle of her silver-back brush, she stroked the tangles out of her hair. Walker pounded the front door, hollering for Marvela.

Slipping into a white cotton skirt, Linden arranged her lilac shirt over the waistband.

The hammering continued until, with an abrupt screech of the hinges, Marvela threw open the door. "What in the name of . . . ?"

Linden wedged her feet into a pair of Montego Bay espadrilles.

From the shouting, it became apparent through the can't-flush-a-toilet-in-this-town-without-everyone-hearing-about-it grapevine, Walker had learned Linden had finally condescended to entertain one visitor.

And it wasn't him.

Underneath the frustrated anger, his voice also held a note of hurt. A rush of tenderness threatened to undo her high-minded resolve.

Chewing her lower lip, Linden yanked at the matted sections of her hair. What had ever possessed her to keep it so long? Nothing but a bother and a nuisance, especially when she was in a hurry. Winding the length of her hair into a messy bun, she jacked it up to Jesus—as Gram phrased it—balling it into a webbed hairnet from her ballet days.

Overriding her grandmother's modulated tones, Walker shouted, "And I know you can hear every word I'm saying to you, Linden Birchfield."

She pictured his face upturned toward her second-story bedroom. She imagined the splotches of color in his cheeks. Flustered, she grabbed her keys off the dresser.

"I'm a patient man," he yelled.

She envisioned his teeth bared in a snarl.

"I've had to be patient whether I'm sniping or watching trees grow . . ."

Her hand trembled as she fitted the shoulder strap of her purse over her arm.

"But I'm about up to here—" he'd probably made a rude gesture, "—waiting for you to let me try to help . . ."

Yeah, like this was helping.

She cast a nervous eye around the room. Had she forgotten something? She patted her purse.

"If you won't come downstairs, then I'll . . ."

The timbre of his voice changed, as did the location. And she suddenly realized Walker was on the move, that he'd hurtled past what limited resistance Gram had offered and sprinted his way up the staircase.

Panicked, Linden dashed down the back stairs as the top of Walker's head crested the front staircase landing. Holding her breath, praying he hadn't spotted her—no foxhole atheist here— she skittered toward the kitchen.

Kicking open the screen door, she raced to the *porte cochère,* thanking God Walker had parked alongside the curb, leaving her exit unhindered. Backing down the drive, her tires spinning, she caught sight of Walker, his head hung out of her open window, bellowing her name.

Linden fishtailed onto the street and thrusting the gearshift into drive sped off toward safety in the form of Dottie Swimmer.

Which promised to be about as much fun as a root canal.

Fifteen miles into the Snowbird, Linden pulled onto the rutted dirt path that passed for Mrs. Swimmer's driveway. She noted the hip-roofed barn across the pasture where installation of the Carolina Lily block would occur this weekend.

A *gadugi* event she had no intention of attending.

She eased to a stop in the grassy turnoff at the front of the house. Slinging her purse over her shoulder, she stomped her way around to the back. Where people—she'd learned courtesy of Marvela and Walker—did most of their living.

And sure enough, in a faded floral housedress, Mrs. Swimmer waited for her on the screened porch, her gray head encased in a traditional red kerchief.

"Humph." The old woman rose amidst the creaking of joints. "Took you long enough."

And a fine how-do-you-do to you, too.

Mrs. Swimmer jabbed her thumb at a brown paper-wrapped parcel on the worktable beside a chipped, white metallic bowl that held beans waiting to be snapped. "The quilt's ready to go, but first I wanted to show you something."

Linden's eyes flickered from the quilt to the old woman's face. Her fingers itched to hold the parcel and make a run for it. Because she had a feeling the old lady had something on her mind.

Something Linden probably would rather not hear.

Mrs. Swimmer sidled between Linden and the parcel. "You want that quilt, you'd best follow me."

Linden's hand tightened on the strap of her purse. Was the old woman psychic?

Mrs. Swimmer chortled. "The look on your face . . ." She bent over, cackling, her hands on her knees. "You wear your thoughts all over your face for everyone to see."

Linden swallowed hard.

Mrs. Swimmer held the screen door open. "Those with eyes to see." She glanced at Linden's feet. "You're going to have a doozy of a time picking your way to the family plot in those things."

Intrigued despite herself, she straightened. "The Teesateskie burial ground?"

Mrs. Swimmer nodded. "Why your generation wants to ruin its feet in those six inch instruments of torture, I haven't a clue." She stuck out her own sensibly clad feet, her big brown toe poking out of scuffed, canvas sneakers. "Feet need to last you a lifetime."

Old Lady Swimmer sniffed. "Who cares about fashion if you break an ankle? Maybe that's the problem." She led the way into the yard, past the chicken house and into the orchard. "Your generation don't know the meaning of real work. Never had to."

The tirade about the current generation—both races fair game—continued past succulent, ripened peach trees.

"Remind me," Mrs. Swimmer motioned. "I've got a basket of peaches for you to take home to your grandma. I hear she and that Wachacha boy have finally gotten around to sparking."

Linden thought about laughing out loud. But it was all she could do to keep up with the nonagenarian who clambered up the rocky slope leading to the bald bluff without breaking her stride or pausing for breath. Which Linden had to do every hundred feet, her lungs burning.

Profusely perspiring—Mrs. Swimmer seemed not to have broken a sweat—Linden clung to the crooked ninety-degree angle of a loblolly branch once they reached the flat terrace at the base of the overhanging granite bluff. Ten or so headstones nestled under the shelter of the rock. Mrs. Swimmer pointed at the tree against which Linden reclined.

"That angle in a branch doesn't occur in nature. Cherokee made." She thumbed her wrinkled, liver-spotted hand at the crest of the Great Smokies in the distance. "One of the Cherokee hunting trails that meanders over the mountains."

Linden squinted over the incline they'd traversed, afraid to let go lest she fall.

"Do you want to see Touch the Clouds's grave or not?"

Linden responded by taking a breath and pushed off from the rough bark. She grasped hold of Mrs. Swimmer's hand for support.

"Good girl. Takes courage to overcome the mountains in our path. But once you do?" Her old eyes studied the mist-covered hills. "The view is spectacular."

Mrs. Swimmer paused beside the first row of grave markers. "I've lived long enough to bury my grandparents and my parents." She rested one gnarled hand on top of a stone that read, Malcolm Swimmer. "Buried a husband." A smile quavered at the corner of her lips.

"A good man," Mrs. Swimmer whispered. "A good man." She gestured at an empty space. "And I'll lie here one day."

Linden made a face.

The old woman planted her hands on her hips. "You think I'm morbid?" Her eyebrows arched. "Only one thing more important than understanding where you've come from, Missy, is knowing where you're going."

Linden remained silent, knowing until she allowed Mrs. Swimmer to say her spiel, she'd never see Touch the Clouds's final resting place.

Beckoning, Mrs. Swimmer stepped behind Malcolm Swimmer's headstone to three smaller markers. "Come see the worst thing I ever had to do."

Linden dug her heels into the rocky soil.

"That pretending it never happened thing working for you, Linden Birchfield?"

Linden gasped. "How did . . . ?"

The old woman stroked the carved lamb at the top of one of the headstones. "'Cause I remember that same wild, inconsolable grief. The panic when somebody's newborn would be dedicated at church. The fear I'd never hold another one of mine in my arms. The Mother's Day Sundays I faked illness to avoid church."

Linden moved closer to study the tiny etched remnants of too short a life. A sudden quick memory pierced her heart at the recent trip she and her mom made to a small grave in Charlottesville.

"That one's easy." Linden tightened her lips into a straight, hard line. "I just don't go to church."

"So you're mad?"

Crossing her arms, Linden kept her tone as light and soft as the breeze blowing onto the skin of her arm. "Mad He let her die."

"And mad, too, if you're honest, He let you live. Welcome to the club none of us asked to join."

She stared at the old woman.

"Has anger worked any better for you in the long run? Brought you any peace or closure?"

Linden plodded from one baby headstone to the next, reading the names and the dates. An infant. A four-year-old. A six-year-old.

Her breath caught. All three in the space of one terrible month in the 1930s.

Mrs. Swimmer sighed. "What was your baby's name?"

Linden wheeled toward the gravestones. "What happened to your children?"

Mrs. Swimmer grunted. "The Snowbird have a legend that when the soul leaves the shell the Lord sees fit to give us at birth, the soul flies upward over Singing Creek." She gestured at the faint tinkling of the rushing water below. "Over the mountain, past the clouds to the Beyond."

The old woman took hold of her hand.

And Linden, steeling herself for another's remembered pain, let her.

"Malcolm had gotten a job building the Blue Ridge Parkway north of here. The children and I worked the farm alone that summer. My Wanda," she positioned Linden's hand on the cold, smooth stone of the six-year-old's grave, "caught a cold. Which turned into pneumonia. Two weeks later, she gave up her shell and flew away to the Beyond."

She trundled Linden alongside the four year old's marker. "Ronnie got away from me one afternoon when I was crying over Wanda."

Mrs. Swimmer's eyes glimmered. "My brother found him face down, floating in Singing Creek. I reckon he'd decided to catch himself a fish for our supper like he remembered his daddy doing, to make his mama feel better."

Linden flinched.

"And the baby?" Mrs. Swimmer released a slow trickle of air, a rustling sound resembling autumn leaves falling to earth. "Overcome, I went into early labor. The baby, Virgil, lived four hours and God, in His mercy, took him, too."

"Mercy?" Linden bit her lip until she tasted the coppery, metallic taste of her own blood. "What kind of mercy is that?"

"Come and see." Mrs. Swimmer tugged her farther into the burial plot to where the oldest, weather-faded graves lay. "There's a lot of things worse than dying for those of us who believe."

A screeching call over their heads prompted them both to look up. Letting go of Linden's hand, she shaded her eyes and pointed. "A rare sight, the eagle. The most sacred of the birds to the Cherokee for he is the one who can fly the highest to the Creator. Here," she called Linden's attention to three more graves. "Is part of the answer you seek from that diary."

Linden drew in a sharp breath. "Touch the Clouds . . ."

"His wife, Miry," Mrs. Swimmer acknowledged. "And that poor, old thing, Auntie Walela, whose mind was too fragile to cope with the tragedy of the Trail. She returned from the Trail, her raven black hair snow white."

Linden squatted, examining the information contained on the headstones. "How do you know these things? These people couldn't be part of your living memory."

"We, like many native peoples, have always had a great oral tradition. Family stories passed from generation to generation. My granny knew Miry and Touch the Clouds. And through her, so did I."

"And what did she tell you about them?" Linden rose. "According to Sarah Jane's journal, everyone believed Touch the Clouds had been killed by the soldiers while trying to escape across the river."

"Touch the Clouds, in the confusion, lost hold of his wife in the water. There were screams as bullets found the flesh of the Cherokee. Men, women, some children. In the murky depths of the Mississippi, he found a hand, which he pulled to the other side underneath the river reeds. And using those reeds, he and a few others managed to breathe and hide until the soldiers went away and it was safe to emerge and search for survivors."

Linden gulped. "It wasn't Leila's hand he held though."

Mrs. Swimmer shook her head. "On the riverbank, he discovered he'd rescued a teenage girl, Miriam Teesateskie. They searched among the cane-breaks for hours. Of his wife there was no sign."

"And so believing her dead . . ."

"He believed, Miry told my own granny, Leila's body had most likely floated downriver and so the two of them began the long trek home. He was so broken by loss, it was Miry who begged white homesteaders along the way for food and shelter. She prayed, she said, every step of the way home."

Mrs. Swimmer angled toward Touch the Clouds's marker where it gazed through eternity over the bucolic tranquility of the mountain farm. "And they made it. Here."

"A lot of whites didn't agree with what the government had done. Many people helped them get home. Miry had no one left. Touch the Clouds took her in, married her. He believed he was taking care of her, but she actually took care of him. Rescued him from himself and his despair. He was devoted to her, I understand."

Mrs. Swimmer patted the top of Miry's tombstone. "A good woman. Strong in her faith, despite the difficulties of her life. Five children she bore Touch the Clouds. A courageous woman who . . ." The old woman glanced over at the auntie's grave. "These are the choices I faced when I suffered my own loss."

Her hands swept the three graves. "I hid from Malcolm when he came home. Hid out at my brother's because I couldn't face telling him how I'd allowed his children to die. For a year he begged me to come home to him." She swayed. "Such time I wasted."

The old woman took Linden's cheeks between her hands. In the face of such searching intensity, Linden could not break away. "Same choice all of us have if we live long enough. When we face what we cannot bear."

Linden quivered.

"The bitter choice Pierce Birchfield, whose blood runs through your veins, made." Mrs. Swimmer pursed her lips. "Don't choose what Auntie Walela did, Linden. Avoidance and denial led her to insanity."

"And Miry's choice?" Linden whispered.

"Miry's choice, like in the difficulties your Sarah Jane faced, was to confront the unchangeable, bear the unacceptable with God's strength, and live on in the grace of God."

"Does it ever go away, Mrs. Swimmer? The pain? The sadness?"

The old woman dropped her hold on Linden. "No, my child, but it does get better. With God's help, I promise you, it does get better."

"How?"

Mrs. Swimmer headed for the path toward home. "Three things," she called over her shoulder. "You got to allow yourself to remember." She extended her arm to Linden.

"What's number two?" Linden gritted her teeth and gripped the old woman's arm.

"Let yourself cry. Tears heal the soul."

Hitching her calf-length dress, Mrs. Swimmer picked her way as nimble as a gamboling fawn along the rock-strewn trail.

"And three?" Linden sucked a deep breath of oxygen into her lungs as they reached the level surface of the orchard once more.

"You got to tell your story to those who love you. 'Cause it's in the telling and in the receiving of the love people offer that you lance the wound and begin to heal."

Linden stopped. "My mom and I, we talked recently. But I can't," she lifted her face toward the mountain and its buried pain. "I can't tell him." She waved a hand. "He wouldn't understand. I don't want him to know what I did, who I was then."

"From what I understand of Walker's army days, he'd be the last to throw stones."

"I'm not the sort of girl a man like him needs in his white-steepled church life. There's no future with me."

"What type of life will you make, Linden, if you never allow yourself to love or receive love back?"

Linden trudged toward the house. "A safe life."

"Alone? That's no life, child. No life at all."

Linden paused at the porch steps. "You and Malcolm had other children, I presume?"

"We did." Mrs. Swimmer tilted her head, not unlike a tail-cocked Carolina wren. "Later."

"There's the difference, Mrs. Swimmer." Linden scooped up the parcel. "The difference between you and me."

26

Her hands gripping the wheel, Linden remembered the map to Chestnut Hill. She drew it out of her purse and located the property between Mrs. Swimmer's and town.

Off the highway and "up the crick," as the locals would say.

And not too far from Fred Alexander's. Another item on her to-do list for the quilt barn trail. Maybe kill two birds with one visit?

She steered the car onto the shoulder of the county road that abutted the main highway. Leaving the quilt in the car, she took only her keys, clicked lock and secured them within the confines of her skirt pocket. She glanced at her dusty espadrilles and at the ditch bank. Beyond, the faint outline of a trail meandered and disappeared into a curve of the trees. Mrs. Swimmer was right about one thing at least.

These shoes weren't meant for country living.

Good thing she'd be returning to Raleigh soon. She took a deep breath. The sooner the better in the case of one irate Cherokee sniper.

She clip-clopped her way down the bank. The doily tops of Queen Anne's lace brushed against her bare shins. Scrambling so as not to lose traction, she hauled herself up the other side and entered the raucous symphony of a Southern forest. The croaking chorus line of frogs. The riotous cacophony of a dozen woodland birds.

Why she'd ever believed it was quiet here in the Snowbird, she couldn't begin to remember.

After about a half mile, she emerged from the tree cover and into a clearing. Her foot caught and she stumbled over something protruding from the ground. She grimaced at her stubbed toe.

Round two—Mrs. Swimmer.

Bending, she pried at the block that had bloodied her toe and after much tugging, a broken brick came loose in her hand. Frowning, her eyes swept the grove. Catching sight of another submerged brick, she went to examine it further. And found another beyond that. And another.

Doing a complete three-sixty, she stood in the middle of what had once been the foundation stones of Chestnut Hill, Leila Hummingbird's home. What was left after the looters set fire to the place.

Linden dropped the dirt-encrusted brick and wiped her hands across her white skirt before she thought. She scanned the surrounding area, trying to imagine what the once bustling plantation would've looked like in Leila's day. She envisioned slave quarters, tobacco fields, and barns where now wilderness subdued all signs of civilization.

But 180 years later, only the clearing where the house stood remained. Linden shivered, noticing for the first time how quiet, unlike the forest, it was here at Leila's old home. Not the sound of a bird or the whir of an insect broke the eerie hush that hung over this place.

Spooky. Sad. More desolate by far than Mrs. Swimmer's family cemetery.

At the crackle of twigs nearby, she whirled as an unkempt, crazy-eyed man strode from the distant trees—his age indeterminate due to the grime encrusting his long-bearded face. For a moment, she wondered wildly, if she'd somehow stepped back to Leila's time and come face to face with one of the murderous looters.

But as he circled the foundation stones, she noted the cell phone clipped to his filthy jeans. A shotgun rested casually against his shoulder. The hair on the nape of her neck rose.

"What're you doing on my property? Spying on me?"

She blinked as the man spoke in the drawled mountain twang common among the white Appalachians.

"You not see those posted 'No Trespassing' signs?"

Her heart pounding, Linden shook her head. The pins in her hair gave way as tendrils of hair —and her stomach—fell.

The man's eyes fixated on her hair and glinted.

He eased the gun off his shoulder, leveling it at her. "Maybe you and I, little lady, should do some talking about respecting private property." He spat a stream of chewing tobacco, landing inches from her foot. "Among other things."

Linden took an abrupt step back, afraid to take her eyes off him. Because to look away from a wild animal like a bear, she'd been told by the Colonel, only encouraged their dominance as predator over prey. Retreating, her heel caught against one of the bricks.

Stumbling, she thrust her hands behind herself in a futile attempt to halt her momentum. In a bone-jarring tumble to the ground, her hands scraped against the sharp bricks and took the worst of it.

He laughed, the sound echoing against the isolation of the place. He kicked the bricks out of the way with his boot. "Get up, girl."

Staring down the black holes of the double-barrel, Linden heard rather than saw his finger click the safety off.

"Jesus," she whispered.

"Or we can have our little 'talk' right here. Makes no never mind to me. Only haints in this place." Standing over her, the gun never wavered from the target he'd positioned on her chest.

"If you ever point that gun at her again . . ." rumbled a mountain behind Linden.

The man's head shot up as he peered into the trees. She twisted her torso, following his gaze.

"If you ever point that gun at her again, Fred," repeated Walker, lumbering out from the trees, empty-handed. "You won't point anything at anyone ever again."

Fred's eyes narrowed to beady slits, but he stepped back a pace.

She scrambled to her feet. Her foot caught in her skirt, ripping the hem.

"You got no call to threaten me, Crowe." Fred jerked his head at Walker's relentless-as-death advance. "This is my property, and you're both trespassing. 'Sides," his bushy mouth contorted. "You got nothing agin me, but empty threats as far as I can see, Featherhead."

His eyes flat, Walker curled his lip. "Oh, I won't need a gun to deal with you . . ."

She jolted at the menace in this Walker she'd never seen before.

Walker reached for her and helped her over the circle of stones. She trembled. But he never took his eyes off Alexander.

He pulled her closer, crushing her spine into his chest. "I'm not with the law, Fred. I'm not interested in your recreational farming activities or your militia munitions cache. But I hear the sheriffs of two counties are looking for a gang that broke into an old man's house in Murphy, robbed and beat him." His hands gripped her shoulders.

Fred spit another wad of chewing tobacco. "Back in the day, no sheriff cared when one of you prairie n——"

Linden cringed at the racial obscenity. As for Walker? Rage radiated off his body.

She felt the heat of his skin through his shirt.

"Big talk from a small-minded man." If anything Walker's voice grew softer, deadlier. "Recompense will have to wait another day until you've got your skinhead sons to back you up, so you and me will be more evenly matched."

Alexander's mouth worked but no sound emerged.

Walker cocked his head. "I'm advising you as a Cartridge Cove neighbor you'd best pack up your operation and take those inbred sons of yours farther into the hills before the good citizens of Cartridge Cove—Cherokee and white—give you and your boys a taste of real justice."

Alexander let loose a stream of curses that blasted every squaw ancestor in Walker's heritage.

"Drop the gun and back away, Fred, 'cause right now I'm debating not only how I'm going to kill you, but how long I'm going to let you suffer before I finally snap your neck."

Alexander's face sagged. He threw down the gun and held his hands palm up. "Didn't realize the gal belonged to you or your kind. Thought my boys might enjoy a taste of sweet—"

With a roar like thunder, Walker shoved Linden behind him and lunged. Linden grabbed at his shirttail.

"Okay, okay." Alexander hopscotched backward. "I'm going. No need to go ballistic."

Walker held his ground until the sight—and the stink—of the man faded into the brush. He removed a handkerchief from his pocket. "Start walking toward the road, Linden. He'll return with his boys and more firepower."

Bending, he hefted the shotgun. "Make that start running." He turned the shotgun over in his handkerchief-draped hands. "Sheriff might find this interesting in a few cold cases he's investigating."

"Wait. What about you?"

He cradled the gun against his shoulder, closed one eye, and squinted down its sight. "I'll be behind you covering our flank. Get going."

"But, Walk–"

"Move, Birchfield."

So she ran.

Panting, she reached the Toyota, Walker's truck parallel to hers. She scrabbled in her skirt for the keys. She trained her eyes on the perimeter of the woods and counted the seconds.

She'd give him ten, Linden decided, her hands shaking. Ten seconds before she dialed 911.

But in five, he emerged, backing until he came to the ditch-bank. In a leap, he crossed over, his hands gripping the shotgun.

His eyes, still wary, broke his sweeping scrutiny of the woods to rest on her face for the first time. "You okay to drive home?"

"I'd rather ride home with you," she whispered low in her throat. She leaned against the hood. Her knees wobbled, unable to support her weight.

A flicker of something came to life in his hard eyes. She watched his pulse jerk in his neck. "So had I, but I don't think we ought to leave your car here."

He studied the deepening twilight engulfing the gap between the mountains. "I'll follow you home, I promise." His eyes returned to her face, this time with more signs of the Walker she knew.

Linden nodded. Laying the gun aside, he opened the driver's door and buckled her in when her hands refused to cooperate. She dropped the keychain on the floorboard.

Extending one arm, he reached for the floor mat and leaning over her, inserted the key into the ignition. "Adrenaline rushes out of your body through your extremities. It's normal."

She breathed in the Fraser fir, the sweat of honest labor, and the unique smell that made Walker, Walker. "I don't see your hands shaking."

He pushed a wisp of hair from her forehead to behind her ear. "I'm a trained operative."

She gripped the steering wheel to steady her hands. "You would've killed him, wouldn't you?"

"To protect you?" Walker straightened, a strange look passing over his face. "Without recoil and without remorse."

Walker waited until the red taillights of Linden's car disappeared down the highway before he cranked his engine. Shifting into drive, he got as far as Mercer's Auto Body Shop before the shaking of his hands forced him to pull over to the side of the road.

He flexed his fists around the wheel. God—and that tracking instinct God had for whatever reason equipped Walker with at birth—had allowed him to spot her car. He should've known she'd want to visit the ruins of Chestnut Hill. He'd deliberately forestalled her earlier attempts to contact Alexander about the quilt barns. Somebody—he—should've warned her away. He'd give the sheriff a call when he got to Marvela's.

If Walker lived to be as old as Mrs. Swimmer, he'd never forget the horror of sighting Linden on the ground and that monster salivating over her.

Walker laid his head on the steering wheel.

Suppose he'd not been there in time or at all? His stomach heaved. He took in a lungful of air and blew it out between his lips.

He murmured a fervent prayer of gratitude for God enabling him to be the right man in the right place at the right time. Opening his eyes, Walker veered back onto the road.

And considered if perhaps his mother was right. If perhaps because of the way God made him—not as a natural-born killer but as a natural-born warrior for the protection of others—it was time.

Time to apply for a law enforcement position no one else in this county wanted because they were too afraid of the likes of the Alexanders. Time to do what Walker did best.

For the good of all.

An all-out manhunt over five counties and a tristate area ensued for the Alexander clan. The realization God had been there for her in that clearing, answering Linden's feeble one word prayer in the form of Walker Crowe, did not escape her notice, either. Gave her something to ponder during the dark hours when the nightmares intruded.

Linden embarked on a long, painstaking journey home toward God. Problem was, that issue had nothing to do with resolving the dilemma of her mixed-up feelings for Walker. So, in the weeks that followed, she reverted to form. Avoidance and denial.

She did everything she could think of to post her own 'No Trespassing', arms-length signs at him. Which he persistently ignored.

Cheerfully, often whistling, ignored as he dropped by to "escort" her to Mrs. Swimmer's barn installation. Since using the Alexander barn was now out of the question, he volunteered his own barn for the Cherokee Rose block.

Surrendering with no shots fired, his splendid isolation, Walker spent most of his after farm work hours in town—she had no idea when he slept—pestering the you-know-what out of her.

Let's get ice cream, Linden. How about coming to watch the guys scrimmage with me before the festival next week, Linden? Can you coach me if I agree to do the voice-over for Touch the Clouds in the tree talk trail, Linden?

All of which, she did.

Because despite her best intentions, Walker Crowe had a curious, deleterious effect on her grandest resolutions. Against which Walker seemed to have declared a war of attrition.

"I'm just keeping you company for the summer, Cherokee man," she reminded him, day after day. "If this hick town of yours had malls or . . . or a putt-putt course, you'd already be history."

That double bracket of dimples almost broke his face as he grinned. "Your words say one thing," his lips nibbled at her earlobe. "But your eyes . . ."

It took both her hands to wrench back his head so she could look him square in the face. "My eyes are saying you, Walker Crowe, dwell in a world of self-delusion."

He laughed again. "Can't help it if I'm in—"

"Don't say it."

She squirmed away to the other side of the truck cab and crossed her legs.

"Okay, okay." He tugged at her sleeve. "Skittish as a newborn foal, I forgot. Come back over here."

She remained unyielding. For about five seconds. But at the imploring look in his eyes, she allowed him to inch closer.

"Please . . . I promise I'll behave." He held up a hand. "On my Cherokee Princess grandmother's honor."

She rolled her eyes. "The People had no princesses or kings, Crowe. Only chiefs."

He sighed. "Give 'em a little education and their head swells with self-importance."

She rounded on him. "Are you referring to my femaleness or my whiteness, Walker Crowe?"

He rolled his eyes. "Neither. Hardheadedness knows no ethnic or gender boundary."

"Exactly," she nudged him in the ribs. "Glad we understand one another at last."

She dropped her gaze to her toes.

"Hey." Walker lifted her chin between his thumb and forefinger. "Where'd you go?"

She shrugged off the melancholy. "How about you escort me to Meetinghouse Road? I still haven't taken a look at the Birchfield plot."

"Aye, aye, Captain," he saluted.

Smiling, his eyes sparked as he scooted to the driver's side, leaving her feeling unaccountably alone. Uncrossing her legs, she shifted over till her hip edged his.

One corner of his mouth quirked as he put the Ford into gear.

Problem with Walker Crowe, she gazed out the windshield as they drove down Main, was he'd gotten to be a habit. An addictive habit. Like potato chips and chocolate.

Or, like oxygen and H_2O?

A need or a want? Which was it?

She pursed her lips. And crooked her arm around his resting on the steering wheel.

Time enough to soldier through Walker-withdrawal after the festival. No sense, she rationalized, in rushing the lonely days to come.

Noticing his collar partially turned up, she reached to fix it. As her fingers grazed his neck, his breathing changed. A muscle in his cheek jumped.

Giving him a sideways glance, she gave his ponytail a playful tug. "Nothing I hate more than a man with prettier hair than me."

He laughed, the sound deep and husky. "If you don't quit that, Linden Birchfield, we're not going to make it to any ole cemetery. Not today."

She withdrew her hand, held it palm up in an imitation of him earlier. "I promise I'll behave." But inside, she thrilled to know she could disconcert him as much as he disconcerted her.

He glanced over to her. "Yeah, right. That will be the day."

But she did behave for the remainder of the ten minutes it took to reach the church graveyard. She handed Walker the map with the location of the graves and followed him through the cluster of trees.

"Most townspeople are buried in the cemetery adjacent to the funeral home," he explained. "Nobody's been buried here as long as I can remember."

Pushing through a stand of mountain laurel, they emerged into a sun-dappled glen filled with lichen-covered marble white and granite-speckled headstones. Some were broken in half, covered with vines of ivy. Not she prayed, poison ivy. Other stones had sunk into the ground, leaving a recessed depression. A few leaned to the side, upended by tree roots.

She surveyed the enclosure. "Maybe a future *gadugi* project?"

The glen—unlike that other clearing at Chestnut Hill— permeated peace and a serene quiet. As different from Leila Hummingbird's old home as the difference between darkness and light, hope and despair. Her heart thrummed. A despair Linden understood too well. A hopelessness she wearied of carrying.

Walker, scrutinizing the plot map, picked his way among the fallen stones. "Here," he called. "This one's got a Southern Cross on it. C.S.A."

She hurried over. "Johnathan Birchfield," she read. "Died at Lookout Mountain, 1863." She glanced up. "Sarah Jane's Confederate flag."

He pointed at the dates. "He was twenty-three. The pain she experienced must've been unimaginable."

Not so unimaginable.

A weariness settled upon Linden's shoulders. Her eyes darted around the burial ground, all of a sudden anxious to find Sarah Jane and be done with the whole business. She'd already spent far too much of her life in places such as these.

"Look, Linden." Walker motioned to a tombstone. "Pierce."

She joined him as he read out loud.

"Assistant Surgeon. C.S.A. Sixty-Ninth North Carolina. Pierce Birchfield. 1816-1900." He scanned the nearby stones. "No marker for the son the Union flag belonged to. Probably buried where he fell. Quincy can locate that information now we have the family name and census records."

She knelt by a smaller stone, older by decades than either Johnathan's or Pierce's. "Do you think . . . ?" She scraped away a vine obscuring the details. "There's a cross carved . . . No . . . It's—"

He squatted beside her. "It's a dove superimposed over that medical thingy. The snakes and the winged symbol."

"Caduceus."

"Right. Your family would know that." His eyebrows raised. "Who—?"

"Dr. Hopkins," they said in unison.

She rose. "But where . . . ?" She brushed her hands against the sides of her cargo shorts. "Where is . . . ?"

Walker strolled around to view the Birchfield stones. He paused on the other side of Pierce Birchfield's final resting place. "I've found her, Linden." He beckoned. "I've found Sarah Jane."

Her eyes widened at the name carved into the same stone as Pierce. Sarah Jane Birchfield. Beloved daughter, wife, and mother. 1822-1908.

"We shall live and love again . . ." he read.

"She's buried in the same grave as Pierce. After what he put her through." Linden shook her head, bemused. "Can you imagine such love and devotion?"

"I can."

Her eyes swung to his face.

What she beheld there took her breath.

She stepped back. "No, Walker. You mustn't."

"What're you afraid of, Linden? God? Me?"

"These graves," she gestured, "are like me."

"What does that mean?" Confusion on his face, he reached for her.

Avoiding his touch, she put herself on the Pierce side of the gravestone. "It's myself I'm afraid of. Of hurting and disappointing . . ." She swallowed. "I've seen everything I needed to see here."

He crossed his arms over his chest. "No, I don't think you have." His black eyes pinned her in place.

"We agreed . . ." She jutted her jaw. "Just the summer."

He dropped his arms. "Linden, wait—"

She moved off, hurrying past the dead. "I'm going to the truck." She sat in the truck a good fifteen minutes before he rejoined her.

Linden cut her eyes over to him. That remote, set look of the early days had returned. He refused to look at her, his lips clamped together.

Mission accomplished. In the nick of time, too.

Before he said the words that could never be taken back.

He didn't say anything on the way to Gram's.

She got out of the truck, and in her room, she ended up toasting her victory alone with her tears until she fell asleep exhausted in the dark hours after midnight.

27

2018—Cartridge Cove

I wish you'd come with Ross and me to watch the parade."

Linden shook her head. "I promised Quincy and Em I'd help them at the Center. They returned from Oklahoma last night with the Western delegation. I can't wait to see the visitors' reactions to our talking tree trail."

Marvela pinched her lips together and applied an even line of fire engine red lipstick. She batted her eyes in the mirror before giving Linden's reflection a look. "You've done a wonderful job with the first annual Cartridge Cove Trail of Tears Commemoration."

"First annual? I thought we were commemorating the 180th anniversary."

Marvela tweaked the white Ralph Lauren sweater tied around her neck. "We are, but after the media got hold of Sarah Jane's story, the Council figures it might be a good idea to keep the visitors coming and the financial coffers rolling every year."

Linden sighed. "I couldn't believe AP picked up the articles we ran in the local paper."

Sarah Jane had gotten more than her fifteen minutes of fame. Her name, her story linked with Leila Hummingbird's tragedy and the larger tragedy of the Cherokee removed to Oklahoma, had flashed across almost every television screen in America. Four major networks conducted interviews of the mayor, Irene Crowe, the Colonel and, yes, Marvela who'd thrown her two cents in, too, determined for the B & B not to be left out.

Over the last few weeks, Quincy, Em, and a small band of Cartridge Cove citizens—Cherokee and white Appalachian—retraced the land and water route from Blythe's Ferry, Tennessee to Oklahoma. State and national news crews marked their progress each step of the way.

"What I don't understand," Gram smoothed the navy blue, sleeveless polo over her white linen slacks. "Is how Touch the Clouds came into possession of the Carolina Lily quilt?"

A knock sounded downstairs.

"Oh, Honey Girl," Marvela breathed in a rush. "Do let Ross in for me. I can't allow him to see me in this state."

Linden smiled at the R-r-r-os-s-s-s. "You look beautiful as always, but yes, I'll let him inside." She pivoted in the doorway, wagging her finger. "Just don't keep him waiting too long."

"Never again." Her grandmother grabbed a brush off her dresser.

Downstairs, Linden opened the door to find a dapper Colonel dressed in chinos and an Oxford shirt.

She shook her head. "Y'all realize it's July outside, even if this is the mountains?"

He laughed and gave her a hug. "Got to keep up with that fashion plate of a grandmother of yours."

"R-r-r-ross-s-s-s," trilled her grandmother from the landing.

That grandmother of hers knew how to make an entrance.

Joining them, Marvela offered her cheek for a kiss. He planted one, smack on her lips. Which Marvela returned.

With gusto. And giggled.

She was so happy for Gram and the love of her life who'd decided to help Marvela run the inn. There was talk of a Christmas wedding.

Linden was so happy for Quincy and Emma who'd returned from their adventure aglow with love.

She was happy for every stinking person in the livelong world who'd ever loved and hoped to love again.

Really.

She was.

"Linden? Earth to Linden?"

Her grandmother stood one hand on her hip. "Did you not hear what Ross asked you?"

Linden shook her head. "No, ma'am. Sorry. What did you ask, Colonel?"

He gave her a crooked smile. The likeness to his great-nephew pierced her heart. She dropped her eyes to her sensible, Mrs. Swimmer-approved, low-heeled flats.

The Colonel and Marvela had been good about not asking nosy questions since she and Walker had parted company a long, lonely week ago.

"Linden Elizabeth Birchfield."

The rising decibel in her grandmother's voice wrenched Linden to the present once more. She'd missed the Colonel's question again.

"I'm sorry . . ." Linden tucked an errant strand into her topknot.

Marvela's fire engine lips pursed. "The Colonel wondered the same thing I did about the quilt and Touch the Clouds."

Ross clasped Marvela's hand. "Just thinking how Touch the Clouds escaped. How a quilt would fare dragged through Mississippi mud."

Linden frowned. "You're right. It's in remarkable condition. Not like something that scraped the bottom of a river."

Marvela extracted her house key from a drawer. "But Mrs. Swimmer said she received the quilt from Touch the Clouds and Miry?"

"Yes . . . No . . ." Linden's brow furrowed as she tried to recall Mrs. Swimmer's exact words. "She said her auntie passed it to her when she was a little girl. The aunt who returned from the Trail, too. Walela."

Ross's eyebrows arched. "Walela? The aunt's name was Walela? Are you sure, Linden?"

Marvela looked between him and Linden. "Ross? What is it?"

Linden nodded. "Yes, I'm sure. Mrs. Swimmer said her auntie came back from the Trail with her hair snow white and her mind broken. I saw the name on the grave marker myself. She died . . ." She put a finger on her chin, picturing the Teesateskie burial plot. "About 1925." She sighed. "She was 103. So sad to be that lost for so long."

The Colonel blanched. "You don't know, do you?" He dropped his hands to his side. "Mrs. Swimmer must've assumed you'd understand the Cherokee or Walker would explain . . ."

"I don't think I ever got around to telling him Walela's story. Why?"

Marvela gripped his hand. "Yes, why, Ross? You're being maddening."

"Walela . . ." Pity glimmered in his eyes. "In Cherokee, it means 'hummingbird'."

Linden lifted her face to the sky above the town commons and listened to the chanting. A drum pounded, keeping time with the erratic thrumming in her head. She'd avoided attending the gospel sing last night as she avoided the parade this morning. Due to the still looming Alexander threat, extra security ensured the events had gone off without a hitch.

But she wouldn't miss this event if she attended no other. Cartridge Cove residents lined the edges of the circle. In this place where the area Cherokee had been rounded up on that long ago June, today representatives of the Eastern and Western bands gathered once more. To pay their respects to the dead, to remember, and to celebrate their spiritual reunification, the Principal People divided no longer.

The Colonel, several Oklahoma friends of his, Irene, and Mrs. Swimmer, among others, did a slow circle dance. Halting, but sure-footed. Deliberate and purposeful. Their dance, as Sarah Jane once explained, a prayer.

Marvela stirred beside Linden as the Colonel offered Gram his hand, to join him in the dance of remembrance.

Linden risked a darting glance across the circle at Walker's face. And wished she hadn't. His eyes bored into her soul.

Smoldering. Probing. Angry.

Linden was angry at herself. Angry at her inability to be what he deserved . . . at her inability to move beyond what happened ten years ago.

Irene and other members passed around turtle shells filled with dirt from the Snowbird and Oklahoma to the onlookers as the drums ceased and the plaintive notes of a reed flute began. One by one the watchers became part of the story, piling the shells on top of each other. Bit by bit building the mound. Linden thought she recognized the tune but couldn't place it.

Mrs. Swimmer positioned her shell on the growing structure and shuffled to where Linden stood frozen. "Miry was pregnant with their oldest son when Walela returned three years later with Junaluska's band that walked home from Oklahoma."

Linden clutched the turtle shell. Empty like her.

Ross and Marvela added their contributions to the pile.

She remembered Mrs. Swimmer's emphasis over and over again at the Teesateskie plot at what a good woman her great-grandmother, Miry, had been. "How horrible for the both of them to realize his wife . . ."

Mrs. Swimmer shook her head. "Not his wife. An empty shell that had once been Leila Hummingbird."

"Leila brought the quilt with her." Linden watched Quincy, his arm around Em's waist, deposit their shells onto the mound. "So, Touch the Clouds lived with the both of them?"

Which explained why Mrs. Swimmer had been opposed to the festival, reluctant to dredge up her family history.

Mrs. Swimmer's lips tightened. "He did the only thing an honorable man could do. He took care of Walela, he and Miry, until the day he died saving your Birchfield ancestor in battle. And then, Miry did the caretaking until my granny took over eventually."

Sarah Jane had mentioned how Pierce returned the body of Touch the Clouds to his farm. "Pierce saw her. Saw what Walela became, didn't he?"

Explaining the inexplicable change Sarah Jane noted in Pierce. An encounter with Walela that resulted in his change of heart toward his own wife and the devotion he'd displayed for the remainder of their marriage. In the end, Pierce had recognized and treasured the love Sarah Jane so selflessly offered him.

"I'd guess so. We'll never know for sure." Mrs. Swimmer shrugged. "I do know he bought the land the Teesateskies farmed and kept the title in trust until it was legal, years later, for the Cherokee to own land again in North Carolina."

Irene, holding Walker's arm, placed her shell on the pile.

Mrs. Swimmer jerked her chin in the direction of the mound. "It's an Ebenezer."

"A what?"

"Listen." Mrs. Swimmer cocked her head and finally, Linden recognized the old hymn, "Come Thou Fount of Every Blessing." "A memorial altar."

"Here I raise mine Ebenezer. Hither by Thy help I've come," the old woman hummed. "And I hope by Thy good pleasure safely to arrive at home."

Mrs. Swimmer's foot tapped out the beats. "An altar to which I believe Sarah Jane, Pierce, Miry, and Touch the Clouds would've joined us today in raising. In acknowledgment. In faith with eyes set on the Beyond."

Tears pricked at Linden's eyes. She dashed them away with the back of her hand. "But not Leila."

Mrs. Swimmer sighed. "Who knows what takes place in the human heart between a person and God, Linden? There's only Him and His mercy where you have the greatest need."

Linden stared, glassy-eyed, as Walker's boys deposited their offerings on the altar, too. "Leila turned her back on God when she needed Him the most."

Mrs. Swimmer inclined her head. "Granny said they used to find her barefoot in her nightgown wandering around the desolate ruins of her old home."

Linden remembered Alexander's mocking reference to the haints, or ghosts, of that place. To children, she might have seemed a ghost or a witch. And over the generations the stories had probably grown.

"Were you afraid of her?"

A sad smile flitted across the old woman's lips. "A little. Now, at my age, I no doubt resemble her more often than not. Granny said she always called for her father or her baby. I don't think she even remembered Touch the Clouds."

Mrs. Swimmer's voice hitched. "I think I reminded her of her lost baby. That's why, Granny explained, Auntie gave me the quilt. And she seemed to settle, Granny said, after I was born. She became calmer. Didn't wander again until that last time."

"The last time?" Linden sniffed and wished she had a tissue.

She must look a right fool, tears running down her face. After a decade of bottling her emotions, once she'd opened the door, she couldn't seem to stop. These days she cried over everything.

"Granny and Granddad found her lying in front of the altar at the meetinghouse. It burned later during the seventies, I think."

Mrs. Swimmer waved to some preschoolers and their moms at the mound. "Such a long way for the Old One to walk. They thought at first she'd fallen asleep."

Linden swallowed. "The altar, you say?"

"Her heart gave out, and she flew, I've always prayed, to the Beyond." Mrs. Swimmer gave her a long look. "'Cause that's how far mercy reaches."

Silence ticked between them as the fluid notes of the flute drifted away on the breeze.

"Let Him help you, child," whispered Mrs. Swimmer. "There are no outcasts from God."

Prone to wander, Lord I feel it. Prone to leave the God I love.

She'd come to the realization of all the long-dead characters who peopled Sarah Jane's world, she, Linden Birchfield, resembled Leila Hummingbird the most.

It was a thought that woke Linden in the middle of the night. And kept her awake.

Here's my heart, her spirit sang. *Take and seal it. Seal it for Thy courts above.*

Linden took a step forward. And another. And laid her empty shell on the knee-high mound.

The cell shrilled from the depths of Linden's purse. Blowing a strand of hair out of her face, she dug into its confines until she located and retrieved her phone.

"Hello?"

She held one hand over her ear and moved away from the craft bazaar set up down the middle of Main, closed to traffic for the festival.

Women of all ages sat behind tables demonstrating the basket-making techniques for which the Snowbird Cherokee were renowned. They chatted as they wove bloodroot and yellow-root stained strips of cane, honeysuckle, and split oak together.

"I can barely hear you, Quincy," Linden yelled. "You want me to what?" She sidestepped the grape Popsicle a toddler clutched in his sticky hands. She smiled at his purple-smeared cheeks. Surprising herself, she patted him on the head. His mother with an apology swiped at his face with a wet wipe.

"Meet whom?" Linden shouted into the phone. "This day is your show and the mayor's and the Snowbird. I'm just here to work behind the scenes and make sure—"

An overhead airliner frustrated Quincy's attempt to articulate his thoughts via the phone.

"Never mind. I'll be at the Center in five."

She clicked off and accessed the throngs, plotting the nearest route through the crowd. But by the time she actually arrived at the Center, more like twenty minutes had elapsed. And her heels against her flats were feeling the blisters formed from her unaccustomed physical exertion across town.

Em bounced up and down like a Cherokee pogo stick on the porch. She grabbed Linden's arm. "Finally. Quincy and I have been dying, waiting for you to meet her."

"Meet whom?" Linden allowed Em to shuttle her inside the air-conditioned interior, delicious on her overheated skin.

Jam-packed with tourists, through the French doors that opened onto the talking tree trail, Linden spotted families grouped around successive boxes and felt a surge of pleasure at the work they'd accomplished for Cartridge Cove on behalf of all its citizens.

Em hustled Linden toward Quincy's office and flung open the door.

Where Linden found an old woman—not as old as Mrs. Swimmer, more like Gram's age—ensconced within the overstuffed leather chair. Quincy grinned from ear to ear.

"At last." He vaulted out of his chair behind the desk.

Quincy took the old woman by the arm and steadied her as she rose. As stylish as Marvela, the woman wore a white cotton blouse, a knotted scarf of sea colors at her throat, and turquoise linen capris. Large chunks of turquoise dangled from her ears.

She was beautiful, too. Beautiful in a way age could never erase. Beautiful in a way that transcended ethnicity.

The woman smiled, her high, sculpted cheekbones lifting. The smile reached all the way to her deep brown eyes, the corners of her eyelids grooved as if over a lifetime by such smiles.

"Mrs. Redman, I'd like to introduce you to Linden Birchfield who found the diary with Sarah Jane and Leila Hummingbird's story." Quincy angled toward Linden. "And Linden I'd like you to meet Mrs. Garnet Redman, from California, who caught the story on the national news."

Linden cut her eyes around at Quincy, but accepted the woman's cool, dry hand in hers. "I'm glad to—"

"Mrs. Redman is LilyRose's great-granddaughter, and she's brought the Cherokee Rose quilt home."

"What?" Linden frowned.

Mrs. Redman squeezed her hand. "All these years, the stories were handed down about the crying baby found along the Trail in a dead woman's arms. Wrapped in a quilt signed with the initials, L. H. 1838."

"Kweti," murmured Linden. "But who found the baby?"

Mrs. Redman's serene countenance shifted toward the chair. "Forgive me, Linden. I hope you don't mind if I sit, but my granddaughter convinced me to hike Yosemite with her again last week, and I'm not as young as I used to be."

"No, no, of course." Linden gestured and took her place across from Mrs. Redman, perching on Quincy's desk. Quincy joined Em in the doorway.

Mrs. Redman's face puckered in thought. "The way I heard the story was that this family came along not long after . . ." She glanced at Linden. "Kweti?"

Linden nodded.

"After she died on the side of the road. No one seemed to be paying the screaming infant a bit of mind, but kept trudging on, head down, step by step toward exile or until they dropped along the way."

Quincy pursed his lips. "So many died, not all of them were buried right away."

"The couple lost their own babe days before. The woman's milk . . ." Mrs. Redman blushed, not of the generation that spoke of such things in public.

"The Jamesons," breathed Linden. "Sarah Jane mentions the Jameson baby dying."

"Jameson," Mrs. Redman's lips curved. "That's right. They settled in Oklahoma, farmed, and raised LilyRose with their other children. Here." She rummaged through the Prada bag at her side. "I brought some family photos I thought you'd enjoy seeing." She withdrew a manila envelope and handed Linden the packet.

A sepia-toned photo revealed an apple-cheeked young woman with Leila's piquant-shaped face who also possessed penetrating dark eyes. Perhaps resembling Touch the Clouds? "She's beautiful."

"Let us see. Let us see." Quincy and Em jockeyed for position over her shoulder.

Mrs. Redman smiled. "I've read the newspaper accounts of the diary. LilyRose's story touches something inside all of us, doesn't it?"

Linden nodded, fascinated by the young woman in the picture.

"Of course, the family had no idea about the Hummingbird connection until I saw the newscast and put the pieces together."

"So LilyRose wasn't lost forever?" Linden blinked back tears. "Someone found her." She handed the photo to Quincy to examine further.

"Was she—?" Linden choked past the lump in her throat. "I know it was so long ago. But do you know if LilyRose was . . . ?" Her lips quivered.

"Happy?" Mrs. Redman patted Linden's knee. "I think she was. She married another Cherokee farm boy whose family endured the Trail, too. He and she, their farm, and their children survived the dreadful uncivil war that followed. My family farmed that land until the Dustbowl. In the 1950s, my husband took the Relocation offer the government issued, and we resettled outside of San Francisco where we've raised our family."

She pointed Linden's attention in another photo to an older LilyRose surrounded by children and grandchildren in front of a large, two-story, white farmhouse. "Some of her daughters married preachers. One of her sons spent his life as a missionary in Africa. She lived a long time."

"Like her mother," whispered Linden.

"A long, happy time."

Unlike her mother.

"I was born in 1941. She held me, I'm told, that Thanksgiving Day. She died the same day the Japanese bombed Pearl Harbor. She was one hundred and two."

Mrs. Redman fumbled for the large canvas bag at her feet. "And here I am about to forget to show you the Cherokee Rose quilt." Linden gasped as Mrs. Redman removed the quilt from the bag and unfolded it across both their laps.

"I've told Dr. Sawyer I want to donate the quilt to the Center, which has done so much to honor the suffering of the people who once loved my LilyRose."

"Oh, Mrs. Redman . . ." Linden traced the outline of a white petal on the turkey red background.

"It's only right that quilt and in a sense, LilyRose, comes home at last to her origins. Back to where her parents both rest." Her fabulous dark eyes crinkled. "But rest assured, this is the first of many trips as my family and I become reacquainted with our ancestral homeland." She laughed. "Wait till you meet my sisters and their clans."

"I can't thank you enough for taking the time to come and tell us the rest of LilyRose's story." Linden felt those treacherous tears again. "To know she was okay . . . You couldn't possibly know how much this means to me."

"Sure, she was okay." Compassion melted Mrs. Redman's eyes. "She was just okay someplace else."

Like Linden's baby?

When Mrs. Redman's daughter and granddaughter loaded with shopping bags came to retrieve her, Linden made her excuses to Em and Quincy. Consumed with the urgent task of finding the perfect spot to display the Center's new acquisition, they barely noticed her exit.

Just as well. Because it was time to go. Away from this place that undid every ounce of self-protection she possessed. She'd email them later. She'd give Gram a call when she was on the road.

Before she reached Raleigh, but far enough away she couldn't be talked into returning.

Limping down the sidewalk, her feet and her heart sore, she reached one other decision. It wouldn't take long to pack the scant items she'd brought for the duration of her time in Cartridge Cove. And then one more stop before she left town, the Snowbird Mountains and the haunting reminders of what she'd never possess.

She'd promised Matt and Jake she'd watch them play stickball and beat the tar out of the Big Cove team. It wasn't fair to break a promise to children, Linden told herself. This had nothing to do, she argued, with her compelling urge to gaze upon Walker Crowe one more time. Her last glimpse would have to last forever.

Because, God help her, she had to leave. For his sake.

28

2018—Cartridge Cove

Walker knew the exact moment Linden arrived to watch the game though he faced the field and his guys. But his antennae, attuned to her since that first day, went on high alert. He'd pondered what he'd do—if she gave him the chance—for a week. He'd thought and dreamed and planned.

Because quit wasn't in his vocabulary, especially when it came to Linden Birchfield.

After the game—which the Cartridge Cove team won, naturally—he had to practically jog to catch her in the parking lot.

"Linden. Wait."

She kept her back to him.

A glance at the piled boxes inside the Toyota sent him into a panic. And put his plans into overdrive.

"Were you going to leave without saying good-bye?" His voice held a note of hurt.

"Might be the wisest thing to do." She looked at him. "Em told me how your guys tidied up the Meetinghouse cemetery this week. Thanks." She flattened her hand on the roof of the car.

He shrugged and placed his hand close to, but not touching, hers. Her fingers flexed, drew back. In the end it wasn't race or faith that parted them.

Not city versus country, but this . . . this thing from her past that held her in a claw of fear. Which she refused to explain.

She cleared her throat. "I wondered if you and the boys would plant Cherokee lilies there for me? And roses at Mrs. Swimmer's place?"

"Best time to plant lily bulbs is in the fall. And roses in late winter or early spring. Why don't you stick around and help me plant them?"

Her lips tightened. "No."

"God Almighty, Linden."

He banged the car with his hand. She blinked.

"Is no the only word you can say to me?" His mouth worked. "I want to tell you . . . I wanted to ask if—"

"Stop. Don't say it." Her eyes grew wide with alarm. "Believe me when I tell you this is for the best."

"Best for me? I don't think so." He laughed, the sound without mirth. "Or best for you? To protect yourself so you can continue to hide from the truth."

She cut her eyes away over the mountains.

Walker raked a hand over his head. Stick to the plan, Crowe. "Okay. Whatever you want."

Her gaze returned to him, fraught with suspicion.

"For old time's sake, one more Cherokee lesson? There's this place I wanted to show you . . . a cooling-off place."

A shadow of a smile ghosted her lips. "This will involve trees, won't it?"

He nodded. "But mainly water."

She let her shoulders rise and fall. "I'm not dressed to go swimming."

Walker surveyed the cut-off jean shorts, light blue t-shirt, and flip-flops. "You're perfect for this place. Rocks would rub the bottom off of a swimsuit."

Her eyebrows rose. "What exactly is this place, Crowe?"

"A fun place," he promised. "Cherokee style." He gestured toward his parked truck. "You can ride—"

"No." At the scowl he couldn't keep off his face, she started to touch the lines between his eyes and thought better of it, dropping her hand to her side. "I'll follow you there."

Her terms or no terms.

Fine. At this point, he'd take what he could get.

Linden parked behind his truck at the graveled turnoff in the mountains beyond his place and Mrs. Swimmer's. She wondered if they were still in North Carolina or in Tennessee.

He waited for her near a path that led into the woods, towels tossed over his shoulder.

Why was she doing this?

She extracted herself from her car. This was probably only going to prolong the agony. But she owed him an explanation. So when he'd thrown her an opportunity to make things right—or right as they could be . . .

And she wanted to squeeze every ounce of every moment she could from being with him.

"It's not far," he promised and set off down the trail. He held back a branch and allowed her to pass through. Stepping over a fallen log, he offered his hand.

She hesitated. Her heart pounded. But she took it, relishing the strength of those warm, brown fingers wrapped around her own. The smile he sent her way almost broke her resolve.

Almost.

The sounds of burbling water reached her ears before her eyes found its source. They emerged onto level ground at the base of a gigantic, slanted slab of rock. Water cascaded down the length of it to empty into the deep pool at their feet.

She rocked back. "What is it?"

"Local watering hole." His eyes twinkled at her reaction. "Best sort of watering hole in the summer." He pointed to the slippery hewn path, which continued up the side of an overhanging bluff.

"A God-made water slide. Sixty foot long. The pool," he peered over the embankment. "Maybe seven-feet deep. Come on, it'll be fun."

She made a face. "On my butt?"

"That's the way I'd advise." He rubbed a hand over his gray NCSU t-shirt. "Unless you want to lose some skin." He dropped the towels and toed out of his sneakers.

She jutted her chin at his khaki shorts as she stepped out of her flip-flops. "What about you?"

"Grass-cutting shorts. Sacrificed to a good cause." He tugged at her hand and led her to the wall of the cliff. "Keep your balance by hugging the rock face," he advised. "Pretend you're a monkey and grip each step with your toes before you ascend to the next level."

He positioned himself behind her. "You go first. I won't let you fall."

Problem was, she'd already fallen. For him.

But she did as he instructed and found herself at the top. She stretched forward on her tippy-toes to gander at the flumes of water disappearing into the pool below.

The water rushed over her toes. She sucked in a breath at the coldness. If this was any indication of what the pool felt like . . .

July in the Snowbird Mountains.

The coiled muscles in his arm hugged around her. A solid buttress of dependable.

Like the mountains.

He caught her around the waist as her feet slid out from under her. "Best not to look too far ahead," he cautioned. "Take it as it comes."

She tried to inject a lighter tone into her voice. "Your philosophy of life, I take it?"

"Instead of trying to force life around my plans," his breath fanned her neck. "I just allow life to happen and with God's strength, adjust around it."

She pondered that difference between them.

"You want to go first or me?"

She edged away. "You."

He lowered himself to a sitting position in the gushing water. "Give me to the count of thirty and you go next." He deposited his hands, palms down upon the surface of the wet rock, and shoved off. Moments later, a splash below.

Imitating his movements, she crouched at the brink, then settled her bottom onto the slick rock. "Here goes nothing." She gulped.

She scooted downward, her feet traveling first. She raised her arms to keep them from scraping. Her eyes fixed toward her final destination, she spilled downhill, plunging earthward. Allowing gravity and the rush of the water to have their way.

The ride proved fast, uncertain, out of control. Totally exhilarating. Just as Walker promised.

Her toes dipped into the pool, and the rest of her followed. She closed her eyes as her head ducked under.

And she dropped. Sank. To the bottom.

His arm went round her waist and, with a jerk, he halted her downward spiral, dragging her upward, till once again she opened her eyes and beheld the sun.

With a spray of water, both of their bodies rocketed from the nether regions. Water streaming down her face, she threw back her head and laughed.

Spurting water out of his mouth, he favored her with a smile and towed her to the edge of the pool.

The corners of her mouth curved. "Again?"

He heaved himself out of the pool, water running in rivulets down his bare legs. "Of course." Grinning, he extended a hand to her, the wild girl he'd unleashed on a ride upon the Cherohala Skyway.

Standing beside him with her tee plastered to her body, she squeezed the dripping, straggling strands of her hair, the clasp, miraculously, still in place.

He cocked his head, a question mark forming with his eyebrow.

She undid the clasp, throwing it on the towel, and shook out the rest of her hair. "Satisfied?"

He smiled. "Not by a long shot."

They took the plunge down the water slide, not once, but five more times. After the fifth time, as he helped her out of the pool, this time he caught her in his arms. His eyes, she noted with a catch in her heart, went opaque. Linden trembled, but not because she was cold.

Rising on her tiptoes, she swayed against him as he brushed a tendril of her hair across his lips. Her arms draped around his neck, and he threaded his fingers into her hair. His body pressed against hers. As exhilarating as the water ride, as frightening, as promising. A wave of feeling crested over her.

How she loved Walker Crowe, for his grin, his gentleness, for the spirit of adventure he aroused within her. For his willingness to share his pain with her. For his strength.

In fitful starts and stops, he lowered his mouth. She tilted her head in anticipation. He cradled her face, pulled her tight to his chest. The sunlight played on his hair.

His hands dropped to the curve of her back, kneading her shirt against her spine. She soaked in his warmth. His lips skimmed over her jaw line and caressed her lips ever so softly.

Tentative. Exploring. Asking.

She answered by pressing her mouth against his, returning and deepening his kiss. She drank him in like the soil drank in rain after a long drought. Fervent. Impassioned. Wasting no time.

Hungry. Devouring. Memorizing with her lips the hollow of his cheekbones, the hard line of his jaw, the taste of him.

Saying good-bye.

As if he sensed her intent, he retracted his mouth and feathered his lips against her cheek. "Linden," his voice rough and pitched low. "I love you. Don't leave . . ." His mouth quavered. She could feel the pounding of his heart. "Stay here in Cartridge Cove. With me."

She lowered her heels to the ground and dropped her eyes. Her throat constricted, and she bit back the words that had risen in response to his.

"You belong here." He gripped her shoulders. "I've been wrong about so much. Full-blood, half, quarter, or none at all. To be Cherokee is about the spirit. And your heart, Linden? I feel it. I know it. It beats . . . like a Cherokee."

Her forehead against his shirt, she listened to the rhythm of his heart. Somehow she needed to make him understand. She'd allowed herself over the past weeks to remember and to cry. Time to do the last part of what Mrs. Swimmer had instructed her to do to lance the wound and to heal.

Time to tell her story to the one who loved her.

"She's been dead longer than she was ever alive."

Walker's eyes jerked to where Linden sat, cross-legged, beside him on the towel. Her voice void of emotion, she trained her eyes upon a distant point above the rim of the mountains.

"Ten years ago."

About the time that last mission of his had gone horribly wrong.

"I was nineteen when she was born. At UVA. My parents had abandoned me again for the less fortunate." She kicked the spongy moss at the end of the towel. "Not an excuse for the choices I made." She shrugged. "Maybe I just wanted to get their attention."

He swallowed past the lump in his throat. He clenched his fist into his lap. He longed to touch her, to hold her in the circle of his arms. But she corralled her apartness from him as if a shield.

God, help me help her.

"What was her name?"

293

Linden sighed. "The courts continue to debate in cases such as hers that she was even a person. A valid, viable human being." Her eyes welled.

He captured her hand. She didn't pull away.

She took a deep, steadying breath. "I called her Lily, and she was born with anencephaly."

He looked at her with a blank expression.

"A genetic abnormality that occurs when the neural tube at the head fails to close during pregnancy, which results in a major absence of the skull and brain. No scalp." She recited the words as if quoting from a medical textbook.

Perhaps, she was.

"Most babies do not survive birth. Lily lived for two weeks. Two—" She bit her lip. Dots of blood appeared.

He was almost afraid to speak, lest he say the wrong thing. "There was nothing that could be done?"

"I hid the pregnancy from those closest to me geographically—Gram and Granddad—and put off going to a doctor who might've known Dad . . . everybody knows Dad, you see."

Her voice choked. "He specializes in genetic disorders. Not that I expected anything like that. But I skipped the usual ultrasounds and routine prenatal exams because by the time I realized I was pregnant, I was embarrassed about what I'd done."

"Lily's father?" he whispered. "You told him? He stayed with you when . . ."

"I told him." She shook her head. "He couldn't backpedal fast enough. Suggested I take a paternity—"

She stopped when Walker went motionless.

He made a growling sound. "What did you say the jerk's name was?"

She squeezed his hand, her lips flitting upward. "My valiant defender, I don't think I ought to tell you his name."

Linden planted a quick kiss through the fabric of his shirt onto his bicep. "Prison wouldn't suit you, Walker Crowe."

At her unspoken invitation, he nestled against her side. He inhaled, slow through his nostrils. "You were alone then."

She nodded. "I'd never wish that kind of alone on anyone." Her eyes skittered at the flash of a bluebird on a branch. "The obstetrician recognized the name on my emergency contact form and called my grandfather, Congressman Birchfield. He and Gram drove to Charlottesville from D.C. Gram called Dad and Mom."

"Would you," he hesitated. "Would you tell me about Lily?"

She favored him with a genuine smile through a veil of tears. "Thank you for asking. Most are repulsed. Don't want to know. Mom couldn't talk about it until a few weeks ago when I met her in Raleigh. Mrs. Swimmer was right. It helps to tell it."

Closing his eyes, he cupped her face with his hands and kissed her forehead. "Tell me," he whispered against her skin.

"She was small and born blind and maybe deaf. Comatose-like. Dad said . . ." Her voice wobbled. "Dad said babies like her were unable to feel pain." She clutched his arm until he wanted to cry out in pain.

For her pain.

"But she breathed and responded to touch and . . ." Her body shook with a repressed sob. "I'd like to think, to the sound of my voice."

He'd never felt so helpless. "I'm sorry, Linden."

"Me, too, Walker. For her. For you. For us because you see why I need to leave."

She shifted on the towel, an arm's length, an eternity removed. Shutting him out.

"No." He frowned. "I do not see what this has to do with you and me."

She rose and slipped her feet into the flip-flops. "It's a genetic condition. I can't risk ever having another child. Putting myself or a child through that again."

He stood. "You've had the tests run on yourself?"

She shook her head.

"Then how do you know this would happen again? Perhaps it wasn't you but that—" The name he called The Jerk he didn't learn in Sunday school. "Maybe it was his gene pool."

"I can't do it." She threw out her hands. "Any of it. You saw what happened to me in the church nursery." Linden gestured at the pool. "I almost went under all those years ago."

She shot him a look. "You asked me once about my job in New York and why I left. I quit before I was fired after I came unglued in the middle of a photo shoot involving babies and diapers."

Linden held her thumb and forefinger inches apart. "I'm this close to being Leila Hummingbird. It's been a slow, slippery climb toward sanity. I cannot—I will not—do it again. I won't do it to you."

He took a step toward her. "What about adoption? I don't care about biological children." He grasped her upper arms. "This doesn't have to be an either/or with me, Linden. I love you. You. And that's not contingent upon any yet-to-be-realized offspring."

"I've seen you with those babies at church. With your guys."

"None of whom are my biological children."

"You deserve a real wife who can give you your own children." She removed herself, gently, out of his reach.

"So you're going to walk away?" He ground his teeth. "Make a life-altering decision not just for yourself, but change the course of my life as well, based on your fears?"

"On a certain reality I've already experienced."

His mouth quivered. "A decision not based in faith, not guided by Him but instead on your fears of what might happen."

She flinched.

"There's a safety in living, breathing faith, Linden." Walker lifted his face to the sky. "A security in knowing whatever lies ahead God will determine your footsteps across that mountain. He will give the courage to keep on keeping on. To approach the future with the hope of Christ."

She averted her eyes.

"How big is your God, Linden? If you focus on Him," Walker pounded his chest, "the problems and the fears, I promise you, become smaller."

"I'm not there, Walker." She tossed her head. "Maybe I won't ever be."

Bending, he retrieved the hair clip at their feet. Before she could protest, he gathered her hair into an untidy bun and secured the clasp.

He backed away. "'I go among trees and sit still.'"

Linden's lips trembled. "What?"

"It's another poem I like by Wendell Berry. Maybe you should look it up when you go ho—back to Raleigh."

Linden's eyes, as blue as an April sky, shimmered with tears. "Good-bye, Walker Crowe."

He clamped his lips together. Walker refused to ever say those words to her.

Without a backward glance, she disappeared into the tree line.

Dropping to his knees in the pine needles, he buried his head in his hands. Praying for God to ease her heart.

And his.

29

I go among trees and sit still.
All my stirring becomes quiet
around me like circles on water.

. . . .

Then what I am afraid of comes.
I live for a while in its sight.
What I fear in it leaves it,
and the fear of it leaves me.
It sings, and I hear its song.

. . . .

I hear my song at last,
and I sing it. As we sing,
the day turns, the trees move.
—Wendell Berry

Late October 2018—Raleigh

A drought-stricken summer evolved into a dry autumn.
Between—God be praised—client consultations and publicity
campaigns, Linden paid the monthly rent on the apartment
she acquired near downtown. She became a faithful attender
of Jesus Our Redeemer Fellowship. And the GriefShare group,

which met there on Tuesdays, provided no small measure of comfort. Her vision of God grew larger. They were strangers no more.

But there was no comfort to be had when her thoughts veered to Walker. Like the masochist she was, she tortured herself wondering how he was getting the trees ready for the Christmas harvest. Wishing she could see the view above the ridge with its glorious display of autumn color.

Like a fool, she caught herself following the fall foliage reports for the Blue Ridge Parkway on WRAL each night. And most surprising of all, she found herself longing for a glimpse of the wild, mysterious beauty she'd found in the Snowbird.

On Sunday afternoons she'd gotten into the habit of bicycling to Raleigh's Greenway, propping herself under a particularly enormous oak with her Bible and the poem by Berry. And with only the music of Crabtree Creek gurgling alongside her special spot and the compelling call of the crow, Linden learned to listen again to the quiet—what passed for quiet in the city—and to God.

She also tossed and turned—not so much over thoughts of Lily these days, again God be praised—but over how long before Walker would give in to the inevitable. How long before he'd give in to the well-meaning matchmaking of the Snowbird aunties. A right outcome for Walker that caused Linden's heart to ache.

Then, her thoughts wandered to who—that lovely veterinarian, Myra Ropetwister from Andrews? Or Wendy Panther from Yellow Hill? And her stomach would clench, even dreaming once she walked into the old Meetinghouse church as it stood in Sarah Jane's day to watch him take a bride.

Feeling crabby after another such night, she was less than polite when she snatched the shrilling phone from her bedside table at six in the morning. "What?"

"Is this how you speak to your grandmother, Linden Elizabeth?"

No Honey Girl today.

A weird, inexplicable feeling took hold. "Gram? What's wrong?" She sat straight up in bed. "Is it Walker?"

"Why would you think that?" Even over the phone, Linden would've bet money Marvela smirked at her from across the state. She'd not been pleased Linden had "run away"—Gram's words—again.

"Is something wrong with Walker, Gram? Tell me."

Marvela huffed. "I called because I thought you might like to be aware of the fact the Alexander brothers were arrested at the Mercantile last night."

Her grandmother called at the crack of dawn to tell her this?

"Good, I guess . . ."

"Did you know Walker's taking a job with the Sheriff's department after he finishes some classes at the police academy? With his military training, he'll be an asset to the county."

The sinking feeling escalated. "No, I did not. He and I . . . We . . ."

"Ross, if you'll start those blueberry pancakes for me on the griddle that would be marvelous." Gram laughed, the mouthpiece tilted away, at something Ross said on the other end.

Linden gritted her teeth. "Is he okay, Gram?"

"Sure. He'll serve as a sharpshooter with the Graham County Sheriff's Department. Sharpshooter . . ." Marvela repeated in case Linden hadn't caught it the first time.

Her grandmother's tone turned smug. "Ross tells me that's what they call a sniper in civilian law enforcement."

"And Walker was involved in the incident at the Mercantile?"

"Yep. He was at the fire station next door, and the situation escalated before the county SWAT team arrived. Thought you'd like to know. Oh, and . . ." Marvela removed the mouthpiece, calling out further instructions to the Colonel about serving the inn's guests.

"What?" Linden snarled. "What else?" She held her breath as the most illogical idea flitted through her mind.

Like maybe her grandmother had called to warn Linden of Walker's pending engagement.

"Gram," she shouted.

"Lord-a mercy, Honey Girl. You don't have to scream in my ear," chided Marvela. "All I was going to say was Fred Alexander escaped custody and has vowed revenge on Cartridge Cove and Walker Crowe. After one of his sons took the cashier hostage—"

"Walker took care of it."

Linden fell onto her pillow.

Marvela sighed. "He did, Honey Girl."

But was he okay? Really? Having to pull the trigger after what he'd been through . . .

An aching to be there for him almost consumed Linden, but she couldn't be there for him in the ways that mattered most. She lowered her voice. "Thanks for calling, Gram."

Silence percolated across the phone line.

"When will I see you again, Linden?"

She jutted her jaw. "When you and Ross visit me in Raleigh, I guess."

Marvela muttered something uncomplimentary about stubborn parts of a donkey's anatomy and hung up.

Two days later, Linden dashed into her apartment with a bag of Grand Asia takeout. She flung her purse on the countertop and switched on the television. She flopped on the sofa to watch the evening news and eat her moo goo gai pan. The anchor started the broadcast with the news of a massive forest fire in the Snowbird Mountains of western North Carolina. Dropping her chopsticks, Linden leaned forward.

"Fourteen thousand acres have already burned . . ." The screen shifted to a live report, the television chopper revealing pictures of fire crews battling the flames.

Smoke billowed from the mountain range. Autumn's splendor wasn't the only thing consuming the treetops. Hellish orange tongues of fire shot high in the air, turning loblolly pines into sulfurous matchsticks.

"Out of control . . . Grown exponentially since Monday . . ."

Her knees buckled.

"Residents are being advised to be ready to evacuate at a moment's notice."

"Where?" Linden yelled at the screen. "Which residents?"

"The cause of the fire has been determined to be arson." The live report shunted from the news crew to the co-anchors at the station desk in Raleigh.

"Wait." She bounced, accidentally upending the coffee table with the moo goo gai pan. "That's it? That's all you're going to say?"

"More coverage at the eleven o'clock news cast," promised the female anchor.

"No . . ." Linden raced to her purse, digging to find her phone. "Don't leave me hanging. You can't do this to me."

She speed-dialed her grandmother. "Pick up. Pick up," she bellowed into the receiver. "Where are you, Gram?" Her fingers drummed.

Visions of the Victorian burning down around her grandmother and the Colonel's bodies seared her mind. "Pick up," she moaned. Her lips tightened.

Irene's quilt shop. The church. The Center. Mrs. Swimmer. The homes of the people who'd welcomed her into their town and their lives. The Christmas tree farm.

Walker . . . He volunteered with the local fire department. She inhaled sharply.

Did that mean he battled the blaze on the front lines? But what about the National Park Service? Didn't they have fire crews?

Her mouth pulled downward.

Of course, Walker Crowe was on the front line battling this fire. It's what he did. It's who he was.

Marvela's number went to voice mail.

"Gram? If you're there, please call me as soon as possible. I heard about the fire. Are you okay? Is everybody . . . ?"

Who was she trying to kid?

"Is Walker okay?" Her voice trembled. "Please Gram, call me as soon as you get this message. Please . . ."

Linden stared at the phone in her hand for a good five minutes before she realized the only thing she could do—the best thing Marvela would've advised her to do—was to pray.

So she did.

For the next three hours, she prayed for everyone she could think of in Cartridge Cove. She prayed while she cleaned the sauce off the carpet. She prayed as she scrubbed the bathroom grout free of mildew.

She didn't vacuum, though. Because she might not have been able to hear the phone ring —which she kept only an arm's length away the entire duration of her cleaning frenzy.

At ten, Marvela called. She sounded tired, but resolute. "Honey Girl—"

"Gram? Are you okay?"

A long sigh. "Ross and I . . . the town . . . we're fine. I'm sorry I wasn't here to take your call. The ladies at the church, we've been working with the diner to provide meals for the firefighters when their shift ends and they rotate to town for some shut eye."

"Firefighters?" Linden gulped. "Who?"

"Multiple agencies. Our boys plus the stations in Robbinsville. The woods have been tinder dry." Marvela took a breath. "The National Park Service. The Bureau of Land Management. The fire crews have gained control of seventy percent of the conflagration, the chief said a few hours ago. They've contained most of it, except . . ."

"Except what, Gram?"

"It jumped the fire break they established at Singing Creek, swept over Chestnut Hill . . ." Marvela paused. "Kind of ironic when you think the arson investigator believes Fred Alexander set it. He's still out there somewhere. Burned his own place down in the process."

That haunted place needed to be swept clean of its old fears and tragedy.

Like her?

"That means the fire was headed toward . . . ?" Linden closed her eyes. "Mrs. Swimmer? Walker?"

A long, agonizing moment ensued during which Linden believed her head would explode before Gram finally answered.

"The fire beast was so fast. Devouring everything in its path, Honey Girl."

Linden sank to the floor, her back against the wall. "Gram . . ."

"There weren't enough firefighters on site to stop it. You know how remote it is there in those hollows."

Linden rocked, her chin on her up-drawn knees, the phone smashed against her ear. Back and forth. Back and forth.

"They only had the manpower and equipment to save one place . . . Mrs. Swimmer's or Walker's farm."

"No . . ." She let the breath trickle out.

"It's okay, Honey Girl. Walker made the choice himself to save Mrs. Swimmer's property."

Of course he had.

"The trees?" Linden groaned. "All his work."

"Just the trees. They saved the house and the horses in the barn."

Not just trees to Walker.

"But is he okay?"

"Why don't you come see for yourself?"

She shook her head, sending her hair spiraling out of order, as if Marvela could see her across the miles. "You know I can't."

"I know you won't." Marvela exhaled, a slow gust of air. "And I won't tell him you called, either."

Linden bit her lip.

"He's asked all of us not to speak your name in front of him anymore."

Sucker-punched, Linden clicked off. She lay face down upon the kitchen linoleum and cried with wrenching, gut-twisted sobs. For herself. For him.

And for his trees.

Gunfire raked the crew digging the fire line. The firefighter beside Walker jerked and collapsed to the ground. Blood spurted from a wound in his chest. Walker dropped to his knees, trying to stem the flow of blood with his leather gloves.

Another blast shot like forked lightning through smoky haze connecting with his buddy from the Cartridge Cove squad. His friend jolted and clutched his thigh.

"Shooter," Walker shouted at the handful of men frozen in various positions on the slope. "Find cover."

He dragged his fallen comrade behind a still-smoldering, blackened log. The winds shifted and picked up speed.

"I promised I'd settle with you, Crowe . . ." yelled a gruff voice.

Walker closed his eyes and heaved a breath. "It's me you want, Alexander. Me that took out your boy. Let the rest of these men go. They're trying to save the town."

Alexander's off-kilter laugh floated out. "What do I care about those featherheads in town?"

Walker hefted the axe end of the pulaski, wishing for the first time in a long while he had his scope and rifle.

Sporadic rounds kept the firefighters pinned in place.

"Walker," hissed his friend. "Get down. Get back." Removing the radio from his belt, Billy sent out a terse SOS to the base camp.

"I'll draw his fire." Walker waved two fingers in the direction of the spike camp where they'd established a temporary base. "Get the wounded out of range."

"No." Billy caught the sleeve of his jacket. "You'll be killed. Don't throw your life away just because Lin—"

Walker yanked his arm free. The anger and pain surged through his heart. "I got this." He gave a bitter laugh. "Trust me. If anyone can deal with Alexander, it's me. Now go."

The trees—his trees—were ruined. Linden forever gone. But someone had to stand up to the likes of the Alexanders of the world.

Walker belly-crawled over the log, expecting any minute the white-hot pain of a bullet to score his flesh. Behind him, he detected the sounds of the other guys loading the wounded onto makeshift litters. The wind whipped and howled.

Gripping the axe, he rose, blocking the litters from Alexander's sight. "You got me, Fred. Like you wanted."

Alexander sidled out from behind the trunk of one of the giants. How it had hurt Walker's heart to see the Standing People ignite one by one this week, almost as much as it had ripped his soul when Linden walked away.

Fred pointed the gun, aiming at Walker's chest. "Hands where I can see them. Drop the axe, Crowe."

The axe settled with a dull thud against the drought-stricken, fire-ravaged earth at his boot. He lifted his hands, palms up, at his sides.

Fred smiled, a gargoylish caricature of a smile. "I'm in the vermin extermination business these days." He tightened his hold on the barrel stock, rammed against his shoulder. "Completing the business my forebears neglected to finish with your kind."

Walker swallowed. The air stifling, his eyes watered and his nose burned.

Fred nudged the rifle in the direction of the ridge, away from base camp. "Up there, Crowe. And prepare to meet your Maker."

At the sudden roar of a hundred jet engines, both men swiveled. The wall of fire had changed course. A mushroom of billowing smoke and ash plumed. The wind shrieked and took on a life of its own. A vortex of flame gyrated a mile upwards into the blood-orange sky. A primeval rage engulfed the giant ones, moaning in agonizing death throes and popping like a thousand exploding mortar shells. The earth shook with the aftershocks, nature's own version of a nuclear meltdown.

"Firestorm tornado," he yelled at Alexander whose face reflected Walker's own raw fear.

"Singing Creek," Walker gestured. "Over the ridge. Get to the water. Only chance. Can't outrun—"

Alexander dropped his rifle. And on all fours like a Great Smoky Mountain black bear, he clambered up the sixty-degree slope.

Walker scrambled up the incline, his boots slipping in the dry soil. His hands scrabbled for the exposed roots of upended trees. His muscles strained underneath his protective gear as he hoisted himself out of the path of the fiery whirlwind.

Licking tongues of fire towered and curled like a wave, crested and rained embers ahead of him. Debris blasted the top of his hard hat. He lurched around the erupting smaller brushfires.

Gaining the ridge seconds after Alexander, Walker ran for his life toward the drought-sluggish water of the creek. He flew past Fred like he was standing still. The monster at his back, Walker leaped across a gulley. An unholy primal shriek erupted from Fred. The roaring furnace accelerated, the flames closed in.

His muscles cramped with fatigue. Heat seared his lungs, sucking out the oxygen. If he didn't make it to the creek soon, he'd drop from suffocation before the flames ever reached his body.

Maybe, he grimaced pushing on, a mercy.

Walker waded into the ankle-deep water of Singing Creek. He pawed at the yellow pouch on his back containing the silver tent shelter. He shook it open, wrapped the shield around him and plunged face first into the water.

The icy cold mountain stream took his breath, but he fought to keep the shelter tucked around his body. The spiraling winds buffeted, trying to rip the life-saving shelter from him. He used the weight of his arms, legs, and feet to hold it down.

With the air too hot to breathe inside the silver foil, he felt microwaved. Holding his breath, Walker hunkered into the bottom of the sandy creek bottom. His lips cracked from lack of moisture, he recited the Twenty-third Psalm in his head and regretted the life he'd never get to live.

The life he'd wanted to live with Linden Birchfield.

He remembered the legand that, after leaving their shells, the souls of The People crossed Singing Creek here before flying over the Snowbird to the Beyond.

But Walker's last coherent thought was of Linden's eyes.

The color of an April sky over the ridge of his farm.

30

The next day, Linden stepped out of a client meeting at RTP, the chrome and glass building gleaming in the morning sun. She'd applied lots of makeup after another fear-driven night to cover the shadows under her eyes. The waistband of her knee-length, pleated gray skirt she safety-pinned a notch tighter.

When she worried, she ate too much.

When she grieved, she ate not at all.

Hearing the buzzing of her cell—she'd turned it to vibrate during the meeting— Linden ran to the parking deck. She flung out the contents of her purse onto the hood of her car in a desperate compulsion beyond rational thought to answer her phone. She knew, somehow, it'd be Gram.

And it was.

"Gram?"

Her grandmother's voice quivered. "Honey . . . I . . ."

"What? Tell me. Anything's better than not knowing."

"I'm afraid not knowing is still all I've got to give you. Walker and a fire crew were working the backcountry road beyond Turkey Hill when Alexander appeared out of nowhere. He shot two of the fireman. Walker gave chase. The others transported the wounded down the mountain pronto. They were losing so much blood, Ross said."

"Walker, Gram. What about Walker?"

"By the time they made it down the mountain to a place the men could be airlifted out, the fire had gained momentum. The squad had to fight their way back up the mountain, foot by foot."

"Where's Walker?" Linden wailed.

"They . . . I don't know. The Forest Service has airplanes dumping retardant to extinguish the blaze. But the wind from the firestorm . . . They can't . . . The planes are grounded now. The deputies are right behind the fire crews searching. They found Alexander's body this morning."

Linden didn't trust her voice to speak.

"Walker had on his gear, Honey Girl. He's trained for this kind of thing."

Her voice when Linden found the words sounded dull. "But they can't find him."

"They're looking as we speak. They won't give up. Walker won't give up. He's tough. He's smart."

He could be dead. A barrier crashed and tumbled in Linden's heart.

Too late?

"As soon as I hear the first word, I'll upd—"

Linden clicked off. Gathering her belongings, she found her car keys and once in the driver's seat, inserted the key into the ignition. What had she been thinking to leave him? To leave everything she'd grown to love in Cartridge Cove?

Home—Sarah Jane, Touch the Clouds, even Leila had somehow known—home was where you belonged. Home was the place where the people you loved lived. Home was full of the people who loved you back.

Images of his body, burned, unrecognizable—

"Not that, God," she prayed against her too vivid imagination. "Please, not that."

Before she realized it, she'd driven close to a hundred miles and found herself on the outskirts of Winston-Salem, where she was forced to refuel her tank. She also bought a bottle of water, prayed Walker had some, too, and because she refused to give into grief yet—three Moon Pies, Nabs, a Milky Way bar, and a pack of Big Red gum.

With a wrenching twist, Linden tossed her hair clasp in the trashcan beside the fuel pump.

Hurry, hurry, hurry.

She fumed at every delay. She wove around clusters of cars on I-40, blasted past exit ramps. Prayed her headlong rush wouldn't be delayed by a speeding ticket.

At four o'clock, she pulled into Mercer's Auto Body shop on the fringe of Cartridge Cove. Only his wife was on duty, manning the cash register. Main Street, like Mercer's, appeared devoid of cars.

The air hung thick and heavy with smoke. And though the sun should be sinking into the horizon by now, the sky and the mountains glowed a distant red. Gladys Mercer didn't seem surprised to see Linden.

"I don't know any news about your man, sweetie."

Not for the first time, Linden wondered if it was the Cherokee in them or the sprinkling of the oft-touted Scottish second sight that accounted for the things these people in the Snowbird knew without being asked.

"Where are they looking?"

"They've got roadblocks on Berry Bush Road." Gladys pointed out the window in the direction of the hills. "The information officer hangs out there, waiting for the crews to come off the mountain for a shift change. If they've found him, that's where they'll know first."

Linden inclined her head in thanks and headed for the door.

"But they're not letting folks venture that far, hon."

Linden didn't break stride. "Just let them try to stop me."

She parked behind a line of trucks, some sporting 'Red Pride', others with Dixie flags and gun racks. A new rotation of firefighters stood at the apex of the road, awaiting transportation to the hot spots. Two Sheriff's Department cars, their front ends toward each other, blocked the road from further traffic.

"Miss Birchfield?"

She recognized one of the guys who'd often manned the station with Walker over the summer.

"What in the world are you doing here?" His plump, pinked face peeked out at her from underneath the bulky yellow and black helmet, chin-strapped on his head.

She squared her shoulders, wrapping her arms around herself in the cool, mountain air of October, no matter that hell raged five miles away.

"I've come to find Walker."

The twenty-something shook his head in disbelief. "Miss Birchfield, we can't let you up there—"

"I'm going if I have to walk every step of the way by myself."

A deputy she didn't know joined the firefighter, catching the tail end of the conversation. "Nobody," he jabbed a finger. "Is going there but authorized personnel."

Static crackled at the radio clipped to his belt. He stepped away to answer.

"They're coming down," he shouted to the men. "They've done it. Contained it. It'll be a mop-up operation now." The men cheered, some flinging their helmets into the air.

Linden elbowed her way to the narrow space where the patrol cars faced each other. "Did they find—? What did they say about—?"

A plume of dust arose. Tires rolled across the dirt surface of the tertiary road, which led into the national forest. All eyes swiveled to watch the incoming vehicle. Conversation halted.

The Forest Service pickup ground to a stop fifty feet away. The dust added to the smoke particles kicking over her and the men. She coughed, shaded her eyes, and peered into the throng of men disembarking from the pickup bed.

One man, then three made their way around the side, their black boots crunching the gravel underfoot. The neon yellow strips on their brownish jackets radiated in the pickup's headlights.

She examined each soot-begrimed face, looking for the one she loved. It was hard to distinguish one man from another, in their gear and covered with grime. They passed Linden, heading for a water cooler and platter of sandwiches on the tailgate of a truck.

Walker's friend on the relief crew jumped into another truck pointed toward the mountains. He tapped on the back window. The driver set off, raising more dust, obscuring more of her vision. She held her ground, waiting for the dust to settle, holding her breath, praying.

Two. Three. Four more emerged from the first truck. They emptied out from the Forest Service vehicle until she was sure no more could appear. But two more firefighters materialized in front of the truck's headlights.

One of the men clapped the other on the shoulder. A tall man, he stripped off the heavy, thick-fingered gloves and stuffed them into a cargo pocket above the padded knees of his pants. Laughing at a remark from his companion, he angled his face. The light bounced off high, blunt cheekbones. Sparking off clean, even white teeth.

The whitest thing in his smoke-blackened face.

Linden took a step forward.

The deputy caught her by the arm. "You can't—"

"Walker!" she screamed, rising on tiptoe. She squinted over the officer's shoulder.

The firefighter jerked, strained forward, searching through the coming night. His eyes, the whites contrasting with the rest of his face, widened. "Linden?"

Linden threw off the restraining arm of the deputy and flew beyond the patrol cars.

She ran all the way, closing the distance between them. She sprinted right out of her sensible, gray suede flats. The gravel rocks cut the soles of her feet, but she was beyond feeling that kind of pain.

Three feet away, she leaped straight into his outstretched arms, knocking his helmet with a clatter to the earth.

"Lin—"

She claimed his mouth with a kiss that sought to burn away the pain of lonely weeks without him.

"I love you," she whispered when she came up for air.

She knotted her hands around Walker's neck. Her feet dangled.

"I'm filth—"

"I don't care."

She allowed Walker one breath before kissing him again, her fingers sifting through his hair on the back of—

Gasping, she pulled back far enough to look him in the face. "You cut your hair."

Her fingers threaded through his locks, no longer bound with the leather band, but close-cropped as in his army days.

She pounded his chest. "What did you do?"

His hand traveled over her spine, across her shoulder blades and under her mane. "Didn't realize I needed your permission. It was hazardous and hot fighting the fire." He wound his fingers through her hair and hauled her closer, his breath mixing with hers.

The corners of his mouth twitched. "Besides, you always said you didn't much care for a man with hair prettier than yours."

She drew back to reassess.

There was a lot to be said for a man in uniform. Army. Cop. Firefighter. She feathered her fingers through his shorn locks again.

He'd lost that barely civilized look—on second thought—she took another look at his eyes, dark and opaque.

And then again, maybe not.

"It'll grow back." His eyes locked onto hers. "If you'll be around to watch."

She tightened her hold. "I'll be around." She couldn't stop her lip from quavering. "If you still want me to be."

He crushed her to himself in answer.

She pressed her forehead against his. "I'm so sorry about your trees and . . ." She choked back a sob. "Everything I said or didn't say. Or should've said. Or—"

"Trees grow back, too. We managed to save that little linden tree close to Mrs. Swimmer's." Walker grabbed a hank of her hair and brushed it across his jaw line. "And I've got a house left."

He smiled. "To bring home my bride."

"I missed you, Walker Crowe. Desperately. You have no idea . . ."

The muted pain in his eyes gouged at her heart.

"Oh . . . I imagine I can." He swung her around. "Because I love you, Linden Birchfield." His voice hitched. "Forever and Beyond."

"You were right about my picture of God being too small." Her eyes dropped. "I'm tired of living in exile, allowing my fears to control me rather than allowing God to direct my steps."

She kneaded the shoulders of his jacket. "I'm sorry it's taken me so long to come home to you. To God. To where He wants me to belong."

Her voice wobbled. "I'm better, but I'm still not sure I'll ever be able to . . ."

"I don't know what the future holds, Linden. All I know is I'm committed to loving you as long as I draw breath."

Walker cupped her face in his hands. "But as much as I love you, you have to know ultimately I'm not the end of your journey. Nor is this place. The end of your journey, the repository of all your fears, hopes, and dreams, must be with Him. And His mercy."

"Streams of mercy." Linden nodded. "The gentle Savior who gave me a second chance after all my mistakes. To love and be loved by you."

Linden kissed one side of his dear face and then the other. "And blessed be God, I don't want to waste a minute of it."

Walker swallowed as she watched his face transform. "Someone once told me the further you've traveled, the sweeter comes the end of the journey."

Linden twined into him. "Better than Christmas trees?" she teased. "Sweeter than tea?"

He threw back his head and laughed. His eyes beckoned. Her pulse raced at his lopsided smile.

Walker trailed his thumb down her arm, brought her hand to his mouth and brushed his lips against her ring finger. "Allow me to show you, Miss Birchfield, just how sweet."

And he did.

Group Discussion Guide

1. "Guide Me, O Thou Great Jehovah" became an anthem for the dispossessed Cherokee in 1838. How has God guided you on your life journey? Upheld and sustained you? Delivered and healed?

2. What about Sarah Jane's story so captivated Linden? What resonated with you?

3. How you ever felt like an outcast or a stranger to God? What trail of tears have you trod?

4. After Afghanistan, Walker longed for trees; after heartbreak Linden longed for peace. Touch the Clouds and the Cherokee longed for the mountains of home. What do you long for? What price are you willing to pay to attain it?

5. Linden and Touch the Clouds struggled to believe in God's goodness; Walker struggled with unworthiness. With what do you wrestle?

6. What surprised you? What made you laugh? What made you cry?

7. If you had one hour to pack your life into one green trunk, what would you take? What would you leave behind?

8. How had life taught Linden to "hedge her bets" with Walker? What has life taught you?

9. The Trail of Tears serves as a metaphor in the novel. Describe the spiritual journey upon which Sarah Jane, Pierce, Touch the Clouds, Linden, and Walker embarked. Describe your own.

10. After the horrors of war, the trees were Walker's "fallback." What is yours?

11. How does God show Himself as Sarah Jane's Consolation over the course of her life? How have you found Him to be yours?

12. Broken by guilt and pain, Linden believes she's thrown away her chance for a happily-ever-after. What would you say to her?

13. Would you have forgiven Pierce?

14. If you were to record a final entry into the journal of your life, what would you write?

15. Mrs. Swimmer said, "Takes courage to overcome the mountains in your path." What mountains have you overcome? How?

16. "Only one thing more important than understanding where you've come from is knowing where you're going." Do you agree? Why or why not?

17. When you've faced trials and loss what choices have you made?

18. Is there something in your past you need to remember? mourn? tell to those who love you?

19. How did Walker surrender his splendid isolation and come to a place of acceptance of who God made him to be? Have you?

20. What would you offer on your own memorial altar—your Ebenezer—to God?

21. How far did mercy reach for Sarah Jane, Pierce, Linden, Walker, and Leila? How far has it reached for you?

22. What holds you in the claw of fear? What have your fears cost you?

23. In what special place—like the trees—can you sit and listen to God?

24. If home is the place where the people you love live and is filled with the people who love you back, where is home for you?

Want to learn more about Lisa Carter
and check out other great fiction from
Abingdon Press?

Check out our website at
www.AbingdonFiction.com
to read interviews with your favorite authors,
find tips for starting a reading group,
and stay posted on what new titles are on the horizon.

Be sure to visit Lisa online!

http://www.lisacarterauthor.com

OCT 21 2015